VILLA AMERICA

LIZA KLAUSSMANN was born in New York and lives in London. She is the author of the *Sunday Times* bestselling debut *Tigers in Red Weather*.

'[Klaussmann] entwines her fact and fiction with a smooth, near seamless stitch, and the end result makes for exhilarating and moving reading'   *Observer*

'Klaussmann writes beautifully . . . [A] gorgeous, melancholy novel'   *Sunday Express*

'Immersive . . . a memorably tense, seductive fiction from many perspectives'   *Sunday Times*

'Glitteringly alive'   *Independent*

'An equally tragic and compelling tale . . . The moments of painfully recollected radiance provide confirmation that something precious has been at stake in the tragedy'   *Guardian*

'A brilliant novel about love in all its forms . . . A deeply moving portrait of a marriage and of a world'   *Irish Times*

'In Liza Klaussmann's skilled and sensitive new novel, *Villa America*, the Murphys' famous sociability becomes intriguingly fraught, the expression of a loving, complicated marriage whose intricacies she investigates with the same emotional acumen displayed in her 2012 debut novel, *Tigers in Red Weather* . . . [An] empathetic, beautifully written novel'
                                                      Washington Post

Also by Liza Klaussmann

TIGERS IN RED WEATHER

Liza Klaussmann

VILLA AMERICA

PICADOR

First published 2015 by Picador

First published in paperback 2016 by Picador
an imprint of Pan Macmillan
20 New Wharf Road, London N1 9RR
Associated companies throughout the world
www.panmacmillan.com

ISBN 978-1-4472-1209-6

1 3 5 7 9 8 6 4 2

A CIP catalogue record for this book is available from the British Library.

Printed and bound by CPI Group (UK) Ltd, Croydon, CR0 4YY

Visit www.picador.com to read more about all our books
and to buy them. You will also find features, author interviews and
news of any author events, and you can sign up for e-newsletters
so that you're always first to hear about our new releases.

These things I know:
How the living go on living
and how the dead go on living with them . . .
so that nothing is wasted in nature
or in love

> —Laura Crafton Gilpin

The ordinary novelist has only one message:
"I submit that this is one way we are."

> —Eudora Welty

WHAT WAS LOST

1935

The sky was as blue as a robin's egg on the afternoon they pulled Owen Chambers' body out of the Baie des Anges. It had taken three days before they could reach him—spring tides off the coast of Antibes; a lack of proper equipment—and he was almost unrecognizable when he was finally recovered, seaweed wending its way through his tangled blond hair.

He'd left a note before taking off in his plane on a March morning so warm it seemed like summer. But the letter had been spirited away by his friend Vladimir Orloff and its contents were lost.

Little was known about his life, except that he was an American who had fought as a pilot in the Great War; that he lived alone; and that, for a time, he'd been part of a circle of American artists and writers who had colonized the Côte d'Azur, before they'd scattered, blown back to their home country.

He had few friends among the locals, save a mechanic who'd worked for him, a couple of pilots from a nearby airbase, and Vladimir, a White Russian transplant. So the funeral was a small, brief affair, and his stone was inscribed only with his name and the date of his death. The rest vanished with him.

❊   ❊   ❊

3

On the same day that Owen was dragged from the sea, thousands of miles across the Atlantic in a dark hospital room in Boston, the heart of fifteen-year-old Baoth Murphy stopped beating.

His mother, Sara, and his father, Gerald, had kept watch for ten days while their son struggled to keep breathing, his body twisted in agony. When he was gone, Sara refused to believe that it was over and had to be forcibly sedated so that they could remove her from her child's side.

Sara, a friend would say later, fought all her enemies at the gate and once that was breached, she had no doors left to close.

Gerald, on the other hand, quietly slipped out of the room, and stood for a while in the silence of the corridor, nodding gently, almost graciously, at anyone who passed by.

THE AWAKENING

1898–1918

1898

Gerald thought about Pitz all the way home from school—
he thought about him from the moment the bell rang at the
Blessed Sacrament Academy, during the long walk through
Central Park, Nurse's hand clamped painfully on his wrist,
all the way to his house on West Fifty-Seventh Street—so
that by the time they reached his brownstone, his excitement was so great that he felt he might pee in his pants a
little at the thought that the dog would be waiting for him
behind the heavy black door.

Pitz had been his special birthday present when he
turned ten, almost a year ago now. Mother had been sick
with Baby, whatever that meant, and Gerald had been given
Pitz. To teach him responsibility, his father had said. Gerald
had heard the words, but they'd barely registered, because
at the same moment the wiry-haired fox terrier had bounded
through the door into the drawing room.

Today his friend was exactly one year old and Gerald had
smuggled him two butter biscuits from his lunch. He'd been
very careful not to let the biscuits crumble in the pocket of
his wool coat, or to let Nurse find them.

Nurse hated Pitz. She said he was dirty and that he would
bite them all one day and might even smother Baby in its
sleep. Gerald knew this was a lie. Pitz was special. He had
been his special present and now he was his special friend.
Pitz was all around special. Best of all, the dog could read

his mind. He saw him doing it: Pitz would cock his head when Gerald was thinking something secret, and Gerald knew that Pitz knew what he was thinking.

Now, as the black door was opened at last, Pitz was waiting and Gerald almost cried with relief. He didn't know why, but he feared that one day the door would open and Pitz wouldn't be there.

"If you want to play with that filthy beast, it will be out in the garden," Nurse said.

Gerald looked at Pitz, gingerly feeling the biscuits in his pocket. It was January and the wind bit into his nose, but he'd rather be freezing outside with Pitz than warm indoors with Nurse. He made towards the back door.

"Gerald Clery Murphy." Nurse could make her voice tower. That was the only word Gerald could think of for it—the way it seemed to grow bigger and bigger until it was looming over him. "What do we do first?"

Gerald reluctantly turned and headed for the stairs to change out of his uniform. Pitz just looked at him. He knew better than to try to follow Gerald upstairs when Nurse was around.

The house was chilly and the curtains were drawn against what was left of the day. His father said only invalids lived in warm houses. Murphys, he said, didn't get sick, although Mother had been sick with Baby. Gerald had seen Baby, and Baby looked fine to him. Mother was very white, though, and would call out often for Nurse, in a high voice, saying Baby was unwell, or that Baby was strange.

On the second floor, Gerald had to be very quiet when he passed Mother's door or the nursery, so that Mother wouldn't get upset. Nurse was marching behind him and he hoped she wouldn't try to take his coat, with the biscuits, because then he would be punished and Pitz would be banished to the cellar again. Pitz was supposed to sleep in his basket in the little room off the kitchen. But it was so very cold there; it even seemed cold in summer. At night, if it was quiet, Gerald would sneak downstairs after his prayers and spirit the dog back to his own bed on the third floor.

Sometimes Nurse checked and on those occasions, if she found Pitz, his friend would be locked in the cellar. Sometimes Nurse wouldn't let Pitz out until the following afternoon, and Gerald would see his friend's eyes—haunted after a day down in the dark with no food or water. When this happened, Gerald knew it was his fault and he wouldn't try to smuggle Pitz upstairs for a while. But inevitably, after a week or so, he would chance it again.

"Give me your coat," Nurse said, holding out her strong hand to Gerald. "You can wear the play-coat outside in the muck."

Gerald was trying to think of an excuse to hold on to it, when he heard his mother's voice from behind the nursery door.

"Nurse," his mother cried. "Nurse. Come see to Baby. She has a color on her. A most unnatural color."

"Now, we must stay calm, Mrs. Murphy," Nurse called out briskly, turning from Gerald. "Baby is well. I will be with you directly."

"Nurse, come. Do," his mother said, but her voice was less agitated. Then a few moments later: "Yes, yes," as if she was talking to herself.

Gerald didn't wait to hear any more and raced up the next flight of stairs, his coat and its precious cargo safe from Nurse's grasp.

He took off his uniform, laying his knickerbockers over the chair and folding his shirt and sweater for the morning.

Changing into his play clothes, he slipped his wool coat on again, and made the perilous journey back down to Pitz.

Kneeling on the floor at the foot of the stairs, Gerald wrapped his arms around the little fox terrier and laid his cheek against the dog's neck. There was the earthy, animal smell—fresh bread and leaves—and Pitz's coat, coarse like his hairbrush, pricking his nose.

The dog let himself be held by the boy, patient, unmoving, despite the smell of the biscuit in the boy's pocket. The boy made a small sighing noise, like a prayer.

It was the first warm thing Gerald Murphy had touched all day.

✻

Gerald ate his supper alone at the small table in the nursery. Besides the table, the room had one little chair, a board to do sums on, a rocking horse with an uncomfortable seat (a present from his uncle), and a couple of ledger books in which Gerald was supposed to practice his handwriting before meals.

There used to be two chairs in the nursery, but the companion had been removed when his brother Fred had gone away to school. Gerald didn't really miss him; Fred had never been unkind, but he spoke to Gerald the same way the streetcar conductor did. Politely, as if he were there but not there, somehow. As for Baby, she was too small to eat in the nursery with him, but Gerald hoped she might get big enough soon so that he would have someone to talk to.

The one good thing about the nursery was that it had a large window, rounded at the top, that looked out over Fifty-Seventh Street, and Gerald could watch the people go by and wonder about them while he ate his boiled beef.

Tonight, halfway through a particularly tough nugget of

meat, a hansom cab drew to a stop two doors down. Gerald shifted his chair around the table so he could keep his eye on it. A man in evening clothes alighted, followed by a woman in a dark blue dress, her gloved hand resting lightly on his. A single brown, wrinkled oak leaf fluttered down onto the man's hat. The lady tipped her head in slightly towards her companion and Gerald thought he could see her smiling at something the man had said. The way she smiled reminded him of Father's friend in Atlantic City.

Father had taken him there last spring so that he could see the boardwalk, and also to get some fresh air. Mother had said that she didn't like the look of Gerald's pallor, which she put down to a bilious nature. This frightened Gerald a little, because he didn't know what it meant, and it sounded dangerous. He wanted to ask Father about it, and almost did when they were on the streetcar on their way to the ferry slip. But once on the steamboat that would take them across the North River to the train at Paulus Hook, he forgot all about it.

At first, before the boat blew for departure, Gerald was absorbed by the advertisements in frames hanging on the walls of the long mahogany cabin. He kneeled on the bench to get a better look, before Father rapped him slightly with his cane. Gerald quickly righted himself, but it took all his effort to keep from swinging his legs.

When the ship set off, Father rose and, beckoning him, strode out to the deck. It was a raw morning and the sky hung very gray over the harbor, the Manhattan piers spreading like tentacles reaching out through the mist, saying *Don't Go, Don't Go*. There was a huge steam liner docked at one of them. There was also a thrilling tugboat, with a big, fat "C" painted on its stack, which passed so close to them that Gerald thought if he reached out he might be able to touch it.

He wanted to lean into Father's side, to feel the gray, lightweight wool of his suit. Father always wore the same kind of suit, but Gerald could never remember actually touching it. He thought he might risk it, it was so cold. He inched slightly closer, but Father moved away at the same time, his arm extended, his finger pointing at something.

"Gerald," Father said. "Do you see that big building there? If you walk up six blocks, that is where I work."

The Mark Cross Company, Father's company. They made leather goods and saddlery, Gerald knew, *for the discerning gentleman*.

"What is that big building?"

Father looked at him, annoyed at having been interrupted.

"That is the American Surety Building."

"Why is it so much bigger than the others?" Gerald asked, chancing it.

"It just is," Father said.

"How did they get it to go so high?" He knew he was on thin ice.

"It's called a skyscraper. They could build it so high because they wanted to."

Gerald looked at his father. He was staring out across at the big building. Gerald could tell he was thinking something. He saw that expression sometimes when he was brought into Father's study to say good night and his father would be reading something, his hand resting on top of his smooth head.

"That is something you must learn, Gerald," his father said now. "You and your brother. To decide to do something and then follow it through to its end. That's how they built

12

that. That's how anything worth doing gets done." Father tapped his cane against the railing and then turned and walked back inside. Gerald followed, still wondering how they had built that big building and who had climbed that high into the sky without falling.

After the boat, there'd been a long train ride, during which Father read the quotations of a man called Ralph Waldo Emerson to him at great length (Gerald knew this was the man whose bust sat in Father's study, giving him the beady eye every time he snuck in when he wasn't supposed to), and then they'd arrived in Atlantic City.

Gerald had been to the seaside before, but never one that looked like this, with its enormous hotels and busy wooden sidewalk right next to the sand, and piers standing high like clowns on stilts, stretching for miles out into the water. Also, there were shops selling all sorts of things Gerald couldn't make out, and couples whizzing by in rolling chairs made for two. There was a huge ice water fountain at the entrance of Young's Pier. Gerald got a pickle pin from the Heinz Pier, which had just had what Father called "a grand opening."

He stayed very close to Father on the boardwalk, but then Father pointed to a large building, with a giant flag on top, and told him that was their hotel. It was the United States Hotel, which sounded very impressive to Gerald.

In the evening, Father said he was going to the theater to see a famous French actress in a play. Gerald didn't want to be left alone in the room by himself, but Father never liked fuss, so Gerald didn't say anything when his father left the room in his evening clothes, extinguishing the light as he went.

Gerald lay in his bed in the darkness and thought about a game he was teaching Pitz to play. Gerald would line up his set of toy soldiers, the ones he'd gotten in his stocking for Christmas, and the dog would knock them over with his nose, one by one. Gerald shut his eyes and tried to picture his friend. Then he rolled his pillow up next to him and put his arm around it, pretending it was Pitz, and went to sleep.

The following morning when Gerald woke, he heard laughter coming from the sitting room that separated his bedroom from Father's. Rising, he opened the door and wandered out. In the fresh light he saw a lady in a mauve dress with dark hair, lying over Father's knee laughing. She immediately went quiet when she saw Gerald, but Father's expression never changed. For a moment he wondered if Father was Father; he didn't look like himself. He looked lighter somehow, nicer.

"Miss Church was just looking for her glove, Gerald," Father said, giving the lady a gentle push off his lap.

"Oh," said Gerald, rubbing his eyes. He stole a glance at his own pajamas; they were rumpled.

He looked back at the lady. She had a nice face and a very nice smile and Gerald wondered if she was to spend the day with them. But then Miss Church gathered her cloak and, holding up a glove, said: "Well, I've found it. Goodbye, Patrick," and then: "Nice to meet you, Gerald."

Gerald smiled. "Goodbye," he said.

"We're leaving," Father said, after Miss Church had gone. "The bellboy will be here soon. Pack your case." Whatever joke Father had been sharing with Miss Church he seemed to no longer find funny, his face set back to its usual place.

"May I have breakfast?" Gerald asked, suddenly feeling very hungry.

"Breakfast is for ladies and invalids," Father said, "and

people who miss trains." Then he rose and went into his bedroom, shutting the door with a small clack.

Gerald looked at the door. He liked closed doors, liked the way they looked, so neat and quiet, and so smooth.

❖

He had finished his boiled beef and the lady and gentleman from the hansom cab had long since disappeared inside the house two doors down. Gerald rose from the small table, retrieved one of the ledger books and a pen and began to draw—a door, with panels for eyes. But he couldn't make it come out right, so he began to draw a leaf, trying to capture all the small bones in it. That's how he thought of dead leaves, like small brown skeletons, but made from lace. Finer even than the lace his mother wore to church.

The light from the lamp near him had dimmed a little by the time he finished. He looked out and realized that it had begun to snow, big heavy flakes, covering the branches of the trees like white moss. He wondered when Nurse would come to get him to say good night to Mother and Father. Perhaps she had forgotten. Out the window, another man, this one with a dog, strolled past and Gerald imagined himself and Pitz one day, walking together on a January evening, snow falling on them, exchanging their thoughts on the world.

Gerald hadn't brought Pitz upstairs for a while, but when Nurse came to fetch him from the nursery, she complained of a cold and Gerald saw his opportunity. After saying his prayers, he tiptoed downstairs, scooped up Pitz and, heart hammering, took him to his bed.

He lay there, with his dog, its body curved against his. He put his face to Pitz's neck and breathed in and out. He listened for the sound of Nurse's footsteps, and when he was sure it was all quiet, he relaxed his grip and closed his eyes.

It must have been very late and Gerald had been dreaming he was a pirate. Or he had been dreaming he was on the streetcar with Father and then he was a pirate. Then his arm hurt and he opened his eyes and saw Nurse, her face twisted in the light of her lamp. She was pinching him. Then it was loud and Nurse was screaming about the devil and his ways and dirty beasts, her spittle flying on his face, and Gerald sat up and saw Pitz cowering in a corner near his bureau, his back curved and tail tucked under him, making himself as round and unnoticeable as possible. His friend looked so very small. Gerald cried out and tried to get off the bed, but Nurse pushed him back and flew at the dog, striking him. And then again, and again.

Then Father came in and Nurse was talking and Gerald couldn't say anything. He didn't say a word to save his special friend. Father picked Pitz up and left the room. Nurse pointed one big horrible finger at Gerald. "You could have killed Baby," was all she said, before slamming the door behind her.

The next morning Father called Gerald into his study before breakfast. Gerald scrubbed his face hard before he went downstairs because he knew Father would be angry if he thought Gerald had been crying.

"You have not shown responsibility, Gerald," Father said. "Since you are unable to manage the dog, it can no longer stay in this house. Animals have a place and once they are elevated beyond that place it not only makes them dangerous, but it reflects poorly on the master. From this day on, you are not to go near that dog. It will live in the yard. It can make itself useful by catching rats. You can make yourself useful by learning to live up to your responsibilities. Is that understood?"

"He'll die outside," Gerald said.

"Nonsense," Father said. "It will have a shelter; I've already instructed Harold to make one. The dog, Gerald, will be a dog."

"No, please. Pitz. He's . . ."

"Enough. Don't blubber. You look like Nurse. Do you remember what I told you about seeing something through to the end? Well, this is just one of those times. You must be a man, accept this as a lesson and see it through to the end. That's the last I want to hear on the subject. You will eat your breakfast in the nursery this morning. Good day, Gerald."

For the next week, every night, Gerald would open his bedroom window and speak softly to Pitz, who sat looking forlornly up at the house. For the first few days Pitz waited until Gerald couldn't stand the cold any longer and would be forced to shut the window, before creeping to the wooden shack Harold had built in the corner of the garden. By Friday, though, the dog no longer waited for Gerald to finish telling him about his day, and by Sunday, he didn't even come out of his shelter at the sound of the sash going up.

When Pitz still didn't appear Monday evening, Gerald opened the chest-on-chest in his room where they kept spare blankets. He pulled out the oldest one he could find and went and lifted the window.

"Pitz." He kept his voice low and hushed.

The sky was so dark that it was a kind of black-blue.

"Pitz," he called again, a little louder.

Finally, Gerald could make out a small head appearing from the shelter.

"Pitz. Come."

The dog moved warily out towards the sound of Gerald's voice.

Taking a corner of the blanket, Gerald dangled it out the window and, swinging his arm, tossed it as far as he could.

Pitz moved slowly toward it and sniffed it. He looked up at Gerald and Gerald knew what his friend was asking.

"Go on, Pitz. Go on and take it. It's for you."

Pitz looked at him a moment longer, and then grabbed one end of the woolen cover and dragged it back to his shack, pulling it in after him.

"I love you, Pitz," Gerald called across the garden. "I love you."

By the beginning of February, Gerald had thrown a total of three blankets, a couple of pairs of winter socks he thought Pitz could make a pillow with, various tidbits from his lunch and suppers, and a box of sweetmeats that he had stolen from the drawing room. But one night, he had nothing useful to throw down to his friend—he had been so very hungry at lunch and there was nothing left over. So, in desperation, he threw down one of his toy soldiers. Pitz came out and snuffled it, before looking up at the window. For a moment Gerald thought he was disappointed because it wasn't food, but then the dog nudged the lead figurine with his nose and looked up at Gerald, letting out a small bark. Gerald began to cry.

The next day, after school, when Nurse was busy with Baby, and Cook was out running errands, Gerald decided to brave punishment and went out into the garden.

He stood in the doorway and called Pitz's name. At first there was no movement, and then a small head popped out of the shelter. Gerald, afraid and elated, moved across the hard ground towards his dog. Pitz emerged slowly and Gerald knelt down and held out his hand. He had brought a bit of biscuit.

"Come, Pitz," he said.

The dog moved closer and Gerald saw that his coat had grown quite matted, and also coarser than he remembered. Pitz smelled the food and cautiously approached, first sniffing from a little ways away, then darting in and scarfing the tidbit from Gerald's palm.

The pink slip of the tongue, the heavy fur; Gerald couldn't wait one second longer to touch him and feel him and smell him. His friend, his special, best, brave friend. On his knees, he reached out his arms, and as he did, the dog turned, and got low. In his rush to get to him, though, Gerald didn't notice or really know what the strange noise meant. He reached out and the dog whipped around and sunk his teeth deep into Gerald's hand.

"No, Pitz. No," Gerald cried softly. He tried again, to hold him, to touch him, despite his bleeding hand and the pain, but the dog just growled and bared his teeth.

Not knowing what to do, Gerald ran back to the house to look for a place to hide his tears. But it was no use. His hand swelled to the size of an onion and Nurse saw it, and knew it for what it was. She reported him to Father, and finally, the judgment came down: Pitz was to go. Where, Gerald didn't know, and Father wouldn't tell him. Only that he himself was to be banished to the nursery at all hours that he wasn't in school.

When Nurse came up later to the nursery to bring his dinner, Gerald couldn't even look at her.

"At least that's settled once and for all," she said, setting a baleful piece of lamb pie down in front of him. "And you, you got nothing less than you deserve, Gerald Clery Murphy.

I warned you about that beast. Dirty, vicious thing." She tapped her fingers next to his plate. "Your father showed too much mercy from the beginning, in my opinion."

"You hit Pitz," he said, staring down at the table, balling his fists in his lap. "You hit him, and then made him go outside and hate me, and now he's gone. My only friend in this whole world. And now I hate you."

Nurse dug her fingers into his shoulder and forced him to look up at her. Her eyes looked like the shiny gray pebbles on the beach in Southampton, which looked smooth but hurt to walk on. "If it had been up to me," she said, "I would have made a hearth rug out of that filthy animal. Something to keep my feet warm."

The memory rose of a terrified Pitz, desperately showing his soft belly to Nurse before she beat him, and in that moment Gerald Murphy made the first real decision of his life.

The boy turned in his seat and, in the coldest voice he could muster, said: "You are a wicked woman and I don't care what anyone says. From this moment on, I will never, ever speak to you again."

And, despite his parents' exhortations, he kept his word. Like the men who built the skyscrapers, he decided to do something and he followed it through to the end, because that's how anything worth doing got done.

Three weeks later, Gerald was shipped off to boarding school.

❖　❖　❖

Sara Wiborg loved the feel of earth in her hands, the humid texture of it between her fingers. She was in the garden of their home in Clifton, Ohio, selecting grasses and bits of things for a diorama she was making for her class at Miss Ely's.

This was to be their last month at Miss Ely's, before they moved to Germany in July. Her father had made great friends with the Kaiser and they were to spend a year there while he expanded his business abroad. At fifteen, she was too old, really, for Miss Ely's anyway and if it wasn't Germany it would have been some other school, although her mother refused to send the girls away. She loved them too much, she said.

For the diorama, Sara had decided to make a farm. Her middle sister, Hoytie, was a few feet away, staring up at the sky, neglecting her work, while Olga, the youngest at nine, was with their nurse in the hothouse picking flowers for her tropical scene.

Carrying a celadon bowl full of pebbles, Sara found a shaded spot under an oak tree where the moss was growing dark and wet, making it malleable. Carefully, she peeled it off in strips, placing them over the pebbles, until she had created a miniature, glistening green hill. She believed the perfect home should be on a hill, but it should also be near the sea, so she had dug a small moat which would serve as the curve of a seashore.

Next she selected small tips of pine and black maple and dogwood and witch hazel to make a copse for her farm. Then she made a collection of the tender heads of Indian grass and planted them in rows in the moss: her wheat field.

She was collecting violets when the storm came. It swept with a sudden violence over the stables and the sunken garden and the hothouse and the pasture beyond, clattering across the house like horse's hooves hitting the ground.

Sara quickly picked up the bowl, as well as the violets, which she held lightly in her hand so as not to crush the petals, and hurried towards the house. When she looked back to make sure Hoytie was behind her Sara saw that her sister was standing staring up at the deluge.

"Hoytie," she called out. "Hurry up. You'll be soaked."

Hoytie turned to her. Then she stamped her foot angrily, and raising her eleven-year-old fist to the sky cried indignantly: "It's . . . raining . . . on . . . *me*."

Sara laughed. "Oh Hoytie, it's raining on all of us. Come on."

❖

When they reached the entrance hall, one of the maids came running with towels. Sara took them and began drying her sister off, catching glimpses of the two of them in the flashing mirrors that hung on the walls.

She wondered at her sister's declaration, how it was some people seemed sure of their place in the world. For her part, she had no idea where she belonged or where she would end up.

When she'd dried off a bit, Sara retrieved the small farmhouse she'd painted—wooden sticks brushed white, the windowsills yellow—and placed it atop her green hill. Then she took her diorama into the Turkish smoking room, where her parents kept all their Middle Eastern treasures.

Setting the bowl down on the polished wooden floor, she went to one of the glass cases and pilfered two gold Egyptian figurines: Akhenaten and his wife Nefertiti.

She placed the king and queen in front of the yellow and white house. They sat there solemnly presiding over their beautiful, lush farm.

Then, as the last touch, she took the delicate purple flowers she'd carried through the storm and floated them on the moat she'd carved. A perfumed violet-blue sea.

1910

It was still dark when Owen rose and collected the eggs, warm from the hen house. He milked the two cows, loaded the aluminum milk vats onto the cart along with the potatoes, butter and cheese, harnessed the mare and began the journey into town. His hands on the reins were stiff from the cold. His balls had shrunk back towards the heat of his body. He shifted on the wooden seat, watching the lantern lighting his way, willing its flame back to him.

He thought about breakfast. The faster he delivered, the faster he would be home and the faster his mother would put that plate in front of him. He urged the horse on. He could smell the fallen pine needles as her hooves hit them, but it was a thin smell; the early March air was still too cold.

He went over the names on his list of deliveries. Mrs. Violet Pease; Mrs. Camilla Thurston; the Drakes; the rectory at St. Andrew's; the old schoolmaster, Mr. Cushing. There was one more, who was it? His head was still thick with sleep and stunned by the cold. His feet had long since lost any feeling and he tried to scrunch his toes in his boots, but he couldn't tell if they were even moving.

To distract himself, he counted how much they would make from this round. One of their cows, Lettuce, had to be dried off soon, so the deliveries would be much smaller for a couple of months, until she could be milked again.

Lettuce was Owen's favorite, a Jersey cow, caramel-colored. He'd been the one to pick her out two summers ago. His mother hadn't wanted to buy her—all that difficulty calving such a small thing. They were smaller and more sensitive than other breeds, the Jersey cows, but, as he'd argued, they ate less and produced such fine milk. They were also soft to the touch, although he didn't say this to his mother; softness was no reason for keeping a working animal.

The other thing he didn't tell his mother was how he talked to Lettuce. It had started off as just something he did before milking, as it seemed to make her less anxious. But over time, he'd begun to believe that she wanted him to do it, that she understood, that she waited for their conversations. She seemed to produce more milk and Owen became convinced that there was some real connection there, despite his shame in believing it. He didn't like to think about it; it was just something he did.

If all went well, Lettuce would calve in May. Hopefully, they could get a good price for the calf, either for veal or dairy, which would make up for the shortfall in milk. But it meant the coming month would be lean.

Then it would be planting season. Because of the sea air, they had a long fall, but spring came late, the beginning of April, when they would plant for corn, as well as some sugar and shelling peas. In May, he'd skip school, there would be too much to do: turning the vegetable fields and plowing down the winter rye and gathering the first potatoes. The hay harvesting would be done in June. The real back-breaking work. But it also meant lovely soft summer evenings, tired, driving the hay back to be baled. Letting the working steers plod along, while he stared up at the changing sky.

Sometimes when he was in the classroom, bored, he

24

would think about all the bigger farms on the island and do the sums of how much it would cost to buy one. Sums were one thing Owen was good at—they arranged themselves naturally in his head—but even he couldn't make the numbers come out right for that. There weren't enough eggs in the world.

When he was younger, he used to imagine a rich relative of his father's showing up and showering them with money. Sometimes the relative would be a railroad magnate, other times a Chicago industrialist. His father had died of smallpox when Owen was three and he had only the barest recollection of him, an odor really, the smell of leather and wet blue from the tanning factory he'd worked in. His mother had set him straight, when he'd mentioned one of his daydreams, the Chicago industrialist: "He was a decent man, your father, but he had no money, except what he earned, and no connections to speak of. He was a good husband, but there's no use thinking on him anymore."

His mother was an islander. She'd left her family to find work in Boston and ended up marrying a man from the mainland. After Owen's father had been hauled off to the pest house to die, his mother had returned to her parents' small dairy farm and eventually took it over when they were gone. Owen had been old enough to work when his grandparents died, four years ago. Now, at fourteen, he was strong enough that they only needed to hire men twice a year to help out.

She was a smart woman, his mother. He loved her. He could remember when she'd been handsome. It wasn't that she was ugly now, just a little weathered, like everyone on the island. She was strong, stronger than him sometimes, birthing calves and even loading hay when they couldn't get a second man in.

Owen looked up at the sky. There were no stars, too misty. The milk cans pinged behind him. The sun wouldn't be up for another hour still, not until he hit town. Then five deliveries, then another hour home, then breakfast. No: six deliveries; the new one. The mainlander. His order would help make up the shortfall, bring the ends closer together.

Mr. Glass, that was it; that was his name. There'd been talk when the mainlander had bought the land out Katama, and then more talk when he'd built the big house. Married with a son and daughter, if the talk was to be believed.

The order was for four dozen eggs. It was a big order for a man with a small family, but apparently they were for dyeing. For Easter. Still, as his mother said: "I don't care if he wants to bathe in them, so long as he pays."

Owen sighed and hunched further into his coat, urging the mare on.

First stop was Mr. Cushing's house. Hopping down from the box he pulled a sack of potatoes out of the cart and brought it to the front door, knocking twice before going back for the milk jug. Mr. Cushing, lean as a bean pole, opened the door and squinted at him.

"Making good time this morning," he said, as Owen placed the milk on the front porch.

"Extra delivery today."

"Who's that now?"

"The mainlander out Katama." Owen held out his hand for last week's empty jug, hoping the old schoolmaster wasn't gearing up for a chat.

"Mr. Glass."

"That's the one." Owen made a show of impatiently stamping his feet against the porch boards.

"They say he's got a flying machine out there. Got it stashed away in a big barn."

Owen stopped stamping. "You've seen it?"

"No, I heard that from Carey. He built the barn."

"How'd he get it to the island? He couldn't have flown it all the way." Owen had read all about the Wright Brothers' flying machine—all the boys in town had—but Wilbur Wright had only managed to fly it for twenty-four miles. And that was out in a field, not over the Atlantic.

"I have no earthly idea, Owen." Mr. Cushing's calm smile annoyed him.

He lifted the jug and hauled it back to the cart. Mr. Cushing called something after him, but Owen was already pushing on, his mind on this new, incredible information, and the schoolmaster's voice was lost.

The road to Katama ran the other way out of town, which meant a detour, and Owen thought perhaps he would put Mr. Glass first on his list of deliveries next time. The Glass place had been built toward the end of Katama Bay and Owen waited until the second to last cut-off to turn in through the pines, as instructed by his mother.

The path was smooth, newly hewn, and the cart barely rattled as he drove over it. After a bit, the trees disappeared and an over-sized barn came into view on his right. Behind it ran a large, cut field, covered in snow. He stopped a moment, thinking about the flying machine, hidden away there like treasure. Then he continued until he saw the house, perched on the edge of a small cliff. At the top of the circular drive, he pulled the horse up in front of a grand-looking porch.

There was no sign of the help, or anyone else for that matter. Pulling out the baskets of eggs, he made his way around the side of the house to a door with a small portico. He set the baskets down on the pathway and looked out to the sea, slate winter-gray in front of him, and returned for the two jugs of milk the mainlander had ordered.

When he came abreast of the barn on his way back up the road, he couldn't help himself. He pulled over. He glanced around, and back at the house: everything was still, the snow on the field muffling the noise of the sea.

He decided to chance it. He opened the barn door a crack and peered inside; it was too dark. He pulled the door wider and stepped in, just a little ways. He still couldn't make out very much, so he went in—just a bit further—and then a little more, and a little more.

It took shape gradually, as his eyes adjusted. An enormous monster of a thing, all white fabric and shiny wood and glinting, cold wire. Aeroplane, that's what some of the newspapers called it, but Owen thought flying machine was a much better description. It was shaped like an arithmetic problem: all rectangles; isosceles triangles; half moons; right angles, straight angles and curves. And the wings. Two sets of them, one on top, one on bottom. Altogether huge, spanning at least the length of six men. And in the center, like an ugly heart, was a mass of metal, with chains and other twisted things, and two shining propellers behind it. In front, a pair of impossibly small seats that reminded Owen of the ones he'd seen in the theater in Boston. The whole apparatus sat atop a pair of long slender pieces of wood, curved like skis.

How many eggs would someone have to sell to buy a thing like this?

"It came in boxes," said a voice from behind him.

Owen turned to see a man standing in the doorway, his broad thick body dark against the sun.

"Pretty big boxes, too." The man adjusted his britches

28

and began striding towards him. Owen was rooted to the spot. "And who might you be?"

"I'm Owen," he said. "Chambers. From the farm."

Up close, he could see the man had a crimson tinge to his buffed skin and his hair was slicked back, like an advertisement, a big full mustache dominating his face. His head reminded Owen of a horse, sinew and bone and meat. A strong head. A rich man's head.

"Aha. So you've heard about my plane. News travels fast, I suppose."

This was Mr. Glass. "Yes, sir, I'm sorry. There was no one . . ."

"Thought you'd sneak a look, did you?"

Owen wondered what the penalty was for breaking into someone's barn to look at a flying machine.

"Don't look so stricken, Owen Chambers, boy from the farm. I'm not going to report you." He turned his gaze to the machine. "She's something to behold, all right."

"Does it fly?"

"Does it fly?" Mr. Glass snorted. "Of course it flies. Why in darnation would I have it, otherwise?" He looked at Owen, as if he were sizing him up. "Would you like to touch her?"

He nodded.

"Go on, then."

Owen approached it carefully, like he would a snake. Tentatively, he stretched his hand out and touched the material on one of the bottom wings. It looked like heavy canvas, and he'd expected it to feel like a sail. Instead his fingertips met with something spongier, tackier. He pulled his hand away, surprised.

"It's rubberized," Mr. Glass said. "Clever, isn't it?"

Owen looked at him and, at that moment, realized all the

things this man must know, and by extension, all the things he himself did not.

"This is *Flora*," Mr. Glass said. "Named after my daughter."

"Like a boat," Owen said.

"Ha. Like a boat that flies." The man ran his hand over one of the wooden poles that separated the lower wing from the upper.

"How does it . . ." He couldn't imagine getting this complicated giant of a machine from where it sat into the sky.

"Come with me." Mr. Glass led him to the doorway and pointed to a conical structure across the field. "You see that derrick out there? You push her out and get her on those rails, attach that weight, and when it drops: whoosh," he made an upward movement with his hand, "she rushes forward and up, up and away."

"Have you flown it . . . her . . . here?"

"Well, now, you need at least six men to get her going. And the right conditions." Mr. Glass scratched his chin. "But in spring, when the weather gets finer, I'm going to rally some troops for a maiden voyage."

"So you've never flown her?"

"Oh, I did. Went with Orville Wright himself, when I bought her." The man's eyes were fixed on some unknown point in the distance. "Quite a man, that Orville Wright. And when you're up there . . . Couldn't get my son to go up, though. He wasn't scared, you understand. Just . . . well, Charlie's more of a scholar. Interested in books and such." He scratched his chin again.

"I could help," Owen said. "When you decide to do it, I mean."

Mr. Glass shifted his gaze to Owen, almost as if he'd forgotten he was there. "We'll see." He seemed suddenly to have lost interest. "I'm sure you must be off, now. Have a farm to run, don't you?"

"Yes, sir." He flushed.

Still, he found it hard to leave the sight of the glorious monster—to get back in his cart, do his chores, go to school. The idea seemed impossible as he stood there, edging out of the barn backwards, his eyes riveted to the whiteness of the wings, the cruel, graceful propellers.

He didn't tell any of the boys at school about the machine, guarding his secret jealously. But he wanted to talk about it to someone, so after his evening chores he sat in the warm kitchen, the island dark and hushed outside, and said to his mother: "The mainlander has a flying machine."

"Does he, now." His mother didn't turn away from the stove.

"In his barn. He's going to fly it in spring."

"It's spring now," his mother said.

"Later, when it's warmer," Owen said.

"When it's warmer," his mother said, "it will be summer."

"Well."

"That's not the same thing." She looked at him. "People don't always mean what they say. In fact, it's often not what they mean at all."

So, Owen talked to Lettuce about it.

"It's like a giant bird skeleton," he told her, running his hand down her back. "And in the center is metal." His hand reached her thurl. "But really, it's mostly wood and cloth." He traveled down her rear flank. "But it's not like any cloth you've ever seen. It's gummy." His hand reached her teat. "I wish you could see it. But then, maybe you wouldn't like it. Maybe you'd be afraid." Her milk came out, pale yellow, thick, like honey, into the pail.

That night he would dream of *Flora*, of flying in the air,

of rising. He would dream of sticky fabric and men with large rectangular mustaches, the color of spruce. Owen would dream of all the things he didn't know, all the things he might.

1913–1914

They had been in London since the beginning of June, Sara, her two sisters and her mother. *The Three Wiborg Girls*, as the sisters were tiresomely known in the columns. Sara was "the chic one," Hoytie, "dark and refined," while Olga, the youngest, was "the delicate beauty." These words felt like intricately made corsets, squeezing them into arranged shapes, pinching at the sides where they met with resistance.

Sara pressed her finger to her eye, seeking out the soft spot on the lid that had been leaking infection on and off since their arrival in Europe in March. A maid, fitting the gown Sara planned to wear that evening, stuck a pin into the light green silk and its tip pricked her, right beneath her armpit. Sara felt the pain like a tiny streak of lightning. She remained still. A stray drop of rain hit the pane of the large window overlooking Hyde Park.

Tonight would be her mother's final victory in the long march through the European Season. The Vegetable Ball at the Ritz. The cream of society had lobbied Adeline Wiborg for invitations to the event, first politely, then a little less politely. Sara's mother received bribes daily in the form of invitations to a *dîner intime* or the offer of a place in someone's box at the opera, each one causing Adeline to smile and hum to herself.

Sara looked at the wreath of carrots, tomato vines and

sprigs of mint, lying on the chaise longue next to her. It was absurd, decorative, useless. *Like me.* She felt very tired.

She consoled herself with the thought that this evening, at least, she wouldn't be expected to participate in any *tableaux vivants* or sing with her sisters—a staple in her mother's arsenal. They had been doing these performances for years at their houses in Ohio, New York or East Hampton, and at drawing rooms all over the East Coast and Europe. Last night, they had done their rendition of the Rhine Maidens' lament from *Das Rheingold* for guests of the Duchess of Rutland. This particular act stood on the fine line between decorum and titillation, but her mother had said: "This is London, after all. Tastes are generally more *piquant.*"

The lights began dimmed, the room thrown into near-darkness. Then: gasps from the audience when, as the lamps were slowly turned up, their eyes adjusted to the sight of Sara and her sisters standing bare-shouldered, motionless behind a gauze curtain. Ever so slowly, the three Wiborg girls began to undulate their arms, the backlight catching their exposed skin like pale water and throwing rippling imitations of their figures across the transparent fabric. They started to sing the song of the nymphs, a lament of loss and reproach, their torsos swaying gently from the waist, forward and back. It wasn't exactly shocking, but it had a languid sensuality that was unexpected, and obviously slightly thrilling. Which is exactly what their mother counted on.

But something had happened last night: Sara had let her mind wander, just a little, then a little more, until there was only the gently flowing curtain, her sisters' familiar voices, a remembered scene from the nursery, the gaslight warm on her back. For some reason that she couldn't fathom even now, Sara had tipped her head into Hoytie's shoulder, breathing in her sister's perfume. And then she was gone, back to her childhood home in Clifton, Ohio, and it was spring and she was comforted by all the small things she knew: the place in the hedge where the rabbit with the missing ear lived; the dark patch under the yew tree where the ferns were shyly uncurling themselves, green and fuzzy and new; the spot next to the cellar door that smelled like violets.

Then, all at once Hoytie was elbowing her, pointy and cruel, and she was brought back to the drawing room and the smell of moldy carpets and half-eaten beef on the sideboard, and Sara realized she had fallen into a deep sleep. Only for a few moments, just a few, insignificant moments.

Yet, if they were so insignificant, why was she still thinking about them now, as she watched the maid reach for a bit of cloth to wipe the blood from her side?

She was twenty-nine years old and most of her friends were already married, setting up their own households, running their own lives. For a while, on the cusp of womanhood—and for some time afterwards—Sara had felt like she was living in a state of suspended animation, waiting for life to really begin. Waiting for the pivotal moment when, like the fairytale, a kiss would awaken her and she would stir her frozen limbs and everything would be set in motion. After a while, however, it had dawned on her that this *was* life, what was happening right now. And with that revelation, she had just gone back to sleep. No, not sleep exactly. It was more precise than that: it was the kind of dozing where you think you've been awake the whole time, only to realize that hours have passed, and that, after all, you must have been asleep.

But things—well, she—had gotten worse over the past year. It had started last summer: she began to find it harder and harder to get out of bed, and sometimes she didn't bother at all, instead spending the mornings staring out the bay window of her bedroom in the beach house in East Hampton. She would squint her eyes to blur the line between the lawn and the ocean beyond. Squint, release, squint, release. Until blue became green and green, blue.

In the fall, she'd gone to see the Whistlers at the Metropolitan Museum of Art. Sara could remember those paintings, *Mother of Pearl and Silver: The Andalusian*, that dark swath of hair, her swirl of silver skirt brushing the floor, the sliver of face turned toward the viewer. But it was the *Nocturne: Blue and Gold—Southampton Water* that had made Sara's breath catch in her chest. The smudgy, luminous harbor seen only by the light of an orange moon (or was it a setting sun?). The painting was obscured, melting, light drowning at the edges.

Sara felt like the light in that painting, always sinking, never rising. Her feelings had not escaped her mother.

"This oppression of yours, Sara. It's unbecoming and it's straining my nerves," her mother had told her one day over breakfast. "And when I say unbecoming, I mean untoward."

"Indecorous?" Sara had helpfully offered.

"I mean, stop it," her mother had said.

Only Olga had been kind. On the days when Sara didn't come downstairs, her younger sister would come up and sit on Sara's sleigh bed and plait and unplait her hair for hours, the two of them watching the waves outside the bay window. "You have such lovely hair," Olga would say. "So heavy."

✻

"I think that's it, Miss," the maid said to Sara, bringing her back to the hotel room, the London rain, her throbbing eye.

"Yes," Sara murmured.

She walked over to the glass and looked at herself. Staring

back was a youngish woman in a cucumber-green dress with heavy hair and sleepy eyes. Decorative. At least that.

⁂

The ball was a success. Sara could see that almost instantly, having learned over the years to be able to judge her mother's hits and misses by the telltale signs. In the case of a failure, there would be whispers, and the whispers could grow so loud that the whole room hummed, like a grist of bees caught in a glass box.

With the Vegetable Ball, though, her mother had outdone herself. The main ballroom was swathed in vines, with squashes, or miniature eggplants, or zucchinis sprouting from their tangled arms. The enormous crystal chandelier hanging in the center had also been covered with growing things: tomatoes, carrots, corn, all arranged from smallest to largest. The Ritz's livery stood against the walls, holding trays of champagne with apples and pears dipped in gold paint. It was opulent and imaginative and grotesque.

Sara was standing off to the side of a group that was jostling for attention, talking with the Duchess of Rutland's daughter, Diana.

"Well," Diana said, giving Sara a sly look.

Sara laughed. "Yes, well."

"I think your mother may have made a few enemies tonight. There's nothing these women hate so much as a *succès fou*. Or being made to come on bended knee to America. This isn't 1905, after all."

That had been the boom year for conquering British titles. America, swelling with heiresses of ink, paper, coal and steel, had seen no fewer than twenty-five members of the House of Lords take its daughters to the altar. Sara remembered her mother putting down the newspaper in disgust after reading about one or the other of these matches.

"Imagine," Adeline had said, "selling your daughters into serfdom. No running water, no money, only cows and horses and dogs. They should be ashamed of themselves." Adeline never liked the idea of marriage, let alone twenty-five of them.

Diana scanned the room, then turned her attention back to Sara. "Let's talk about something infinitely more interesting," she said: "*Me.*" Her friend smiled. "What do I remind you of?"

Diana was fitted in a sleek white ball gown, with thick seams of red, green and yellow.

"I don't know," Sara said, feeling weary. "A vegetable patch?"

"A vegetable patch, indeed. That might be all right for some." Diana eyed Sara's bright green dress and preposterous wreath. "No, these, lovely Sara, these are racing stripes. I plan on winning your mother's vile ragtime potato race."

"Oh Diana," Sara said, laughing. "Don't."

"Why not?"

"You know why not. It's just one of Mother's antiquated games. The joke is always on someone else."

"Oh, it's all how you look at it. There's art in everything." She winked at Sara. "Even antiquated games."

Olga opened the ball with Prince Colonna, who, rumor had it, was as ridiculous a gambler as his father. They were trailed by a servant in blackface, dressed in the garb of a Southern plantation slave, frantically pushing a wheelbarrow full of vegetables.

The guests laughed uproariously at the spectacle and Sara saw her mother's face shining in triumph. More faux-slaves blew green and gold dust out of small handmade cornucopias from the sidelines.

Her eye began to throb again. As the guests pushed forward to join in the ball, she was claimed like lost luggage by the first gentleman on her dance card. He introduced himself, but while his lips moved, no sound seemed to reach her. She nodded anyway and gave him her hand. He swept her into the crowd, turning her round and round, his arm close at her waist, his breath champagne-sour.

Her eyes wouldn't seem to focus, so the room spun, a whirl of color over her partner's shoulder. She felt panic rising up, couldn't remember her steps. *What was this? Yes, a hesitation waltz, that was it.* She was reminded of the story of *Little Black Sambo*, how the vain tigers stole the child's clothes and then chased each other jealously round and round a tree until they melted into butter.

She felt sick. Round and round, round and round. The room glistening indecently from the gold dust, champagne tipping onto the floor. The band quickened its tempo. She forced her eyes to adjust. The guests themselves seemed to have taken on a freakish quality: rouged lips smacking, arms jerking up and down like puppets. Even Diana, in a corner of the room, laughing and goading her suitors into betting on her in the race.

"Nothing like a ball at the Ritz . . ." her partner was saying.

She could see one of his front teeth was slightly discolored.

"I was saying just the other day to Frank . . . you know Frank Wallis, don't you, Miss Wiborg? Solid chap."

Sara had the most sudden and furious desire to see the room consumed in a great fire, one that would sweep down upon them and swallow up the vegetables and the livery and the awful people-puppets in one cleansing scourge. Burn it all down.

Sweat broke out on her upper lip and she was sure the same damp was staining her green silk dress. She had to leave the ballroom right that instant or she would die.

"Excuse me," she said to her partner. "I . . ."

"You're not ill, are you, Miss Wiborg?"

"No. Yes. I just feel slightly faint. I think I should sit down."

"Oh, by all means." He escorted her to the edge of the dance floor, where Sara fled his solicitation.

As she squeezed past yards of chiffon and satin and feathers, pressing on her, suffocating her, she saw Hoytie making her exit with a young woman in a yellow tiered gown, a hunter-green silk flower pinned to her bosom. She hurried to catch up with them.

"Hoytie," she called when she made it to the ballroom's antechamber, her pulse throbbing.

Her sister turned, her dark eyebrows curving only slightly, more in curiosity than recognition.

"I can't stand it anymore," Sara said, as she caught up with them. Yet, as the words left her lips she realized that she actually felt nothing of what had come over her only moments before. As if unseen fingers had pinched the wick of that emotion and extinguished it as quickly as it had been lit. She was left only with the emptiness of knowing that she couldn't even sustain her own despair.

Wearily, she greeted Hoytie's young friend with the flower: "Hello," she said.

The young woman didn't meet her eyes, but answered: "Oh, hello."

"This is Irma," Hoytie said, waving her hand as if that wasn't really the point. "Anyway, why are you so undone?"

"I . . ." What could she say? *I wanted everyone to die in a fire, but now, actually, I feel extremely sanguine about the whole thing. Just a little numb, really . . .*

"Well, not to worry. You can just have a nap if you're bored. Seeing as you can just pass out anywhere." Her sister gave Sara her most insincere smile.

"Yes, yes," Sara said, tired of the joke already. "Anyway, I thought I'd just escape to the ladies' sitting room."

"How funny," Hoytie said tightly. "That's where we're going, as well."

"I can't read your mind, Hoytie," Sara snapped. "I'm not following you, for heaven's sakes."

The mirrored room, with its lingering odor of powder, glowed in the lamplight. Once ensconced—Sara lounging in one chaise, while Hoytie and Irma shared the one across— her sister produced a cigarette, fitting it neatly into an ivory and gold holder. Hoytie leaned back and gave her lighter to Irma. The girl, after fumbling a little with her glove, lit the cigarette and then stared wide-eyed at her sister.

Sara knew Hoytie smoked in secret. Adeline did not approve: she thought it stank and that it polluted the girls' hair. Lately, however, Hoytie had become less and less secretive about it. Sara had even found her smoking on the terrace in East Hampton.

"Those vegetables," Hoytie said, exhaling.

Sara smiled. "I never knew Mother harbored ambitions to run a plantation."

Hoytie snorted. "Well, after all her talk about lords really just being farmers, I suppose she thought a vegetable ball might suit them."

"Yes," Sara said. "I'm not sure they got the joke, though. Diana was going to run in that potato-sack travesty."

"No."

"Mmm."

"And Olga with that prince," Hoytie said. "I hope he knows Mother wouldn't let him get within ten miles."

"I don't think he's interested. Father's pockets aren't deep enough to cover his debts."

"No, you're probably right. Men. All their buying and selling. It's disgusting." Hoytie turned her head and looked at Irma. She reached out a long-fingered hand and began playing with the girl's green silk rose. "Don't you think, Irma?"

"Yes," the girl said, in an almost-whisper.

"There's always Gerald Murphy," Hoytie said laughing. "He never seems to go a day without writing." She snorted. "A Catholic. As if Father and Mother would even dream of letting Olga go to a papist."

"Sweet Gerald," Sara said.

A friend from childhood, a little brother of sorts. His father had a house in Southampton, not far from their own in East Hampton, and they'd come to know him the way children come to know each other in a summer place. He'd been fourteen when he'd first visited them at the Dunes, for a party—all awkward limbs and big, deep eyes. He'd grown into his body, even if the eyes remained the same. He was often paired off with Olga for dances and the like, but there was no romance between those two, just an appropriate age gap and a geographical closeness.

Sitting there now, she could still picture his sad face in the crush of people on the quay in New York, seeing them all off when they set sail for Europe in March. And the last letter she'd had from him had been full of melancholy. He was looking after his brother Fred, who had fallen ill while the rest of the family was away on the Continent.

It seems Gerald had even called on her father in East

Hampton, although he'd written that, without them there, he'd felt like he was haunting the house.

Sara watched as Hoytie moved her hand from the rose on Irma's bust, up the girl's collarbone and neck, and pulled a wisp of hair free, coiling it around one finger.

Sara put her head back against the chaise and closed her eyes. She could feel the rustle of silk against the upholstery under her. The smell of talcum in her nostrils. She thought of the opium dens she'd read about in the newspaper and wondered if this was the "dangerous indolence" they spoke of.

"Dangerous indolence," she murmured, as the sounds of the room around her mingled with the thoughts in her head.

It was so, so quiet. There was only the sound of Irma's shallow breathing, as Hoytie ignited some unseen passion in the girl. What did Sara care?

"Good night, Sara," she heard Hoytie say softly, as Sara felt the wreath slipping from her head and, from far away, heard the small *tish* as it hit the floor.

⁂

The following evening, Sara found herself descending from a motor cab into a crush of tails and top hats and beaded gowns all gathered outside of the Theatre Royal at Drury Lane.

As she picked her way across the damp pavement through the crowd and into the marble lobby, her sisters and mother following in her wake, she heard someone call: "Hello, Sara darling," and looked up to see Stella Campbell waving at her.

They'd met the English actress last year on the *Mauretania* on their way to London for the Season. Mrs. Pat, as she insisted on being called, had smoked and drunk her way through the voyage, at once scandalizing and amusing her fellow passengers.

"Hello, dear Mrs. Pat," Sara said, when they all reached her. As she leaned in for a kiss, she felt the older woman's thick, dark mane brush her cheekbone and had a strange desire to bury her face in it.

"Adeline, your girls are a marvel, really," Mrs. Pat said. "So *inviting*." She gave Sara a wink. "What do you think, Sara? Does this dress *walk*? Or does it make me look like a cigar?"

Sara could see what had made her one of the most popular leading ladies of her time; she wasn't beautiful, but she had a shape that dominated (curved, almost indecent arms) and a face supple enough to run the gamut from soulfulness to irony. Sara laughed. "Oh, it walks."

"And Hoytie, dearest, how are you?" Mrs. Pat turned to her sister.

"I'm bored," Hoytie replied.

"You can't be bored," Olga said. "Nothing's even happened yet."

"Yes, Olga," Hoytie said tightly, "that's why I'm bored."

"Stop differing, girls," Adeline said.

"Bickering?" Olga said, taking their mother's arm.

"No, Hoytie," Mrs. Pat said. "This is thrilling. Stravinsky's scandalous *Rite of Spring*. We're hoping for a riot, darling, just like in Paris."

"Well, I'm not," Hoytie said.

Sara looked around at the crowd milling about the lobby: women in delicate lace and draped bodices; men, stiff-spined, nodding. The image of flames licking at the Ritz ballroom returned. She said, "I think I'd quite like a riot."

By the time the Duchess and Lady Diana arrived, the five of them, including Mrs. Pat, were already in the Grand

Saloon. They were seated at a table next to a Doric column, drinking sherry out of small, green glasses, like little luminous thimbles, while the gas-lit chandeliers hissed overhead.

Sara was concentrating on not letting any of the golden liquid drop onto her white evening gloves when she heard Diana whisper in her ear: "Careful, or you'll get a reputation."

"A reputation for what?" Sara asked, wondering fleetingly if she cared.

"Oh, I don't know." Diana smiled and absently touched her pink silk headband. "Anything, nothing. Drinking, keeping company with a fallen woman. Anything worth doing, really."

At this, Sara saw that Mrs. Pat had risen and was collecting her opera glasses and the fan with the large lapis "S" carved into its handle.

"Well, darlings, I must be off. I absolutely *hate* to be late for the conductor." As she squeezed past the approaching figure of the Duchess, Mrs. Pat said: "Violet."

The Duchess, with her sad, round blue eyes and high cheekbones, nodded her head: "Stella." Sara thought she caught just a glimpse of a smile pushing itself onto the Duchess of Rutland's lips.

"Oh," Diana said, taking Mrs. Pat's vacated seat, "it really is too awful that Mrs. Pat can't join us."

"Yes," the Duchess said, "but there it is. Until Cornwallis-West gets his mess cleared up, well . . ." She trailed off as Olga stood to give the Duchess her chair.

"I don't know what they're all fighting over, really," Diana said.

"Oh," Sara's mother said. "I don't know if I really *want* to know."

"I do," Olga said, eagerly.

"Oh, you must know that Mrs. Pat has been having an *amour* with George Cornwallis-West. Didn't you all? Oh, really," Diana said. "But, of course, he's married to Jennie, née Jerome, more recently Lady Randolph Churchill. It's been going on forever. Since you met her on that boat . . . which one was it?"

"The *Mauretania*," Sara said.

"An *amour*?" Adeline said vaguely.

"An affair," Hoytie said, casting an impatient eye at their mother.

"Yes, well, since you met her. And now the Cornwallis-Wests are separated, but divorce . . . that's proving more complicated," Diana said. She rubbed her thumb and index finger together.

"Why would anyone want to be married twice?" Adeline's hand rose to clutch her mauve evening bag. (Sara hated that bag, a relic of the 1890s; cold drawing rooms and mutton.)

"My feelings exactly," the Duchess said. "Once is most certainly enough."

If Sara liked Mrs. Pat, she was in awe of Violet Manners. She had never known a woman like her; she could remember the first time she met the Duchess at a weekend party at Belvoir Castle: she had descended the staircase in a midnight-blue gown, a string of the most glorious pearls Sara had ever seen twined about her neck and fastened, curiously, with diamond earrings at each shoulder. That small touch, that tiny, frivolous fragment of creativity, had moved Sara. (Why? Why? Who cared about earrings? It was just *that*, Sara reasoned: they were *supposed* to be *earrings*, not clasps, not epaulettes, not a ring, not a spoon, not a chair . . . but by reinventing them, she'd given them importance, somehow.)

The Duchess had been an artist when she was younger

and part of a bohemian set called The Souls. It was said, and not that quietly either, that she'd had a number of lovers throughout her marriage to the Duke, and some of the more persistent gossip-mongers suggested that neither Diana nor her elder sister were actually the natural children of their father.

Sara thought there was something grotesque about affairs or *amours*, or whatever one wanted to call them, as if romantic love and family were not compatible, as if logic and just plain good taste demanded they be separated. She wasn't naive enough to think that great matches were made for love, but she wondered about the worth of great matches at all.

She had only a nebulous notion of what she'd like her future to look like, but it looked nothing like any of the society drawing rooms she'd seen. Still, once ensconced in Belvoir Castle, she couldn't help admiring the way the Duchess and her daughters lived their lives. There was an artistry to everything they touched, discussions—not just of gossip, but of painters and musicians, of politics and writers—that she had rarely experienced at home or anywhere else. And she had added that to her indistinct dream, filling in a small part of the bigger picture. "Oh, I do hope there'll be some sort of scandal," Diana said as the box conductor led them around the grand circle to their seats.

"I wish everyone would stop talking about riots and scandals," Adeline said.

When Stravinsky had debuted his *Rite of Spring* in Paris the month before, the music, along with the famous dancer Nijinsky's choreography, had caused an out-and-out brawl to erupt in the theater. Women had thrown themselves at men on the other side of the aisles, beating them with their fans, and, in one reported case, a shoe. Men had fallen to slapping each other across the face with their programs and calling for duels.

Sara, however, was expecting a tempest in a teacup and the possibility of a nice long nap. She was slightly disappointed to find herself seated at the front of the box, rather than the back where it was darker and more discreet.

As the lights went down, Diana was still scanning the room with her opera glasses, and Sara could hear Hoytie sighing behind her. The Duchess let off just the faintest rustle of satin and Narcisse Noir.

The introduction began with the melancholy notes of the bassoon, all at once sliced viciously by a set of flutes. They trilled, stopped and started, like the rev of a motor car engine. The woodwinds played so high and so sharp that Sara winced and the Duchess dramatically placed a gloved hand over her right ear.

Then the curtain went up. A group of dancers clad in furs and small pointy hats, all pagan and hideous, began stamping up and down on the stage in time to the horns and strings.

"Oh my," Diana whispered.

An old crone-like figure, her face painted entirely white like a death mask, stood in the foreground, bent at the waist, clutching her stomach. Then, she too began jumping up and down and throwing herself around, falling on her back with her legs sticking up in the air.

Sara straightened her spine.

This was not ballet. Gone were the delicate, airy costumes, the movements fluid as water, toes pointed to follow the muscular line of a dancer's calf. Here, feet stuck out at right angles, dancers rounded their backs when they dipped to the floor, ordinary and inelegant as anyone picking up a scrap of paper, their arms angular as they pumped angry raised fists.

She understood what had made the Parisian audience so angry. To have one's own love of comfort and beauty thrown back in one's face in such a public way. It made the audience feel small, shallow.

But there was something else Sara recognized here, which they must have seen, too: a kind of rage. Sara's pulse flicked at her temple like a horse crop and her palms began to sweat.

Drums accompanied the pounding of feet, sending up vibrations so violent they scaled the orchestra and made the floorboards tremble. More primitive costumes filled the stage as the dancers began to clap.

"Are they actually clapping?" the Duchess mused from her seat, to no one in particular.

Sara heard her mother say something, but it was drowned out by the noise and the humming in her own head. When an elder was brought in, the whole group threw themselves down again and again onto the stage. She could hear their bodies hitting the floor; flesh and blood connecting with the dusty boards, the crush of joints and ligaments.

She wanted to be down on the stage with the dancers, feel her ribcage meet the planks, feel the sickly ache of having her breath knocked out. She was reminded of the first time she tasted blood in her mouth (a skating accident), the surprise that *it tasted good*, rich, tangy on her tongue, the even more startling revelation that she wanted to taste it again.

The maiden chosen for sacrifice now stood alone in a pool of light on the stage, motionless and knock-kneed, as the score dropped to a hush. Sara held her breath, until it was almost unbearable.

She was dizzy by the time the girl began to dance, a death spiral. Full of helplessness, compulsion. Running from pillar to post in a desire to escape her fate, to be let out of the circle. Jumping and turning herself in a frenzy.

She could almost smell the soil, hardened, awaiting spring. She was vibrating, with the lack of oxygen, the warmth of the theater and the strangeness of the music. Then the maiden, exhausted, shivered and stamped. And fell down dead.

Sara only realized the lights had gone up when her mother pressed her hand, a look of alarm in her eyes.

"Are you quite well?" she whispered.

Sara could only shake her head.

❖

"Oh dear," the Duchess said, as they made their way to the street. "It looks like 'the nice evening at the theater' is going out of style. I suppose we must all adjust."

"I thought it was horrifying," Adeline said, mauve evening bag firmly in hand. "Sara practically took ill."

"I don't see what all the fuss is about," Hoytie said. "What was that anyway? Just a bunch of unappealing people in unflattering dress hurling themselves around, as far as I could tell."

"That," Sara said, her breath only now beginning to come easily, "that was *new*." At that moment, she felt like she might never sleep again.

❖ ❖ ❖

Gerald was lying on the beach in East Hampton at five o'clock in the afternoon watching the September sun illuminate the outline of Sara Wiborg's legs beneath her white muslin dress, the swell of her breasts stamped against the horizon. The Wiborg women had only just returned from Europe, and Sara, lying on her back, hands under her head, ankles crossed, was talking about London, about the Ballets Russes and art and the people she'd met. She had a way of recounting things that he liked. She didn't gossip, but nor did she leave out any of the story.

Earlier in the day, Gerald had driven to the Dunes from Southampton to see the Wiborgs. But really it was to see her. He'd written to her while she'd been abroad for the Season, but when he was finally confronted with her this afternoon, he found he'd gone quiet. After some fairly formal greetings, Gerald, at a loss, had wandered into the dark-paneled library that looked over the lawn to the sea and carelessly picked a book. Only when he'd settled in one of the Westport chairs on the terrace did he take in the title: *Camping & Tramping with Roosevelt*. Not exactly scintillating stuff. He knew he couldn't very well go back and get another without being noticed, so he pretended to skim through a chapter about the Mammoth Hot Springs. It didn't matter. His mind, his ears and even his eyes, when he could manage it, were on her, as she worked only a few feet away in the garden, chatting to her father.

"What's this?" She was showing her father one of the string beans, running her gloved fingertip along its unnatural curve.

"Tomato thrip," her father said, taking it from her and throwing it into a refuse basket next to him.

From where he sat, it seemed to Gerald that at times they were whispering, but really he knew it was just the wind carrying their words away from him. Under the mass of her hair, he could see moisture gathering at her nape, dampening the starched collar of her dress. After a while her father went inside and she'd looked up to the terrace, unpinning her sun hat. "Shall we go down to the beach for a while?" she'd smiled.

Gerald knew that if he was considered a natural companion for any of the three girls, it wouldn't have been Sara, the furthest in age from himself. But it was Sara he'd missed while she was away, Sara he'd longed to talk to. As they lay together now, looking out over the ocean, she told him about *The Rite of Spring*.

"I wish I could describe it better, how it made me feel," she said. "It was so . . . primitive. No, that's not it. That makes it sound like it was all chickens pecking at the earth and ugly peasants. It *was* ugly, but not in any kind of simple way. Do you have any idea of what I'm talking about?"

"Animal," Gerald said.

Sara turned over on her side and looked at him, hatless, squinting in the orange blow-out of the sun. "Animal?"

"I mean, maybe that's what it was. Something that's primitive, but also . . . physical." He didn't dare say sexual.

"Yes, that's exactly it. Animal."

He liked how she rolled the word around in her mouth, as if that's what she was doing with it in her head.

"You should have seen it. *You* would have understood it." She settled back again.

"Yes," he said, nodding, but really he was thinking back to last summer, when they'd lain on the beach together almost like this, except it was dawn and they had slept there all night.

It had been after the last of Adeline Wiborg's summer parties at the Dunes, and Gerald Murphy had come over to be Olga's date. The three girls had sung and then the evening had grown into night and the rest of the guests had gone home, and the family to bed, all except Gerald and Sara and Frank Wiborg. He'd watched as she'd risen from the sofa where they'd been sitting and gone to the window and looked out at the sea, illuminated by a sliver of moon. Then she'd come back and put her hand on Gerald's shoulder and said: "Let's go sleep on the beach."

He'd nodded, but Frank had grumbled, because of course, he would have to sleep with them, too, on the cold sand.

They gathered blankets and Sara's father took a flask of whiskey and they walked to the edge of the beach grass and lay down, staring up at the stars, cold silver holes in the night sky.

Gerald didn't know when he'd fallen asleep, but at some point, he felt dawn light on his face. He'd been aware at the time, through partially closed eyes, that she was watching him. He'd kept still. After she'd gone, he'd stayed awhile, thinking of her. It had moved him, how she'd looked, or rather the knowledge that she *was* looking. What had she seen? He would have liked to have seen himself through her eyes, find his own contours. Not the hidden, shadowy ones he tried to keep buried, nor the image reflected in his father's exasperated and disappointed expression. He'd felt that what she'd seen might be something better, stronger. He couldn't say why, only that perhaps with her, he was right. The true Gerald Murphy, the one he didn't even know yet.

A year had passed since that night, a year since he'd graduated from Yale and started work at Mark Cross. And yet, that other person he longed to see in himself had yet to emerge.

A shadow passed over him and Gerald looked up. Hoytie was standing there, a large white hat shading her dark features.

"Sara," she said. "Mother's looking for you."

"Oh. What time is it?"

"Well, *I* have no idea." Hoytie looked at Gerald. "Are you staying for supper, Gerald?" She smiled at him.

When he'd first become acquainted with the family eleven years before, he'd been as attached to Hoytie as to Sara or Olga. They'd all palled around together, a fourteen-year-old Gerald blushing at Hoytie's teasing. He knew Hoytie had no real interest in him. She just liked everyone to like her best, to think of her first. He didn't mind; he found her amusing, but he felt no real closeness to her now.

"No," he said. "Father wants me back for supper."

"Oh, shame." Hoytie's gaze lingered, before she turned her attention back to her sister. "Sara."

"Yes, yes," Sara said, rising and brushing the sand off her dress. She gave Hoytie a little shove as she passed her, and Hoytie stumbled.

"How . . ." Hoytie went pink under her hat.

"Ha," Sara cried out as she ran up the dunes and onto the lawn.

Hoytie took off after her.

Gerald stood, shading his eyes with his hand, watching them push each other as they rushed up toward the house. Two white dresses, two ghosts running up the lawn, their heads inclined as they tried to keep their balance, laughing. Sara's ungloved hand, suspended in the air like a pale leaf. He had that sick feeling he often got when he watched physical intimacy, an ache in his stomach. Outside, looking in. Nose to the glass.

✦

October came crisp and self-righteously to New York City, and on this Tuesday Gerald snuck quietly out of the house, a good half an hour early, to walk to work. This allowed him to avoid "going over business" with his father on the twenty-four-block walk from their home to the offices of the Mark Cross Company, a tedious, sour morning ritual that always left him less prepared for the day, rather than more. It was something his father had instituted when Gerald's brother, Fred, started working with the firm, and a habit he continued with Gerald. The truth was that Patrick Murphy liked to harangue his sons bright and early about their lack of business sense. Fred, quite sensibly, had taken to leaving the house an hour before their father was ready, setting out on foot or in a taxi cab. But Gerald generally felt a curious inability to defy his father's plans. It was that same inability that had found him, upon his graduation from Yale the previous year, agreeing to work for his father's leather goods firm, despite the fact that the prospect smelled of death.

Today, however, Gerald craved the busy, impersonal noise of the pavement. There was a thought that wouldn't let him go. And although he couldn't say when it had begun, it had been slowly taking root. It was simple. It was this: Sara Wiborg.

An early shower had bathed the pavement, which now shimmered pigeon gray and gave off that slightly warm smell of clean tar. Sun hit the windows of Spalding Bros. as he passed, framing Gerald's reflection against a football jersey and making him think fleetingly, and painfully, of Yale, of all the ways you were in or you were out.

In the end, despite a spotty academic record and no sporting talent to speak of, he'd managed to "make it" at Yale. In his senior year, he'd been tapped for the secret society of Skull and Bones, and he'd left college with an eclectic group of friends, some of whom he continued to see in the city. Although, if he was honest, outside of the Skull and Bones fellows, many of those friends, like Cole Porter and Monty Woolley, were considered "too artistic" to be the thing.

By Forty-Fourth Street, the crush of people hurrying to work—or meetings or appointments with tailors or milliners or great-aunts—grew more dense, as if a great hue and cry of "Upwards, to the destination!" had been heard all around the city, and Gerald was swept along with them.

At the corner, the crowds relented and he stopped for a moment. He saw the red awnings of Delmonico's billow like sails in the wind, could hear the snap of the canvas in the crosstown breeze. The red, like a sash worn by Sara at one of her mother's evenings. It was all Sara: the smooth marble of the New York Public Library, her forehead; the curve of the colonnade at the Waldorf-Astoria, her calf; the elegant automobiles clogging Fifth Avenue, the shape of her spine; the golden yellow of the fallen leaves, the color of her hair.

Gerald was surprised to find that he'd arrived at the Mark Cross Company. Smoothing down his coat, he entered the building and took the lift up to his office on the third floor.

A brass plaque attached to his door read: Design Manager. It wasn't a real title, but his father said that was probably fitting. Fred had started out as treasurer, moved into the position of general manager and then secretary. Gerald, as Patrick Murphy often pointed out, was suited to none of these roles. His grasp of business was limited, and he certainly wasn't experienced enough to be general manager. His father doubted he ever would be. Still, he was insistent that Gerald should blow the cobwebs out of his mind and decided on a role that allowed his youngest son to think up designs for new products for the company. There was talk of a safety razor, and perhaps some new leather accoutrements.

After hanging up his coat, Gerald took out a pile of drawings from the bottom drawer of his desk and went over them. He loved the beauty and simplicity of the leather and saddlery they commissioned from the factory in England, but his father's withering criticism made him feel too embarrassed to show him any of his personal ideas.

He pulled out his correspondence cards and sat, idly tapping his pen, before setting it to paper.

Dear Sara,

I know you are so very busy with all the happy luncheons and teas with the ladies of the large-hatted variety (such wonderful conversation), but I was wondering if I could reserve just one day, Wednesday next, to spirit you around town.

I opened the newspaper the other day to find that there is a show of Leon Bakst's prints, his drawings for the Ballets Russes, and thought that of all the people in the world, you must see them in all their Oriental glory, before you see the real thing in India.

I thought I would make a date for the two of us to sup on Delmonico's Lobster Newburg afterwards, because as we both know, that is what the very best people do after seeing art.

Will you be tempted? I hope so.
     Yours,
      Gerald

He reread it, hoping it struck the right note between humor and sophistication. Then, feeling too nervous to delay, he put it into an envelope and went to the door, calling for the office assistant, Mr. Guise.

"Please have this delivered to Miss Wiborg." He looked

at the letter again before handing it over. "Her address is on the envelope," he added.

Shutting the door, he sat back down at his desk, only to rise again instantly. He opened the door to call for Mr. Guise, but found him standing where he'd left him, still holding the letter, a bemused expression on his face.

"Look," Gerald said, taking an annoyed tone, "will you please have one of our large drawing cases sent up from the floor and also ask one of the cutters to come to my office."

Then he sat and waited. He was setting something in motion and now that it had started he was impatient that it should all happen at once. The smell of the wet tar outside was still in his nostrils, the impression of everything being connected to itself and to her still fresh in his mind. A soft knock on the door and the cutter arrived, carrying the drawing case. Gerald noticed the man, now standing still in the doorway, had exceptionally strong-looking hands.

"Please, come in. I . . . I know you must be busy, but this is very important." Gerald fidgeted, his palms sweating.

"Sir."

"I want this drawing case altered. It's for a young lady, who will be traveling. So," he opened the case, "I want the backing taken out, so it can be rolled up. She doesn't use paints; these will need to be stitched up into compartments," he pointed to the spaces reserved for pots, "to make them small enough to hold pencils. Also, the strap: I want a buckle added, to make it more secure. Brass, I think." He could already see the case in his mind's eye.

"Yes, sir." The cutter hesitated. "I think though, sir, that the leather will be a little stiff to roll. Would you like me to oil and stretch it?"

"I see, yes," he nodded, then looking up, "thank you."

"It's nothing, sir." The cutter took the case from Gerald,

their hands brushing. Gerald pulled away quickly, but couldn't help watching the back of the man, the softness of his chambray shirt as he walked away. He seemed purposeful, Gerald thought, comfortable in his own skin.

❖

Two days passed with no response. Nothing either at home or at the office. He'd tried to be nonchalant when asking their maid, Evers, if there was anything in the post for him, but she'd just pressed her lips into a white line and gave a sour, "No, Mr. Gerald," leaving him feeling both sorry and, for some reason, humiliated.

At dinner, he asked his mother whether she knew if the Wiborgs were in town.

"I have no idea," his mother said, "although those awful papers are full of Adeline's troubles with customs." She sighed. "Luckily, your father got that Mr. Stanchfield on to it."

When the Wiborg women had returned from Europe, Adeline had made something of a stink with the customs officials, steadfastly refusing to pay the duty they demanded. She'd swiftly been indicted for smuggling, delighting the tabloid newspapers, which ran lurid headlines about the affair. Gerald's father had helped with a lawyer.

Perhaps, he thought now, they'd left the city for a while to avoid the publicity. He was wondering if he should send a letter to Sara at the Dunes, when his mother put a hand to her head, as if feeling for an impending headache, and said: "There is something, Gerald, that needs attending. I'd forgotten, because, as you know, I've not been well lately."

Gerald looked over his soup at Fred, who gave a small flicker of his eyebrow.

"Esther and I were asked to attend Mrs. Farrow's evening

of chamber music tomorrow," his mother said. "But Esther has a poem to finish." Anna Murphy stopped and stroked his younger sister's lank hair. Esther took no notice, continuing to scribble in her tattered book, her soup pushed off to one side. "And," his mother continued, "I must be here to see that she does."

Esther was their father's favorite. She wasn't a beauty—at fifteen she was gaining on six feet tall and had a lazy eye. Still, she had been deemed a genius at eleven and had recently begun publishing her poems in some of the best magazines. Their mother really understood nothing about what Esther wrote, or said, but insisted on Esther as her companion through her depressions, under the guise, of course, that she was helping her daughter. Gerald felt that Esther's formidable brain and patchy attention to her personal appearance were her way of exerting some form of limited independence, as if her physical and mental geography were the only terrain that she had under her command, and she would command ferociously. He loved and admired her for it.

"So," his mother continued, "you must go in my stead, Gerald. We really can't disappoint Mrs. Farrow."

The subtext, Gerald knew, was that they were lucky to be invited at all. Mrs. Farrow was a terrible snob, and while his father could be quite charming when he wanted to be, he still came from modest beginnings, had made his money in trade and was a Catholic. Three strikes in Mrs. Farrow's drawing room. And his mother, who distinctly lacked her husband's charisma, couldn't stand the stress of the required performance. So he was being sent. It didn't really matter; he was used to it.

"Yes, Mother," he said, but when he picked up his soup

spoon again, it seemed his appetite had deserted him. He could see Fred smirking into his own supper.

"Good," Anna Murphy said vaguely, reapplying pressure to her temple. Then after a moment: "Oh, and Fred, you must go, too."

*

The next evening was bitterly cold. Fred was hunkered down in his coat in the back of the taxi cab, sighing, his dark hair combed back from his forehead.

"Well, this should be a fine time," his brother said. He blew into his collar. "I could be at Delmonico's instead. Mother and her headaches."

The mention of Delmonico's caused Gerald a small prick of pain. He put it out of his head; she didn't feel the same, and that was all right. Why should she?

"I bet you're very much looking forward to fielding questions about the finer points of Catholicism from Mrs. Farrow."

Gerald groaned. *"Do you think you Catholics will get another saint this year? I hear the pope is just awfully busy* . . . What is there to say? One can only pray, Mrs. Farrow. God, that woman is a bitch."

"Well, perhaps if they made old New York blue bloods saints, she might consider a conversion." Fred chuckled.

"Maybe, I'll float the idea to her."

They were silent awhile, then Fred said: "Are you going to this board meeting tomorrow?"

"No," Gerald said. "I'm just the design manager."

"Whatever that means."

"Yes."

"I envy you, I really do. You don't have to listen to these

bores go on and on, or Father tell endless limericks. God, I hate this job."

Gerald looked at his brother.

"I just keep thinking that there must be something more than this," Fred said.

It was unusual to hear him speak so openly. It wasn't that their relationship was strained, exactly. It was more that he and Fred seemed to have an unspoken agreement to keep to certain topics. And those didn't include an honest appraisal of their feelings.

"Yes." Gerald leaned his head back against the seat. "There must."

Fred clapped his hands together, as if to warm them, then looked at Gerald. "Well, what's wrong with you, then?"

"Nothing."

"Yes," Fred said, turning toward him, a knowingness in his eyes. "Oh yes, there is. A girl?"

"I beg your pardon?"

"You heard me. A girl?"

"No," Gerald said, "no girl."

"Hmm," Fred said, still regarding him.

"We're here," Gerald said, and pushed the door open before his brother could ask him any more questions.

Mrs. Farrow's blue-silk drawing room was crammed full of hothouse lilies, making Gerald feel as if he was at a state funeral. The sideboard was laid out with sliced veal, jellied salmon, preserved whole fruit, small tender green beans and a large glistening bowl of grapefruit salad dotted with pimentos. He picked a sherry off a tray and looked for a spot where he might stand unseen while he gathered his strength.

He'd only had a sip from his glass when Fred came up next to him, saying: "Let's just get it over with." He steered Gerald toward one of the large windows, where their hostess stood, encased in mauve taffeta, looking like the prow of Nelson's ship. She was talking with a gentleman of the same age but slightly less girth.

"Mrs. Farrow," Fred said, taking her hand. "Our mother sends her regrets. She's devastated not to be able to be here tonight. I hope we're not too disappointing as replacements."

"Lovely to see you both." Mrs. Farrow turned towards her companion. "Mr. Beardsley, I don't think you know Fred and Gerald Murphy. Their father is the Mark Cross man, you know, all that lovely saddlery. Patrick Murphy. Do you know him?"

"I don't believe so."

They all shook hands, although Mr. Beardsley appeared relieved to have an excuse to sidle off, which he did fairly smartly.

"I hope your mother isn't unwell," Mrs. Farrow said.

"Not exactly top form," Fred replied.

Gerald, facing the entrance to the drawing room, felt his attention wander to the other guests milling about.

"It's funny you two should show up at this instant," Mrs. Farrow continued. "Delphine Conrad and I were just discussing that Saint Rita—Saint *Rita*, really too prosaic— that the pope canonized a few years ago. Do you know Mrs. Conrad? Where has she gotten to? Oh, there she is, by the sweet sherry. Well, no matter. Do you know the one I'm talking about, Gerald?"

Gerald felt her hand on his arm and he turned back. "Mrs. Conrad?"

"No, the saint, with the funny name. Like a shopgirl. Anyway, apparently she's the saint of abused wives." Mrs. Farrow smiled at Gerald and then Fred. "We were saying, Delphine and I, that really, perhaps we could all use a little saint like that."

Gerald knew Fred was trying to keep from laughing; he could feel him almost vibrating next to him.

"How's that brilliant sister of yours?"

He didn't listen to Fred's response. He was looking across to the doorway, where a shape in cream silk was passing, face turned away. He knew that shape: the large breasts, the small waist and all that hair, the color of aster honey, piled up. She came back and was standing, listening to something. She saw him and he saw her. She didn't smile and Gerald's chest felt tight. And then, without realizing that it was going to happen, he said: "Sara."

"What's that?" Mrs. Farrow turned in the direction of Gerald's gaze. "Ah yes, Sara Wiborg. Goodness, is she still unmarried?"

Fred was looking now, too.

"You're quite close with the Wiborgs, aren't you? They often have you to stay in East Hampton."

"No," Fred said tartly. "We visit them, and yes they are friends. But our father has his own house in Southampton. I believe you lunched with us last summer."

"Did I?" Mrs. Farrow asked sweetly. "I don't remember."

Gerald didn't care about Mrs. Farrow's sudden amnesia or Fred's annoyance or the saint with a name like a shopgirl or any of it; he only cared that she was walking towards them and any second she would be with them.

Her expression was serious until she was about three or four steps away, when her face lit up in a smile, like an actress coming on stage. She took Mrs. Farrow's hand and must have been exchanging the usual pleasantries, but Gerald was fixated on watching her mouth move and the words spilling out were meaningless to him. Every moment that she didn't look at him or speak to him was an agony. He felt like demanding in a loud voice if she'd received his letter, if she gave a damn about him. Instead, he gently clasped his hands behind his back and looked at the floor.

"Gerald?"

He looked up.

"Won't you take my hand?" She was smiling at him. He wondered if it was the stage smile or a real one.

"Of course," he said. He tried to feel the warmth of her through her glove, but wasn't sure if what he felt was only the heat of his own hand. Aware of Fred's gaze on him, he released her.

"I must check that the musicians have everything they need," Mrs. Farrow said. "We'll be starting shortly. Sara, do get yourself a sherry."

"I'll get it for you, Sara," Fred said gallantly, leaving Gerald both helpless for not offering first and alone with the only person he really wanted to talk to.

"How have you been?" Gerald asked, trying to sound as neutral as possible.

"Busy," Sara said. "There's this uproar with Mother's customs." She colored a bit. "Well . . . you know."

"Yes."

"Your father was wonderful, you know," she said quietly. "She pleaded guilty in court yesterday. It was actually quite awful . . . Anyway, this is a dull topic."

It hadn't occurred to Gerald that Sara would take such a thing so hard. She always seemed impervious to societal judgment of this sort. But of course, reputations were everything. "No," he said, "I'm the one who's sorry. My invitation must have seemed so trivial and insulting with everything that's going on."

She looked up at him, still a little pink, and said: "No, not at all. It was quite dashing and wonderful. I just wasn't sure if it was out of pity and then things got a bit busy and I didn't know what to say."

"It wasn't out of pity." He looked at her seriously.

"Oh, no. Of course. Well . . ."

"Sara, your sherry," Fred said, joining them. "And Mrs. Farrow has sent out the word to take our seats."

❋

They stood in the glass-fronted gallery, not speaking. The graceful shapes of Leon Bakst's Eastern demi-gods, priestesses and fairytale characters—their pointed toes and voluminous costumes, heavy headdresses weighing on slender necks, all colored in indigo and emerald—hung on the white walls before them.

Gerald could hear the sound of ladies' shoes and gentlemen's canes hitting the walnut floorboards, the whispers and occasional giggles as they glanced at the images. Swollen brown bellies and peacock feathers created by a Russian Jew for the holy trifecta of the Ballets Russes: Stravinksy, Diaghilev and Nijinsky. But he and Sara were quiet.

They moved slowly and stopped in front of each watercolor, as the other spectators outstripped them and disappeared.

The Blue God was waiting for them at the end. When they drew up in front of him, Gerald could hear Sara breathe a little harder, saw her chest rise, all the tiny buttons on her daydress shivering. His own breath seemed caught somewhere in his chest.

The knowing face and cruelly drawn eyebrows, the satyr's smile. The skin, starting out green like the Atlantic, deepening into an almost black smoothness. The forearm and biceps of a man, but the delicate, elongated fingers of a woman. Male and female in one. Dressed in gold, with pink

66

over the chest, where a bosom might have been, and balancing on one leg like a lotus. It was the shape, both powerful and graceful; the watercolored texture of the flesh; but mainly it was in the Blue God's eyes looking directly at you, as if he knew everything, judged everything, was everything.

He couldn't say why exactly, but Gerald felt he might cry and was ashamed. As if whatever he saw in the image before him echoed in some secret place in his heart. Then he felt Sara take his hand in hers, clasping it tightly, reaching across the wide black space of all his longing and loneliness.

The Wiborgs had set sail in December and the first letter Gerald received from Sara was posted from London, where the family had stopped to spend Christmas on their way to India. They'd stayed at Belvoir Castle with the Duchess of Rutland, whom Sara seemed to worship, and her daughter Diana, whom she loved. They'd ridden to hounds, she informed him, and dined outdoors, and been forced to eat burning plum pudding at every meal, even breakfast. In short, she'd written him, he wouldn't believe just how picturesque she'd become. Although Sara mocked the experience, Gerald felt slight panic at the thought of all the things she had done and seen, all the people she knew, that he had not and did not.

Still, the thought of her hand, its pressure in his grasp, pushed him to persevere.

New York
January 1, 1914

Dear Sara,

However picturesque you may have been on
horseback, it is nothing compared with the vision
I would like to present to you of young Gerald

Murphy, sitting useless at his large, dust-covered
desk at Mark Cross, endlessly trying to make heads
or tails out of sums and papers. Sometimes, even, he
goes so far as to sketch something that will no doubt
end in a wastebasket hidden in a closet at the farthest
ends of the building. From there, he may go to
Delmonico's or Rector's for dinner, perhaps on to the
theater, with other equally distinguished young men,
where he will be forced to talk of nothing but sums and
papers. Talk about picturesque; it is truly a glorious
sight.

Sometimes, just sometimes, he catches a glimpse
of a painting illuminated from the inside, the hoof of a
horse so shiny it looks like it's been treated with polish,
a woman with heavy hair pressed in a doorway in the
sleet, and is reminded that all is not lost.

Tell me more of your adventures.

Sending love and New Year's wishes to everyone,
Gerald

* * *

Port Said
January 15, 1914

Dear Gerald,

We have reached Port Said, where this letter will
be making its journey back to you. Lights, lights
everywhere as we crossed that invisible line between
Europe and the Orient. The smell of something black
and burning—rubber?—fills our nostrils and, while
Father complains dreadfully, it excites me. When the
sun comes up, what shall we see? Even the air feels
different here. I will try to get another letter off before

we make for the Suez Canal, so that I can sketch these
thin lines in.

I'm sure work is a bore, but you must persevere.
Your father is wrong about you—you have an eye, Jerry.
Laziness is having a gift and not using it. But you are
using it.

As for the company you're keeping, well, it does
sound dull. Perhaps some new companions, who share
your excitement about even the smallest thing, are
called for.

Hoytie and Olga send their love, as do I.

Sara

❋

New York
February 3, 1914

Dear Sara,

After your last letter, I waited patiently for the
suite. I imagined your Port Said full of markets of
silk and camels and turbans, covered in a black mist.
Sadly, it seems your missive is an orphan.

I don't know why I can't get on, as other men do.
Even Fred, who loathes the work perhaps more than I,
seems content to go about his life, while I feel like
there must be something out there that I'm missing.
Something more . . . complete. I am going to stop
writing. If I go on, you'll only think of me as weak-
minded and complaining.

Somewhat foolishly, but not without fondness,

Gerald

❋

New York
February 15, 1914

Dear Sara,

It is a beautiful, soft day in New York, the kind that mercilessly fools you into believing that spring is just around the corner, and the cherry trees are busily making their buds. Or so I like to imagine.

A woman passed me in Central Park yesterday in a dress nearly the same color those blossoms will be: delicate, warm pink, almost fading to white. As if she herself were spring, or trying to tell me something of it. And I thought: I wish you were here to talk this over with. I can't very well chat to the men I see about such a small thing, without being thought effeminate. Wilson, Panama, and the Cadillac 1914, yes. But something so slight, which weighs so heavily on me afterwards, no. Yet, you are not here. And I long to know what your eyes are seeing, something brighter and bolder, no doubt.

The Black Service—that darkness that descends on me without warning, and which had me in its grip in the last letter—has passed. I can write to you now with a clearer head and, perhaps, clearer intention.

It is as if I have been living in some shell, some prison, that is shaped like the world, but is actually some false interpretation of it. There are times I could shake with frustration at not being able to make what I feel inside manifest on the outside. I would give anything to be able to taste and see and feel and show things like other people, but I am held in, somehow.

Write to me of your adventures.

Yours,
Gerald

Jaipur
March 10, 1914

Dear Gerald,

Let us talk of small things, then. I sleep with your beautiful drawing case under my head on trains. So soft, it feels as though it has been thumbed a hundred times. A pillow full of sketches that have you lined in them, not your likeness, of course, but things I think you will understand, even if you've never seen them before.

And Bombay, not a small thing, of course, but full of the Blue God. Full of Bakst, and thus full of the afternoon we spent together.

Then Jaipur, the Pink City, all rose-colored, indeed bolder than your cherry blossoms, and warmer. Painted pink for the Prince of Wales—imagine such a thing— and the Palace of the Winds, like an intricate wedding cake, built of blushing sandstone. To see it lit just before sunset, it simply glows. Yesterday, we rode elephants, their leathery gray ears softer than you can imagine— softer even than your case—to the Amber Palace, set like some fairytale castle high on a hill.

It's dryer here than Bombay, and gives one the impression of truly being lost to the outside world.

You should see this, Jerry. Nothing, not even your Black Service, could reach you here.

Yours,
    Sara

Post Script: We have decided to stop in Rome instead of going straight on to Marseille, so send any further post this month to:

Palazzo del Grand Hotel
Via Vittorio Emanuele Orlando, 3

Rome
March 20, 1914

Dearest Wayward Jerry,

What can you possibly mean by never writing?
You have neglected us shamefully. Olga and Hoytie are
reading this over my shoulder, with equal indignation,
having reminded me this afternoon that the last letter
we received from you was as far back as January.
Like Phileas Fogg, we have been round the world and
return to civilization none the wiser to your doings.

Hoytie says she has heard that you were seen
skulking around at a costume ball at the St. Regis,
and we would like to know what costume it was you
were wearing.

India has been magical, really the wildest success,
even if we were accused by the local newspaper in
Delhi of singing "coon song snatches"—a very poor way
of describing our lovely ragtime medley performance
at the Gymkhana Club. Hoytie wants me to tell you that
the reaction "was disgusting." Father felt it was a poor
selection (his words), and remains very huffy about it.
Mother, of course, is thrilled.

Do send news.

Love from us all.

＊

Rome
March 25, 1914

Dear Gerald,

Please forgive the last letter. I know you'll
understand. But, really, what have you been doing?
I have been sketching quite a lot. Spring in Rome truly

is Jamesian and, after India, feels very false and
mannered. I'm pining for the colors—the reds and
greens and golds, the pinks and blues—the smell
of amber burning and the noise of the market calls.
The air was so thick with it, it almost had weight.

    In haste,
      Sara

✿

            New York
            April 16, 1914

Dear Sara,

    It seems your letters from Rome were much
delayed—the slow boat to China perhaps?—so that
all three of them, including the one from Jaipur, arrived
at once yesterday. It was strange reading them in
tandem, like a mask and then the face underneath.

    India—I need more time to respond to what you
wrote. It feels as if my head is full of the sounds, the
touch of the things you describe so eloquently.

    Although you are much missed here, I would not
trade places in that Jamesian paradise you find yourself
in. Instead, I will await your return, which seems
increasingly far off, and content myself with the
company of people who eat chicken salad and nod
their heads at every piece of wisdom trotted out.
My God, this is a bad age for singular thought.

    Work is quite busy—with what I am not entirely
sure. If I figure it out, I will write it in my next letter.

    Yours,
      Gerald

✿

Cannes
May 6, 1914

Dear Gerald,

I am glad spring has finally come to you. Have you seen your cherry blossoms? We have left Rome and are now in Cannes with its extremely muscular Casinos. I've been wondering about something you wrote to me, a small thing, really, but . . .

✿

New York
June 1, 1914

Sara,

Your last letter made your absence even keener. Will you not come back . . .

Deauville
July 6, 1914

Dear Gerald,

It's strange, how finally your voice, the true one you allude to, has reached me over these thousands of miles and many months. Can it be true . . .

✿

New York
July 18, 1914

Dear Sara,

I know exactly how you feel. It's stifling in New York, but all I can think of is that it will be exactly in this kind of weather that you return, and therefore feel extremely amiable towards it. Still, everything here whispers of your absence. What you said has changed how I see things . . .

❖

London
July 18, 1914

Dear Gerald,

Your reply has not reached me (and may never at this rate). But this crossed my mind in the meantime: will you . . .

❖

Southampton
July 31, 1914

Dear Gerald,

I will be with you before this letter is, but writing about this in my diary doesn't seem enough. Perhaps things have started to feel unreal unless I tell them to you. All talk is about war, and as we wait for the *Lusitania* to set sail, we have heard rumors that Germany is preparing to enter the dispute over the murdered Archduke. Everyone on board is twitchy. We've been told that we will be sailing without lights, and they are loading the cruiser guns. She is, of course, a British ship and no one knows where we'll be in five days, so these are the precautions. I long to read an American newspaper to see where we really stand, but alas, we can't get hold of anything less than a week old.

Is it really possible for these great old nations to move this fast? Things always seem just that little bit slower in Europe, a little more refined, and yet in four days it seems as if everything has been thrown up in the air, the music going at a dizzying pace.

I remember once longing for the Ritz to burn. I am sorry for that now. I hope we will get there safely and that yours shall be the first face I see.

S.

✿   ✿   ✿

The day Owen went up in the flying machine broke bright and clear over the island. He'd risen far earlier than he needed to, but he'd been waiting for this day for four years. Four years since he'd stolen his first look at her in the barn.

Europe had just declared war on itself and it was all anyone could talk about. Even Mr. Glass. Well, especially Mr. Glass, who only last evening, on one of their walks, had spoken only of that, as if the next day they wouldn't be flying in an aeroplane in the sky.

"Bad business, what's happening in Europe," he'd said. "Still, they're always fighting about something, some small border or other. It'll be over before you know it. We just have to keep those shipping lines clear and make sure we don't get dragged into their mess."

But Owen didn't care about shipping lines or border disputes in faraway places. All he could think about was that he was finally going to take flight, like the Wright Brothers. But he'd tried to nod thoughtfully, anyway, as they'd ambled through the old cemetery.

They often walked there. Mr. Glass liked looking at the headstones and also it wasn't far from Owen's farm. It had become a weekly excursion, if the weather permitted. Mr. Glass would drive his motor car out to the cemetery and he and Owen would walk its perimeter and chat. Sometimes about the farm, what Owen was planting or harvesting, sometimes about his plans for the future.

In the years since Mr. Glass had come to the island, he'd gained a reputation for being a bit, well, different. He didn't seem to take any notice of age or station when choosing his friends. On any given evening he was as likely to be found playing cards and talking cotton with Councilman Perry, the second richest man among them, as he was to be drinking whiskey and discussing infectious diseases (a particular interest) with the old schoolmaster, Mr. Cushing.

He was generous with his money, even if, for the most part, he stayed out of local politics. His only real cause, and the only thing Owen had ever heard him be unreasonable about, was what he called sexual vice. As far as Owen could tell, this encompassed any kind of unwedded contact. He could work himself red in the face on the subject of perversion.

Owen suspected it might have something to do with what had become of Mrs. Glass, whom the mainlander never spoke of and whose fate was unknown. Other than that one subject, though, Mr. Glass was as kind and warm a man as Owen had ever encountered.

Of all the favors Mr. Glass bestowed, the most unlikely were reserved for Owen, who was far below him in *both* age and station. Yet, Mr. Glass had adopted him somehow, as his own. There had been many kindnesses over the years: a pair of church shoes at Christmas, books for his birthday (this year, the very funny *Ransom of Red Chief* and the somewhat bewildering *Scarlet Plague*), paying the vet bill when Lettuce's calf had breached. And no doubt Mr. Glass would have done more, if Owen's mother hadn't made it clear, through silence and declined invitations, that she didn't approve.

In the four years he'd known Mr. Glass, Owen's life had unfolded as anyone could have guessed it would: he went to school until he knew enough to stop and devote himself full time to running his farm and taking care of himself and his mother. Now, at nineteen, he was strong, tall and built for labor. He would eventually be expected to marry, have children of his own and teach them how to run the farm. The only unexpected things that had happened to him originated with Mr. Glass.

Specifically, Owen's special status when it came to the flying machine. Ever since he'd met Mr. Glass that day when he'd snuck into his barn, Owen had been deemed vital to every launch, every repair, every small discussion of *Flora*.

Owen knew his mother thought it was odd that a man like Mr. Glass would be interested in someone like him. More than odd, he knew she felt it might be dangerous, somehow. But Owen understood, at least he thought he did. There was something missing in Mr. Glass, and he filled it. It was that simple. A need to impart something, to leave something behind. He had his son Charlie, of course. But, well, Mr. Glass seemed disappointed in him somehow. Not like he loved him any less, but just that somehow he wasn't what Mr. Glass had hoped. And Owen could tell that Charlie knew it; in the few times he'd met him, he'd felt the younger man's eyes on him, following him, watching him, with a trace of disgust or mockery or something Owen couldn't quite put his finger on.

This morning, though, he tried to put all these things out of his mind, even his mother's unspoken disapproval of his impending flight. She'd agreed to give him the morning and early afternoon off, and he'd promised he would be back in time to do his afternoon chores, and that the hired man could do the rest in his absence.

To his surprise, though, when he went into the kitchen, she handed him some bread and cheese and let her hand linger on his shoulder.

"Wind's from the south. That'll be fine," she said.

It was the first time that his mother had indicated that she'd been listening to his obsessive chatter about *Flora*: all his long explanations, over the years, about how the machine worked, how the elevator at the front helped control pitch and balance, how the lever controlled both roll and yaw, how it was best to take off into a headwind.

Owen looked at the clock for the hundredth time that morning. Then he gathered up his things and set out.

The farmland went from cool and lush to a fine light green as the dew on the beach grass evaporated and the stalks took on a razor-like quality. By the time he arrived, everything was hot, sharp, bright, and the sound of the beetles whined in his ears.

A small crowd of people stood around the edge of the cut field, drinking lemonade, dressed in their finery: some boaters and some bare heads, depending on which part of the island they belonged to. More boaters than bare heads on the Glass land.

It was breezier here than inland, and off to one side Owen saw Mr. Glass's daughter, the flesh-and-blood Flora, her white dress pushed close against her body in the wind. She reminded him of those blades of beach grass before the sun hit them, slightly curved under the weight of the condensation. She was looking at the ground and her hat obscured her features. But her posture suggested to him that inward quietness, that *waiting*, which seemed to come off her like a perfume.

Next to her stood her brother, also slight, with a mouth

like a girl's. His hands were stuffed in his jacket pockets, his eyes wary.

He didn't really know them, the Glass children. They'd both been away at school in the early days of his acquaintance with Mr. Glass. Now, Charlie was at university, and Flora, whom Mr. Glass referred to as his little domestic angel, lived in Boston with an aunt.

"Owen." Mr. Glass's voice carried from the barn. He was gesturing for him to go over.

Mr. Glass was wearing the same thing he always wore to go up: a one-piece suit, like long-johns, only made of sail cloth and fastened at the front with pearl buttons, and a flat cap secured by motoring goggles, which at this moment rested above the brim. The first time he'd seen this getup, Owen had felt strange about those pearl buttons. But Mr. Glass had explained that they had been sewn on by Flora herself, from her own little sewing box, for good luck.

"Owen, we don't have all day."

He hurried to reach Mr. Glass and the five other men, including Mr. Cushing, gathered to help push *Flora* out and onto her track. He felt Mr. Glass grip his shoulder hard as he entered the barn.

"Perfect headwind." He smiled at Owen. "You ready, son?"

"Yes, sir," he said, but his eyes were on *Flora*, her clean lines and shapes rising before him.

They all took their places and, on the count of three, lifted the machine, her skis just barely off the ground, and stepped her out sideways onto a small trolley. Then they began to push, down the field, the smell of freshly cut grass rising both bitter and sweet, towards the derrick.

Once there, they backed her up onto the track and bridled her with the rope, white as bone and waxed, that attached to the weight. Owen put the trap in place to hold her. Mr. Glass climbed into his seat and opened the compression release and adjusted the spark, while Francis Carey and Mr. Cushing turned the propellers.

The engine came to life, a noise louder than any motor engine, dark and vibrating. The propellers turned on their own, biting through the air, and the machine was pushing against the trap like an anxious racehorse.

"It's time," Mr. Glass's mouth said; he couldn't hear the actual words.

Owen took a look at the crowd, seeing all the pairs of eyes staring back, then climbed up and arranged himself in the passenger seat. His hand brushed the red velvet under him. Mr. Glass touched his arm, making him flex involuntarily. The older man handed him a pair of motoring goggles. Owen pulled them down around his eyes and the world became a little less clear, less stable, like looking through a thin film of water.

Mr. Glass raised his left hand in the air and the men began hauling the weight, hand over hand on the rope. When it reached the top of the derrick, Mr. Glass gave the signal and *Flora* shot forward, pushing wind into Owen's surprised mouth.

The machine cleared the track and lifted slightly, before dropping again and hopping a bit. Then she was no longer making for the ground, but for the sky, and with the rumbling of the engine in his ears, Owen thought: *It's happening, it's happening right now.* His stomach seemed to be pulling downwards, as if it didn't want to be separated from the earth. The weight of his heart, however, felt strangely light, like it was traveling in the opposite direction.

The sun was on his face. In the horizon, past the farmland and beach grasses, he could see Katama Bay to the left and the open Atlantic in front of him, growing from light to a blue darker than winter pine.

Mr. Glass kept the lever pulled back, and *Flora's* nose pointed ever upwards. They were clearing the property now, and Owen looked at Mr. Glass; Mr. Glass smiled at him, his teeth a brilliant white, and Owen felt afraid and filled with joy.

He looked down. To his left, he saw a flock of Canada geese take flight in a clean V-formation, their black heads like arrow tips. To his right, an expanse of farmland, a patchwork quilt of corn crops and the now-shorn hay fields, the fallow land brown on top. He couldn't believe how beautiful it looked from the sky. Owen thought about his own farm, the land he worked. He knew its edges and colors, its smells. He knew when it was harvest time by touch, knew its quickening beneath his fingers. But never had he imagined that it had this kind of logical symmetry.

Before they reached the dunes guarding the beach, Mr. Glass rolled the plane slightly, and with pressure on the right-hand lever *Flora* began to turn. They were circling round to begin the journey back and the descent. Owen tried to memorize everything he could see, his island, its contours and geography. It was like a body, like his own body, he thought, its curves and dips, the places it was hard and soft, its imperfections.

Mr. Glass was staring at him, then he took Owen's hand in his own. Owen looked down at his hand and back at Mr. Glass, who nodded, as if they were in agreement. And perhaps they were: perhaps Mr. Glass had that same feeling, thrumming, weightless, altered. Like his insides had been scrambled up, changed forever.

The moment hung between them for what seemed a long time, everything suspended, and then all at once they were down, hitting the ground in hard fits as they rushed across the field toward the barn. Mr. Glass was pushing *Flora's* nose down, as if grinding her back into the earth. Then she stopped, and it was all over.

Stepping back onto the firm ground, Owen felt dizzy. He looked around and saw some of the watching crowd moving towards them, men clapping Mr. Glass on the back.

Owen, though, was still up there: the black arrows of the geese, the line of dunes, the outlines of the fields. And then there was the feeling, the feeling of being unbound to anything.

"Would you like a lemonade?"

He turned and saw Flora, swaying slightly in her white dress, holding a cup out to him.

"Thanks," he said, taking it and drinking it down in one swallow.

"Did you love it?" She was talking to him, but looking at the ground.

"Yes."

"Was it like it is in dreams, I mean when you can fly in your dreams?"

"I don't have those dreams," Owen lied.

"Oh." She was blushing a little.

He'd embarrassed her. Then he realized he'd wanted to embarrass her, but he couldn't say why. Maybe it was his irritation at the interruption. Or maybe just to see what she'd do. He felt giddy at the thought.

"You looked very happy when you came back."

"I was," he said. "I am."

Behind her, Owen could see Charlie Glass making his way across the field. He was walking slowly, but Owen could see his gaze was firmly fixed on them. When he reached them, he draped an arm over his sister's shoulders.

"So, was it everything you hoped for?" He smiled lazily.

Owen frowned. "It was."

"I'd like to go up," Flora said. "I think it must be wonderful."

"Father won't let her," Charlie said. "Too precious, aren't you?" He looked at his sister. "We can't have you miles up in the air. We need you here."

"And you? Have you never wanted to go up?"

"Oh no," Charlie waved his hand, dismissing the idea. "We're earthly beings, Flora and I. Unlike Father. And you, of course."

"I'm just a farmer." Owen shifted his feet. He felt uncomfortable. He couldn't tell if Charlie was making fun of him or being serious.

"Well, you're a farmer who flies in aeroplanes and talks to cows."

Owen looked up sharply.

"Don't be angry," Flora said. "Father told us about your cow. Lettuce. How you talk to her. It's perfectly lovely."

"You're like a magical farmer," Charlie said, his eyes on Owen. "Look," he said, running his hand through his hair, "Flora and I have been wanting to take a trip up island for a picnic and a swim. We were hoping you'd join us. Weren't we?"

"Oh yes," Flora said. "Say you will."

"I have my chores." Owen could hear himself, a terse rube, a country bumpkin with no manners. He hated it.

"Well, how about next Sunday? You can't work on Sundays."

"Thank you, but I have church, and the farm doesn't know Sunday from any other day of the week." He could imagine what his mother would have to say, or not say, about this.

"Oh please. We'll arrange everything," Flora said. "We can pick you up after church."

"Exactly," Charlie said. And when Owen remained silent, trying to figure a way out of it, he added: "Excellent. It's settled then. It'll be a grand adventure."

Owen wasn't sure how it had been settled, exactly, but they were quick, he had to give them that. He couldn't help but admire how they'd worked in tandem, like two birds of prey. He was thinking about this when their father came over and, touching his daughter on the shoulder, said: "Are we nearly ready for lunch?"

"Yes, Father," she said.

"Owen, you'll stay, won't you?"

"I can't, Mr. Glass. Have to get back to the farm."

He looked disappointed. Then he clasped Owen's arm and for a moment the three of them stood that way, Mr. Glass connecting them, Charlie off to one side.

"Thank you," Owen said. He was remembering the man's hand in his.

Then Mr. Glass smiled at Owen, as if to relieve him of the burden of having to say anything else.

"Well, come on, you two." He turned to his children, and the three of them moved off towards the small group still hovering near the edge of the field.

Owen stayed. He ran his hands over the machine, her smooth spruce and sticky fabric, her wiring. He held his palm above the engine, feeling the rising heat hitting his skin. In the distance the crowd was dispersing, some back to their regular lives, their chores, perhaps a swim in the bay, others off to the Glass house for lunch.

After a while, he too left, heading home to his mother, to his farm, his chores.

❖

It was the dead of night and Owen was running, running as fast as he could. Sweat trickling down his temples, his back, in the darkness. Running to outstrip the thoughts in his own head. But they wouldn't go. Only a week had passed since he'd flown up in the sky, only a week, but everything was different. Everything was ruined. In the tumble of his mind he thought of his mother, of Mr. Glass. He thought of a kiss. And he kept running, as it burned down his body.

Was he ashamed? No, he was not. But he was afraid. And he was sad; sadness like someone had blown a hole in his heart and now there was only a current rushing where his heart should be.

It had all begun with the picnic, although perhaps it had really started before then, with Mr. Glass's favor. Perhaps inevitable disaster had been building and growing all these years, like a storm. But he couldn't help thinking the turning point had been the picnic. They'd come the next Sunday, as they'd said they would, picking him up after church. And he'd gone with them, despite the look on his mother's face.

They'd ridden up island, where the pine and scrub gave way to the lusher oaks and beech. On the way, they'd eaten raspberries. Charlie had reached into the satchel next to him and pulled out a pouch of wax paper. He'd passed it to Flora, who'd picked a berry, inspecting it, and then to Owen.

They were a bit soft and crushed, warm from being in the bag and then in Charlie's hand. He'd put one in his mouth, and tasted its furry sweetness, then the sting from the acid at the back of his throat.

When they'd reached the small pond, hidden away from the more popular bathing holes, Flora had laid the picnic out on a white cloth: a loaf of bread, some cheese, hard-boiled eggs, beach plum jelly, part of a leg of lamb wrapped in muslin, the congealed fat dotting its surface, and a small bottle of wine.

He was hungry, but he'd waited for Flora to parcel out the lunch. Charlie seemed to have no qualms, though, tearing off a piece of the lamb between his fingers, eating it slowly.

Flora had handed them each a glass of wine. He never drank wine at home, except on special occasions, Christmas and christenings. But that day he'd put most of it down in one swallow. It had been delicious, more bitter than he remembered.

"Charlie, a toast? You're always so clever with them."

Charlie had raised his glass and said: "To the babies."

"Oh no," Flora had said, laughing. "Something prettier."

Her brother had laughed too, choking slightly on his lamb.

Owen watched them. At that moment they'd seemed lovely and mysterious and they spoke in tongues. His earlier discomfort with them, the feeling that he was missing something, something vital in their banter, did little to mitigate his pleasure; he enjoyed them the way you could enjoy a magic trick without understanding how it worked.

"All right," Charlie said. He held his glass up. *"All days of glory, joy and happiness."*

Flora held out her glass to Owen. "Yes, yes, that's good. We should drink to that, shouldn't we, Owen?" Her eyes were lovely, he'd realized, heavy lashes.

"Yes," he said, touching his glass to hers. "We should drink to that."

"Enough mooning," Charlie said. "Lunch."

They ate, Flora delicately peeling the eggshells with the tip of her nail. Charlie was not nearly as careful, leaving bits of food dotted around him. Owen ate everything quickly and was finished before the others. Flora offered him her second egg.

"I couldn't," she said. "Really, you have it."

It was warm and humid, and afterwards, when the food was finished and the wine all gone, they lay in the grass. Owen felt sweat beading his upper lip. He wanted a swim but he was tired and his limbs felt heavy.

"Shall we play hide and seek?" Flora asked.

"No," Charlie groaned.

"Oh yes," she said. "Owen, don't you think we should?"

He did not think so. "It's a child's game," he said.

"I know that. But it's fun to play. To pretend. Didn't you like it when you were younger?"

"I don't know," he said. "I can't remember playing it."

"Well, then we have to."

When neither of them moved, she said: "All right, I'll hide first. Count to one hundred and then start looking."

"That's not how it's played," Charlie said.

"I know. But I'm giving you each one hundred seconds more to rest."

"Mmm. Go on. We'll rest."

Owen, his eyes closed, heard the swish of Flora's bare feet through the grass as she made off somewhere behind him. He started counting in his head and stopped at thirty. He drifted off, somewhere between sleep and waking. The real world was there, but so were other thoughts that had no place in it.

He sensed Charlie moving.

"I think we're at a hundred," he said.

Owen opened his eyes and slowly stood. "More, probably." He wanted to sleep.

He looked in the direction Flora had taken and was

about to set off when Charlie stayed him, his hand on Owen's arm.

"Never mind that," Charlie said. "Let's swim."

Owen smiled, but jerked his head, silently indicating Flora.

"Oh, she'll come back when she realizes no one is looking for her. She's fine. It's too hot to play games, anyway."

Owen looked at the pond, cool and green and still. He undid his shirt, fumbling with the small buttons, and removed his undershirt, before unbuckling his pants and stripping down fully. They were his Sunday clothes, somewhat grass-stained now, and his mother wouldn't like it. He kicked them off to the side.

Looking over, he saw that Charlie was still fully clothed, staring at him.

"Are you planning on swimming with your clothes on?" For the first time since he'd known him, he thought Charlie looked ridiculous and felt a small, pleasurable shock of power.

"No, I . . ." Charlie was embarrassed and started quickly undressing himself.

Without waiting, Owen ran into the water, plunging into its cool depths. It had a silky quality and he felt it gliding off him as he surfaced, washing away the heat and the wine. He laughed.

Charlie stood at the edge a moment, waiting, before running in too, flailing his arms and hooting.

"My God, that's good," he said, slicking his wet hair back off his face.

"It is," Owen said.

Charlie dove down and came up. "It's deep here. I can't touch."

"We can dive from there," Owen said, pointing to a low-slung oak branch off to the side. "It'll hold."

They both swam fast, gasping for air, pushing each other down to get ahead.

As they stood on the bank, Charlie climbed up on the branch. Owen watched his body, wet and curved like a scythe, slicing into the water, showing off.

He went next, pulling his knees to his chest, dropping like a rock, and landing thunderously close.

Charlie skittered off to where he could stand, wiping water out of his eyes. "You ass." But he was laughing.

Owen was treading water, smirking, and after a bit Charlie joined him. Now they were both looking at each other, their arms and legs working invisibly underneath the water to keep their heads up. He felt a real joy, sudden and complete, and it overwhelmed him. He wondered if Charlie felt the same, if it was hanging between them, suspended.

"You look like two seals." They both turned their heads to find Flora standing at the edge. "It seems I turned out to be the one seeking."

"Sorry, Flo," Charlie said. "It was just too hot. And the pond was too cold to resist. Come join us." He slapped the water.

"Oh really," she said, turning and pretending to busy herself with packing up the picnic.

Charlie swam towards her and walked calmly, naked, out of the water, in a display of comfort with his sister that he hadn't shown with Owen. Owen wondered whose benefit it was for. His own clothes were lying in a pile next to Flora, trapping him in the pond.

"Come on," Charlie said, his pretty mouth smiling.

Owen snorted and shook his head. "I don't think so."

"Oh, don't be so shy."

"Charlie," Flora said. "Bring Owen his clothes." Her voice had lost its kind teasing tone, its flintiness surprising Owen.

Brother and sister looked at each other and then Charlie shrugged and picked up Owen's pants and undershirt and brought them over to the oak branch, placing them behind the tree. He waited while Owen climbed out.

"Charlie, come help me wash the glasses."

Only later, when they were on their way home, had Owen noticed the small raspberry stain blooming on Flora's skirt, like a kiss.

❖

That's what he remembered now, running through the darkness. A kiss. But first there'd been a note, a small elegant hand, telling him to come to the barn, a secret meeting in the night. And he'd gone. And in the darkness, they'd found each other, breath hot. Then: the softness of the thigh, softer than Lettuce's flank. The small, low gasp as their lips parted. As his tongue pushed in. That desire he never knew existed. All of it instantly extinguished by the sudden lantern, Mr. Glass's face twisted in front of them: first surprise, then rage, then disgust.

When he'd seen Mr. Glass in the light, heard him say calmly: "I'll kill you," Owen had tensed for a fight. He'd had no intention of running then, at least he didn't think he did. He did think of letting Mr. Glass kill him, that was true. It seemed fair, somehow. But then next to him, he'd heard, "Go. Go now," whispered in his ear and he'd obeyed. As simple as that. Like hearing a starter's gun. And he'd run, like he was running now.

His feet hadn't taken him home, though, but to Mr.

Cushing's house. Why he chose the old schoolmaster, he couldn't say. Perhaps he thought that he, with all his learning, might understand, or maybe because he was a friend of Mr. Glass's, like Owen had been, and he would be able to offer some absolution. All Owen knew is that when he saw Mr. Cushing's house, he went there and woke him.

They'd sat at the kitchen table and Owen thought, momentarily, of how sad that room was. A bachelor's room, with no woman to tend it, it seemed too neat, too tidy, like a place a monk would live.

He tried his best to explain, but the words wouldn't seem to come out right. He told Mr. Cushing about the note, about the kiss, about Mr. Glass's face. About how he had run, like a coward.

"Yes, Owen. I think I see," Mr. Cushing had finally said, his face showing neither disgust nor compassion. "But why did you go there? Lord in heaven, what were you thinking?"

"I only went because she asked. I thought it would be all right. I didn't know it would be . . . But then it happened, and I couldn't stop. I didn't want it to stop."

Mr. Cushing didn't say anything for a while. Then: "You're going to have to go. Tonight. There's nothing else for it. You can't stay now."

Owen nodded. Of course, he was right. He understood the implications of what he had done, of being caught: even if Mr. Glass didn't carry out his threat to hurt Owen, he could most certainly destroy him, their small farm and, ultimately, his mother. He would be branded a sexual villain, a deviant, a rapist.

They all knew the stories of poor boys who crossed rich men, of what happened to them. This was his penance. Penance for the betrayal of Mr. Glass and everything he'd given Owen.

"Come on," Mr. Cushing had said, shaking him. "It has to be done now. I'll take you to your mother to say your goodbyes."

Owen had sat in the cart watching Mr. Cushing, his tall frame stooped and tired, as he spoke words to his mother that Owen couldn't hear. After listening to the old schoolmaster awhile, she'd touched his arm, as if to stay him, and walked inside the house.

Thinking of it now, Owen could feel tears making tracks down his skin, dropping into his collar, cooling and then drying as he ran.

When his mother reemerged she was carrying the satchel that was now strapped to his back. In it were some of their savings and the bread, as well as a sweater and his winter coat. She brought it over to the cart and put it beside him. She looked into his face, put her hand up to his cheek. It was warm. That was all, no words.

He hadn't been able to look back as they pulled away from the house and the farm.

"I can take you as far as the next turning, but then you'll have to make your way to Cottage City on your own from there. The ferry leaves at dawn; you'll have to hurry to make it."

Owen nodded and when they reached the turn, climbed down and took the bag off the seat. He would've shaken Mr. Cushing's hand, but thought the man might not like to. So he just nodded at him and said: "Thank you." Then he'd strapped the satchel to his back and started running.

Cottage City was already busy and the sun hadn't even fully risen. Owen boarded the ferry and stood looking at his island as it pulled away. He thought about all the things he belonged to and how much he'd wanted to get above them, to get away, and how he'd give anything now to have them back. He thought about how it was no use thinking this way, but then what else could he think about? Not the future, not the mainland or what he'd do for work, or food, or what would happen to him. He wondered if he'd ever be able to come back. He thought about the kiss, like lightning smiting the ground, incinerating his past, and changing everything.

1915

Sara saw him first, weaving between the other passengers, his eyes scanning the platform. She touched his arm and he turned, that lovely straight profile framed against the gray stone and hoary steam of the station. She smiled at him and knew he knew why she was smiling. His golfing attire—a dove-colored, single-breasted jacket, knickerbockers, argyle socks and tweed flat cap—all very serious and appropriate.

"Lovely outfit." She laughed.

"Isn't it, though," and Gerald colored slightly.

Their hands brushed, but there was nothing else, no other contact between them as they boarded the train from Penn Station to East Hampton and sat primly next to each other. She glanced at his face from underneath her straw hat and could see he was still smiling, too.

She'd only been back from India six months; six months and everything was different. When she'd set out on the journey, she'd had no idea what was waiting for her; her future had seemed like a flat road, one she could see all the way down. Then Gerald's voice had reached her, his words had *happened* to her. Those letters: her astonishment at being perfectly understood by another person. Not only understood, but delighted in. Of, finally, being *seen*.

Her life was only just now beginning in earnest, in color. And she was terrified that something would happen to snatch it from her grasp.

They'd agreed to keep their engagement a secret until they could come up with a plan of attack. So much about it was problematic that at times she felt it might be hopeless. There was the Catholic question, not to mention his small income from his job at Mark Cross and his father's feeling that he would come to nothing. And then, of course, her mother's vocal opposition to marriage as a general rule.

But today she didn't want to think about that. She wanted to think about the pressure of his thigh against hers: two friends out ostensibly for a healthy round of early spring golf—although, in fact, they were heading for the Dunes. The house would be closed up this time of year and the prospect of spending some time with him alone, away from the bounds of friends, family, servants, made her chest tight. She peered over the back of their seats and at the gentleman across from them.

"There's no one," she whispered. *No one we know*, was what she meant, of course. Then she carefully unbuttoned and slipped off her glove, and pressed her naked hand to his face.

He looked at her. That was all. Nothing more was needed. It was simple: he loved her and she loved him. She loved him in a way she hadn't thought possible, in a way that surprised her and made her glad to be alive. Her own capacity for it amazed her. She had previously thought that kind of love was something found only in novels and sonnets. Worse even, an insidious lie to make one discontented with one's real lot in life. But she was drunk with it, and now she believed. How you could be in someone else's head, really and truly. How it was impossible to be wrong with that person because everything about you was what he wanted.

The last time she'd seen him had been two weeks ago, that February evening at her parents' club when everything had been settled between them. They had managed to steal time before she left for Montreal with Adeline and Hoytie and Olga, and he for Westchester with his parents. She had been sitting on the settee in front of the fire in the club's small library, her head back, eyes partially closed, as if resting, but inside, her heart had been tapping a hard rhythm against her chest. She'd wanted him to touch her, she wanted to feel his lips against hers.

She'd been thinking of all the secret kisses that had passed between them: there had been the first one, stolen, sweet, almost chaste, and then longer embraces, others, hot and hard, her hand snaked around his neck. But the more she'd received, the more she'd wanted.

Yet, that evening, Gerald had been uncharacteristically quiet, and so she was just thinking these things, not moving, trying to keep herself decent and still. They'd remained like that for what seemed an eternity.

"Sara," he said finally, and the grave tone of his voice made her open her eyes.

It wasn't just serious, there was also a distinct edge of anxiety. *Please God*, she thought, *don't let him be changing his mind*, and she felt slightly sick.

"You said . . ." He stopped. "You said you could see me everywhere, doing everything together." He cleared his throat. "I'm sorry," he said. "I'm feeling . . . What I'm trying to say is: *I* can see it. I see you everywhere. I love you. I didn't think I would ever be able to love anyone, be able to show to anyone how I feel, about . . . But now . . . There's only you. Now, there can't be anyone else."

And all she'd said—all she had to say—was: "Yes, I know." And that had been that.

*

Inside the Dunes, Sara drew back the mustard-gold-colored drapes in the large drawing room, exposing dust motes rising from the covered furniture, although the wood-paneling and gleaming floorboards still smelled freshly of wax polish. She set out the food she'd brought on the worn and loved Oriental rug in the middle of the room.

"Do you think you'll be able to get a fire going?" she asked. "I'll hunt us out some plates and things." She fled before Gerald could answer.

In the pantry Sara was a mess. She almost dropped one of the plates getting it off the shelf and the silverware clattered around her as she tried to stuff it all into a gardening basket she'd found in the hallway. When she finally did break something—a glass—she stopped.

She touched her hair, piled tightly, sportily, on top of her head, and took a breath. She knew what might occur; she had, of course, known all along. And she feared it and desired it and thought she might have a heart attack before anything could actually happen.

Earlier that morning, as she lay in her large walnut bed in the city, pulling the linen sheets around her body, her hand warm on her skin, she'd imagined feeling languorous, sensual, at this moment. Instead, she found she felt stiff and nervous and altogether unattractive. She realized she had no idea if Gerald had ever been with a woman before, and she suddenly feared their age difference; how would she, at thirty-one, compare with all those lithe, budding girls? It was too awful to contemplate.

Still, there was no going back now. Besides, they were to be married, so this would happen sooner or later. Mustering her courage, she swept up the broken glass and set it on the counter, before picking up the basket and making her way back to the drawing room.

In her absence, Gerald had managed to get the first flames to catch the seasoned logs, and she could smell the comforting perfume of ash and apple wood. At the sound of her footfall, he turned and smiled. Sara cleared her throat anxiously and busied herself pouring milk into a couple of glasses, trying to invoke an attitude of cool domesticity. Her hand shook so badly that fat white drops fell onto the rug.

He came towards her. Her whole body was shaking and she had a momentary desire to run from the house. Gerald took the glass and bottle from her hands and set them down.

"I'm sorry," she said. "I'm just very nervous."

He pulled her to him and held her and she could hear her heart beating and wondered if he could hear it, too. They stayed like that for a while until she could feel her muscles unwinding, her breathing slowing, then he let go of her.

"That's better," he said quietly, looking down at the floor.

"Shall we eat?" She had no appetite, but the picnic seemed the only way of postponing the inevitable.

They pulled the rug closer to the stone fireplace and sat cross-legged, both of them picking at the chicken, absently eating the grapes. She had placed the basket between them, but perversely, also wished it wasn't there.

She poured herself a second glass of milk and said: "Oh, this is really lovely milk."

Gerald looked at the milk and at her and said: "Yes." Then, carefully, he pushed everything out of the way until they were sitting side by side. He put his index finger to her neck and traced it down her collarbone, around the curve of her breast until he reached her waist. Sara, her heart in her mouth, lay back and uncrossed her legs until she was stretched out fully on the rug.

"You're beautiful like this," he said. "Are you cold?" Now he seemed nervous, doubtful.

She shook her head.

"I imagine you like this all the time. The time when we slept on the beach and then you watched me," he said. "The time when you came back from Europe and had seen the Ballets Russes and you lay like this, and the sun was going down."

She looked at the thin light hitting the wooden floorboards. Then she couldn't stand it anymore and she pulled him to her, feeling his weight, agonizingly, exquisitely heavy on top of her, and found his mouth and pressed her own against it. His hands were light and quick on her hips and her waist. And then they both struggled with jackets and skirts, the tiny buttons on the back of her blouse, petticoats, stockings, socks. But the whole time, turning to see the other, hands on each other's faces, mute, impatient.

He was over her, bracing himself on his palms above her, mouthing words too quiet to hear. Then he was whispering into her ear, his breath humid against her skin, and she found herself whispering back, things she wouldn't be able to remember later. She watched him as he moved above, his throat curved, perfect; he watched her as he touched her, and afterwards he told her things about what had happened and about herself and how he felt.

"I really do love you," he said finally.

Sara knew it was true; she knew it now in her bones, imprinted in her flesh, knew it inside and out, like a perfect truth. And so, because of this, she turned her face away, her hand over her eyes, and cried.

They were quiet on the train ride home, the station names passing like signposts leading them slowly back to reality: Eastport; Bellport; Patchogue; Babylon; Massapequa; Bellmore; Freeport. Finally, Penn Station.

They knew they had to leave each other, but this seemed impossible after what had passed between them.

"We have to speak to your parents," Gerald said. "We can't go on like this."

"Let's give them more time," Sara said, afraid again.

"I'll write you," Gerald said. "We'll figure it out. But we have to do it soon."

"Yes," she said. Then, leaning into him slightly: "I never thought . . ."

"No," he agreed, a small smile curving on the lips she had so recently kissed.

Sara pressed his hand and then they parted.

*

The next day a letter arrived from Gerald. A delicate paper grenade.

My darling Sal,

You have left me awed. And I could never take what happened between us casually. As I held you I felt as if everything that came before, everything I feared about myself and my ability to communicate my feelings, was nothing but terrors in the night.

But now I have to tell you that I can no longer live alone with this feeling, and they all must know our plans for the future. I am coming Wednesday morning to ply my suit with your father.

I know you are afraid; I am not entirely at ease with this prospect myself. But we must be brave. It is the only way. I love you.

G.

Sara put the letter on her nightstand and regarded it. She paced her bedroom, fiddling with the chintz drapes and staring distractedly out the window at the traffic passing on Fifty-Fifth Street. She picked it up, read it again, sighing. Then she went to find her sisters.

❖

Sara slept terribly Tuesday night. For someone whose only problem before had been getting up in the morning, it was a new and torturous experience.

When she did sleep she dreamed of Gerald, of that afternoon at the Dunes, the luminous, whispering hours they'd passed together. She rose before dawn and didn't lie down again. Instead, she took out Gerald's letters and read them, partly to reassure herself, in that unreal hour of the day, that what she felt was indeed real.

The last letter, his most recent, had been sent the day before.

> My darling,
> I got your note and I understand everything you say. But this is the worst of it and it must be got through to get to the other part. Because this is the other part: think of a relationship that not only does not bind, but actually so lets loose imagination. Think of it, my love— and thank heaven.
> G.

Sara was already dressed when her father knocked on her door at nine o'clock.

"Yes," she said, pretending to be arranging her dresser.

Frank Wiborg strode over the threshold and stood there, his large body filling the door frame. "I have received Gerald Murphy's card requesting an interview in half an hour."

"Oh?" Sara inspected a powder pot.

"Do you know what this is about, Sara?" He waved the card at her.

"No, of course not."

"Well, I hope not. For your sake."

When she did not respond, or even turn to face him, he grumbled: "Gerald Murphy," but left her alone after that.

She waited until she was sure he had gone into his study and then she opened the door and scooted along to Olga's room.

"Oh, it's beginning," she said, pacing. "Father knows."

Olga, mid-brush at her own dressing table, shook her small, neat, curly head. Everything in Olga's room was neat, all her little things in perfect order. "Oh Sara. I feel like it's happening to me, I'm so nervous."

"Well, it's not," Sara said.

Another knock at the door and Hoytie came in. "Father's making a racket in his study." She perched on the bed watching Sara. "For heaven's sakes, stop fidgeting."

"Don't," Sara said.

"Is Gerald here yet?"

"No, but he knows. The card gave it away, I suppose."

"Right. When is he expected?"

"Not for another half an hour," Sara said, getting up and pacing the small bedroom.

"Good," Hoytie said.

"Oh, there's nothing good about this. What if he says no?"

"Stop with the dramatics," Hoytie said. "I've been thinking: when Gerald arrives, you go and tell Mother the news. That way it will be a flank attack and she won't have time to change Father's mind."

"Oh Hoytie," Olga said. "How can you be so calm? This is Sara's whole life we're talking about."

"I feel sick," Sara said.

Hoytie rose. "I'll get some sherry."

"Oh, yes, good idea," Olga said. "I think we could all use a little Dutch courage."

Hoytie returned with the decanter and poured them each a glass. "To success."

"Yes." Olga raised her glass.

"Oh God," Sara said.

They were on their second glass when they heard the front door open, murmurings in the hallway and then the snap of their father's study door.

"It's time," Hoytie said.

"I don't want to." Sara hid her face in her hands. "Can't you just do it?"

"Don't be a little idiot."

"Come on," Olga said, "we'll come with you."

Hoytie pushed Sara down the hallway to their mother's bedroom. Quietly she opened the door. She could hear her mother humming, strangely, "The Battle Hymn of the Republic," as she splashed around in the adjacent bathroom.

Sara stood in the middle of the room and Hoytie gave her a sharp shove.

"He hath loosed the fateful lightning of His terrible swift sword. His truth is marching on."

Sara could imagine her mother's rounded body floating and plummeting in the bath water, like some kind of glorious, avenging porpoise.

"Glory, glory . . ."

"Do it," Hoytie hissed.

She knocked on the door and heard the splashing and singing go quiet.

"Who is it?"

Sara opened her mouth, but nothing would come out. She looked helplessly at her sisters. Olga smiled weakly.

"Yes? Who's there?"

She tried again, but again, she had no words. Finally, Hoytie inflicted a swift, mean kick to the ankle and Sara, in a cry of pain and slight insanity, yelled: "I'm marrying Gerald Murphy," at the bathroom door and turned and ran, her sisters in tow.

"That was the best fun I've had in ages," Hoytie cried, as the three of them streamed back down the hallway to the relative safety of Olga's bedroom.

✤

"How could you? How could you do this to me?" Adeline Wiborg, dressed in black, as if in mourning, and lying on her chaise longue, threw Sara an accusatory look.

"Mother," Sara said. "But you love Gerald."

"I do not, I *do* not. Why should I love Gerald Murphy?"

"What did Father say?"

Sara's father was out, lunching with Patrick Murphy, presumably trying to come up with a plan to control the damage. Gerald himself had stormed out before she'd had a chance to confer with him.

"What do you think he says? He doesn't want to sell his daughter and break up the family any more than I do."

"Break up the family?" Sara paced, exasperated. "But we've been together so much longer than most families."

"It doesn't seem that long to me," Adeline said, real sadness in her voice.

"And we wouldn't be far. We'd find a place in the city, of course."

"Find a place in the city? You'd move out?"

"Oh dear," Sara said.

Adeline sat up, brushing aside her tears. "Sara, dearest, be reasonable. He's a Catholic. What do you know about being a Catholic? About raising Catholic children?"

"I don't know. It's never seemed that important." Sara put her hand to her head and went and stood by the small bay window in her mother's dressing room.

"Well, this is just it. You haven't thought any of this through."

"We love each other and we want to make a life together. That's all," Sara said, but she was beginning to feel the weight of her mother's question pressing on her.

"And what will you live on? A place in the city, indeed. Who's to pay for this place? Your father?"

"I . . ."

"No, no. This is all too much. It's out of the question. It's untenable, impossible, it's . . . I can't do without you, anyway."

"Mother . . ."

"I can't talk about this anymore; I'm ill. Let me rest."

Things hadn't gone much better with her father, who'd accused her of naïveté and indolence and profligacy with money.

"I've spoken with Patrick Murphy," her father began when she'd seated herself in his study. "While we're both very fond of you and Gerald, this does not seem like a sound plan. Mr. Murphy in particular seemed extremely doubtful on the subject of Gerald being able to provide for you in any meaningful way."

"Mr. Murphy has never been exactly . . ." she searched for the right word, "favorable to Gerald."

"Well, I think he should know," her father said hotly. "He is his son, after all."

That afternoon, Sara received an invitation from her cousin, Sara Sherman Mitchell, to take tea at her house.

Sara Sherman had lived with the Wiborgs for a time after her parents' death, before marrying her husband Ledyard. If anyone would know about the difficulties Sara now faced, it was her cousin, who had managed not only to marry a Roman Catholic, but to do so with Sara's parents' benediction. Also, Sara was sure—and this was what made her heart beat a bit faster in her chest—that the invitation was no coincidence; Gerald must be behind it.

When the Mitchells' maid opened the door, Sara Sherman was already there, practically pushing the poor girl aside to get to her cousin and clasp her hand, her eyes bright beneath her frizz of dark hair. (Why did Sara Sherman's hair always look like she'd been beekeeping in the hot sun?)

"Come, come. Tea's all laid out," she said, dragging Sara behind her.

Once in the upstairs parlor, Sara looked around to see if Gerald was lurking somewhere, but the room was empty.

"So . . ." Sara Sherman said, patting the cushion next to her. "Gerald Murphy. I'm so glad for you, Sara. Really."

"Well, don't be too glad," Sara said. "It's not on, as it turns out. At least not according to the parental council. There are so many . . . complications. I don't know," Sara said, "I'm beginning to get slightly afraid."

"What are you afraid of? Let's think this through logically."

"Well, firstly, there's the Catholic question. As mother pointed out today, what do I really know about it? About raising Catholic children?"

"Yes," Sara Sherman mused. "Well, it is hard—terribly hard at first—to get used to all that. But it works itself out, eventually. Ledyard was quite fierce about it in the beginning, but we've found a rhythm, if you will. You just sort of get along with it."

"I don't know . . ." This did not seem very clear to her.

"What else?"

"I'm rather ashamed to admit this, but there's the age difference."

"Are you afraid that he won't find you . . ." Sara Sherman seemed to be searching for the delicate phrase. "Feminine enough?"

Sara colored, thinking of herself lying back for Gerald, offering herself to him too quickly, so easily, like a bitch in heat. "No," she said sternly. "Only: what will it be like in ten years, in twenty? And what will people say? Poor Gerald Murphy, caught by the old spinster Sara Wiborg?"

"Now you're just being ridiculous. I can't see that age makes any difference at all. And if it's just other people you're worried about, let Gerald worry about it for you."

"I know you're right—" She was interrupted by a knock at the door.

Sara Sherman rose to answer it, and after conferring with her maid came and sat back down.

"Now," she said, "there's someone here to see you and I must make myself scarce." She squeezed Sara's hand. "What was it the Romans said? Fortune favors the bold? Be brave, darling Sara."

Then there was Gerald's dear, dear face at the door: the long, aquiline nose and serious brow, currently furrowed; the lovely bowed lips, just a bit too full, that kept his expression from ever looking too ascetic.

Sara was scarcely aware of her cousin's exit as she met Gerald across the room and put herself into his embrace.

"What a day," she finally said, pulling away from him.

"An autopsy and coroner's inquest, all in one," he said darkly.

They sat close together on the sofa.

"What did your mother say?" Sara was thinking of her own mother.

"She seems to think we're playing a scene from *Romeo and Juliet*. Never mind her. It's my father that's the real problem. I was told in no uncertain terms what a disappointment I am and continue to be, and that he blames himself for enabling my lack of any fundamental grasp of my duties in this world."

"Oh, I got that, too—a little less harshly perhaps—from both of my parents."

"The trouble is: how is one able to live up to one's duties if one isn't given any?"

She traced a fine line in his brow, trying to smooth it away. "Do you think . . ." She wanted to say this carefully. "I'm beginning to wonder if perhaps . . . perhaps I may not be the best wife for you."

He looked at her sharply. "Do you want to get out of it?"

"No. No, I don't. But . . . well, do you?"

"My God, I do not." He held her gaze.

"We've never talked about religion." She toyed with her tea doily. "Yours, I mean."

He let out a sigh. "Is that all? I was afraid you might be beginning to agree with my father."

"I don't care one bit what your father thinks about you," she said fiercely.

"And I don't care one bit about the Catholic Church. The only thing it has given me is cold, distant parents and floggings in the woodshed by nuns too dense to know when a young boy misses home, such as that home may be. You will never have to set foot in one if I have anything to do with it."

Sara laughed.

"Well, I'm glad you find it funny. You wouldn't have found Sister Martha and her nasty switch all that amusing, I can tell you that." But he smiled at her.

"No, it's just . . ." She felt relief, not only because of his words, but also because they were them again, together against the world.

"Sara," he said, his face serious, "this is important: the only world I want is the one we invent for ourselves. I don't want what my parents have or what your parents have. I want something entirely of our own creation. I've felt inauthentic for most of my life and I want to be finished with that."

She took his hand: "You will never, ever have to be other than you are with me."

"Truly?"

"Truly."

"My God, Sara, we're really going to do it." He was laughing now, a bit crazily. "I feel slightly hysterical."

"Well, don't get too hysterical. We have to come up with a new plan, now. I'm afraid you're going to have to become a serious businessman, at least for a little while, if we're going to convince them."

"I can be anything you want. Anything."

*

In the days and weeks that followed, their parents showed little sign of relenting. Gerald was working hard at Mark Cross to prove to Patrick Murphy that he was suitable for promotion, or at least favor, but to Sara, he seemed to grow more and more depressed, suffering under bouts of what he called the Black Service. She wasn't happy, either, about keeping their secret while the world went on around them, when what she wanted to scream was: *I am loved; I am lovable.* But she had decided: she was not going to be at the mercy of fate one minute longer.

So, in between private lunches at La Goulue and tea at Sara Sherman's and evenings out under the veneer of family chaperones, they wrote to each other.

Dearest Jerry,

I visited the studio of H. Mann (horrible man) yesterday and caught my heel on his unfinished floor and have been thinking ever since how much I love boards with knots in them, unfinished, imperfect. In our house, I don't want everything polished and trussed up. When I think of all the chintz in the world . . .

❊

Dear Sal,

You and I prefer the imperfect, the lady without her corset, to the grand dame roped and hemmed and hoisted. Shabby genteel, as I like to think of our style. I don't want a home that reeks of *Vogue*'s latest hints to the housekeeper. You, Salamander mine, shall never again live in a *tableau vivant*.

Smart chintzed apartments. Bah. None of these for us. I was just at Billy Forsythe's place this afternoon, which is indeed just a bit too "smart apt"—shall this become a popular phrase?—and when I was finally at liberty to flee said abode, I came across a wonderful antique shop. I went a bit nuts and in a fit of optimism, bought the first things that will (they shall!) adorn our home: two milky-white glass vases for your room, a terrifying stuffed pheasant, a silver box for your dressing table, a set of six pewter goblets, an octagonal ashtray, which you'll love, one gold-flecked lamp, a set of glass bottles the color of sea, and a miniature tureen decorated with the bust of a family dog.

I've had them sent to the familial manse, but I have no idea where I'll hide them from prying eyes. It doesn't matter, it gave me such comfort because I felt your presence so clearly while I was choosing them, it was as if you were next to me . . .

Dearest Jerry,

I am coveting a set of Sheraton benches. But where to keep them? I really can't alarm Mother any further. Also—a lovely, sturdy bassinet, made of some kind of reeds that could have come from the Nile.

Does that alarm you?

Dearest Sal,

I love the bassinet already. And what will go in it. My God, can't you see them? Curious, creative, humorous, lithe and clean . . .

Dearest Jerry,

Most of all, loved and kept safe. Their life—our life— will be loaded and fragrant, filled only with everything that is beautiful and different and wonderful . . .

My Darling Sal,

I think it's the details in life that are important, all the small things that create the larger picture. When I think back on my own childhood, it's my father's study I see: the bust of Emerson, the small, mean black notebooks full of his limericks, that smooth cruel desk. All of it adding up to a controlled distance we were kept at. All that contained sadness.

I've never said this to anyone before . . .

❖

Dearest Jerry,

It's so strange to think of our lives before we knew that we loved each other. For me, it's almost unrecognizable, and there are times when I wonder that it took us so long. But I can't be sorry about anything, because it brought us to this point.

I feel only with you have I become an actual living, breathing woman. Dearest Jerry, I want to be the best wife to you, to make a home and a place in the world for you where there are only round edges . . .

❖

Dear Sara,

I fear I am getting nowhere with the paternal figure. I want to believe in these things, but truly I am losing faith. I feel that all the secrecy, the playing of games, playing the bachelor in New York, among men who not only don't understand me but seem to regard me with suspicion, is breaking me down. I'm not certain of anything anymore. I wish I was stronger for you, for us . . .

❖

Dearest Jerry,

None of this is easy; not for you, nor me. It feels unjust, but it will come right. I promise you . . .

❀

Dear Sara,

I know I sound petulant and pouty, which only makes me feel worse, because it's small and I hate anything that's small. But at times you leave me a little frightened—frightened by your goodness, your discretion, your self-containment, while I go all to pieces. At times your perfection leaves me wondering what I can offer you in return . . .

❀

Dear Gerald,

Don't talk nonsense.

The problem was, of course, that she knew exactly what he meant. As the time dragged on, with no resolution in sight, it was becoming harder to sustain the fantasy and, despite herself, Sara began to feel like she was back in that Whistler painting, a sense of inertia slowly overtaking her.

Then, one morning, she found she couldn't, or just didn't, get out of bed. She lay, in between sleep and waking, without even the energy to write Gerald, who, in a need to escape the city and their predicament, had agreed to go off on a retreat with some former members of his Yale secret society.

When she'd missed breakfast, and lunch was threatening to pass by as well, her mother knocked at her door. Sara expected a reprimand, but her mother's voice was gentle.

"Sara, dearest," she said. "May I come in?"

Sara turned on her pillow and regarded her mother. "Of course."

"Are you unwell?"

"No. Yes. I don't know." She felt sleepy, that was really all. Her limbs heavy, sinking into the mattress.

Her mother first sat on the edge of her bed, then lifted her whole self in, and wrapped her arms around her eldest daughter. She stroked her hair.

They lay like that for a while, listening to the traffic outside the window, watching the afternoon sun move against the wall. Sara was reminded of the time, so many years ago now, that her puppy had been run over by a sleigh, its tiny little body crushed and bloody under the cruel metal runner. All the warmth gone out of her pelt. Sara had carried the dog all the way back to the house, before collapsing at her mother's feet. Adeline had lain in bed with her for days, just as she did now, cradling her daughter until Sara's grief had lightened.

She wanted to tell her mother that it might not work this time, but Adeline spoke first.

"Is it really so untenable here with us?"

Sara squeezed her mother's soft hand. "Unbearable, you mean? No. Of course not."

When Sara didn't say anything else, her mother started again. "You are our dearest child, and we want you to be happy. That's all."

"I know that, Mother." She felt safe there in Adeline's arms. "It's just I want my own life. And . . ."

"And children," Adeline finished for her.

"You do know how old I am." She turned and looked at her mother. Then, feeling that hard little shame that had been lodged in her for years, as she'd been passed by, said quietly: "This might be my last chance for happiness."

Adeline looked away, as if she couldn't bear to see it. She sighed and then nodded. "I forget, I suppose, sometimes. You girls have been my greatest happiness; my favorite accomplishment."

"I know."

"Yes," she said after a while, "you're right, after all. You are a woman. You must have a household to manage." She kissed Sara's head. "I'll speak to your father, if you promise to rise for tea."

"I love you, Mother."

"Yes, yes." Then: "My darling girl."

Sara lay there for a while longer, then rose and began to dress herself. She picked through the post lying on the silver tray in the hall and found a letter from Gerald.

My Dearest Sal,

   I am writing this from Deer Island, with an enormous mounted bear head hanging over me. You know that I was rather dreading this retreat; I do hate the awful feeling of being "inspected" when with a group of men, the feeling of being incomprehensible to them, such as I am. But it has turned out to be a relief, for I can finally speak to men I admire about the woman of my life, without the hush and secrecy that has been following us.

   I just wanted to write and tell you: you have kept alive the man in me. Everything else I have done, and appeared to be, has not been real. I will return to you, with the full confidence that what lies before us will be new and good and will erase the smudged years that have gone before.

   All my love,

   G.

When she'd finished reading it, she went to her writing desk and took a pen and a sheaf of stationery. She sat for a moment and then put her pen to paper.

My dearest Jerry,
Do hurry home. I believe the storm has broken.
I love you.
Sal

1918

Gerald was standing in the mess line, the bright Texas sun beating down and making his skin itch in his wool flannel shirt. He was trying to read Sara's latest letter amid the cacophony of hungry, waiting men.

It was a warm January day, somewhere in the 60s he guessed, and the light was bouncing off the flat yellow landscape of Kelly Field, forcing him to squint when he raised his eyes.

He was jostled by some other trainees fooling behind him, and he moved up a bit and redoubled his efforts of concentration. Since he'd shipped out at the beginning of the month to the Ground Officers' Training School, Sara had written him almost every other day, long letters crammed with details of her everyday life, which was mainly taken up by their three-week-old daughter Honoria, as well as her views on the politics of the war and her concern that he would be shipped off to Europe.

What remained unsaid in her correspondence, but was nonetheless apparent between the lines, was Sara's lingering sadness over Adeline's death, from pneumonia, a year ago now. Her mother had never been exactly robust, but her sudden decline came as a shock, and Sara didn't seem to have fully come to terms with her passing, even if she rarely mentioned it.

In her latest "report," as Gerald had come to think of

them fondly, Sara wrote that she'd been dining with some visiting Columbia professor of Russian studies, and was cheerfully passing on his views.

Of course, Father had no idea what he had let himself in for, agreeing to dine with this "friend of a friend." He was quite the radical, but I found him marvelous. Anyway, Jerry, he says that no matter what happens between Russia and the Central Powers, just the proximity of the German and Austro-Hungarian soldiers to the Bolshevik revolution has hurt them. Apparently, hundreds of thousands of workers in Berlin are preparing to strike for peace soon and the idea of revolution has "infected" the armies and navies of the Central Powers.

Imagine! What a triumph it would be for Socialism, if the war was won by psychology instead of steel. Of course, I know you are anxious to do what's right and fight alongside our men, but I, for one, can't say I'd be glad of it.

You see, I can't be happy if you are not with me, and if anything were to happen to you to prolong that indefinitely . . .

Honoria is gaining weight fast and furiously and becoming so beautifully fat. We both loved your night letter wishing her a happy third-week birthday. She must be bathed in front of the fire in my room now, as the bathroom is too cold—the gas is weak owing to the positively arctic temperatures here. Olga and Hoytie are coming to lunch tomorrow, to see myself and the delicious one, and we're planning a stroll around the park. Only a week ago, I could barely walk to and from the nursery, the bathroom and our bedroom. Then yesterday a dinner and a real outdoor tromp tomorrow. So you see I'm getting so much stronger, and you aren't to worry.

We both love you and miss you. Do write, or better yet, send a telegram so that I can have your news soonest.

Love,
Sal

Gerald folded up the letter and put it in his shirt pocket. He was nearing the opening to the mess tent, but he couldn't quite muster enthusiasm for the beans and anemic pork waiting for him inside.

He was now strangely grateful for a childhood that had prepared him for what he found when he arrived at these desolate airfields outside San Antonio. It wasn't that the freezing nights, cold showers and small canvas cot were familiar, exactly. It was more the feeling of isolation, the flatness of emotional life—here reflected in the dusty, open spaces of these former cotton fields—that resonated with him.

The same couldn't be said for some of the men, who took the conditions and the uncertainty hard. One of them, Tom Wilson, had been among the twelve trainees in Gerald's wall tent. No one knew much about him, where he came from, but he'd been softly spoken and always shared his care packages around.

After a week at camp, however, they'd been woken in the night to his cries. He was standing in the middle of the tent, between the two rows of cots, completely naked, screaming: "It drops down. It drops down. It drops down on you," before a medic could be fetched to take him away to the infirmary. They'd all agreed the defect must have been there before, but it had unsettled them nonetheless.

A Jenny passed overhead and Gerald looked up, using his hand to shade his eyes. He watched the small biplane circling over Kelly Field's barracks and tent cities before coming in for a bumpy landing in the distance. He felt a shiver of possibility pass through him. He'd been accepted for Signal Corps' School of Aeronautics in Columbus, and if all went well, he could be up in one of them in less than a month.

Still, he had to get out of Texas first, and he didn't know when that would be. In the meantime, drills, bayonet and rifle training, and field work lay ahead. It was a strange place, this camp. Two thousand acres of drought-afflicted land holding ten thousand men from all over, but it didn't feel like America at all. It seemed more of a twilight country between what had been and what was coming, between his former life and war.

He barely recognized the Gerald Murphy who, en route two weeks ago, had blithely stepped off the train in New Orleans to buy, as he'd written Sara at the time:

> a marble-topped sofa table (for the hall?), a pair of silver grape scissors, a claret jug engraved with the initial "M," a set of ivory oyster forks, a strange lavender pitcher for Honoria's bath, and a small agate box carved in the image of a lady's head, trimmed with diamonds, and inscribed with: "Walk on roses and think of me."

Their home seemed so far from him now, a sort of paradise that felt alien. Sara herself seemed so far. He'd left her three weeks ago, still in mourning clothes and unwell after the hard birth.

The day that Honoria had come into the world, Gerald had never felt so helpless. While Sara had been given sleeping drugs during the ordeal, her pain afterwards was unmistakable. He didn't know the details, of course, but he knew it had been a bloody affair, if the reams of pinkish towels streaming from the bedroom were anything to go by, and the doctor said she had suffered enough trauma that she wouldn't be able to walk for several weeks. He'd cried at the thought of Sara's poor broken body, because that body belonged to him, now, and he was responsible.

But then he'd come here, and started preparing to fight, looking towards war, and all those emotions had become less immediate. It wasn't that he loved her any less, only that at times he couldn't feel it, as if he'd been sent back to a time before her.

After lunch, Gerald started heading back to his tent to collect his soap and towel for his shower. Showers in camp had to be taken in a twice-weekly rota due to the severe drought that had been plaguing Texas for almost eight months. His tent was up this afternoon—the worst time because they had work duty directly afterwards.

A truck passed him and he watched as it came to a halt outside the officers' barracks, a luxury hotel compared to the comparatively flimsy tents the inductees were assigned to. An officer stepped out, but as he turned to slam the door shut, Gerald was shocked to see him get thrown back, a good four feet, as if some unseen force had pushed him through the air. The officer lay there stunned, as Gerald ran over.

"Are you all right, sir?" He put out his hand to the man, who seemed to be having trouble focusing.

"What the fuck was that?"

"I don't know. You just . . . flew back."

"I think it came from the truck," the officer said, standing. He held up his hand as if expecting it to explain itself.

"The engine?" Gerald asked, looking at the truck.

The officer shook his head. "Don't know, it shorted out earlier, but then it was fine."

"Well, at least we're not low on mechanics here, sir."

The officer looked towards one of the aeroplane hangars in the distance. Gerald followed his gaze, all at once aware of a deep stillness in the air. Beyond the hangar, there was something on the horizon, a darkening, far away.

"This is some weird weather," the officer remarked, rubbing his hand.

"A storm must be coming," Gerald said. "I've got to get to the showers. Are you all right, sir?"

"I'm fine. You go on. You'll stink to high heaven if you miss it." He grinned at Gerald.

Gerald had gone about a quarter of a mile when the wind came. He had to keep his head down to shield his eyes from the grit blowing up off the road. He was already late for the showers, getting later, and it felt like he was trying to run through water. His thighs began to ache and small pebbles were stinging his exposed skin.

Then a mule raced past him, almost trampling him in its panic. Startled, he raised his head, and that's when he saw it: what had started as that small darkening in the distance was a mountain, a mile high and as wide as the whole horizon. It was eating everything in its path.

Gerald ran faster, his muscles straining, his lungs hot. By the time he reached his tent city, it had covered half the distance between them, a boiling wall of dust rolling and screaming towards camp. He was paralyzed at the sight.

He had never known this kind of visceral fear, except in dreams. The one nightmare he sometimes had: standing on the edge of a calm shore when, out of nowhere, a gigantic, terrifying wave came crashing down upon him.

At that moment, standing ten feet from his tent, rooted

in place with this hallucination thundering at him, he felt for certain they would all be consumed by it. He looked over at his tent and sprinted. Then, all at once, it was upon them, and everything went dark.

The flap to his tent had been secured from the inside and his yells to open it were drowned out in the noise of the wind and the black filth that was filling his mouth and nose. Trying not to panic, he got down on his knees in the dirt and felt inside the flap for the tie. He fumbled, but managed to get it loose. He yanked the corner back and crawled through the opening, then lay on the floor panting.

"Jesus, Murphy." By the light of the oil lamp, Gerald could see John Plenner, the Philadelphian whose cot was next to his. He was tying the corner down. "You could have filled this whole place up."

"It came too fast," Gerald said.

"You were late." Plenner was yelling above the noise, but his voice wasn't angry. "What the hell is going on out there?"

"It's too dark. There was a . . . a wall, a mountain." He sat up.

By the few lit lamps, he could see that the twelve-man tent was almost empty: just himself, Plenner and Carter, a Texan who pronounced San Antonio "San Antone." Around them, dust was flowing in like smoke under the canvas, and the sides of the tent were buckling.

"Where is everybody?"

Plenner shrugged.

"It's like . . ." He couldn't even say what it was like.

"The apocalypse," Carter called above the wind. "Damn dust storms."

The wall tent was crammed with six cots on each side, facing each other, lockers at their feet, and a corridor running down the middle at the highest part of the pitch. It was fixed with flies outside, which held the top rod stable and pulled the sides down low, forcing the men to stoop as they approached their cots. With every inch of space planned for, it was claustrophobic at the best of times.

Gerald went over to his own locker and pulled out one of the handkerchiefs Sara had sent him, wiping down his face, then using it to clean out his mouth. He sat down on his cot.

"I saw a man touch his truck and fly through the air," he yelled at Carter. "Was that . . . ?"

"Static electricity," he yelled back.

Gerald wondered if any planes had been up when it hit.

Plenner was checking the stakes and supports, carrying his lamp from spot to spot. "There's too much dust coming in."

"How many of those handkerchiefs you got, Murphy?"

"Ten?"

"Give us some."

The three of them tied the handkerchiefs around their faces, leaving just their eyes showing.

"If it gets too bad, y'all have to cover your eyes, too," Carter yelled. "Pinkeye."

"How many of these have you seen?" Plenner's voice sounded hoarse.

"Two in the last year alone. Both bad."

Over the next hour the temperature plummeted below freezing. They put on all their clothes: their extra workshirts; the two service coats, one wool and one cotton; and their overcoats. Then they pillaged their tent-mates' clothing and blankets, which they rolled up and laid against the perimeter of the tent to try to slow the incoming dust. They had no water to drink, nor even to wet their handkerchiefs with, and the sound of their coughing blended with the sound of the storm.

The second hour brought flying debris. First, objects of unknown origin nicked and skimmed across the canvas outside, startling them, and keeping them on edge. What appeared by its shape to be a metal locker flew against a front corner support and bent it, making the tent pitch inwards. Dust spilled in through the weak spot and they decided to move towards the back.

Just as they did, a metal pole skewered the canvas fabric, its tip hitting the exact spot they'd vacated only seconds before. A shaft of sand poured through the hole, like through an hourglass.

They stared at each other over their handkerchiefs, eyes locking then looking away. They were silent, but Gerald knew they were all thinking the same thing.

Plenner got down on the ground and slid all the way under one of the cots and covered his ears, while Carter proceeded to take a sheet and build a sort of tent around himself, pulling the edges under him.

Gerald looked at the two of them and then went and lay on his own cot, face down. After a while, he reached under his pillow and found Honoria's baby shirt, which he'd brought with him from home. He lifted his handkerchief and buried his whole face in it, straining to smell its milky sweetness, the odor of his daughter's soft baby skin, amid the acrid stench of the dust.

By the third hour, they had doused the lamps to conserve oil, and the relentless shrieking of wind was all Gerald could hear. He was thinking about Fred, who had already shipped out to France with his artillery division; he hadn't considered the noise before, the noise of war, hadn't conceived that sound itself might drive you crazy.

By the fourth hour, he could hear Beethoven's Ninth Symphony. The "Ode to Joy." Beginning softly, softly. Gaining pace and depth, building itself. Then filling his head, as if it were hollowing out his skull and pouring itself inside of him. He breathed in the odor from his daughter's shirt. The vigorous presto passage, vibrating through him. He listened very, very carefully, and there it was: the choir. He wanted to cry, it was so beautiful. He had reached the second theme, its high military style, when he felt himself being shaken. He ignored it, concentrating on the thread of the symphony. But when he was shaken again, more forcefully, he reluctantly turned his neck and looked up.

Carter was standing over him, holding a lamp, pointing to the ground. He moved in and shouted in Gerald's ear: "Plenner. Man's covered in dust. He has to come up off the ground, but he won't."

It took Gerald a moment to quiet the symphony and focus on what Carter had told him. But then he nodded and forced himself to rise.

They walked over and knelt down, looking under the cot where Plenner had stashed himself. Gerald could see that he was covered in a fine silt and his body was racked by coughs.

Carter shook his shoulder. "Plenner. Come on now, you have to get up, all the dust's coming in that way."

He didn't move.

"John," Gerald said, finally, "you'll suffocate."

When Plenner still didn't move, Gerald and Carter looked at each other. Then, with Gerald grabbing hold of Plenner's arm and Carter his leg, they dragged him out.

Gerald used what little spit he had to dampen another handkerchief, while Carter began wrapping a sheet around Plenner. Gerald wiped down Plenner's face, gently digging the cloth into his nostrils and around his mouth. Plenner let them work on him, quiet, eyes unmoving.

Having something to concentrate on had hushed the music in Gerald's head, but it hovered on the edges of his mind, and he was half listening for that melody when a dull thumping drew his attention toward the front of the tent. Carter stopped, too. In the dim half-light they could see movement behind the canvas, as if something was being hurled over and over against it. Whatever it was seemed to be gathering force and they could see the ties beginning to give.

Carter was up first, with Gerald behind him carrying the lamp. There was a noise pitched higher than the wind.

"Someone's out there," Gerald shouted. "We have to open it."

"No," Carter yelled. "No way in hell."

"We have to. They'll rip the canvas off."

Carter looked at Gerald and shook his head angrily. "Shit."

They stood there a few moments longer, while whoever it was hurled themselves frantically against the tent.

"All right," Carter shouted. "But just the bottom flap. And quickly."

Gerald put down the lamp and untied the flap. He reached his hand outside and felt the sting of the dust and something else. Hail? Grabbing in front of him, he got hold of what felt like an ankle and all at once the hurling stopped. There was a scrambling and a dark face appeared low to the ground, one wild white eye, and Gerald moved back, clasping an outstretched hand.

Gerald stood, picking up the lamp, and as he did, the stranger stood too. His face was reddish black, masked with dust, making his eyes startling and large. His hair, also coated, stood straight on end, as if he too had received an electric shock.

Moving so quickly that Gerald had no time to react, the man grabbed him by the shoulder, put his face right up to his own and screamed: "It drops down. It drops down."

"Christ," Carter shouted. "It's Wilson."

Gerald tried to wrench out of his grasp, but Wilson held on tightly.

"Get him off of me," he yelled. He was unwilling to drop the oil lamp, but that left him with only one free hand to push Wilson away.

"It drops down on us."

"Get him off."

"Tom," Carter yelled.

Wilson had gotten Gerald in a bear hug and was forcing him backwards towards the line of lockers and cots. He had his mouth up to Gerald's ear now and was whispering into it: "It drops down. It drops down."

Gerald could see Carter over Wilson's shoulder and, out of the corner of his eye, Plenner still sitting on the ground off to the side, unmoving. He felt the back of his calves hit the metal of a locker and Wilson drew away slightly and looked into Gerald's face. There was something in his eyes, not just the panic, but also a kind of pleading, as if it was very important that Gerald understand what he was saying.

"Tom," he yelled.

Wilson nodded. "Yes."

"Tom, it's me. It's Gerald Murphy."

"Yes." And for a moment Gerald felt there was a flicker of recognition there. Then Wilson smiled, revealing dirt-covered teeth. The awful, dumb heartbreak in his eyes. He put an index finger up to Gerald's forehead and tapped: "It . . . drops . . . down . . . on . . . us."

With a startling alacrity, he pushed Gerald aside, causing him to stumble as he tried to hold on to the lamp.

When he'd managed to right himself, he saw Carter standing motionless at Tom's side. Wilson was holding a service revolver, his elbow making a perfect angle, pressing the barrel to his own temple.

There was only the screaming melody of the wind, the sound of hail hitting the canvas and the three men standing in tableau. Then Tom Wilson said very distinctly: "It's something wicked," and blew part of his skull away.

The next day was remarkably fair. Gerald sat on his cot staring at the pen in his hand, the paper beside him. He wanted to write a letter to Sara, but he didn't know the right words.

The tent cities at Kelly Field had been decimated by wind, by panicked mules and by trucks crashing suddenly into barracks and the mess halls. The sound of coughing filled the space the wind had occupied, and the line for the infirmary stretched halfway down the road. Plenner, his eyes pink and swollen shut, was among the men.

Gerald had spent the day with the other boys, cleaning the dust and Wilson's brains out of the tent. He and Carter and Plenner had been forced to spend the night with Wilson's leaking body, until the storm broke and help could be fetched. Carter had covered Tom with a blanket, but when the medics came to take him away, dust had piled around him anyway, filling the hole where his eye had been, like a bottle stopper.

Wilson, they'd learned, had escaped the infirmary, raving, at the height of the storm and no one had dared follow him out into that hell. The medics also told them that he wasn't the only one: three others had taken their own lives during the storm. Gerald wasn't sure if that was supposed to make it better for them or not. The medics had given them this information with an air of instructors contextualizing a battle, as if, yes, this sort of thing happens, all perfectly normal under the circumstances.

He didn't think it was normal, though. And he couldn't rid himself of the image of that arm, its neat precise angle before the trigger went off. Nor of Carter's face, splattered with tissue and bone fragments afterwards, little tiny pieces of Tom Wilson all over it. As if Carter was Wilson at that moment, the same reddish-black face, the same startled eyes, the same dumb animal look of fear. A look he remembered from a long time ago, from his small, feral dog, before it bit him.

He'd wanted to talk to Carter about this, about all of it. But when the Texan had come and sat down next to him outside the tent, and put his hand to Gerald's shoulder and said gently, "How you holding up, Murphy?" Gerald could only turn his face away and answer: "I'm fine, thank you." After that, Carter left him alone.

In the world of other men, he'd always been stiff. Polite kindness and decent interest in their welfare—that was all he had to offer. So self-conscious, it came off as indifferent, his true feelings left unrevealed. It enraged him, it ate him up, how he couldn't make his affection, his camaraderie felt.

How would he be able to live with men, fight with men, die with men at war? In a trench, in an airplane, with a leg blown off, would he say politely: "I'm fine, thanks. You? Your skull does seem to be missing a piece . . ."?

Now, sitting on his cot, pen and paper in hand, he looked over at Carter, who was cleaning his boots, a shock of brown hair in his eyes as he worked away the dust. He had so much to say, to share, but it was too late. The moment had passed. He had to accept that there was only one person in the world who knew him. And she would probably be the only one who ever did. Gerald put the pen to paper.

> My Darling wife,
>
> Forgive this short letter. I am writing now only to say that it gives me such courage to think of you, of us, our family. Thank God for you, the only person in this world to whom I've been able to show the full weight of my love. I believe in it, completely, this dream of ours.
>
> It is my creed.
>
> Love,
>
> G.

❀ ❀ ❀

Sara was sitting in front of the fire in her bedroom in the house on West Eleventh Street, Honoria sleeping in her basket beside her. The heat was making Sara feel drowsy and she stretched carefully on the settee, so as not to tear the stitches again. She'd done that in January, a month after Honoria's birth, and now it was March and she still hadn't healed fully from the second go-round with the needle.

She mustn't fall asleep, she told herself, because she knew Miss Stewart, the baby nurse, would let her go on sleeping and then she'd miss Honoria's bath. Miss Stewart, it seemed, felt almost as protective of Sara as she was of Honoria, and was constantly scolding her to get more rest.

But Sara loved bath time. She loved watching her baby's small body, squirming in pleasure at the warmth of the watery cocoon. She'd heard that some babies hated being washed, but her daughter delighted in it. And in turn, she delighted Sara.

To keep herself awake, Sara reread Gerald's letter, which had arrived yesterday. He was now in Columbus, Ohio, studying for his preflight exams. The letter was short and beautiful and somehow sad, it seemed to her. But she was glad about it. She'd felt lately as if she was the only sad one, and she hated that.

It wasn't just that she missed Gerald's company, his love, his body, the little hollow place at the base of his neck. It was that she sometimes felt such huge loneliness, such isolation, in parenthood. Every change and every new feeling, she experienced alone. And she found herself either weepy or furious: she hadn't just wanted a child; she'd wanted *a family*.

It was at this moment that she needed her own mother so—needed her to tell Sara about how childbirth had been for *her*, about feeding, and the child's weight gain, and what was normal, and below average, and what was extraordinary about her daughter.

She'd become pregnant with Honoria three months after Adeline's death, while still in mourning. It had been such a strange thing to go about all in black while her belly got bigger and bigger with new life. The juxtaposition had disturbed her so much at one point that she'd become convinced that the mourning dress might affect the disposition of her child. Of course, the doctor had told her that morbid fantasy was not uncommon in women who were expecting and that all she had to do was put such thoughts out of her mind.

But those dusky, private suggestions had only deepened —through the pregnancy, then the birth and now motherhood. Her perception of events or people, or even of her tiny daughter, surprised and alarmed her at times.

She remembered Honoria's christening in late December, two weeks after she was born and just before Gerald left for San Antonio. It was their second wedding anniversary. Their townhouse had been full of rosebuds and hothouse flowers for the occasion. What was left of the umbilical cord had fallen off Honoria in the bath that morning.

The birth had been hard and Sara wasn't able to move from her bed; the doctor had cut her open between her legs to help Honoria's passage and the incision had become infected.

So they'd decided to hold the small christening service in a bedroom adjacent to her own. Miss Stewart, standing next to her bed, held up a hand mirror at such an angle that Sara, lying down, could watch the proceedings reflected, without being seen herself.

Hoytie, who was now in France in the Ambulance Corps, had stood as godmother and Gerald's father had agreed to stand in proxy for Fred, who'd already shipped out.

In the looking glass, Sara had watched as Gerald walked into the room, carrying Honoria in her christening dress. It was one they'd agreed on together, but when she'd seen it then, in the mirror—embroidery and lace over bright cherry-colored silk—she'd felt a wave of sickness and terror come over her. The red of the silk had reminded her of the blood on the sheets, and all over her legs, which, in her narcotic state, had made her believe she had been shot down there.

She could remember the visceral panic even now, sitting on the settee, as her lovely girl made her sleeping noises—something between a smacking of lips and a gurgle. She put out her hand and rubbed Honoria's back. Her child's body was hard and soft at the same time. If she pressed a little she felt the resistance of her small muscles and bones, a solidity that comforted her. And, oh, how she loved to smell her, put her nose in her neck, or her stomach, or the sole of her foot, so fragrant—body and skin and warmth and the smell of milk, sour and sweet.

Sara suddenly felt fiercely toward her child and wanted to grab her up and hold her tight and crush her daughter against her own body. For some reason, she was reminded of the Spanish flu they said was spreading east across the country, killing grown men, and what if something happened to Honoria, so small, so unsafe. All those germs, carried on the wind, on breath, on hands, on lips, on sheets, on coins circulating everywhere . . .

"Mrs. Murphy?"

Sara looked up, flushed.

"Is the fire too hot?" Miss Stewart asked, her face concerned.

"No," Sara said, trying to control her breathing. "I was just . . . is it bath time?"

"Yes," Miss Stewart said. "I'll get the maid to bring in the tub and the water."

With the small zinc bathtub placed in front of the fire, and the steaming water poured from the pitcher, its temperature tested carefully by both Sara and Miss Stewart, Sara gently woke Honoria up.

There was a little fussing as her daughter reacquainted herself with the world, still so new and strange to her. But she finally settled down and Sara undid her white dress and got her out of her underclothes and her diaper.

Then she placed her baby gently in the warm water, holding her suspended with one hand, while she splashed her with the other. After a while, she let Honoria down in the water and leaned her upright so she could play. Tiny hands slapping against the surface, so gratified by the noise and the movement and light from the fire reflected in the droplets spinning up around her.

Sara smiled at her, saying, "Yes, yes, I know," to every expression. Then Honoria stopped splashing and for a moment Sara thought there was something wrong. But her daughter just cocked her head a little and looked her straight in the face. Those brilliant gray eyes surrounded by pale bronze lashes. The pupils a little dilated. It gave Sara a jolt, a sensuous pleasure she recognized from somewhere else, in the dark of her bed with Gerald. It swept over her. And she let out a sigh. And Honoria let out a sigh, as if they were thinking the same thing.

Afterwards, when Honoria was dried off, her hair a little red duck's fluff on her head, Sara rubbed oil into her pale skin and she glistened. The baby wiggled at her touch and stretched her toes toward the heat coming from the grate. And she tried to eat the oil off her hands, making Sara laugh.

Then Miss Stewart settled both of them back in the settee, Honoria safe and clean in Sara's arms. And in the warmth of the fire, and the wake of the pleasure, they both fell fast asleep.

❖　　❖　　❖

Owen lay on his cot in a chateau, somewhere near Chaudun, France, listening to the breathing of the other men in his squadron, punctuated from time to time by the sound of night bombers dropping their calling cards on the rapidly moving front lines.

The canvas cot felt tight around him. At six feet, he was

too tall, and his shoulders too broad, for these cots made for Frenchmen. After two years of sleeping in them, he should have been used to it, but tonight it felt smaller than usual. Next to him, he could tell Quentin wasn't sleeping either. He could tell by the rhythm and pattern of his breath, which he now knew as well, if not better, than he knew his own. They were both waiting for daylight.

He guessed it was around three o'clock in the morning, and they would all have to be up in less than two hours to prepare for their mission. They'd been moved from the tip of the salient at Château-Thierry to this place, their jump-off point, to cover the 2nd Marine Division on their advance to retake Soissons. There'd been some fuck-up the day before, at the start of the counterattack, and an advance that should have required three regiments now had to rely on only one, the 6th Marines. Owen's squadron, along with three others, had been brought in to provide whatever help they could from the air.

Their orders were to fly at 100 feet and strafe as much of the German front line as possible, while the Marines advanced behind a rolling barrage. They'd never flown so low and they'd all known what it meant when they'd been informed: all the Boche fighters would have altitude advantage on them, while the generally useless antiaircraft artillery would have a real chance to make contact. It was a pilot's no-man's-land. It also meant that command didn't trust the tanks.

"Something's wrong," Quentin had said, rolling a cigarette after dinner, his dark hair shiny from want of a bath.

"Not enough tanks," Owen said. "Or not good enough."

"Not enough men," Quentin said.

"Too much information," Owen said.

Quentin lit his cigarette, nodding. As a fighter squadron,

they were never given many specifics on their missions. This time, however, they knew a lot, and it worried them. It made them feel insecure as to who was really in charge. Owen could feel it in himself, as well as in the men around him.

"Jesus. Those poor bloody Marines," Quentin said.

Owen reached for the tobacco pouch. He rolled a pinch up and lit it, before running his hand through his hair, cropped close because of recent nits, bleached blonder by the July sun.

They'd sat smoking, silent. Owen could feel the warmth and smell the body odor coming off Quentin. They'd been together for almost two years now, since that November at Pau, their aviation finishing school, a dream after the hardships of training at Avord. Their bodies had hardened, thinned together; the list of their enemy kills, and their own minor wounds, had grown together. The only two Americans in their French escadrille, they'd both opted out of joining their own country's ranks together.

Now, lying in the dark of that room in that nameless chateau, Owen knew what Quentin was thinking, because it was what he and most likely every other man in that room was thinking. It was about fire, the eternal question for aviators. If your machine caught flame, did you jump to almost certain death, or did you risk the agony of burning alive, in the hope that you might be able to land before you were incinerated?

Over the many months they'd flown together, through the winter at Verdun, and the hell of the Chemin des Dames, they'd seen men make both choices. There were so many ways to catch on fire—the fabric, the tank, the wood; they'd debated wings versus tails, engines versus entire fuselage. But in the end, the conversations always concluded one way: Quentin was for jumping, and Owen was for staying.

"Look," Quentin would say, "you have to be realistic. You know when it's bad, when it's too far gone, and you just have to cut your losses. I'd rather go out falling through the air, than with my flesh melting."

"There's always a chance you could land," Owen would say. "Always a chance that you misjudged how bad it is, always a chance you might make it."

"You're talking about a miracle."

"I don't know. Maybe."

"No," Quentin would say, "the miracle would be that you jump and you live."

The longer they survived, the moodier these conversations made Owen. It was said that combat pilots had an average survival rate of three months. Quentin had been flying for fourteen, knocking six months off here and there due to chronic appendicitis, a broken arm and other injuries. Owen, however, had been flying for twenty. It was, after all, only an average.

Quentin was the ace, surpassing the necessary five official kills to score a total of eight. But Owen was the phenomenon. His nickname in the squadron was *La Chance*, for his lucky escapes. While being pursued by three Fokkers, his aileron control rod had been hit, the wires whipping across his face and slashing his scalp, forcing him into an uncontrolled dive, and he'd still managed to land, blood pouring into his eyes, right next to a first-aid station. Then there'd been the time his engine had cut over no-man's-land. He'd crawled through a triangular barrage to an Allied trench before the Germans exploded his machine with heavy shelling. The favorite among the boys in the squad, though, was the time he'd been seen going down, plane smoking, over a forest, only to reemerge hours later over the trees, his plane decked out in flowers and ribbons, supplied by the French peasants who'd found him and helped him repair it.

Owen didn't want to rob the boys of the laughs they got from recounting these stories, from joking about his nickname, so he kept quiet. But he hated it. He thought it was jinxy. Jinxes and superstitions, good luck charms and rituals, these occupied a huge space in the imagination of the pilots, himself included.

Most of the boys carried charms when they went up. Quentin kept a gold cigarette case in the front pocket of his flight suit. He said it had been given to him by an Indian Maharani he'd met during his travels.

Quentin, it seemed, had been everywhere. He'd come from a bit of money, somewhere in Connecticut. After his mother had died and his father took off for South America, Quentin had traveled to France and then worked his way from Algiers to Tunisia through to Egypt, before ending up in Bombay as a ticket agent in a railroad station. He'd seen his first airplane in Calcutta, where he became a mechanic for a stunt pilot, before traveling back to France. There, he'd joined up with the French Foreign Legion.

Owen's own experiences felt gray in comparison: the two years working in a tannery in Boston, coming home each evening to that hovel of a room in Chinatown, the smell of wet blue sticking to him, and staring at the place in the corner of the ceiling where the horsehair plaster crumbled a bit more every day from the oily damp. No friends, no money. Then his mother dying. The farm being sold. He'd found out about the Lafayette Flying Corps at a town hall–style meeting he'd attended out of sheer loneliness, where he'd heard all about the Americans fighting for the French cause in the air. He'd managed to wangle a letter of introduction from Mr. Cushing, who'd taken on the task of disposing of the farm and the livestock, and also from a reputable missionary in Chinatown he sometimes talked with. And eventually, in the spring of 1916, he'd set sail for France. Only then, at twenty years old, did he feel his life had really begun.

Quentin always said it was a strange philosophy, to believe that his life began at the moment he started preparing for death. But Owen knew the difference between dying in an airplane, in a war, fighting with men you loved, and dying in a shithole in Chinatown, watching horsehair plaster crumble in the corner of a room.

In the darkness, he heard a shuffling and a click. He knew Quentin was opening the cigarette case. He often played with it when he couldn't sleep.

He waited. And then it came: "Owen, you awake?"

"Yes."

"I've been thinking about that girl."

That girl could only be one girl and it frightened Owen to hear him say it; they had an unspoken agreement not to mention her.

"Don't think about it."

"No, I know. I just can't help it tonight, for some reason."

"Try."

There was a silence. Then: "Why should I?"

Owen turned over and sighed. "Because . . ." What could he say? There was no concrete reason, at least not one he felt equipped to articulate. Just that, at least to him, she represented the same thing as jumping out of a burning airplane: she represented giving up. "Because she's bad luck," he said finally.

"See, I don't think so. I've been thinking about it and I think she's what we're fighting for. I mean, that's the reason we're here, why we're flying, not sitting behind a desk at Pau or Avord, twiddling our fucking thumbs and waiting for all the fighting to be finished."

The girl would always be *that girl* to them; she had to be, because they didn't know her name. They didn't know anything about her, except what had happened to her. And even then they didn't know why. But she'd become their story, and they owned her motivations now.

It had started seven months ago, this story with the girl. December in Paris. Quentin and Owen had gone up to take their physicals with the U.S. Air Service. The United States had finally joined the war that April, and like all the other Americans in the Lafayette Flying Corps, all they'd wanted was to fly under their own colors.

They'd been given a day of leave in the capital before their exams, but a trip to the Red Cross had made them tense. They'd run into two other Lafayette Fliers who'd just failed their physicals. They were being sent back to the U.S.

"I just had another official kill three days ago," one of them said angrily. "And now I'm blind, according to the U.S. Air Service? Fuck that."

There were more of course—stories about the aces like Lufberry and Thaw, their heroes, being shoved behind desks, forced to train boys with zero experience how to fly a Penguin, or worse, being sent back home to shift paper there.

"They can't make us transfer," Quentin had said as they'd strolled on the Quai de Conti alongside the Seine. "We have the choice. We can stay with the French."

"We can," Owen said. The sun hit his face. The weather seemed particularly mild.

He thought about the men they'd been fighting with. It had come to mean something, this country. They'd watched them send one tide of men after another to their deaths, until they were scraping grade schools for new soldiers to hold the front.

"I don't know, though," Quentin said. "It feels wrong, somehow. I mean, this isn't home."

"No," Owen said. "But they might need us more."

"You going to save the whole of France all by yourself? Quite the hero."

"Don't act like what we do is nothing, Quentin. I can't believe that."

"Jesus, the eternal optimist. *There's always a chance, Quentin, always.* Don't you ever get fucking tired of that?"

"Fuck you."

They were angry, but so many things made them angry now. It might have been a relief to hit each other. Their eyes were locked, their hands tense and itching.

That's when the girl made her entrance. First, a scream from above, then as they looked up toward the sound, she came down from the bridge in front of them, feet first, her black dress like a parachute, a black veil streaming above her. Then, sickeningly, she hit the river.

Quentin didn't move, but Owen tore off his coat, his sweater, his shoes. He was in the freezing December water before he could think. She hadn't surfaced. He dove down. It was dark. He couldn't see anything. It was too cold. He wouldn't last long, he knew. Surfacing into the sunshine, he heard shouting. One more dive and then he'd have to try and get out. Back down under the water, he thought he saw the outline of a pale face and swam towards it, but it disappeared further below. He kept going and then knew he couldn't. He started swimming back up, but was suddenly too tired. He knew that face. It wasn't the girl's face. It was Charlie's face, it was Flora's face. Then someone's arms were around his waist, pulling him up. And in the daylight, he saw Quentin, Quentin holding him.

They were dragged out by a group of men who had rushed down to the quay when the girl had jumped in. They sat there shivering. Did anyone know her? No. Yes: she was a bus conductrice. She just found out her son was dead. No, she was a waitress at the Brasserie St. Louis. No, she was a war widow and she'd lost all her money. It didn't matter.

They made it back to their hotel, sitting on their twin, flea-bitten beds, facing each other, wrapped in blankets.

"You shouldn't have gone in," Quentin said, shaking his head. "She wanted to die. You shouldn't have interfered."

"Well, she did die, so that should make you happy," Owen said, lying back on the bed. He stared up at the ceiling. "I'm staying. With the French, I mean. I'm going to fight. They're sending kids—I mean really kids, Quentin—to the front. I'm staying."

He was quiet for a while, then Quentin said: "Fuck it. What's home anyway?"

Later, when they were falling asleep after drinking themselves into a stupor at the local cafe, Owen said: "Besides, you went in, too."

"It's different," Quentin mumbled, "I went in after you."

°

In his cot, Owen knew they'd run out of time. Ten, fifteen minutes maximum, before they'd be ordered up. Quentin was asleep. He'd heard the cigarette case fall to the floor. They were going to die today.

He wondered about saying things. Living in Boston, he'd heard orators, lesser men, floor bosses, missionaries: all of them spoke, as if to relieve themselves of the burden of their thoughts. But in all the great moments of his life, there'd been no words. He wasn't like that, he couldn't summon them. His farewell to his mother, his shame before Mr. Glass, his gratitude to Mr. Cushing, his brotherhood with Quentin, all these things were left unsaid.

*

On the field outside the makeshift hangars, their mechanic met them, bleary-eyed. The pilots in Escadrille 15, dressed in their fur-lined suits and boots, began to prepare their Spads. They were the best planes, fast and powerful, but also unreliable and impossible to land. They all loved them.

Owen's, the *Lettuce X*, was a beauty. She was the latest in a long line of *Lettuce*s—the others having been sacrificed to *La Chance*'s luck—and kept clean by Arnaud, his French mechanic, a fourteen-year-old kid from Paris whose own superstition was managed through obsessive cleanliness.

At first, when it went around that *La Chance* had named his plane after a beloved cow, the French boys couldn't get enough. He was teased for being a *paysan* and a *plouc* until Quentin had said firmly: "What you boys don't understand is that a good cow is far more reliable than your sweetheart, any day."

Unlike the other pilots, Owen didn't have a good-luck charm. But he did have a ritual. He would run his hand along *Lettuce*, from nose to tail, whispering to her all the good things about her, all the ways in which she would help him. He did it before he went up, every time, without fail. No one interrupted another pilot's ritual.

That morning, as the sun was coloring the sky a light purple, that peculiar dreamy haze, he whispered to *Lettuce*, and they talked about fire. He told her to hold until he was down. All the while, though, he could see Quentin out of the corner of his eye, waiting for him to finish.

When he was done, Quentin walked over.

"Don't talk about that girl again," Owen said, putting on his leather hood and adjusting his goggles.

"No," Quentin said. "But I'm right."

Owen nodded, but only in acknowledgment that Quentin had spoken. He looked up at the horizon. "One hundred feet," he said.

"One hundred feet," Quentin said.

"Poor fucking Marines."

"Poor fucking Germans," Quentin said and he smiled that rakish smile of his.

Owen laughed and held out his hand. "See you up there."

They shook hands, looking at each other, before Owen broke the contact. He signaled to Arnaud, and began climbing into his plane, as Quentin walked away.

The support mechanics joined them and they began the job of purging the fuel line: fueling, ignition, turning the prop, throttling, cutting the engine, and starting again. It was a tedious chore, but failure to purge could mean a sudden stall in the air and with the Spad, which was too heavy to glide, it meant dropping like a brick to the ground. When they were finished, Owen began testing the two Vickers machine guns.

Around him he could hear the rest of his squadron making the same tests. The first wave had left an hour before and their escadrille and the Escadrille 12—thirty mounts all together—were to fly out on the second. If the timing was correct, they would meet the first two squadrons in the air on their way back to refuel. It meant their own group wouldn't have the element of surprise on their side, but would hopefully meet with a somewhat depleted enemy.

Owen closed the radiator and set the fuel gauge to its

thickest level to feed the engine, before calling *"essence et gaz"* to Arnaud, who gripped the prop.

"Contact," Arnaud yelled.

"Contact," he yelled back, snapping the switch.

With a strength that always surprised him, Arnaud braced his thin frame and spun the heavy propeller, and the low growl of the vibrating engine filled his ears. Owen increased the power and let the engine warm up.

To his right he knew, without looking, that Quentin was doing the same, while to his left, he could see Allaire, Grenier and Massart already moving down the runway. Their squadron would fly in three V-formations of five, at 12,000 feet, until they hit the front.

When the tachometer was holding steady, Owen gave the thumbs up and the support mechanics removed the stops. The engine heightened its growl as he put on full power, then *Lettuce X* began to move across the field, bouncing slightly, the wheels beginning to lift, and Owen took flight.

It was a funny thing, when the machine left the ground. Where before the speed rattled his teeth, the minute it lifted, the plane seemed to slow until, finally, it hardly seemed to be moving at all. Then it was only the roar of the engine. That had been the hardest part of training for Owen, not being able to use his hearing to detect his surroundings. Only his eyes were of any use and in that sense, it was like being deaf and dumb. He constantly had to scan all around him, twisting his neck this way and that to situate himself and look out for enemy patrols. It was only later that he realized his ears had become adept at detecting engine problems, that the slightest stutter could break through his consciousness and alert him to possible trouble. In fact, silence was a pilot's enemy because, unless you were in a full dive, it meant something was disastrously wrong.

After leveling out, he closed his radiator and checked his position in the formation. He looked over to his right, and saw Quentin, who raised an arm in salute.

It was a cocoon of engine noise and early morning sun, high above the fields, all human violence swept away at that altitude. No corpses or machine gun fire or breaking shells or screams. Just lines and blocks of brown and green. He checked his clock. The 6th Regiment had been scheduled to jump off at 7:00 east of Vierzy, an hour after an artillery barrage, and just behind a rolling barrage. It was 8:20. Depending on the resistance, they could have made it some good distance by now. Owen calculated twenty to thirty-five minutes to reach them. Ten minutes or so before they should meet the first two squadrons on their way home. Once at the front lines, they would lower their altitude and dive in to strafe the enemy troops.

They were too far behind the lines to expect any German pursuit groups, but he scanned around anyway. They were flying southeast to meet the Marines and the sun was against them at this hour. He squinted into the distance, then again, to make sure his eyes weren't fooling him. A formation of black specks was moving toward them. He looked over at Quentin, who raised his hand to indicate he'd spotted it, too. Then to his left to Allaire.

They held their line. Owen could feel his heart beating in his chest, the rush of chemicals that indicated his fight mode. It was another enemy, the adrenaline, making his nerves jumpy and his decisions impulsive. It had to be conquered before any contact was made. Once, in Paris, he'd heard an ace chastising some eager young flier, saying that flying wasn't sport, it was scientific murder. He'd held on to that, and found his own way of crushing that hopped-up feeling of heroism that got so many pursuit pilots killed.

He looked at his controls, took in everything from left to right, checked all the numbers, did the sums in his head. This calmed him, counting, doing mathematical equations. It always had.

When he could feel his pulse slowing, he looked up again. Then he saw the rudder stripes: they were French planes. Their planes. It was the first two squadrons, but they were heading back too soon.

As his formation passed the last in their line, Owen saw one of the pilots give a thumbs down. Something was wrong, but they wouldn't know what until they got there.

He scanned the ground in the distance and then he saw the problem: there were no tanks moving. The 6th hadn't jumped off yet. The first two escadrilles must have strafed until their fuel ran low, and had been forced to turn around without making any forward progress. It also meant the German machine guns would have had a chance to get a fixed position on their 100-foot flying line.

Emptying his brain, he began to drop altitude to prepare for the dive. He looked over to Quentin, but Quentin wasn't looking at him. Instead, he was craning his neck over the side of the cockpit, intent on something in the near distance.

Owen looked, too, and saw that the French tanks had begun to move. It was a small group of light tanks, too small perhaps. But it had begun. Two minutes more and they'd be just in front of them.

At full throttle, they dove, pulling out at 100 feet over the first line of German troops, well dug in, it seemed, flattening over the second line toward the anti-tank artillery, and opening fire.

Owen's hand vibrated hot on the trigger, his eye fixed to the scope between two mounted guns. The roar of the engine, the hissing thunder of exploding shells, as his guns ate through the cartridges, this was all there was. Then, passing the third line, he pulled out and climbed fast in order to start to circle around and do it again.

He had to look up into the sun to see if there were any Germans coming from above, but all he saw was the Allied circle painted on the wings above him. The change in gravity and direction disoriented him immediately, and only by looking over the side could he center himself. He was heading back to the Allied lines. Keeping his sight fixed on the partially destroyed spire in the distance that marked the town of Vierzy, he began his turn.

When he came back around, he saw the 6th Marines go over the top, in perfect formation, advancing across the open wheat fields. But the tanks were going too slowly, and so the men were unable to avoid the incoming fire. From this height he could see them dropping in their tracks. And yet, still they came, wave after wave. He was mesmerized. The determination, the discipline; it was one of the most beautiful things he had ever seen.

He saw Quentin below him, the black heart and his number, 1566, painted on his plane. Ahead, he spotted Allaire and Grenier; he couldn't find Massart, but that didn't necessarily mean anything.

He made another pass, blew another small hole in the line. Then another, and another. Enemy machine guns had torn their own holes in his wings, but none had hit the fuselage. In the distance, the other formations were swooping, strafing, turning. He saw one go down in a spiral dive and hoped whoever it was had managed to land.

The 6th pushed their costly advance past the first German line, but the Marines under him were now trapped by machine gun fire and the constant barrage. He knew his escadrille were doing little to staunch the flow. They needed bombers for that, and no bombers were coming. He checked his clock: 9:45. They'd been burning fuel for over an hour and the first two squadrons would be gearing up to return. One more pass.

He saw Quentin come in on his right wing. They looked at each other, but there was no way for Owen to read his expression clearly.

Then he heard the dreaded *clack-clack*. Twisting his neck, he saw them: two Fokkers swooping from above, partially hidden in the sun, their machine guns firing. He knew Quentin was some feet above him, somewhere in the glare, but he didn't have time to look. One of the Fokkers was almost on him and he heard a bullet tear into the right-hand side of *Lettuce*'s body. He broke to the side, zigzagging, in an effort to avoid the German's sights. When the noise of the machine gun didn't follow, he rolled around and looked up. The Fokker had abandoned him. Further up, Quentin was preparing to loop the loop to avoid the attack from above. He couldn't see the second Fokker pulling up, underneath.

Before Owen had time to react, the Fokker had trained his sights and raked the belly of Quentin's plane with bullets. Owen saw the flame start at the front, near the propeller. He saw Quentin's plane begin its descent, engine cut.

As it gained speed in the fall, the flames spread across the nose. *Lettuce* was banking, coming round; Owen's mind was waiting, waiting for the jump. But the plane just kept falling and then it was almost on him, and as it passed he saw Quentin, his chest engulfed in flames, his face turned towards Owen. He was alive. Not moving. Burning to death. Then, in a flash, he was past him and gone down to the earth.

The diving Fokker was only seconds behind. Owen prepared for his own loop, flashing up past the German plane, before reversing their roles and diving down on him instead. He had him in his sights, but as he gripped the trigger his gun jammed. He sped down past the German, who now dove to pursue him.

Out of options, Owen took the last chance he had: a spiral dive. It was a dance, the spiral dive, one they'd been forced to practice over and over in flight school. The defender sped towards the earth in a corkscrew. The idea was to cut the engine and force the pursuing attacker to overshoot. At this low altitude, though, Owen's only chance was to try to pull out of the dive at the last possible moment, in hopes of causing the Fokker to crash.

He had no idea which side of the lines he was on, no concept of north or south or east or west. No time to feel fear or to count or to think about Quentin, or anyone for that matter. Just the rush of air that passed him as his plane sped down, ignition cut. He could see the ground rising to meet him, he could hear the faint *clack-clack* of the machine gun above him. And then he hit the switch and throttled her up as hard as he could, both hands willing her to come out in time. But *Lettuce* was responding slowly. He had no glide in this plane. He was now counting in his head as the earth came closer. To his left, he saw the Fokker suddenly swish by, engine smoking. He didn't have time to think about that. *Lettuce's* nose was inching up, little by little leveling out.

"Come on, come on, girl." He didn't know if he was saying it out loud. "Hold with me."

Then he was there and it was too late.

⁂

The darkness in his eyes slipped away slowly, revealing smoking wood around him, something weighing on top of him. It was his wing, he realized, bent over the cockpit.

Pushing it away, he tried to move. The safety belt was still on. He hit at the clasp with his fist and it released. Owen managed to extract himself, sliding his body to the earth. It was slimy. The stench was unbearable, smoke and vegetable rot and something else. Lying on the ground next to the wreckage he listened, trying to ascertain which direction the fire and return fire were coming from. But it got mixed up with the ringing in his ears. He pushed himself onto all fours, but there was something wrong with his left ankle. And then, something wrong with his thigh. There was blood. A bullet? Then a noise so terrible, it shattered every nerve in his body. A moment later, the ground trembled. Where the fuck was he? *Pull yourself together*, he commanded his brain. He looked around. It was a shell. Next to what had been his plane. They were shelling his plane. They were trying to kill him. But he couldn't tell which direction it was coming from. Then another hit, not as close. But from behind. He would go the other way. He was crawling as fast as he could across the wet ground, when suddenly, the earth opened up. One minute he was crawling and the next falling. He heard his bones crunch.

He lay there. Far above him he could see sky. He wanted to just lie there for a while. For a year, or until this war was over. Quentin was dead. Quentin had not jumped. He remembered that. Quentin had not given in. He pushed himself up on his elbows. He was in a small deep hole. Behind him was a thin tunnel. His mind turned this over slowly. He was in a listening post. Jesus, he hoped it wasn't German. Digging his nails into the rocky side, he pulled himself up onto his feet, stumbling against the wall when his left leg gave out. He vomited, bile. Then he started slowly moving towards the tunnel, dragging his left leg with him.

The tunnel was only about as wide as his shoulders, and very dark, with only a thin line of sky and sunlight visible above him. He couldn't hear very well, and now he couldn't see very well. He used his hands to guide him forward. One over the other, as he leaned into his right shoulder. Then out of the darkness came another darkness, a shape more defined.

Only when he was right on it did he realize it was the profile of a man. There was someone standing there, not breathing, or not so he could tell, eyes closed, pressed against the side of the tunnel. Then one eye opened, white, and the profile turned to face him, and the mouth opened, pink and wide, and with a yell, the person made of darkness leapt on him.

Then they were lurching against the side of the tunnel, no room even to fall. The person was speaking German, that much Owen could hear. His hands were around Owen's neck, and Owen's on him. The pain in his ankle, in his thigh, screaming.

He was dizzy and he knew what that meant. He gripped the person's neck tighter, and only then thought about how slender it was. A boy. He pulled the head back and hit it against the wall of the tunnel, praying for a rock in the side. Again, and again, until he could feel a little give. The skull? Then the air moved around him and there was a muffled shot, gun against fabric, and the body beneath the neck he was holding slumped, and Owen let it go.

Next to him was another figure, bigger, lighter. Owen stared, feeling wild and ready.

"It's all right, fella," he heard the figure shout at him. "You're with the Marines."

Later, Owen would learn that he had fallen into a recaptured trench that was being held by only two men from the 2nd Battalion under machine gun fire and constant barrage. They held it until midnight, when they and twenty other men separated from their divisions were relieved, and Owen was evacuated to a field hospital. The boy, shot, was some poor fucking German kid who'd gotten confused and left behind, hiding in the tunnel, hoping no doubt to make an escape under cover of darkness.

Afterwards, and for a long time to come, even when the war had ended, everything felt bleached of color. In the hospital in Cannes, through the numerous operations that left him with a limp, and upon his release, when the future seemed to stretch cruel and endless before him. Yet, something about what the two Marines did, something about what Quentin had done, holding to the end, that kind of unquenchable, ravenous optimism, kept a small bit inside Owen alive. And it would spring back. But that was later, after he'd met them. After he'd loved them.

THE GOLDEN BOWL

1923–1937

1923

Linda Porter sat at her dressing table in her big room in her big Venetian palace, rouging her lips. She was crying, but they were tears of . . . what? Frustration? Yes, that and something else. Not sadness.

Things had gotten bad in Venice, and the Murphys only seemed to make it worse. Ever since they'd come, she couldn't help feeling angry with them. All their damn self-containment and obvious affection. All Sara's talk of how well Gerald's painting was coming along. Yes, yes, she knew he was making something of a reputation for himself, but to bring Cole this ballet, as if Cole needed any help from him, as if Cole weren't obviously the more talented one.

She sighed and put down the rouge pot, not bothering to wipe away the tears making tracks through her powder. Oh, it wasn't about Gerald's success. Or maybe just a little. But that was petty jealousy.

Admit it, she said to herself. Ever since she and Cole had rented the palazzo he'd seemed to feel no need for any self-constraint, no need to hide his nocturnal searches for his bit of rough. *Bit of rough*, that's how she'd heard Monty Woolley refer to it when he thought she wasn't listening. In Paris, Cole was . . . well, perhaps not more discreet. But somehow it was less obvious in a city, with the men out roving in packs under the respectable veneer of drinking and palling around. Venice, for all its sophistication, was ultimately just a small town.

Then the Murphys had arrived and Gerald's intimacy with Cole, their ease together, bothered her. There was a sort of one-upmanship in flamboyance between them, all looked upon with beatific serenity by Sara, who was so clearly secure in her feelings for Gerald, and his for her.

It felt smug to Linda. She also knew that her husband loved her, but it didn't bother her any less, his constant pursuits elsewhere. What had Sara to be smug about when anyone with eyes could see that Gerald . . .

Then there was the constant talk of Cap d'Antibes and their happiness there: how *natural* it all was, what a *simple* life they led, how *quaint*, how *lovely and interesting* their children were. If she heard those names—Honoria, Baoth, Patrick—one more time . . . It made Linda want to scream. *All right, all right*, she wished she were back there with them, instead of here, in this mad merry-go-round of gaiety and parties and darkness. All the darkness in Venice. Oh, she loved it, really. But sometimes it just got too much, especially when it was shown up by people like the clean and shiny, well-pressed Murphys. She was glad Sara was now gone. But she wished Gerald would go, too.

It was unkind, maybe, but they made her sad. Yes, sad it was. Linda looked at her reflection, dabbing the damp around her eyes with a handkerchief. Then she wiped all her makeup off and started again.

Cole swanned—there was no better word for it, preening in white as he was—into the music room of the Palazzo Barbaro and announced to Gerald: "I'm off."

Gerald was sitting at the desk in front of the open windows. He'd been working on the sketches for their ballet, or more precisely fiddling with a sketch for the backdrop decor, his jacket draped over the baroque chair, shirtsleeves rolled up in the damp evening air.

He smiled at Cole.

"Linda is going to some soiree at the Palazzo Papadopoli, if you'd like to join. Supposed to be hideously divine."

"No," Gerald said, "I'm sitting this one out. Thought I'd play around with the set sketches, listen to the gondoliers' love songs."

Cole waited two beats—he was good at that—before saying: "I may compose a few of them myself." His friend smiled slightly, but his large, hooded eyes remained inscrutable. "Well," he said, finally, "if I can tempt you . . . Do you have everything you need? The bar is always stocked, as you know. Despite our best efforts."

"I do," Gerald said. "I'm well fixed." He held up his half-empty martini glass.

Cole nodded and turned to leave, before coming back and placing his hand on Gerald's shoulder. He lit a cigarette. "Strange, I miss Sara already. Awfully. Linda does too, you know."

Gerald knew this last part was a lie, but he patted Cole's hand. "Me three."

"Right. Nighty, night." Then he was gone.

Gerald leaned back and stared up at the ceiling: Roman soldiers were having their way with white-shouldered, pink-nippled women. He rubbed his temples. His hangover seemed to date back at least three days. He took another sip of his martini and thought of Sara, who'd taken the train back to Cap d'Antibes that morning.

The two weeks of parties had had something to do with her early departure. She'd woken two days ago, sat bolt upright in bed and announced: "I can't take one more of these holocausts."

It was true that his old Yale friend's lifestyle had become increasingly lavish, even outlandish, but then many people's had since the war. Paris was no different, nor New York. Yet that wasn't the real reason Sara had gone. Or not only that. It was also Linda.

"I smell a whiff of that unpleasant odor," Sara had said to him after the incident at the Lido, where everything sort of came to a head. "Eau de Disapproval."

She was right. He'd felt it too, though neither of them could really put their finger on the source. It just felt . . . taut, like one of Cole's piano wires, ready to snap. They weren't entirely up for all the nonstop lavish craziness, but nor were they as well behaved, it seemed, as Linda would have liked. And throughout it all Cole sat on the fence; the man who had as many quips on the tip of his tongue as Gerald had handkerchiefs in his drawer was suddenly a deaf mute.

He and Sara had come down to stay, ostensibly for a month, so that he and Cole could work on the ballet they were writing together for the Ballets Suédois in Paris. *Within the Quota*, intended to be a lighthearted curtain-raiser, was to be designed by Gerald, composed by Cole, and written by both. But all the parties and hangovers and sightseeing had gotten in the way of any real work and the conversations had begun to take on a strained quality. Furthermore, Linda and Cole never ended the evening in the same place, which didn't surprise Gerald or Sara, but seemed to aggravate Linda.

Before this trip, he hadn't met his friend in months and he'd missed him. He could still see the Midwestern boy that he'd met for the first time in his junior year in college.

Gerald had happened upon his room, mistaking it for someone else's, and when he'd opened the door he was met with one anemic electric lightbulb hanging from the ceiling, a monstrous hooked rug with a rose border that looked as if it dated back to Betsy Ross, wicker furniture and tacky silk cushions scattered on the floor. And in the center of all this was Cole, sitting at an upright piano, all gussied up in a ghastly houndstooth suit and puce tie, hair parted in the middle—his very best Peru, Indiana, outfit. He'd introduced himself and after consuming several glasses of claret, they'd ended up talking all night about Gilbert and Sullivan. Gerald felt he'd met someone he could be himself with.

They'd remained friends, albeit vaguely, through the intervening years and then really reconnected two years ago, when he and Sara had moved to Paris. Cole and Linda, who'd set up there during the war, had conspired to make what had originally started as a trip for Gerald to study French landscape architecture into a permanent move.

They'd introduced Sara and Gerald to everyone they knew. They gave wonderfully amusing and extravagant parties in their apartment near Les Invalides, dizzying nights passed in a swirl of music and platinum wallpaper and *bons mots*. Although, despite all this, his old friend did seem to be struggling a bit with his career.

So when Gerald had been offered the chance to design and write this ballet, he'd immediately proposed Cole as the composer and cowriter. Thus the trip to Venice had been arranged, as a sort of working holiday.

It had started off well enough. They were met with much affection and kissing and coddling and a description of who'd done what where in the palazzo, and weren't the linen sheets divine, and did they like the flowers in their room and so forth. It had felt good to be back in their company.

For their part, they had tried to entertain the Porters with tales of their time at Cap d'Antibes. The four of them had all gone together last August, and he and Sara had loved it so much that this summer, they'd convinced the owners of the Hôtel du Cap to keep it open out of season with a bare minimum of staff—a cook, a waiter and a chambermaid.

It had been quiet—the only other guests were a Chinese family who'd also decided to stay on after all the fashionable people had left for cooler climes. But, while the Porters had decided not to return, they'd eventually managed to convince Pablo Picasso—whom they'd met in Paris while painting sets at Diaghilev's atelier for the Ballets Russes—to come down with his family and liven things up.

"He's wonderful," Sara was saying over dinner in the palazzo one evening. "Funny, and very naughty. He has this terrible habit of waiting until you've bent over to pick something up, a towel or a glass, or something, and then sneaks up behind you and takes a picture." She laughed. "He's gathering quite a collection of rear-ends."

"My," Linda said, dryly, "doesn't he just sound wonderful." Her fork made a small screeching noise against her Blue Italian dinner plate. "Nothing I'd like better."

"No, Sara's right," Gerald said, backing up his wife. "He's mischievous, but natural."

Cole leaned back, the candlelight making the white dots on his navy silk tie wink on and off. "I have the impression that when he opens his mouth to speak, little squares and triangles and two-headed women might pop out instead of words."

Gerald laughed. "No, he never talks about his art. He's very salt of the earth, very naughty, very fun."

"She's not fun," Sara said. "Olga."

"No, for a ballerina she's oddly serviceable. She begins to speak and you think she's going to say something sparkling and then something entirely banal comes out."

Linda laughed, a harsh short sound, and Gerald saw Sara's head come up sharply.

"Well," Sara said, slowly turning her gaze away from Linda, "banal or not, what I find strange is she seems to feel nothing for the little boy, Paulo. Poor little thing is left to himself to play with Gerald's raked-up seaweed, while she stands around watching her husband's every move."

"Children aren't as interesting as some people seem to think," Linda said. "I find with certain of our friends that the subject becomes positively obsessive, to the point where one wonders if the lady in question's brain has been pushed out with the baby."

There was a silence, then Sara said: "What an interesting observation."

Gerald looked at the two women, and then at Cole, who was smoking a cigarette, brushing some unseen crumbs off his lap. "Well," he said, "when it comes to Olga, I mean really. His mother, who only speaks Spanish—the inimitable Señora Ruiz—has more to say for herself."

"The Spanish always do," Cole said, lifting his head, his face brightening. "Saucy chatterboxes."

"There was one very funny moment with him, though, his only real *poetic* moment," Gerald went on, encouraged. "We were walking, all of us, and there was this lovely old farm dog lying in the middle of the road, in the shade of a fragrant lemon tree. It was hot, you see, midday, and cool under that tree. And up the road comes this big, black car and has to stop because the dog won't move. So the chauffeur honks the horn and . . . nothing. Finally, the chauffeur has to get out, pick him up and deposit him on the side of the road. So, afterwards, when the car has gone on and the dog has settled back into his shady spot, Pablo says: '*Moi, je voudrais être un chien.*'"

"Poof. He's got his wish," Cole said, both hands shooting up into the air. "For I hear he is indeed quite the dog."

Cole's laughter, and Gerald's, was cut through by the sound of a chair scraping against the polished wooden floor.

"He's not the only one," Linda said, rising suddenly. She stood there a moment, almost helplessly, before saying, "I'm sorry," and then walking out of the room.

Gerald looked at Cole, who just smiled back at him.

"You know," his friend said, finally, into the silence. "I think I may go for a little walk, as well."

They'd seen Cole and Linda later, at the party they'd all planned on attending, arms linked, she laughing at something he'd said, and it was once again all smiles and warmth, as if nothing had happened.

That night in their bed—huge, gilded, with an embroidered headboard—he and Sara had mused on it.

"She knew when she married him," Sara said, puzzling it. "Yes, she knew."

"I suppose he's not being very discreet," Sara said. "To paraphrase Mrs. Pat, who cares what anyone does, as long as they don't do it in the street and frighten the horses."

Gerald laughed. "I suppose that's about it. But discretion wasn't really ever Cole's suit."

"True." Then: "Perhaps there's another woman? One could see how much that would hurt."

Gerald couldn't help but laugh a little. "There's not another woman."

"No," she said. "No, of course not." She sought out his hand under the soft linen sheet. "They are devoted. I mean, they always seemed devoted. Although, I couldn't stand what she stands."

"It must be hard on both of them," he agreed. He could hear the noise from the canal through the open windows, the rise and fall of Italian.

She turned to him. "Do you think it's us?"

"Of course it's not us," he said, although he wasn't entirely certain that was true. "How could it be?"

"I don't know," she said.

She snuffed out the lamp on the bedside table and was quiet for a while, leaving him to wonder if she'd fallen asleep. Then he felt her reach for him, her delicate gauzy nightgown brushing against the hairs on his arms.

"Will you come closer?" she asked softly.

Even after eight years of marriage, her need for not just sex, but physical, communicated affection, still surprised him. He felt that need with the children—like her, his love for them was visceral, an ache inside of him. But in his marriage bed, in *that* way, he wasn't as open. It wasn't as crucial to him, he supposed. It wasn't *in* him in the same way.

"Will you, my love?" Even more softly, this time.

She was the best part of them. Of what they'd made together. So his fingers found the hem of her nightgown.

"Promise me: you won't ever fall for another woman."

"I promise," he said.

⁂

"You're more than welcome tonight, you know." Now it was Linda standing in the doorway of the music room, her body encased in a white silk gown printed with what looked like purple nightshade.

"Thank you, but I don't think I'm actually able," Gerald said.

The evening had grown closer, making the sounds of the city seem richer, denser, more resonant.

"You could be my date," she said, smiling.

He knew she was trying to be kind, after Sara's departure, after the scene at the Lido.

"I wish this poor old body would allow me. You look marvelous."

She looked down at her dress, her aquiline nose casting a shape like an arrow across her face in the lamplight. "Oh, thank you. Cole bought it for me."

"He has wonderful taste."

"Yes," she said. "He is wonderful. Isn't he?"

"I think so."

Linda took a big breath, her bosom rising. "Well, I'm going. Once more into the arena." She gazed at him, before turning away. "Good night, then."

"Good night," Gerald said.

When she'd gone, he looked back at the sketches lying before him. He and Cole had agreed on a backdrop painted to look like a huge newspaper, black and white with sensational headlines mimicking those printed in America these days—*Unknown Banker Buys the Atlantic; Ex-Wife's Heart Balm Love-Triangle; Rum Raid Liquor Ban*. It was an exciting project, but Gerald couldn't stop his mind from wandering back to his own work, waiting patiently for him in Paris.

It had taken him a while, but he'd found his vocation. After the war, they'd moved first to Cambridge where he began studying landscape architecture at Harvard, and then to England and finally Paris for the same.

One bright November afternoon two years ago, however, he walked past Paul Rosenberg's gallery on the rue La Boétie and his life changed. There, in front of him, were canvases the like of which he'd never seen: fractured, but strictly ordered, like muddy stained-glass. He'd understood them immediately, like a language remembered from a youthful visit to a foreign country. They didn't represent *the thing*, but the *essence* of the thing; life seen through a prism. He learned later they were cubist paintings by Juan Gris and Picasso. But all he was aware of then was the electricity of recognition: if that was painting, that was what he wanted to do.

So he'd spent two years studying and evolving his own style, and then this spring had selected four pieces—two oil paintings, a watercolor and a sketch—to show at the Salon des Indépendants in Paris. They'd been a mild success with critics, especially *Turbines* and *Engine Room*, the two oils. He was fascinated by the inner workings of the hard, metal hearts of machines, those huge precision instruments.

But what he was working on now excited him most. An enormous eighteen- by twelve-foot painting he'd titled *Boatdeck*. He'd been working on the sketches for it in Antibes, while the original canvas was housed in his studio in Paris. He was anxious to get back to it.

He figured it would take them another two weeks, Cole and him, to finish *Within the Quota*. He was only mildly worried about the two weeks he and Sara would be parted, or rather the two weeks Sara would spend without him in Antibes. Of course it was clear to him that Pablo had fallen in love with her, enchanted at the very least. He sketched her constantly, took photographs, watched her admiringly with the children, or when she danced, or arranged her hair. His gaze would follow her as she went to the changing tent they set up on the beach. All this under the watchful eye of Olga. But Olga, pretty, delicate, young, was no match for her husband's sheer masculinity. Gerald wasn't as intimidated by the man's potent physical presence as he might have been when he was younger. Marriage to Sara created a kind of cocoon against that. But he still felt his own limitations as a man when compared to someone like the Spaniard. Would Pablo try something on? He wondered. He trusted Sara, that much he knew. So the unease was a slight one, hovering just beyond his everyday thoughts, just teasing the edge.

Two more weeks. Then he could return to Antibes, to Sara, the children, to his sketches. Then autumn in Paris and *Boatdeck* and . . .

"First things first," he said to himself.

He picked up his pencil and tried to fix his attention on the work in front of him. He could hear the gondoliers' love songs rising from below, floating over him, and perhaps over Cole and Linda, who were out there somewhere, as well.

      *   *   *

Sara had never felt as relieved as she did when the Train Bleu finally pulled into the Gare d'Antibes in the late afternoon. She couldn't wait to see her children, to hold them, to get back to her rooms at the hotel and bathe and drink a large glass of fresh milk and generally wash Venice away.

She'd been lucky to make the right connection in Menton. The train ran infrequently this time of year, and finding one that stopped at the Antibes station was even more of a rarity, as all the English and Belgians and French aristocrats locked up and fled north for the summer Season. Of course, there were no longer any Russians, their villas long empty and haunted, dotted among the hills of the small fishing village on the Côte d'Azur.

So it was deliciously quiet when she stepped off the train,

the smell of the Aleppo pines, the parasol pines and the *pins maritimes* filling the dusty, dry air. It was like being baked in an evergreen oven.

The platform was deserted except for a few porters and Vladimir, waiting to pick her up and drive her back to the hotel. As with the Picassos, Sara and Gerald had met Vladimir at Diaghilev's atelier. His story had intrigued them: an aristocratic Russian émigré who'd fled the Bolsheviks to wind up in Paris designing sets for the Ballets Russes. So when Gerald set up his own studio he'd hired the Russian to teach him basic techniques of stretching and mounting canvas, and to generally help out.

One evening, however, Gerald had brought Vladimir back to their apartment on the rue Greuze for supper. Sara had been ready to tear her hair out when they arrived. There'd been trouble getting Patrick, then one and a half, down that evening, the cook had quit two days before, and she was desperately late getting supper ready. The minute he walked through the door, Vladimir had just taken over, as if it was all the simplest thing in the world. He'd chopped vegetables, roasted the meat, opened wine.

At one point, after setting the table, Sara had passed by the children's room and sitting on the edge of Honoria's small bed, his hands throwing shadows on the wall in the low lamplight, was Vladimir.

"Let me tell you story," the Russian was saying, "about a rabbit I knew when I was a little boy, about your age. His name was Peter and was very bad rabbit. And he made much trouble for his mother, Mrs. Josephine Rabbit, and for the not very nice Mr. McGregor."

"Why was Mr. McGregor not very nice?" Honoria asked.

"Ahh," Vladimir said. "We may get to that on another evening."

After he'd regaled the children, the three of them had then eaten supper by candlelight, while Vladimir told *them* stories of St. Petersburg before the Bolsheviks. He was magic and Sara decided there and then that they couldn't do without him. She asked, and he said yes. From then on, he was their companion.

He was supposed to have spent this summer in Paris, but he'd come down south while they were in Venice, to look out for the children who were staying with a nurse Sara wasn't entirely certain about. The Picassos had agreed to put him up at their villa, and when he wasn't checking up on the nurse, he was free to do as he pleased.

"Can we take the coast? I'm longing to see it," Sara said when she'd settled into the yellow Renault that always put her in mind of a duck.

Vladimir lit a cigarette. *"Oui."* He spoke very formal French—everyone was *vous* except the children—and a good bit of English, but he could be positively monosyllabic at times.

"How was *Venise*?" he asked once they'd begun to make their way.

"I didn't care for it," Sara said. "Not this time, anyway. I'm glad to be back. How are the children?"

"Fat."

Sara laughed. "Good." Through the pines, she could see the straw-colored cliffs leading down to the sea, itself brushed violet and pink in the afternoon light. Olive trees were pushing out through the crags here and there. "And the nurse? She gave them the fresh milk, from the farmer?"

"Oui. La vache donne son lait avec de générosité," he said. "Also fat."

With the roof off, the sun hit her face, warming her skin.

"And the Picassos?"

"He works, she sulks."

Sara nodded. "All's right with the world, then." Yawning, she stretched her arms toward the sky and closed her eyes, feeling the breeze running through her fingers.

At the Hôtel du Cap, she drank her glass of milk and read her letters: one from John Dos Passos, who described himself as "slowly baking" in the Paris heat and inquiring about their return date; one from the Barrys—Phil was working on the follow-up to his play *You and I*, and Ellen was going mad with boredom—would they come to their villa in Cannes and dine with them; and one from Fred Murphy's wife, Noel, saying they'd found some nice apartments in Paris, but that Fred's health seemed no better.

Sara sighed. She'd wait until Gerald had returned to tell him about Fred. He worried so about his brother, who'd come back from the war a hero, but in shattered health, both physically and mentally.

She was about to compose a response to the Barrys when the children came streaming into the bedroom, the nurse just behind, trying in vain to corral them. Bending low and opening her arms, Sara caught them as they threw themselves at her, and felt that peculiar gratitude of being so missed and so needed. Honoria, five, her wavy hair cut short like a boy's, smelling of milk and salt and fresh bread; Baoth, four, his skin brown like a nut, his upturned nose crinkled with joy, hair like a silken cap; then Patrick, her tow-headed youngest, waddling, his expression serious as always. It seemed that, for him, life itself was a serious business.

"Well," she said. "Have you all been good?" Three heads nodded in unison. She stood, her hand brushing the top of Baoth's head, feeling the fine texture of his hair against her palm. "Did you write us letters? We didn't get anything." She looked at them with mock sternness.

Honoria looked pained. "We did, we wrote to you about the beach, and Vladimir's story about the jungle boy, and about Phillip and Lily." The last two mentioned were the dogs.

"Hmm. Well, I suppose Dow-Dow will be happy when he gets them in Venice."

"Poor Dow-Dow," Honoria said. "He's all alone."

"No, Dow-Dow's fine. He's with Mr. and Mrs. Porter and they're all having a lovely time."

"Did you bring us anything?" This was Baoth.

"No, but Dow-Dow *might* have something for you. You'll have to be very good to find out, though."

"All right, children," the nurse said. What was her name? Rose. She *was* tired. "It's time for baths then supper."

"Make sure you get yourselves very clean," Sara said. "Lots of soap." The influenza epidemic had made her careful about germs, and health in general. Along with plenty of soap and clean bath water, she insisted their milk—and as much of their food as possible—came directly from one of the local farmers, as well as making sure they spent a great deal of their time out in the fresh air.

When Rose had taken them off, Sara thought about Gerald, "all alone" with the Porters, as Honoria had put it. She did feel sorry for him. But he'd seemed less bothered by the tension with Linda and Cole.

Sara, however, hadn't been able to stand it one more day. Not after the dreadful scene on the Lido. It had been the four of them that day, but Gerald and Cole had gone out for a swim leaving the ladies behind on the sand.

"That's quite a swimming outfit Gerald has," Linda had remarked, when the two men had splashed into the water.

Gerald would be naked on the beach if he could; he loved the feel of the sun on his skin and the common woolen knitted swimming costumes irritated him. Sara had found him a pair of light, striped shorts in Cannes, which he loved but which did contrast with the black two-piece costumes still worn by most of the gentlemen. She'd also knitted him a dove-gray cap, which he wore to protect his head from burning. She adored the overall effect: tall and lean, his long muscles visible without the dense clothing. More importantly it made him happy. Linda, however, seemed to feel differently.

"Oh, I think those black heavy things look positively funereal," Sara responded, trying to keep her tone light.

"It's awfully camp," Linda said, her gaze still on the men. "You wouldn't want to give the wrong impression."

"What impression would that be?"

Linda was quiet. Sara could see Cole and Gerald had swum out quite far.

"Well, if *you* don't mind."

"I do not." Sara opened her parasol and shaded Linda from her view.

As Gerald and Cole cleared one of the buoys, Sara heard shouting from off to their left. A lifeguard was standing on the shore yelling at them, waving his arms and trying to beckon them back in. Sara could pick out the word *pericoloso*.

Cole and Gerald had heard him, too. Gerald waved back, yelling: "So is love. Love is very *pericoloso*." Although the two men did turn and start in.

"Oh really. This is too much," Linda said.

By the time Gerald and Cole reached the shore, Sara could tell Linda was spoiling for a fight. She just wasn't sure who was going to bear the brunt.

"Did you really have to make such a scene?" she asked.

"But, darling," Cole said, bending down to kiss Linda on the lips. "Love *is* dangerous."

"It is, the way you make it," Linda said.

Gerald looked at Sara, who gave a small shrug. He lay down, wet, in the warm sand and closed his eyes.

"Gerald, don't you want your robe?" Linda asked.

Sara could tell he was pretending he hadn't heard her.

"I'll wear it," Cole said gaily. "Look. It's got stripes. How exciting." He donned Gerald's robe and then snatched Sara's parasol out of her hands, twirling it over his shoulder. "Where's my hat?" he said, before locating his white straw hat and placing it jauntily on his head.

Sara reached into her bag and pulled out her Kodak. "Don't move," she said, laughing. Cole placed his hand on his waist and jutted out his hip. "Don't move," she said again, before snapping his picture.

"Oh, for God's sake." Linda stood, turning angrily on Sara. "Perhaps you don't care how your husband behaves in public, but *I* do. You're all children."

"My husband behaves just as he pleases, and just how he should, in public and private," Sara said coldly.

"Keep telling yourself that, darling," Linda said, before storming off in the direction of the lagoon.

That had been that, as far as Sara was concerned. That evening they'd gone off to yet another party, pretending the incident had never happened. But the next morning Sara had told Gerald she was leaving.

And now she was back, in a place where there was no yelling and no recriminations, thank God. Just the quiet village and its hills and the sea and the children and Vladimir and the dogs. Where everyone could be just who they were.

*　　*　　*

He was sketching her on the beach where she lay, the straps of her coffee-colored swimming costume visible, pushed down off her shoulders, her legs wrapped in a bright printed cloth. A long strand of pearls hung down her back. The beach, the sea, was good for them, she'd said, because that's where they came from.

He squinted under his Stetson, and then looked back at his pad. With his pencil he outlined the curls that fell down around her shoulders, then shaded them, smudging the lead with his thumb. Some days she wore it pinned up, and he had a sketch of that too. Also of her wearing a turban. But today he would capture the form of her hair loose, undone. He was already thinking of using it in a composition with two other nudes, with her in the center, three Greek muses.

Off to his left, the three Murphy children were raking seaweed, taking over their father's usual daily job of clearing the small beach inch by inch of the briny carpet. He could hear their voices pealing, call and recall.

Aside from sketches of Sara, his pad was also full of studies of the things the Murphys took to the beach every day: two fringed umbrellas; a pink and white striped tent for changing in; cotton cushions of various colors—rose madder, Naples yellow, celadon, *blanc-neige*—popping against the cerulean blue of the sea; blankets to lie down on; cloths to wrap up in; silk scarves to wear as turbans; bottles of wine and sherry and tins of biscuits from Paris; serving trays, crystal glasses; and a basket full of clothes to dress up in if the mood struck.

Sara stirred, sitting up a little more, looking over her shoulder like Ingres' *Odalisque*. His blood quickened. He turned the paper and quickly outlined the pose, so as not to lose the image of it, still fresh in his mind.

He squinted again at the frame. His pencil made a

cross-hatching where the blanket was, creating a grid around her reclining figure. He knew the outlines of her body now, after a long summer spent watching her. Full breasts, curved hips, perfect, muscular calves. The heavy, dark honey hair, the upturned nose, the cupid's bow of a lip. And those eyes, canted downwards like a lion's.

As he watched her, she held the sherry bottle out to Olga, who tipped her head forward in complicity. Then she called out to the children.

Three naked little brown bodies ran to her and sat patiently as she rubbed them all over with coco cream, the unctuous, jungle smell carrying over to where he was sitting. He watched her strong hands, mother's hands, knead and smooth it over her little natives' skin, before releasing them one by one back into the wild. She lay back down.

Minutes passed. She toyed with her book, not really reading. He thought about how different she was to Olga, marveled at all the ways women could be made; his wife's lithe body, like a stream of water, and dark smooth head stood in contrast to Sara's heavier, rounder, blonder form.

He slept for a while in the afternoon heat. Then the Murphys' nurse, Rose, gathered up the children and the dogs—a Scottie the color of ink and a spotted small one—to take them all back to the hotel for lunch and a nap. Paulo was at home sick with a summer cold, being tended to by his grandmother and his *nounou*.

When they'd gone, Sara filled a tray with a small bottle of chianti, a large slice of pâté and hunks of baguette, a bowl of olives, three colored plates, and a garland of ivy.

"Lunch is served," she said. "Oh, wait." She rummaged around and produced a small vase filled with flowers picked from the succulents outside the hotel, and placed it in the center. "Now lunch is served."

He liked that detail. It was feminine, gay. He admired that in her.

The three of them ate and then bathed. Olga went into the tent to change into a dry costume and then lay down and fell asleep in the shade of one of the umbrellas. Sara was reading a novel sent to her, she'd said, by Gerald's sister, who was a friend of the author.

She'd held the cover up to him when he'd asked about it.

"The Beautiful and the Damned," she'd said. *"The Disorganized and the Drunk* would be more apt. I do wonder at Esther's taste sometimes."

She seemed absorbed in it now, though. He moved closer to her.

"Perhaps you can take me to see this house you and Gerald have bought," he said.

Sara looked up. "Oh, yes."

"This evening?" He cocked his Stetson over his eyes, shading them.

"If you'd like."

He would like. He wanted a chance to be alone with her. He had nothing against Gerald Murphy, whom he found quite original, but he was drawn to Sara. Perhaps it was her Americanism. It was true that he'd never been exposed to this kind of American woman before—married, rich, a mother, but also a muse. He knew the young stupid ones and the old ones and the Sapphic ones. None of those appealed. This one was sensual in a way that was unselfconscious.

He wouldn't go too far: perhaps a hand on the small of her back, leaning close. Just run his hand over her figure, to feel what until now he'd only drawn. He thought about the moment just before something begins, just before the hourglass has tipped and time begins to run out. He loved that moment and once it passed, it felt like a death.

He was thinking of this, and of what might happen, when Olga opened her eyes, and stretched. Sara put her book down again and said: "Would you like to see our house this evening? We were thinking of going for a viewing."

"Oh, that sounds nice," Olga said lazily, and looked at him. "That's a good idea, isn't it?"

✻　　✻

Owen was sitting at one of the rickety tables at the Café des Pêcheurs, overlooking the Port d'Antibes, drinking a *Remplaçant*. He'd acquired a taste for anise; liked watching the liquid cloud over when he added water from the little carafe on the side.

There were only a few other people at the cafe: some fishermen relaxing after a haul; a group of those bohemian artists who seemed to flock to the region in the summer; and a drunk war invalid—the Riviera used to be full of men like that, but they were becoming less and less visible. It was six o'clock in the evening, but it wouldn't get more crowded than this.

The village was too small to attract fun-seekers, who had Saint-Raphaël, Cannes or Juan-les-Pins, with its new casino and smarter restaurants, to choose from. Here there was nothing except a couple of cafes, a movie theater that was open once a week—if the piano player could be located— and some fine beaches.

It was a good hour's drive, at least, from Owen's rooms near Saint-Raphaël, but he liked to come here to escape. Just to be quiet. He rented space for his plane at the Fréjus airbase and from there ran his business of flying in goods from London, Paris and farther-flung places across Europe for the rich who couldn't be without their caviar or silk handkerchiefs during the winter Season. He sometimes ran pleasure trips along the coast to supplement his income.

Because he was always at the base, he'd come to know the young aviators stationed there and, along with the proprietor of the cafe below his rooms, they made up his circle of friends. But there were evenings, like this one, when the joviality and youth of the French pilots depressed him. None of them had served in the war and they looked upon his experiences as the pinnacle of glory. Yet Owen had started to become frightened of relating his own stories; they'd come to feel like they no longer belonged to him, like they had happened to someone else, in a book, perhaps.

After Chaudun, he'd been sent to Cannes, to a convalescent hospital, while his leg healed. It had been broken in three places and after five months, one operation and a few metal screws, the war was basically over and he'd been discharged. He'd been in no hurry to leave, anyway: he was burned for combat flying, and it had been beautiful there—the Croisette and beaches, the palm trees, the converted hotel with its big turrets.

So he'd taken some of the money he still had from the sale of the farm and bought one of the army's surplus planes, going cheap, and an old Citroën, which he'd fixed up. He'd struck a deal with the commander at the Fréjus airbase for hangar space and eventually taken rooms in Agay, on a perfect little bay surrounded by the Esterel Mountains. There, the cliffs were pink instead of golden. Along with the one cafe, there were a few villas, some smaller houses and a handful of fishing shacks. It was eight miles from the base, but the calm was worth the price of the petrol.

The *patron*, a squat brown man with shoulders like planks, came to refill his glass. Owen had been there often enough for the man to know he took two refills before leaving.

The sun was changing the color of the sea from light to dark, as it made its way west. He looked over at the group of artists talking, his attention drawn by the mix of English and French he heard.

They were a group of three: a stocky man with a big nose and dark hair parted deeply from the right, a black Stetson on his lap; a taller, slender man in a striped fisherman's shirt whom he recognized as a Russian he'd spoken with one evening; and a woman in a flowing gown, like some Greek goddess. She was older than himself, he thought, but beautiful. And seemed very still. She had sloping kind of eyes. She was staring at him.

He looked at the port and then back at her, to see if she was still looking. She was. It gave him a sort of funny feeling, like being memorized, in the way he'd memorized arithmetic problems in school. Her gaze was very frank, for a woman, and he had the impression—one long-forgotten and only vaguely, and anxiously, remembered—of something about to happen.

❖

The sherry at the cafe was very bad, Sara decided. But after they'd all gone to see the house she and Gerald had bought, Vladimir had suggested an *apéro* there; he'd apparently become very fond of it in their absence. Picasso had come along, while Olga had begged off in order to change for supper.

It had cheered Sara to see the villa again; every time she fell in love a little more. It was a place that people could be happy in, she decided. Perfectly nestled in the hills of Cap d'Antibes, a bit below the old lighthouse, it sat on seven acres of sloping terraced gardens, overlooking the Golfe-Juan, west towards Cannes. It had been owned by some military attaché or other who'd brought back what seemed like an entire botanical garden from the Far East. Gerald knew all the names. When they'd started on renovation plans, they'd both agreed that the gardens must remain intact.

The villa had been purchased on something of a whim, but hadn't cost very much. Her father had decided to dole out proportionate amounts of his capital to Sara and her two sisters before his death—an effort to circumvent inheritance tax. The funds, along with a strong dollar against the franc, had made the price-tag seem a pittance. (At least to her and Gerald who, she granted, weren't very clear about money.)

It had been especially beautiful that evening, with the hills below them the color of elephant skin, the gulf turning from turquoise to jade as it spread towards Corsica. And it had pleased her to win Pablo's approval.

He'd found the garden *très belle* and the view perfect for a painter, he'd said. Of course, she'd known the real reason he'd wanted to go up there, and in fact she was flattered. He was charismatic, there was no doubt, and such a physical presence, and she liked being around him. But what he had in mind was out of the question. So she'd invited Olga and even roped in Vladimir as an extra precaution.

Now, at the cafe, the two men were carrying on a long discussion about the different types of boats moored in the port. Vladimir, who'd been studying to be a naval architect before his flight from St. Petersburg, was very interested in that sort of thing. Sara was not.

Instead, she watched as a drunk war veteran got drunker and eventually went to sleep. Then she fixed her gaze on a young man, perhaps ten or fifteen years her junior, sitting by himself, sipping from his drink. He was built like a classical statue, an inverted triangle, his long legs stretched out on either side of the cafe table, the muscles in his arms faintly visible beneath his cotton shirt. He was tan and quite blond. He didn't look local, or even French, but nor was he dressed like a wealthy Englishman, or an American. Couldn't be a German.

She stared at him awhile, before he noticed. He looked back at her as if he expected something from her.

She turned to the two men. "Who is that man over there, do you think?"

Vladimir looked over. *"Un pilote américain."*

"Truly? You know him?"

"One evening, over an *apéro*," Vladimir said, clearly anxious to return to his yachting explanations.

Sara continued to stare at this young blond aviator. She knew it was a bit impolite, but this was a village, and open curiosity was tolerated by the French in a way it would never have been in England or America. "What's he doing here?"

Vladimir, now resigned to this line of questioning, shrugged. "What is anyone doing here?"

She liked the way the young man looked back at her—slightly nervously, slightly eager—like Baoth when he was learning to swim.

"I think I'd like to meet him," Sara said.

1924

Owen was dreaming. In his dream, he was a blade of wheat, green and unfurling, pushing out of the ground with sun and moisture. As the sun grew warmer, he grew longer, taller, stronger. He was shooting up and then he stopped. But the sun kept on. And as it became hotter, he began to change color, he turned from green to golden. He was drying up. And then he was burning. All at once, he was cut down, quickly, with a metal blade. He was dead and rolled up and turned into feed, and he couldn't stop it any more than he had been able to stop himself from growing in the sun.

He awoke covered in sweat. The small bedroom with the linen curtains felt close and yet it was only just dawn, the air cool and dryer than usual. His yellow bedspread was damp from his body.

He got up and put on his swimming trunks and a shirt and his espadrilles and shut the door behind him. He walked down to the beach and dove into the water. There were only fishermen up at this hour, but they were far away on their boats, tiny dots on the horizon. He swam for a while and then went back to his rooms above the Café d'Esterel.

He took a quick rinse in the bath on the landing then dressed for the day in his chinos and chambray shirt. The sun was up, but not high, and he went to take his coffee with Auguste.

The Frenchman was already finishing his first *café au lait* when Owen found him at the zinc counter. Upon his arrival Auguste, without a word, prepared the same for Owen and then slid it over to him. They stood there in silence, but it was the good kind, and it reminded him of early-morning breakfasts with his mother, who'd also known about quiet. After a bit, Auguste made him a *tartine*, which Owen wrapped in a napkin and took with him out to his car, to eat on the drive.

At the base, most of the aviators were at breakfast and the hangars were deserted. He pulled up in front of his own and shut off the motor. Inside, in the semi-darkness, she was waiting for him. *That Girl*. She was a modified Spad, a two-seater built for durability and distance, instead of speed like *Lettuce*.

Off to one side was a wooden desk where he kept his accounting and appointment books, as well as the maintenance calendars for *That Girl*.

He checked these over now, knowing already he had nothing on. Still, it grounded him to see everything in order. Afterwards, he went over to his plane and began the ritual of running his hands over her wooden body, speaking to her, telling her what a beautiful day it was turning into.

By the time he reached her nose, the sound of the aviators and the mechanics descending on the hangars filled the air. Owen went out and flagged down Eugène, the mechanic he shared with one of the pilots, Edouard Jozan. Eugène, with the blessing of the French military service, received a small stipend from Owen for helping him out with *That Girl*.

Eugène moved quickly, always—one of the things that Owen liked about the man. And when he'd first met him, he'd been glad to see that he *was* a man, not a boy like Arnaud, his mechanic during the war.

"Just going out for a turn," Owen said. "Won't be up long."

Eugène nodded and waited while Owen pumped the throttle. When Owen called out, he cranked the prop, Owen made contact, and the mechanic stepped away. Owen lifted a hand in thanks, before beginning to taxi.

Once up, he made for the Golfe de Fréjus and the open water. In the morning sun, the colors of the sea were sharply delineated: first a mossy green near the line of the shore, then a band of turquoise, and finally a deep indigo.

The sun above and water below, and the hum of the engine, so much quieter than the fighters he'd flown, made the dream finally disappear and he felt a contentment come over him. The day was before him and he could do as he pleased. After this, perhaps another swim and then lunch in Saint-Raphaël. He checked his controls, all the numbers and arrows waiting only on his decisions.

❊   ❊   ❊

The champagne was finished before they'd even left the Marseille train station.

"We should have brought more than one," Zelda sighed.

"You shouldn't have let me forget my billfold and then we could have bought some," Scott said irritably, although he knew it was as much his fault as Zelda's.

They were making the move down south to *e-con-o-mize*, as Zelda called it. In New York, they'd been running through the money as fast as the *Saturday Evening Post* could pay, and Paris hadn't been much better. Scott needed to finish *Trimalchio in West Egg*; Scribner's was losing patience, despite Max Perkins' assurances that everyone had faith he could pull it off. So when Sara and Gerald had extolled the virtues—and cheapness—of the Riviera, the plan was made to go down in June in search of some peace and quiet. They'd settled on Valescure, on the northern edge of the town of Saint-Raphaël, about an hour-and-a-half drive from their friends in Cap d'Antibes.

The car had held out until they were almost at Marseille, when it had begun to smoke and cough and then, finally, just die. He and Zelda had grabbed what luggage they could manage, along with one bottle of champagne from the crates in the backseat, and made a dash for the Train Bleu. Someone would have to go deal with the car and the champagne later.

In the melee, he'd forgotten his billfold in the glove compartment, and he and Zelda had had a time of it scraping together the money—loose change from his pockets, errant bills in her handbag—to buy tickets for the salon car.

"Let's talk about this summer," Zelda said, breathing on the window and then drawing waves in the condensation.

"All right." Outside, the edge of the city disappeared as the train rounded a turn.

"You're going to work very hard and I'm going to get very brown."

Scott nodded, his eyes wandering around the car, taking in the marquetry patterns of floral baskets, the polished ceiling fan and Lalique lights, the navy blue carpet and toffee-colored velvet seats. He wondered how much it had cost to put this car together.

"But," she said, turning away from the window and poking her finger into his shoulder, "I'm going to work too."

"On what?"

"On my swimming, and my dancing."

"I see."

"And," she said, "you're not going to drink too much."

"*You're* not going to drink too much," he said.

This was a dangerous conversation. They both knew it, and so were silent for a while.

After a bit, Zelda said: "Let's play the game."

"All right. Who?"

"Sara and Gerald," she said.

"You go first."

"If I were a Greek goddess, I'd be Demeter, in charge of all the golden fields and the harvest and fertility. An avenging mother."

"That's good," Scott said.

"I don't like what's *in fashion*, but I like beautiful things. All my clothes are soft and clean and made out of delicious fabrics. I'm graceful and my touch brings loveliness even to the smallest, itsiest, bitsiest things."

"I'm sensuous," Scott said.

"I am?"

"Well, she is," he said. "In that sort of motherly way."

"Hmm," Zelda said. "You never said that before."

"Well . . . never mind. Go on."

"I like things that are *new*: new art, new inventions, new people. But really, I'm very old-fashioned. I don't ever get crazy. Maybe," and here she fixed her eyes once again on Scott, "maybe it's because I'm forty."

"She's not forty. She's thirty-seven, I heard Gerald say so."

"Oh, I'm forty, all right. A woman knows."

"Fine. My turn. I'm tall and lean and Irish. I'm a painter and I'm getting quite famous—I'm the one who did *Boatdeck*, after all, and got myself on the cover of magazines."

"Don't be jealous."

"I'm not, I'm in character. Everything I do is precise,

without waste, and designed to be generous and original; I like to give pleasure. I can be friendly, but also cold, when someone least expects it."

"Yes, that's true, I've seen that. Like when we turned up at Saint-Cloud and said we were leaving on the *Lusitania* . . ."

"Don't interrupt. I'm like one of those machines I paint. Perfectly elegant, with lots of gears and fitted parts, and look oh-so-finely tailored. With all my straps and buckles, I must be a masochist." Scott slapped his hand on his knee. "Ha."

"Oh, I don't know how you got masochist."

"You saw how."

"I think it's a mighty big stretch."

"Now who's jealous?"

"All right. Let's do Esther Murphy."

"Too easy: I'm distorted to look at, I smell like the gutter and I'm brilliantly clever. I'm a cubist painting."

"You are canny sometimes." Zelda smiled at him. "Let's do Dos."

"Dos Passos?"

"Do you know another Dos?"

"No, but I don't see why we should do him. You're picking some awfully dull ones." Scott wasn't sure how he felt about John Dos Passos. That book of his had been all right, just. But Dos judged him and Zelda, he could see it behind his eyes, in his silences. He might also be squeamish about sex.

"He's very canny, too," Zelda said sweetly. "*And* . . . They say he's writing a book of genius—and getting on with it very well."

"He doesn't have a wife," he said, hating himself for his prissy tone.

"You're a big one for excuses." She stretched out in her seat, satisfied as a cat.

"Oh, shut up."

They were quiet until the train trundled into the station at Saint-Raphaël, whereupon another problem presented itself: with no car and no money for a taxi, they had no way of getting themselves and their luggage to Valescure.

"It's very hot," Scott said, looking dubiously at Zelda's leather case.

"Do we not even have enough for a lemonade? I'm awfully thirsty. How is it so dry here? I feel like a tumbling tumbleweed."

"We might be able to beg one," he said. "A lemonade. Not a tumbleweed."

"I could put on my gypsy scarf," she said, "and moan and gnash my teeth."

Scott picked up his suitcase in one hand, and Zelda's in the other, and they walked out into the bright sunshine. They were greeted by a magnificent Byzantine dome, the color of pencil lead, rising above a church in front of them, and beyond, the old port. They turned left onto the promenade, palm trees standing sentry in between the beach and the red, red buildings, with their red-tiled roofs. They passed the Grand Casino, blindingly white, and walked a bit further, dazed by the heat and the newness of their surroundings, before concluding that they were going in a loop.

Scott was sweating in his white linen suit and Zelda picked up a palm frond from the road and began fanning him with it.

"I think we should have taken a right outside the station," he said.

"Maybe we'll just have to sleep on the street."

"We should look for a Banque de Paris." He stared up and down the promenade.

Zelda looked longingly at the shady cafes swelling with people taking their lunch. Then she stopped fanning.

"Scott, isn't that the Murphys' man?"

He followed her gaze. "Where?"

"There at the cafe, table on the left. With the blond man."

"Yes," he said, placing the face. "Yes. The Russian . . . what's-his-name . . ."

"Vlad the Impaler," Zelda said.

"That's the one. How marvelous. We're saved."

"You could have saved us, Goofo."

"The odds were long," he said, picking the cases back up. "Come on."

"Hello," they said, almost in unison, when they reached him.

"Vladimir," Scott began, "I don't know if you remember . . ."

"Madame and Monsieur Fitzgerald, *bonjour*." The Russian said it as if he'd been expecting them, as if it were the most natural thing in the world that they had wandered, sweating, carrying luggage and a palm frond, up to his table at this cafe.

"Yes," Scott said brightly. "Look, we've had a problem with our car and then I left my billfold . . . in short we need a lift to Valescure."

"I'm going that way," the blond man sitting with Vlad the Impaler said. An American, apparently. "I can give you a ride."

"This is Owen Chambers," the Russian said. *Un ami.*"

"Well, that would be awfully good of you."

"I'm just going to finish my drink." The blond man indicated his full glass.

"Join us, madame, monsieur," Vladimir said.

"Oh, that would be heaven." Zelda exhaled dramatically. "We're desperate for refreshments. We're not camels, after all."

"No indeed." Vladimir bowed his head.

"You're American?" Scott said, when they'd pulled over chairs and sat down.

"Yes," Owen replied.

"Where from?"

"A small place. New England. You wouldn't have heard of it."

"Try me," Scott said.

The blond man just shrugged.

"He's from here, now," Vladimir said.

Scott didn't like mysteries or people who pretended they had them. He was about to get into it when the waiter came over. Zelda ordered a champagne cocktail and he followed suit with a gin and tonic. "We'll pay you back. Awfully good of you."

"You're very blond," Zelda told the American. "Like a moth."

The man smiled at her. "Thank you."

"And very tan," she said. "I'm going to get very tan, too."

"It'll look nice," Owen said.

The blond fellow was admiring his wife. He liked that; he admired her a lot, too. Perhaps he would let it drop, the mystery or whatever it was.

"Do you know the Murphys?" he asked.

"I do," Owen said.

"Don't you want them to adopt you?" Zelda took the champagne off the tray herself, before the waiter even had a chance. "Scott and I do. They're so comforting."

"I think I know what you mean," Owen said, seemingly amused.

"Oh good. Then they can adopt all three of us. It would be nice to have a moth in the family. Wouldn't it, Scott?"

"That's always a good thing," Scott said. "Who doesn't like a moth?"

The American's car was a Citroën that looked like it had seen better days. Unless he was that certain type of old-money that pretended to be poor, he was far from flush. But he had nice manners, the way he handed Zelda into the back carefully, as if she might break.

They made their way noisily as they climbed into the scrubby hills of Valescure. Owen had said he knew where the Villa Marie was.

"Is it lovely?" Zelda asked.

"It's quite a place," he said.

It was indeed, like some grand Moorish fortress, with a sort of square turret rising from the top. The iron gate was open and they navigated the sweep of the gravel drive. When Owen pulled the car up front, Zelda hopped out, landing perfectly on her dancer's feet, and ran off.

Owen helped Scott get the cases out of the back, before they were greeted by a young French girl, their cook, she explained. Through the open door, Scott could see a flash of blue and white tile. It was perfect. This was where he would finally finish the book. Locked away, with no distractions, only the calm of the sea below and the sway of the trees on the air.

Zelda came running back. "Oh, Goofo, you should see the gardens: palms and olive trees and pines. It's Eden."

"Thanks very much," Scott said, turning to Owen. He felt anxious that their summer should begin right now, in quiet.

Owen nodded.

"Perhaps we'll see you again? With Sara and Gerald?"

"Sure."

"Oh, and we have to pay you for the drinks."

"Don't mention it," Owen said, getting in the car and shutting the door after him.

"No, I insist," Scott said. "Soon."

"Goodbye," Owen said.

"Goodbye, Owen," Zelda called, waving her arms furiously. "When we see each other next, I'm going to be as brown as you."

Owen just lifted his hand in a wave and drove off.

When he was gone, Scott drew Zelda close and kissed her pretty bow mouth. "This is going to be so good for us," he said. "You'll see."

*   *   *

The Fitzgeralds had been on the Riviera for two weeks before they agreed to Sara's invitation to join them for lunch in Cap d'Antibes. Apparently it had taken them that long to recuperate their car from Marseille, where some misadventure had forced them to abandon it.

By the time they arrived at the hotel that afternoon, Honoria, Baoth and Patrick had eaten and taken their cots out into the grounds of the hotel, accompanied by Henriette, the replacement for the rather ordinary and uncreative Rose, who they'd gotten rid of after the previous summer. ("I think, astoundingly, she's making them stupider, rather than smarter," Gerald had said.) The children loved picking just the right spot among the acres of pines and tropical gardens surrounding the hotel.

Sara had asked lunch to be served on the terrace of the Pavilion, settled a quarter-mile behind the main chateau on

Eden Roc. It was perfect for a luncheon party as it over-
looked the sea in front and, to the left, the saltwater
swimming pool blown into the basalt rock, giving it the best
breeze in the height of the afternoon. The curved terrace
was set on the upper level, shaded by navy blue awnings and
surrounded by white metal railings decorated with lifebuoys,
like an ocean liner.

She and Gerald were already sitting in the sun when the
Fitzgeralds walked down, Zelda surveying everything with
those Indian eyes of hers.

"Say-ra," she called out, disentangling herself from Scott
and running the rest of the way.

Sara loved the sound of her name on Zelda's lips. It
always sounded breathy and more romantic with that southern accent. Zelda engulfed her in a cloud of white chiffon
and gardenia perfume, kissing her once on each cheek,
before laughing and repeating it all over again. She looked
tan and muscular, her hair a fluffy bob.

"Oh hello," Sara said. "We thought you'd never get here."

Gerald was standing, shaking hands with Scott, who
looked a little green around the gills, then taking Zelda by
the shoulders: "How lovely."

"Oh, it's so entirely magical here," Zelda said once they
were all seated. "Like a castle in a fairytale."

"We're so glad you came," Gerald said. "Did you bring
things to bathe in?"

"Oh Gerald, we can always go naked," Zelda said.

"We did," Scott said.

"Have you settled in?" Sara put her hand over Scott's,
while Gerald poured the sherry. "Are you getting a lot of
work done?"

"Yes, it's going well, I think." He leaned back a bit in the
canvas chair, exposing the wrinkles in his white suit.

Sara thought she detected a hint of uncertainty, or perhaps moroseness in his tone.

"He's positively a monk," Zelda said.

"Well, that's what you came for," Gerald said.

"I suppose I *have* been pretty boring." Scott drank down his sherry in one go.

"You have," Zelda said.

"But luckily Zelda's found a nice group of people to go to the beach with."

"Yes, also some aviators," Zelda said, looking at Sara.

"They're actually quite dashing," Scott said. "And they have a lot of ideas about valor and glory and the physical life. It's not just a routine with them, because they're in the military, it's some kind of moral philosophy. It comes with no gray shading, all black and white and hard edges. I've become a little fascinated."

"We both have," Zelda said.

"Well . . ." Sara said, glancing at Gerald, who gave an almost imperceptible shrug. "Wonderful. Perhaps we'll get to meet them."

"Oh, but you know one of them," Zelda said, fixing her with her eyes. "Owen . . ."

"Well, he's not one of them, really," Scott said, waving his hand. "We don't really see him."

"I do," Zelda said airily. "I've been swimming with him a few times."

Sara saw Scott look sharply at his wife.

"Yes, Owen Chambers," Sara said.

"When?" Scott demanded.

"When what?" Zelda held her glass out to Gerald.

"Anyone else?" Gerald asked.

"When did you see him *a few times*?"

"I will," Sara said. "Scott?"

"Oh, you know. Once in the morning by accident. When you were writing I took the car to Agay, to see the beach. And the other times? Well, I don't remember exactly. We might have had a drink together. But you've been so busy." Zelda pushed her hair out of her face with her palms, positioning herself better to catch the sun.

"How did you both meet him?" Sara asked, trying to defuse the situation.

"He gave us a lift to the villa. He was with your man Vladimir," Scott replied.

"We've become quite . . . well I don't know if fond is the right word . . ." Sara said, searching. "Because he's so . . ."

"We like being around him," Gerald said. "He's emotionally economical."

Scott laughed at this. "I wondered if he wasn't faking it."

"No, I think he is truly contained," Sara said. "He's like the quiet person you keep hoping will talk just to see what they'll say."

"I don't think we're doing him justice," Gerald said, shifting in his seat. "He's better than that."

"No, we're not," Sara said. "But I'm glad you met him. He's original."

"He's a fantastic swimmer," Zelda said. "That's what I like in a person."

Sara smiled. "Me too." She touched Gerald's arm. "There's nothing better than a man who likes his beach . . ."

He kissed her hand.

"I want to kiss Sara's hand, too," Zelda said, taking her other arm and pressing her lips to Sara's wrist. "Oh, what is that smell? You smell like a Tahitian seashell."

"Coco butter," Sara said, laughing. "I'll give you some. Wait," she said, rummaging in her straw basket. "Here." She handed the bottle over to Zelda.

"Really?"

"Yes, take it."

Tristan, the hotel's one waiter, appeared carrying a tray.

"Ah," Gerald said. "Lunch. Finally."

They had marinated sardines and grilled provençale tomatoes and chicken stuffed with garlic and figs, all washed down with copious amounts of white wine. Washed down most copiously by Scott, Sara noticed. It was a pain for poor Tristan, who had to carry the dishes from the main kitchen, but he was generally a sport about it and she felt lazy and warm when they'd finished.

"Shall we all go for a walk, then a swim in the pool?" Gerald asked, standing and stretching.

"I want to stay here with Sara. Alone," Scott said.

"Well, I want to be alone with Gerald," Zelda said.

"I guess that settles it." Gerald offered his arm to Zelda, who did a curtsy.

"I do want a swim," Sara said. "Come back for us when you've finished your walk."

"All these difficult decisions," Gerald said, before taking Zelda off with him.

Sara leaned back and looked up at the awning, rolling gently in the breeze.

"I want her to be happy," Scott said. "I want her to have friends."

"Who? Zelda?" Sara looked back at him.

"Yes. I do. And I like the group she's found. But she doesn't understand about work."

"She seems happy to me." Sara didn't really like confidences from married couples. It wasn't that the intimacy bothered her, but no good seemed to come out of conversations like these. It always seemed like a betrayal to her; she would never talk about Gerald that way. Nor he about her, she knew.

"Well, she's not happy. You see how she goads me. And she lies about things. She never saw that Owen friend of yours."

"Scott," Sara said, laughing now. "What a ridiculous thing to say. How do you know that?"

"I just do," he said darkly, but didn't elaborate. "Is there more wine? God, it's dry here. Is it always this dry?"

"Oh." Sara looked around. "I don't know. We could call for some, maybe. But I think we'd have to go back to the main house to do that."

"Anyway," he went on, as if he hadn't asked and she hadn't answered, "she's not like you. She can't just be *content* with her life. And let me get on with it."

"I think you're being unfair," Sara said, as gently as she could. "You seem to call all the shots. And she follows you."

"You see," he looked close to tears now, "that's what everyone thinks. But it's not like that. Look at her with those friends and her trips to Agay."

"You just said you wanted her to have friends, and that she didn't see Owen. Honestly, Scott. This conversation is getting tiresome."

"You are perfect. The perfect woman," he said, and then buried his face in his arms, making snuffling noises.

"Come on," Sara said. "Let's go for a swim, cool off your head."

Scott wouldn't swim, but he lounged while she bobbed in the pool.

Eventually Gerald and Zelda returned, she carrying a bottle of wine.

Zelda presented the bottle to Scott as if it were the

Crown Jewels. He hopped up, a broad smile transforming his delicate features, and threw his arms around her. "You are the most wonderful woman in the world. Perfect," he said.

Gerald joined Sara in the water.

"Everything all right?"

"It seems to be now," she said. "Scott got a little bent."

"Well, it's hot. It can go to your head," Gerald said. "Zelda gave me a glorious dance performance on the lawn."

"You are a lucky man," Sara said, sliding her arm around his waist, feeling his skin soft and smooth under the salty water. A shock of pleasure still came over her when she realized that she could do that whenever she wanted.

Zelda, who had gone off to change, returned and dove into the water with a grand splash. "Ta-dah," she said, swimming over. They hung on to the rocky edge of the pool, overlooking cliffs that sheared off into the sea.

"Gerald was telling me all about the house you're building. I wish it were finished. I want to go to a party there. It sounds darling."

"Oh, it's taking forever," Sara said. "I think it will be done by spring. We hope. Everything moves a little more *doucement* down here."

"Oh, but I wish we could. You could give a party for Scott and me. And herald our arrival."

Sara laughed. "What can I say to that?"

"Say yes."

Gerald was shaking his head.

"Well," Sara said. "I suppose we could give a garden party. Couldn't we, darling? On the grounds . . . Let me think about it."

"Thinking is no good for the mind," Zelda said, serious now. "Just ask Scott. His mind is rotten." And she swam away, her green swimsuit zigzagging like a lizard under the surface.

Gerald leaned into Sara's ear. "Your mind is rotten," he whispered and she burst out laughing.

"What's so funny?" Scott called over from his lounger. "I want to know."

"You two," Sara called back. "We're so glad you've come. It's like joining the circus."

"I always wanted to join the circus," Zelda said, and did a little underwater somersault.

"Sara, you can ride the elephant," Scott said, "and Gerald can be the lion tamer."

"I'll be the tightrope walker," Zelda screeched.

"And I'll be the sad clown," Scott said. "I do sad very well."

"You do it very badly," Sara said.

"Oh God, you're right," Scott said with mock glumness. "I'm awful at it."

After Scott had finished his bottle, she and Gerald walked them back to their car.

"You won't forget your promise?" Zelda said, climbing into the passenger seat and tucking her white dress around her legs. "About the party."

"I doubt you'll let me," Sara replied.

"What party?" Scott said, taking the wheel.

"We're going to have a party at . . ." Zelda stopped. "What are you calling your house again?"

"It's called Villa America," Gerald said.

Scott revved the engine, which coughed a bit before turning over. "Villa America," he called over the noise. "Just perfect." And then they were off.

"Goodness, I felt like we were homesteaders being raided by a band of Comanches." Night had long since fallen and Sara was changing out of her dinner clothes.

"I hope they made it home alive," Gerald said, removing his cuff links.

"That car," Sara said. She went and looked out over the grounds, at the inky sky.

This June had been drier and hotter than the last two, but there was a nice breeze coming through the French windows, swishing the hems of the drapes against the parquet floor. They had the loveliest set of rooms in the hotel, a corner suite with a sitting room that looked south towards the sea and west over the gardens. Sara was listening for the nightingales when she realized Gerald hadn't answered. She saw him turning the gold links over in his palm.

She rose and went to him, wrapping her arms around his chest, leaning her cheek against his back. "Are you all right?"

"Of course," he said. "I just sometimes wonder why I don't miss him more."

"There's nothing wrong with you," she said, knowing she'd said it all before. When Gerald didn't respond she went on: "Fred hadn't been himself for a long time. He'd gone before he actually . . ."

"I'm not sure I missed him then, either." Gerald laid the cuff links, his brother's, gently on a side table. "I keep wearing them, thinking I'll look down at some point, in an unguarded moment, and feel *something*."

"It's only been a month. Perhaps it will come later."

"No," Gerald said. "No, it won't."

"Come to bed."

"I'm going to check on the children," he said, turning and kissing the top of her head.

She watched him wander slowly out of the room, before stepping out of her underclothes and slipping on her night-gown.

✽

Gerald stood inside the large bedroom where his three children lay sleeping: Baoth, his sturdy brown five-year-old leg thrust out from under the sheets, snoring like a bumble-bee; Honoria, her tawny head in profile on the pillow, fingers curled delicately around the tip of the sheet; and Patrick, still as a rock on his back, silent in sleep.

He wanted to touch their heads, give a kind of benedic-tion, but he was afraid of waking them. They were so tired at the end of their days spent swimming and playing with the dogs and scrambling around the rocks and raking seaweed and building up worlds for themselves. It made him proud that this was their life. He briefly thought back to his own childhood: Pitz; a cold trip once to Atlantic City with his father; Fred off at boarding school, leaving the playroom empty.

Gerald hadn't been at the Hôpital Salpêtrière when Fred had died in late May. He and Sara had taken the children there a few weeks before so that they might have some sort of goodbye, but only Honoria seemed to have retained any vague notion of who he was.

He'd been off his head for some time, an after-effect of the war. Whether his mental condition was due to the con-stant pain he was in or because of what he'd endured on the front was unclear. But either way he'd been ruined. They hadn't seen much of him and Noel, even though they were all in Paris. Fred just wasn't up to anything, really; he pre-ferred to keep to himself rather than socialize with Gerald and their circle. Noel had tried, organizing family dinners and such. But it had never felt right, somehow; Fred wasn't all there, oftentimes rambling incoherently throughout the whole meal. Even if Fred had been in the best of health, what did they have to say to each other, anyway? Gerald had reasoned. They'd never really been close, always watching each other from a distance, only one shared thread—their childhood—which Gerald would rather forget.

The day Fred died Sara had arrived, breathless, at his studio. He'd been working on a new painting, a canvas estate title for Villa America, and Vladimir had been mixing paint. All at once she was there, knocking on the door, her lovely face terrified, carrying what she thought was a bomb.

But when she told him what Noel had phoned to say, he'd felt nothing. He'd let her hold him, as she'd done this evening, but really it had been more for her, or maybe a bit for himself, to appear normal.

The funeral had been small and for some reason the only image or feeling that stood out from that day was his astonishment at the beautiful shadows the sun had cast on Noel's high cheekbones. After the service she'd walked over to him, like a six-foot-tall blond Amazon, an avenging Valkyrie, and had handed him the box with the cuff links and Fred's fountain pen, a Parker Big Red.

"I didn't know what you'd want," she said. "But I heard you admire his pen once."

"It's lovely," Gerald said, putting it inside his breast pocket.

"I've given Esther his books," Noel said.

Gerald saw his sister, newly arrived in Paris, off to one side talking animatedly with some friends of Fred's.

"And I've sent your father his medals, though I doubt he'll reply."

"I shouldn't think so," Gerald had said.

They never spoke about Fred's falling out with their father, although he knew Noel would have liked to. Whatever it was—and it was about business, and personal failure and their father's never believing that any of them, except maybe Esther, was any good—it had died with Fred.

Baoth stirred and Gerald realized he'd been standing there for some time. His son let out a small groan, and then his snoring resumed. Gerald was about to turn to leave when he heard a small, quiet, "Dow-Dow?"

It was Patrick. His younger son hadn't moved from his position, but Gerald could see that his eyes were open. He went over and sat on the edge of the bed.

"What are you doing awake?" he asked, smoothing the sheet over his child.

"I was having a dream."

"What was your dream?"

"It was about a big fish," the three-year-old said, wriggling upright, his blond hair smushed up in the back.

"Was it now."

"It was a good fish. But then I woke up and I saw you and I thought you were the fish."

"No fish. Just Dow-Dow."

"What are you doing?"

"Just thinking. And listening for night fairies," Gerald said, smiling.

"Night fairies?" Patrick's eyes, so like his own, went slightly round.

"Sometimes, if you're very quiet, you can hear them. The hum of their wings," Gerald said. "They like children, you see. So I came in here to find them."

Patrick lay back down, listening. "I don't hear anything," he whispered after a moment.

"It works better if you close your eyes," he said, rubbing Patrick's arm. So soft. "Why don't I just sit here and we'll close our eyes and see if they come."

"All right."

When Patrick's breathing had gone hushed and regular, Gerald carefully lifted himself off the bed. Then he stood a few minutes longer in the room, waiting, until he knew for certain that his own bedroom would be dark, that there'd be no hand searching him out. Until he knew for certain that Sara would be asleep.

✿   ✿   ✿

Sara and Gerald were preparing to go to La Garoupe beach when the telephone in the sitting room rang. It was Tristan explaining that he had Madame Fitzgerald on the line for Madame Murphy. Could he put her through?

It had been over a week since their lunch at the hotel and they hadn't seen hide nor hair of them since.

"Say-ra," came the breathless voice down the line. "The awful beast of a car has broken down. I've had to absolutely beg the nice man at the cafe to let me use his telephone and Scott isn't answering."

"Where *are* you?" Sara asked, putting her hand over the receiver and mouthing *Zelda* to Gerald's inquisitive face.

"I'm in Agay, but the car is . . . well, I don't know where the car is. In the middle of the road, I guess. A little before that. Oh, Say-ra, what am I to do?"

She laughed. "Stay where you are. We'll come rescue you. What's the name of the cafe?"

"There's only one tiny, little one," Zelda said. "Oh, thank you. Thank you."

"Well, the car has broken down again. And Zelda is in Agay," she said, raising her hands in exasperation.

"I suppose we'll just have to go get her," Gerald said.

"We'll send the children and Henriette on to the beach. It would be a shame for them to have their day spoiled." Sara looked at the bags she'd packed. "Shall we take our picnic with us? We'll all be hungry when we get there."

"A car picnic. Grand. We can act like Scott and drink our sherry stash dry on the way down."

"I'll do a dance performance atop the backseat." Sara smiled. "You know, I once drank a whole bottle of champagne myself in a smart red Simplex with someone else's husband. Imagine."

"Thank God I found you before you got a reputation."

"Oh, I don't know," she said, toying with one of the damask pillows, "I wouldn't have minded a bit of a reputation. But, yes," she said, plumping and setting it back in place, "thank God you found me." She walked over to him and twined her arm around his. "I like that shirt on you. A real fisherman's shirt."

Gerald disentangled himself and picked up the lunch basket. "Let's go break the news, no use putting it off."

She watched his retreating figure a moment, before picking up her own straw bag and following him.

"You'll have to rake the beach for Dow-Dow today," Gerald told the three children, standing in a line, faces serious with attention. They'd been waiting impatiently in the lobby for their parents to come down.

"We will," Honoria said.

"But who will lead the exercises?" Baoth asked.

"You can do that," Gerald said. "Do you remember them all?"

"I think so."

"I do," Patrick said and stretched out his arms, moving them in a kind of circular motion, like a drunkard trying to imitate a seagull.

"You're very clever," Sara said, leaning down to pull him to her.

"Can we take the canoe out?" Baoth asked loudly.

"No, I don't think so," she said, straightening.

"But Mamzelle will be there," he sulked.

"No whining," Sara said. She turned to Henriette. "Don't let them take out the canoe, will you, Henriette?"

Henriette shook her head crisply. *"Ne vous inquietez pas, madame."*

"Fine, then," Sara said. "Have a lovely afternoon, children. And be good."

"And wear your hats after bathing," Gerald said. "You don't want to go bald like Dow-Dow."

"You're not bald, Dow-Dow," Honoria said, highly amused by this. She rushed at her father, squeezing his legs.

"Getting there," Gerald said.

Sara noticed he didn't push her away.

When they reached the car, she placed her bag on the backseat, and then turned to Gerald. "You know, I think we might go on to Nice after rescuing Zelda. To the bookstore, to get the *Transatlantic Review*. The one Scott's been going on about."

"The Ford Maddox Ford thing?"

"Mmm. I also thought we might pass by the airbase, to see Owen. There are some records he could pick up for us on his next trip to London."

"Fine," Gerald said, settling into the yellow Renault that the children had nicknamed Iris, for some unfathomable reason.

An hour and a half later, they found Zelda sitting at a

small wicker table in the front of the Café d'Esterel, drinking a milky-white anisette. The cafe, which looked out across the road to the beach and the bay beyond, was clean, but spare, and dead quiet this time of day in the summer. The only other soul was the *patron*, a man in his mid-forties, brown with a weather-beaten face, polishing the bar top. He greeted them and then went back to his business.

"Oh, Dow-Dow, Say-ra, thank you for coming to get me." Zelda looked like an advertisement for a beach holiday, all tan and fresh.

"Well, we couldn't very well leave you stranded, could we?" Gerald said.

"Where were you going?" Sara asked.

"Well, here, to swim in the bay. Isn't it just the most perfect bay you've ever seen?"

"By yourself?"

"Well . . . yes. I thought I might drop by and see Owen. But he isn't here."

"Oh," Sara said.

"Where did you have that dress made?" Zelda touched Sara's navy and pink paisley silk shift. "I want one just like it. You know, you have the most amazing clothes."

"Paris," Sara said, confused. "Zelda, I don't think you should be taking this car for long trips by yourself. It isn't safe."

"It really isn't," Gerald agreed. "Ten more minutes and you would have missed us."

"Another hour and the phone service would have been shut down for the afternoon," Sara said.

"Oh, I know. I just get so bored. I can't stay locked up in that Moors' prison all day."

Sara shook her head. "Go to the beach at Saint-Raphaël, then."

"You both are so right," Zelda said brightly. "About everything."

"Come on," Gerald said. "Let's get you back to your Moorish prison. Scott can send for a mechanic later."

"Do you want to swim?" she asked hopefully.

"No," they said in unison.

On the drive back to Saint-Raphaël, Gerald turned to Sara. "I think I'll get out at the base. You can take the car on to Nice and swing by and pick me up on your way back."

"Really?" She looked at him.

"You're going to the airbase?" Zelda piped up from her position in the back, between the picnic basket and Sara's straw bag.

"Yes," Gerald said. "I might go into town after and have a look."

"Oh, can I go, too? With Gerald?" Zelda had rummaged through the picnic and was eating some of the *biscuits sablés*. She offered one to Sara.

"Don't you want to get home?" Sara took one and bit into the buttery shortbread, before putting the rest into Gerald's mouth.

"Oh no. Scott will still be working."

"Fine with me," Gerald said, swallowing.

"How will you get back?" Sara asked.

"Oh," Zelda said. "I have money for a taxi."

Sara and Gerald looked at each other, he apparently as speechless as she was.

"Oh, for Christ's sake, Zelda," he said finally, and Sara burst out laughing.

❖

When they arrived at the Fréjus airbase, Gerald stopped at the entrance and got out, while Sara took the driver's seat,

211

honking once before calling: "I'll pick you up at five? At the cafe by the square, next to the church."

"Bon voyage," Gerald said. "Be careful on the roads."

They made their way across the quadrant in silence, heading for the hangars. Gerald could see a fine line of brick-colored silt beginning to cling to Zelda's green-and-white striped hem, like a slash of rusty lipstick, as they walked. She seemed to be concentrating hard, on what, he didn't know. But there was a determination to her expression and her walk that made him slightly uneasy about what awaited them.

In Hangar No. 9, they found Owen leaning against a wooden desk, smoking. Next to him was another young man, whose form and curling hair made him look like a model for a neoclassical sculptor.

In the center of it all, dominating everything around it, was the airplane: about twenty feet long and twenty-five feet wide, with a royal blue body and white wings and tail. *That Girl* was painted in stark block letters along the fuselage. She looked like the sea, Gerald thought.

Owen put out his cigarette, without a word, as if their arrival had been expected.

"Hello," Zelda said, dropping a curtsy and then turning into a pirouette. All that determination was still etched into her features. It made the move look practiced instead of graceful, and he felt a little sorry for her suddenly.

"Good afternoon," Gerald said.

Owen smiled at him. "Hello. Do you know Edouard Jozan?" he asked, indicating the flesh-and-blood statue. "We share a mechanic."

The dark-haired man stepped forward and shook Gerald's hand vigorously. Then he turned his attention to Zelda. "It's always the greatest pleasure," he said, kissing her fingers.

"Yes. Isn't it?" she said, her voice catching in her throat. She turned away quickly. "Owen, I went to Agay looking for you. At your rooms. But my car broke down and Gerald and Sara had to come rescue me."

"That car isn't safe," Owen said.

"That's what we told her," Gerald said. "I've come to ask a favor. Do you think you'll be making a trip to London anytime soon?"

"Oh, business," Jozan said. He clapped his hands. "You Americans."

"I *am* running a business here," Owen said. "Or trying to."

"But business without a drink?" Jozan's muscular face wore an expression of mock agony.

"It's Jozan's day off," Owen explained. "He wants a playmate."

"But now I don't have to bother with you anymore," the Frenchman said. "Madame Fitzgerald can be my victim. Shall we leave them to it?"

"Oh, I don't know." She looked at Gerald then Owen. "It was really Owen I came to see . . ."

"He's being too boring," Jozan said. "He can join us when he's finished."

"Oh." She looked at Gerald. "Shall I?"

"Do as you like," he said. Her girlishness could be tiresome sometimes and he'd had enough babysitting for one day.

"As long as you promise to come find us," she said.

Jozan offered her his arm, which she took. "*A bientôt, messieurs.* Look for the gay people at the cafe."

Owen didn't say anything, just lit another cigarette and watched them go, before turning his gaze back to Gerald.

"His English is very good," Gerald said, because at a loss, alone with Owen, it was the first thing that came into his head.

"It's for Zelda's benefit," Owen said. "You had a favor?"

"Well, of course we'd pay you for it." Gerald shifted uncomfortably. "But Sara wanted some records from London. Clara Smith and Al Jolson."

"I'm going next week," Owen said. "A pick-up from Harrods for an English couple in Cannes. I can get them then. Just tell me where to look."

"Do you have a pen?"

Owen pulled a pen and sheaf of paper from a drawer and set them on the desk. Gerald bent down to write out the address of the music shop. He could feel Owen's body next to his. He and Sara had met Owen two or three times since last summer, but he'd never been alone with him, nor this near. Owen's thigh, where he was leaning, brushed slightly against his own as he wrote; it surprised him how tall and broad he was up close. Gerald himself was a tall man, but Owen had a kind of mass he lacked.

"There," he said, screwing the cap back on the pen. He moved away a bit and surveyed the airplane. "She's beautiful. May I look at the engine?"

"You can't really see much of it," Owen said. "You see the nose?"

Gerald nodded.

"That's covering the engine underneath."

"Do you mind if I . . . ?"

Owen picked up a stepladder, which was leaning against the wall. He carried it over and set it up under the propeller.

"I almost became a pilot myself, during the war," Gerald said. He smiled ruefully. "But I only ended up on desk duty."

He climbed up, placing his hands on either side of the metal nose. It was smooth and globe-like beneath his palms. He peered over the lip. "I can see a bit," he said, turning back to Owen, who, he noticed, was holding the ladder very carefully, as one might for a child or an old lady. "Below the nose."

Owen nodded.

"Is that copper?"

"It's a Rhone 9C. They have those copper induction pipes. That's how you recognize them."

"They're lovely," Gerald said.

"I suppose." Owen furrowed his brow slightly. In the semi-shade of the hangar, Gerald could make out the color of his eyes, like pewter. "I've never really thought about them that way."

Gerald climbed down. "An instrument of precision," he said.

"Not all the time," Owen said. "In fact, they can be pretty damn imprecise."

"No, I mean engines, in general," Gerald said. "They work just as they should. Precisely; each piece fits another piece that puts the whole thing in motion. Well, that is until they stop working at all. Then you have to build them all over again."

Owen shrugged, but Gerald saw him looking up towards the nose, quickly.

"Sorry," Gerald said. "It's just what I've been spending much of my time thinking about. Engines, the inner workings of things. My paintings, I mean." He stopped, slightly embarrassed. "Perhaps that sounds a little pompous."

"No," Owen said, folding up the stepladder.

Gerald watched him lift it over the desk with one hand, as if it weighed nothing at all.

215

"Well . . ." he said.

"Zelda showed me a picture of your painting. In a magazine." Owen turned. "*Boatdeck*, right?"

"Right," he said.

"I liked it. It was like . . . arithmetic. Clean, I guess." Owen looked up at him. Now he was the one who seemed uncomfortable. "I don't know."

"No, no," Gerald said. "You're right. But on a grand scale. Like an airplane, I suppose."

Owen held his gaze. "Look, I was going to take her up. Just to run her engine. Late afternoon is a good time for it, warm, but not too hot."

"Oh," Gerald said.

"Do you want to come along?"

"Go up in the plane?"

"Have you ever flown before?"

Gerald shook his head. "No. I never actually made it up."

"Will you be afraid?" Owen was leaning against the machine now.

"I . . . I don't know. I don't want to be afraid. But I might be."

"An honest answer," Owen said. "Don't, if you don't feel like it."

"No, I do," Gerald said. "Feel like it, I mean."

"Good," Owen said. "We just have to wait for my mechanic. He'll be along soon."

✿

Vladimir was sipping his coffee on the Place Formigé in Fréjus, across from the old cathedral. From his spot on the terrace of the Café des Julii he could see Jozan and Zelda drinking cocktails on the other side of the square. They were sitting at another cafe, closer to the Hôtel de Ville, whose orange-stucco front washed pink in the late afternoon light.

He was not surprised to see the young, dashing naval aviator with the young, reckless Madame Fitzgerald. Nothing could be more natural really. However, he was surprised when, some time later, he saw Gerald and Owen Chambers walking towards them down the rue de Fleury.

It wasn't the fact that they were together that he found strange, it was *the way* they were together.

Walking in stride, side by side, their heads leaning in towards each other, Gerald was listening and nodding as Owen talked. One of the things that Vladimir liked about his blond American friend was that he rarely talked very much. He just seemed to let things wash over him, good, bad, indifferent. But here he was, obviously expressing some stream of thought as if that was the most natural state in the world for him.

He knew some of the story of Owen's life, although admittedly he knew few of the details, the bigger picture drawn from small comments and deductions: a romantic scandal when he was young, followed by a flight from home; work in a factory; dangerous and heroic acts during the war; the loss of someone close to him; an injury that ended in him staying on in France, here on the Riviera.

It was the kind of story that Vladimir understood, the reason he believed they'd become friends; his own past was also writ in large and dramatic terms. His father had been the banker to the Tsarina, shot in front of his own eyes by Cheka during the Red Terror. After his father's murder, he and his mother had been forced to leave everything behind—wealth, status and what connections they had— and flee to Paris, where she now worked as a cleaner and he as a sort of attaché to the Murphys, who had become like family to him.

He thought of his own story as a quintessentially Russian one, in the tradition of their great poets and the drama of their novelists. Likewise, he thought Owen's story belonged to the American fables of loss and expansion, tales of how the West was won and such. And now, they both sat comfortably on the sidelines, like two old men watching the world go by. They fit together, he and his friend, two parts of the same idea.

Yet, seeing him talk with such determination to Gerald, so out of character, Vladimir wondered if he truly understood his friend's ambitions.

The two men spotted Zelda and Jozan, their posture changing in recognition, then they looked around, away, as if to avoid them. When they saw Vladimir, they walked in the direction of his table.

"May we join you?" Gerald asked, always polite, an attribute Vladimir appreciated.

"Please." Vladimir spread his hand across the small iron table.

"I didn't expect to find you in Fréjus," Gerald said, sitting down.

"He's come to see about a girl." Owen smiled slightly at him, before taking the seat on his other side.

"A girl, you say? You're full of mysteries," Gerald teased.

Vladimir shrugged. He didn't want to talk about Irene. That was his business, and maybe even then it was nothing at all.

"Owen's taken me up in his airplane. It was marvelous . . . the most marvelous thing I think I've ever seen. I'm still not composed enough to speak of it," Gerald said.

Sometimes, Gerald had a way of over-talking things, a

style that made it seem like he was trying to cover something up, his true feelings perhaps. He'd wondered at first if this was an American trait, but he hadn't seen it in the others he'd come to know. Of course, the Russian way could also be grandiose, but it was direct in its passion.

Owen ordered a *Remplaçant*, Gerald a sherry.

"You should try it," Gerald said to Vladimir. "The feeling of ascending and the way you can see everything."

"I've never had the pleasure of a request." He glanced at Owen. "Anyway," he went on, "I'm more for the sea than the air. A boat, that would be my vessel."

When the drinks arrived, Gerald continued: "Like a bird, gliding through the air. Buffered by the wind. The pulse of the motor . . ."

Vladimir couldn't help but arch an eyebrow.

"And Owen, in complete control. It was marvelous, wasn't it?" Gerald looked at Owen.

Owen just looked into his drink.

"He was telling me how it all works," Gerald said, turning to Vladimir. "All the little rituals one has to go through before you can actually take her into the sky." He shook his head in what seemed like wonder. "Thank you," Gerald said, putting his hand on Owen's shoulder. "It was truly an experience."

"Don't mention it." Owen downed his drink. "I have to go."

"Oh?" Vladimir saw Gerald's face cloud over.

"Mmm hmm." Owen dropped some francs on the table before rising. "I'll let you know about the records."

"Oh, of course. Well, whenever you can. There's no real rush." Gerald was clearly pained.

Vladimir felt for Gerald, his embarrassed confusion. But, really, it wasn't in his nature to understand a man like Owen.

"Goodbye, my friend," Vladimir said.

"Goodbye," Owen said and started off, back across the square.

They watched him until he disappeared around the corner of the Hôtel de Ville.

"I said something." There was no mistaking the misery in his tone. "I just don't know what it was."

Vladimir shrugged. "Who knows?"

"I only wanted him to know how much I enjoyed it."

"Of course." It wasn't his place to explain how sometimes personal things need to be kept personal. There was no telling a man a thing like that.

Gerald sipped his sherry and they were quiet for a while. Then Gerald said: "I shouldn't have talked about it. I shouldn't have asked questions. It was . . ." But he didn't share the rest of his thought. Instead, he looked at Vladimir. "What do you make of him?"

"I think," he said carefully, "he's someone who lives very much in here." He tapped his temple.

"Yes," Gerald said. "That's what I think too. We'll have to help him with that."

Vladimir shook his head, smiled a little.

"What?"

"It's only that, *des fois*, help is not helpful at all."

"Nonsense," Gerald said, and finished his drink.

✿

Jozan watched Zelda watch Owen walk across the square.

"You shouldn't waste your time on that one," he said. "He's not for you."

Zelda turned her face slowly to him. "Whatever do you mean?" she asked sweetly.

She was a strange one, this Madame Zelda Fitzgerald, a

sort of woman-girl, with a slow violence operating underneath a sweet exterior. He found her exciting and nothing like the girls around here. But he'd have to be careful. He shrugged. "I'm not sure he likes girls."

"You're just being nasty," Zelda said, but continued to eye him over the rim of her glass.

"Maybe," he agreed.

"Has he ever had a sweetheart?" she asked.

"None that I've seen," Jozan said. "And plenty of women would have liked to."

"So he's deliberate," she said, satisfied. "He chooses carefully. Unlike some."

"Now you're just being nasty. To me."

"Maybe," she said, and laughed.

"Instead of driving your car to Agay, you should just drive it here," he said, putting his hand over hers.

"I think," she picked the lemon out of her drink and nibbled on it, "I'd like that."

"Yes?"

She nodded brightly even though, all at once, she seemed close to tears.

❖

That night in bed, Sara was reading her *Transatlantic Review*, while Gerald lay on his back thinking.

"You know," she said, putting the magazine down. "I read the piece by that writer Scott's always going on about, Ernest Hemingway. It's very good. Different."

"Mmm?" He turned to face her.

The bedside lamp threw a golden cast across her already tan face, making her look lit from the inside like a Vermeer.

"You aren't listening." She placed her hand on his cheek.

"No," he said. "Sorry. I was just thinking about being in the plane."

"Yes. You've been rather quiet about that. I go to Nice and you get to go up in an airplane. Very unfair."

"I said too much about it already," he said.

"What do you mean?" Her eyes had the quizzical look they took on sometimes when she was worrying about him.

"Just earlier. When we ran into Vladimir at the cafe. I went on in this awful way." He rolled back over onto his back. "I don't know why I have to be like this."

"Oh Gerald. You're you. That's enough."

"You say that. But we both know. All the things . . ."

She slid down in the bed, propping the pillows under her head. "I'm sure Owen understood. He's very . . . he doesn't seem to judge people very much."

"The things I want to say . . ." He suddenly felt furious. "Christ, what the hell is wrong with me?"

"Stop it," she said sternly. "You're working yourself up. Everything is fine. Life is good. Don't spoil it."

"Is it? Sometimes it seems to be, but then there's this emptiness inside of me. How is that possible?"

"Gerald," she said. "Maybe Fred's death . . ."

"No." He felt full of all the things he couldn't say, even to himself. Unarticulated, dark things, suspicions about his nature, his character, his abilities . . . God, he could go on forever with that list.

"Darling," Sara said after a few minutes. He felt her fingertips against his face again. "Tell *me*," she said. "Tell *me* about the plane."

He thought back to the afternoon, climbing into the passenger seat behind Owen in the cockpit. Watching the mechanic turn the propeller, the calls back and forth between Owen and the Frenchman, a mysterious language. The sound of the engine, louder than he expected. The feeling of adrenaline in his blood before they'd even begun to move. From behind, seeing Owen's arms working the lever, tapping the controls. The tan line where his neck hit his collar. His head bent in concentration. Moving along the runway, past the other hangars, gaining speed, lifting, lifting, just before the beach. His stomach muscles working against the pull of the ground. Gliding, whirring over the short strip of sand, and then out over the sea.

"What you see from up there," he began. "All the places you thought you knew, you never knew them. What they really looked like. All the pieces make a whole, Sara."

"Go on."

"I could hear my heart in my ears, as if it had traveled up my body. And then there's the feeling of being pulled in two, part of you wants to go higher, and another wants to come crashing down." He looked at her. "And something else: I felt so close to him, and alone at the same time. It's one of the most perfect feelings I've ever had."

"I see," she said. She held his gaze for a while. "I'm glad. I'm glad you did that. And you express it just right. I'm happy you told me about it."

He smiled. He felt overcome with love for her, and then gratitude, and then desire, as if in telling her it all became true, as if nothing was real until he told her. He looked at the white of her gown against the white of the sheet, and the brown of her skin. He took her face in his hands and kissed her. So much love, and so much gratitude.

✧　　✧　　✧

By late July, forest fires had broken out in the Esterel Mountains, and the morning air was tinged with the smell of burning pine and eucalyptus as Owen drove along the coast to deliver the records Sara had requested.

The cliffs above the coast were a tinderbox. Owen had seen the ravages of the flames when he'd flown over: black pockmarks where trees and scrub had been eaten away. The visibility was bad inland, as the fire threw up pink and violet smoke. At night, the sky glowed orange in the distance.

It had been a bad month for Owen, although the summer season was always slow. But then there'd been trouble with the plane's engine, that so-called instrument of precision, which had grounded *That Girl* and delayed the few runs he did have. He'd only managed three trips in four weeks: Switzerland and Belgium and London. Mostly for edibles and dry goods that the foreigners in the grand hotels in Nice and Cannes couldn't seem to live without. So he'd been glad of Gerald's errand, if only for the extra cash.

He drove through Antibes and down the boulevard du Cap, which ran the length of the peninsula below the old town. He'd never been up to the hotel where the Murphys lived. The few meetings he'd had with them late last summer had been on their preferred beach, La Garoupe, sometimes with small gatherings of their friends, who treated him kindly but mostly just left him to his own devices. He couldn't be sure if that was his doing or because their friends didn't really know what to make of him. He wasn't an artist or an intellectual or rich. Nor was he a servant. That must confuse them, he'd decided. Either way, it didn't bother him. Not really.

He didn't regard his acquaintance with the Murphys as a friendship really, just the type of connection Americans had to each other down here, on the basis of being from the same place and not being tourists.

When Sara had first introduced herself, she'd seemed genuinely interested in what he did, but hadn't asked him any questions about his past, which had been a relief to him. She'd ended the brief conversation by saying: "I'd like to know you, if you'd like to know us. We'll be at the beach almost every day for the next couple of weeks. Come see us if you'd like."

She'd seemed frank and uncomplicated and without any real motive beyond what she'd offered. So he'd gone. Once and then again, when Gerald had been there. And then again. But mainly he'd spoken with her. They'd been long days in the sun, with their friends and the children and their dogs and the nannies and Vladimir, and as much or as little conversation as you wanted. And that had been that. Until Zelda had come along, bringing Gerald like a pilot fish. And then the flight.

He drove his Citroën through the wrought-iron gates of the Hôtel du Cap and parked just before the steps that faced toward Eden Roc and the sea. Four storeys high, capped with a slate roof—what Vladimir called a mansard roof—the hotel reminded him of a tiered wedding cake he'd seen once in a shop window in Boston. It didn't have the mass and curved flourishes of the Belle Epoque hotels in Cannes or Nice; it was more ladylike, less can-can girl, in its manner. And what he could see of the grounds was full of well-kept, lush-looking plants, despite the drought.

With the records tucked under his arm, he took the steps two at a time and entered the large lobby with its shiny white marble floors. There was a young boy at the front desk. His brass nameplate read: *Tristan*.

"Bonjour," Owen said. *"Je passe voir Monsieur et Madame Murphy."*

The boy looked at him and nodded, before picking up the telephone at the desk. He spoke briefly into the receiver and then told Owen. *"Madame Murphy arrive."*

Owen looked around. The lobby gave way to a grand sitting room draped in orange and blue fabrics. The hotel had the hush of emptiness to it, that out-of-season feeling of having been deserted.

Sara came down the wide staircase, her hair pinned up and tied back with some kind of silk scarf, her white dress loose.

"Owen," she said as she approached. "We weren't expecting you. We would have made more of a fuss. Gerald's down at Eden Roc doing exercises with the children." She held out her hands to him.

He took them briefly, before letting them go. "I brought the records," he said. "I thought you'd waited long enough."

"Oh, wonderful," she said, taking them and turning them over, looking at the covers. "Oh, perfect. You found just the right ones."

"Good," he said. "I'm sorry for the delay. Engine trouble."

"Hmm?" She looked up. "You've come all this way and it's awfully hot. Let's have a drink of something outside. I know a shady spot."

Before he could answer she took his arm and began leading him through the lobby to the back of the hotel. She smelled sweet. Behind him he could hear the sound of Tristan's footsteps.

They went through a wide set of double doors and over to a corner table on the terrace, beneath an umbrella pine growing from the earth below.

"It's not as breezy as the ocean side, but there's more shade here," she said. She looked up at Tristan. "Two sherries and some *biscuits sablés*," she said, before turning back to Owen. "I hope you don't mind me ordering for us. It's what we have every day at this time. For some reason, it's the perfect antidote to eleven o'clock in the morning."

Owen smiled. He liked her very much.

"So." She settled back. "Tell me everything you've been doing."

"Not much, actually. Trouble with the plane. Business is slow."

"Can you fly through all that smoke?"

"I can," he said. "It's not perfect. But it's not the first time I've done it."

"No." Her face clouded. "Of course not. The war."

She was quiet as Tristan set down the drinks and the shortbread. She went on: "Was it quite bad for you?"

He wasn't sure how to answer that.

"I'm sorry," she said, "perhaps that's indiscreet."

"No, it's fine," he said. "It's more . . . it's as if I've talked about it too much. And then it just becomes a story."

She seemed to think about this. "That does seem to be the way. We have these experiences and then they just turn into something we tell somebody, to amuse them or frighten or titillate them. Like performing. It can make one feel numb, asleep . . ."

"Like you're disappearing," he said. He'd never spoken to anyone about it in this way before, and he was surprised how easily it came with her.

"Yes, like disappearing. Like being invisible." She bit into one of the biscuits. "That's it exactly."

On this side of the hotel the only sound he could hear

was the dropping of dry pine needles in the heat and the purring of a turtle dove in the distance.

"It's parched," Sara said, brushing off some of the needles scattered on the table. "You may not be bothered by the smoke, but those fires are a bit of a worry."

"It's strange," he said, "I kind of like it."

"You would think," she said slowly, "after everything you've . . . you would think it would be the opposite."

"I find excuses to fly over it." He didn't know why he was telling her this. "Like I want to be close to it."

Sara looked at him, those sloping eyes of hers fixed on him. "That's terrible," she said.

"Is it? I don't know. Maybe."

"To be attracted to something dangerous like that."

"I guess that's not how I think about it. It's more that it's familiar."

"Intimate," she said.

He laughed. "I wouldn't get that fancy about it."

She laughed too. "I'm being overly romantic. I can get carried away."

"I don't see that," he said. "You seem pretty level to me."

"Well, thank you." She put her hand over his. "That's a high compliment."

Again, he found himself withdrawing from her touch. He didn't know when this aversion to physical contact had started, maybe in the hospital when he'd had to submit hourly to having doctors poke and prod and test his body, like it was an experiment. Maybe before that. He'd noticed, though, that Gerald seemed to have it, too, moving away quickly when his thigh had accidentally brushed him in the hangar.

"Well, so no work," Sara said, either not noticing or

pretending not to notice his reaction to her touch. "But have you been having any fun? Who have you been seeing?"

"I don't think I'm like you. I don't keep that much company," he said.

"Yes, we do like being around other people," she said, thoughtfully. "I know some people think that's because we don't like to be alone among ourselves. But that's not it," she said. "Everything is better when you share it, I think. That flow of ideas between different people, the chaos of it all, makes life so exciting. And when someone new comes in, the chemistry changes and you see things in people you hadn't seen before."

She'd clearly thought a lot about this. She spoke so confidently, the way some people spoke of God. He didn't believe in God; only luck, good and bad. And perhaps some choices. So listening to her, he couldn't help but doubt this religion of hers.

But all he said was: "I don't mind being alone."

"You're not alone all the time, though, surely. Vladimir speaks of you often."

"Vladimir. Yes, I see him."

"And the Fitzgeralds? Do you see much of them? We saw them for a beach party in Saint-Raphaël awhile ago, but I haven't heard from them since."

He wondered how much she knew about what was going on up at the Villa Marie. He pulled out a cigarette and lit it. "I haven't seen them in a couple of weeks," he said carefully.

"You share a mechanic with Edouard Jozan, don't you?"

"I do," he said, forcing himself not to look at her.

"What do you think of him?"

"He's young. Brave." He finally looked up and grinned. "French."

She wasn't smiling back. "Don't judge Zelda too harshly," she said. "It's hard for her, running after Scott all the time."

"I don't," he said, honestly. "I don't judge her at all."

⚬

After Owen had left, Sara remained on the terrace. She knew she should prepare for the beach, and yet she stayed, toying with her empty sherry glass. She was thinking about Owen, about what he'd said about the forest fires and about his war stories.

She'd mentioned once to Gerald that Owen reminded her of a lake, smooth, showing nothing except the reflection of its surroundings. Now she realized she'd been stupid about him.

She'd been given a small glimpse of what was underneath, a brief allowed closeness, and it moved her. Like when one of her children unfurled a hot little hand to reveal some precious collected treasure—a bottle cap, a beetle.

That was what Gerald must have felt, too, when he went up in the plane with him. That unexpected vulnerability.

Sara supposed she shouldn't be surprised to find something softer, broken even, in Owen. She'd heard from Tristan, who'd heard from God-knows-who, that Owen had been in some dangerous and tragic accident during the war. Apparently saw his best friend burned alive. But she'd also heard that his nickname had been 'La Chance', which she regarded as foolhardy. Perhaps, she thought now, if anything, she'd expected to find a man more like Edouard Jozan. Not that she minded a man like that; in fact, some part of her found that kind of virility exciting. Clearly, Zelda did too.

When she and Gerald and the children had gone to Saint-Raphaël for the day at the beginning of the month, it had already been evident that something was afoot between Zelda and Edouard. At least to everyone, it seemed, except Scott.

There'd been too much liquor, as was always the case with Zelda and Scott, and the nannies had been left to amuse the children, although little Scottie Fitzgerald, who'd only just arrived from Paris, seemed pleased as punch to have playmates.

Zelda had been gay, a crown of roses on her head, speaking to everyone. But most of her attention had been fixed on Edouard and their physicality had attracted Sara's notice. The two had spent a lot of time swimming together, racing and splashing and pushing each other. Later, as Zelda lay on her blanket, quite close to Edouard, eyes closed, Sara noticed her pinky reaching out and twining around his hand.

Scott, meanwhile, had sat under an umbrella, his skin greenish white, drinking from a bottle of gin.

Gerald told her later, on the ride home, the children asleep in the back, that Scott was having an awful time with the book and that any time away from it, like a day at the beach, made him feel anxious.

"But did you see Zelda?" she'd asked.

"Yes," he'd said. "I think you'd have to be blind not to have noticed that display."

"Scott didn't seem to notice," she said.

"No."

"I suppose if it's not about Scott, he wouldn't," she said. She'd begun to tire of Scott's antics, his ferocious sociability. She'd thought he might drop some of it once he and Zelda left the melee of Paris, but he'd only seemed to pack it along with everything else in his trunk.

"That's a bit tough," Gerald said.

"You're right," she sighed. "They're young."

"Still," he conceded, "I wouldn't want to be in Zelda's shoes."

Since that day, she'd had no reply to her invitations or correspondence. She and Gerald had both assumed, or wanted to, that it was only because Scott was hard at work and Zelda busy with Scottie. But now, after what Owen had said, she wondered.

Clearly, she'd have to try something else. She asked Tristan to bring her some writing paper and when it arrived she set about penning two letters. The first was to Scott and Zelda, inviting them to a party on the grounds of Villa America in two weeks' time. The second was to Owen, telling him she hoped he'd join them, too, "because no one should be alone all the time." At the bottom of each letter she wrote: *Dinner-Flowers-Gala*, and underlined it twice.

     ❊   ❊   ❊

The evening of the party was dry and warm, with just a hint of a breeze rustling the plantings on the grounds of Villa America. Sara could name them all now: Arabian maples; persimmon; white and black fig trees; phoenix palms; date palms; cedars of Lebanon; desert holly; mimosa; pepper trees; lemon and orange and olive trees. Their most precious, though, was the linden tree that grew close to the house, high above the tiered terrace gardens. The large old tree with its silvery leaves would eventually shade the gray and white marble terrace that would run along the back of Villa America, and they'd given specific instructions to the architects and builders to take the utmost care with it.

The construction on the house was coming along: the pitched red-tile roof had been removed and the third storey erected. Still, the flat sunroof they'd wanted had yet to be built and all along the perimeter of the house, the earth was all turned up and untidy.

The gardens, though, were in perfect condition, if not a little dry, and that's all the space they needed for the party. They'd had furniture brought from the hotel and set everything up on the first three terraces, each separated from the next by a small flight of stone steps.

On the highest tier, closest to the house, were a series of small tables, and wicker chairs covered in bright beach cushions, and off to the left, the gramophone and the records.

On the next tier down, they'd set up a banquet. Sara checked the dishes—cold sliced duck with fresh plums, courgette *tartes*, wild lettuce, stuffed artichokes, a few lovely fresh cheeses, and for dessert *millasson*, sprinkled with caster sugar. There was also a large bar table: champagne, anisette, peach wine and a rhubarb cocktail that Gerald had spent two days perfecting in the kitchen of the Hôtel du Cap.

The guests had been asked to come at five p.m. for a cocktail and the Salon de Jeunesse, a show of paintings by Honoria, Baoth and Patrick, under the tutelage of Vladimir. The children would stay for an hour and then be ferried back to the hotel for supper and bed. Sara saw them crowding around Gerald now as he arranged their artworks against a stone wall.

Sara walked over and placed her hand on Gerald's back. He looked beautiful in his bone-colored linen suit. He'd had it made for him in Paris in the spring, saying he didn't want to fuss too much with dinner clothes in Antibes. "We're not going down to mix with *sheer society*," he'd said.

Sheer society, *holocausts*; she smiled to think of the private language that they'd been inventing between themselves over the years.

"What do we have here?" Sara asked, now putting her hand to Honoria's head. She loved the feel of her daughter's soft, cropped hair beneath her palm.

"This one's mine," Honoria said, pointing to a purple and blue canvas, with mounds of green dotted through it.

Sara bent down. She could see that small flowers and bits of leaves had been pressed into the green paint. "My goodness," she said. "That's beautiful. What do you call it?"

"I call it 'Fleurs in Antibes,'" she said proudly.

"Very ambitious," Sara said, trying not to smile.

"Mine's here," Baoth said, pulling her hand.

Sara exchanged a look with Gerald: their middle child's painting looked like a muddy, gloopy nothing. This one was not going to be an artist. "Very manly," she said. "What is it?"

"Beef stew. The way Mamzelle makes it." He guffawed when he saw her expression.

Patrick was sitting in front of his piece, playing with a tin soldier, marching it up and down the canvas. Sara had to squint at it. It was just a small pen drawing, of a stick figure —a man she assumed, from the hat—on what might be a beach, given the squiggly lines that could resemble seaweed.

"Who's this, my love?"

"Monsieur Picasso," he said, not stopping the march.

"Oh, I think he'll be honored. Would you like to give it to him when he comes tonight?"

"All right," Patrick said, seemingly unconcerned.

"I think you've all done splendidly," Sara said. "Some more graciously than others," she added, eyeing Baoth.

"Yes, I think tonight you can be spared the switch," Gerald said.

All three children laughed and shrieked a bit at the thought, Honoria crying: "Dow-Dow, no."

"Well, you never know," he said. "The switch may be produced at any time."

"Children, I want you to go up to the gate, now," Sara said, restoring order. "And be ready to greet our guests. Honoria, you may ask them when they come in what they'd like to drink and then tell Dow-Dow. All right?"

"Yes, Mother," she said.

"Maybe they'd like the switch," Baoth said.

"Enough of that. Get along." She shooed them off, then turned to Gerald. "Really, you and that switch."

"They must be aware of the harsh realities of life."

She linked her arm in his. "As if you'd ever teach them that."

"No," he said, serious now. "I would never teach them that. You look marvelous, by the way."

Standing on her tiptoes, her Louis heels digging into the ground, Sara put her mouth to the hollow of his neck and kissed him.

＊

By eight o'clock the sun had just begun to set. The clouds at the far edge of the horizon were a shocking coral and the date palms made dark fingers against the sky. Nightingales competed with the sounds of Clara Smith, her supine voice stretching against the scratch of the gramophone.

A warmth had risen in Gerald, the kind he felt when he was glad about all the people around him and with his efforts to make them happy.

The children, long since bundled off, had shown off their paintings proudly and he'd photographed them next to their works, promising a Villa America art magazine later on.

Now, amid the music and birdsong, there was the pleasant hum of the guests. Dos, who'd joined them last week at the Hôtel du Cap on his way back from Spain, was here, as were the Picassos, and the Comte and Comtesse de Beaumont, along with their very decorative, but drunk, houseguests. By the banquet table he saw Philip Barry and his wife Ellen, beautiful in a salmon-colored gown, talking with his sister Esther, and next to them, Don Stewart in conversation with Vladimir and another young writer whose name he'd forgotten. In the middle of it all, Sara in a white draped linen dress, backless and shot through with silver thread, her long pearls spilling down her spine.

The only ones missing were Owen, and the Fitzgeralds, of course. But as he'd told Sara, he doubted that anything short of murder would keep those two away from a party billed as *Dinner-Flowers-Gala*.

He walked over to the banquet table to join the Barrys and Esther, catching the strand of their conversation.

"Yes," Phil was saying, "but what interests me is whether to have—and maintain—a happy family, one must give up art to seek money."

"I'm surprised," Esther said, towering over the play-wright. "I didn't think money would be a question for you, at all."

Ellen laughed, throwing her dark head back. "She's got you there, Phil." Gerald loved her throaty chuckle, her sardonic temperament.

"No," Esther said. "I think the more interesting question is whether an artist can truly make such connections, such intimacies, as a family. An artist will always be an artist, whether she sublimates it or not." She waved her hand— ragged nails, Gerald noticed—as if to dismiss Phil's thought. "But can a true artist be part of a collective, or will she always end up striving for individuality? That is what we must focus on. All we know is . . ."

Gerald could tell his sister was gearing up for one of her blue streaks and he interrupted before the monologue took on epic proportions.

"Aren't you in a collective?" he said, putting his hand on her arm.

"A circle," Esther began, "is different than a collective. A collective . . ."

"I see," Gerald said, before she could continue. Esther was a monumental intellect, but party conversation wasn't her strong suit.

"Ah," Phil said, turning to Gerald. "Here's a man who's an artist and a family man, and successful at both."

"Yes," Esther said. She moved unconsciously closer to Gerald. "But that's because Sara doesn't go tinkering around inside his head. She doesn't play Dr. Freud with his motivations. Thus, in a way, he is able to live both the examined and the unexamined life."

"Is that true, Murphy?" Phil seemed highly amused. "No Dr. Freud at bedtime?"

"If Dr. Freud came to our bedside," Gerald said, "we'd offer him a warm milk and brandy, have a nice little chat, and send him back to his own room, like we do with all naughty little boys."

"Even in that comment . . ." Esther began, but she was cut off by a commotion coming from behind them.

❖

Dos had been half listening to Esther Murphy from his spot a few feet away near the peach wine. Esther was one of those talkers that could leave you both irritated and spellbound at the same time. Ditto her appearance, with that ungainly figure and lazy eye and bad smell. He knew not all lesbians were like that. In fact, Esther's circle had some positively elegant women, not to mention young nubile girls, in it.

But, whatever her looks, there was no doubt that Esther was terrifyingly bright. He just couldn't stand the way she talked *at* you instead of with you. This was what he was thinking, anyway, when Scott and Zelda arrived, bringing all that drama and staginess in their wake.

They were noticeably stumbling and arguing loudly as they entered, and of course, everyone turned to watch.

Scott was trying to take Zelda in his arms and she was pushing him away. "You almost killed us," she hissed loudly. "Don't talk to me."

"Fine," he cried. "Although it was you asking for a light for your cigarette when you knew that turn was coming up."

Dos saw Sara walk over quickly, but not too quickly, and take Scott by the arm. Smiling and speaking softly, she led him away. Then Gerald did the same with Zelda. Like referees separating boxers. Afterwards, the rest of the guests began to resume their conversations, but half-heartedly, as if they were disappointed that the match had ended so soon.

With Zelda and Scott off in their respective corners— the spectacle cleared—Dos noticed someone else who had come in behind them, a tall blond man, with just the hint of a limp. War vet, he surmised.

The man walked over to the banquet table as if nothing unusual had just happened, and picked up a glass. He poured an anisette and lit a cigarette. He didn't greet anyone, or even really look at any of the other guests. He seemed to be fixated on the horizon. Dos had to laugh a little, the man seemed so much like a decorative extra in a play.

He picked up his own glass, along with the bottle of wine, and walked over to the other end of the table, where the man was standing.

"Hi," he said. "That was quite an entrance. You part of the act?"

The man looked at him, smoking his cigarette. "I was the driver. They had a little car trouble."

"Bad luck," Dos said.

"Not for them," the man said.

"No," Dos laughed. "Not for them. They do like an audience. You're American. Sorry," he held out his hand, "John Dos Passos."

"Owen Chambers," the man said, taking his hand.

They stood in companionable silence for a while, the last of the evening light and the newly lit hurricane lamps making everything sort of glow. Then Dos said: "It's kind of like being in heaven, isn't it? You can only bear it for so long."

The man smiled. "I'm not in it very often."

"Ah," Dos said. "Do you know the crowd? Do you want a run-down? I've had just enough to drink to be indiscreet."

"Go on then."

Dos could tell he was amused, if only slightly. "OK, do you know the Picassos?"

The man nodded.

"Right. And you know Scott and Zelda. And I assume you know Gerald and Sara."

"Yes, I know them." The man stubbed out his cigarette.

"So, the tall weird one over there, the woman? That's Gerald's sister, Esther. Sapphic. Smart. They say she's in love with Natalie Barney. Follows her around like a puppy dog. Do you know who that is?"

Owen shook his head.

"Never mind. I digress. So, the tall one over there by the gramophone . . . the one with the glasses? That's Don Stewart. He's a writer. Funny stuff. One about a tourist.

239

We just got back from Pamplona together. Bull-fighting with some fake bohemians. He cracked his ribs, that's why he's standing funny." Dos looked around. "Where's that bottle?"

The man handed him the peach wine.

"Thanks. I don't know who that young guy talking to him is. The woman by the tree, with the dark braided do? That's Ellen Barry, she's a portrait painter, and that," he said jutting his chin, "is her husband, Phil. Playwright. You'll like them. Or I like them." He sipped his wine. "I think that's it . . ."

"It felt very complete," the man said, finishing his second glass of anisette.

"It did, didn't it?" He liked this fellow. "Here, have some more anisette. Wait. What are you drinking out of? That's way too small. Have a wineglass. It's a party." He filled a wineglass with anisette and passed it over. "So—Owen, is it?—your turn to tell a story."

"What kind of story would you like to hear?" Owen took a larger gulp from the glass.

"One about car trouble and Scott and Zelda."

"I don't know how interesting it is."

"I'll be the judge of that," Dos said.

"All right. Scott crashed the car into a post next to the cafe where I live," Owen said.

"Where's that?"

"Agay."

Dos nodded; he knew vaguely where that was.

"Zelda knocked on my door and said they needed a lift. I was coming anyway, so . . ."

"How did Scott crash it?"

"He says that Zelda asked him to light her cigarette on a turn."

"And did she?"

"I don't know," Owen said, tipping his wineglass back. "She says he did it on purpose. She seemed pretty upset."

"What's your theory?"

"I don't really have one."

"You're not very good at this," Dos said, refilling his glass.

Owen laughed. "No, I guess I'm not."

"Never mind, we all have our talents," Dos said. "So, what's your talent, Owen?"

"I fly planes."

"Damn good talent. Do that in the war?"

"In the Lafayette Flying Corps."

"Flew for France. I was with Norton-Harjes. You know, the Ambulance Corps." Then, before he could stop himself, he added: "Fucking mess that war."

"Yes," Owen said.

"Well," Dos said, wishing he hadn't started this conversation and wondering if he was obliged to finish it. "Well."

He was saved from continuing the thought about the fucking mess of a war by the arrival of Don Stewart, and that younger man, the one he didn't know.

❖

The sun had almost dipped completely below the horizon and Sara was trying to reason with Scott, or at least calm him down enough so that she could release him back into the party. Out of the corner of her eye, she saw Tristan's brother, hired to help out, lighting the last of the scattered hurricane lamps, which Gerald had painted all different shades of blue and silver. High above them, the lighthouse blinked on and off, and the wind was beginning to be audible.

She'd taken Scott down to the last level of the garden, away from the guests, and he was now leaning against an Arabian maple, his curly head hung like a dog.

"Scott," she said gently. "It sounds like it was all a misunderstanding. You love Zelda and I know she loves you. That car was worthless, anyway."

"Oh, it's not the car," he moaned. "You don't understand."

"What don't I understand?"

"She wants a divorce," he said, lifting his mournful eyes to her. "She doesn't love me."

"Nonsense," Sara said.

"It's that Jozan. She's fallen in love with him."

"I think she just needs a bit of attention, that's all, with you working so hard." She did think this, but she also felt slightly alarmed by Scott's words.

"No, no, no." Scott shook his head.

"She's young, Scott. It's only natural that men will be attracted to her."

"You're not listening." He started banging the tree with his fist. "She *doesn't* love me, she *loves* him. She wants a divorce. She's had carnal knowledge of him. She *told* me."

"Scott . . ."

"She said he made love to her like a man." He looked like he was about to cry now.

"When was this?" Sara took Scott's fist in her hand. "And stop that or you'll hurt yourself."

"I dunno." He hung his head again.

"Scott, when did she tell you this?"

"A week ago, maybe more. It's all over. The dream is over. It was there for a while, but now it's gone . . ."

"What did you say?" Sara wanted to keep him to the concrete details, away from the hysteria that seemed to be threatening.

"I forbade her to see him again," he yelled, hitting the tree once more.

"And did she?"

"She couldn't," Scott said. "I made sure she couldn't."

Sara wondered just what exactly had been happening at the Villa Marie. "What do you mean, Scott? What do you mean, you made sure?"

"I need a drink," Scott said, and he suddenly stood and swerved towards the stairs.

⁘

From his spot next to the gramophone, Gerald could see Scott heading unsteadily in the direction of the bar.

He turned back to Zelda. "You're sure you're all right?"

"I'm marvelous, Dow-Dow. Whatever do you mean?" She looked like a pale pink tulip, her silk dress cut in the shape of petals from the waist, like a dancer's skirt.

In an effort to separate her from Scott, he'd asked her to come help him pick out a record. But he hadn't been able to get much out of her. Gerald had to admit, that was one of the things he liked about Zelda: she didn't talk behind Scott's back.

Zelda held out an Al Jolson record. He put it on and then said, as nonchalantly as possible: "You and Scott. You're getting along?"

"Swimmingly," Zelda said. "We've spent so much time together lately. More than ever."

"That's wonderful," Gerald said warily. "And the car?"

"Oh, the car? I've forgotten about the car. What happened to it?"

"I don't know," Gerald said. "That's why I'm asking you."

"Well, I'm sure *I* don't know." She looked at him incredulously.

"Oh," Gerald said. "But you're all right."

"Of course I am," she said, putting her hand gently on

his forearm. "Why wouldn't I be? Scott's been keeping me locked up in the villa."

"Excuse me?" He couldn't have heard her correctly. The wind seemed to be picking up somewhere on the other side of the hill, and it carried some of her words away from him.

"It's been like a dream, Dow-Dow. Although Scott says it's the end of the dream. Beginning, end, who knows?" She was looking off in the direction of the half-finished house.

He didn't know what to say; she must be out of her head with drink.

"Dow-Dow," she turned back, those eyes leveled at him, "don't you think Al Jolson is just like Jesus?"

"I'm sorry? Like Jesus?" He was confounded. Still, he couldn't help loving her. She was like someone who was perpetually moonstruck.

"May I have one of your lovely cocktails, please?" she asked sweetly.

"Of course," he said, offering her his arm. "Of course you may."

◦

"I'm Whit Clay," the young man introduced himself to Owen.

Owen guessed he was around twenty-two, twenty-three, perhaps. Young. But maybe that's because he felt older than his twenty-eight years. He'd heard someone say once that you were born a certain age and that you'd remain that age, in spirit, all your life. Who'd said that?

Owen realized he was getting drunk. Then he realized that he'd just been standing there, mutely staring at this Whit Clay. "Sorry," he said. "Owen Chambers."

"Don Stewart." This from the tall bespectacled man who reminded him of a young Mr. Cushing, his old schoolmaster.

He who'd saved him from . . . from what exactly? Ruin? Shame?

"We've been swapping talents," his new friend, John Dos Passos, said. "It turns out I'm damn good at summing up party guests."

"And filling wineglasses," Owen said.

"Yes," Dos Passos said. "Owen here was drinking out of a thimble. I was forced to step in and rectify the situation."

"Good for you, Dos," the Mr. Cushing–Don Stewart man said. "A man in a crisis."

"And what do you do?" Dos Passos pointed a finger at Whit Clay.

"I'm a writer," he said. "Working for the *Transatlantic Review*."

"Christ, who isn't?" Dos Passos laughed.

The young man shrugged and returned his attention to Owen. Owen looked away, and then couldn't help looking back. Whit Clay was slim, slight almost, with smooth, clear skin and a strong mouth. He reminded him of some of the college boys he'd flown with.

"What do you do?" Whit asked him.

"I'm a pilot," he said. "I run a business . . ."

"Pleasure flights?"

"Sometimes. I mostly fly in goods." He shifted under the young man's gaze.

"I've never been up in a plane. I'd like to."

Whit's eyes were green, he noticed. "Oh," Owen said finally.

Whit smiled. "How much do you charge?"

"Well, well," Dos Passos said, seemingly entertained. "Quite the journalist, there, Whit. Big interest in flying?"

"Leave it, you idiot," Don Stewart laughed.

"Sorry," Dos Passos said. "Peach wine?"

"Thanks," Whit said. Then to Owen: "Do you live down here?"

"I do," Owen said, as Dos Passos also refilled his glass.

"It's beautiful. I can see why you would. Paris is a swamp this time of year. And then cold in the winter." Whit drank from his wineglass, wind catching his hair.

"I liked Paris," Owen said. "Sometimes."

Whit shrugged. "It's fine. Lots of Americans. Some of the bad kind. But lots here, too."

"I guess." Owen looked around. Dos Passos and Don Stewart seemed to have moved off, somehow, now in their own conversation.

"I'd heard about Sara and Gerald Murphy," Whit said. "Seems they know everyone."

Owen felt he didn't really understand the comment, what it meant, where it was leading. He put his glass down. He never over-drank and now he was definitely drunk.

"You look like . . ."

Owen could see Whit's jaw, all the muscles and tendons and bone. He wanted to touch it, run his thumb along the contours. Whit smelled like cologne, but it was a good smell. They seemed very close together, and Owen was wondering if they were too close, when he felt a hand shove him aside.

"Excuse me, excuse me." It was Scott. "Excuse me, Owen. I saw you two talking and I thought . . ."

"Hello, Scott," Owen said, moving closer to the table, hoping to brace himself a bit.

"I saw you two talking . . ." Scott also looked like he could use the table.

"This is Whit Clay," Owen said.

". . . I thought I just had to ask this young man . . . Whit Clay is it?" Scott peered rudely into Whit's face.

"Yes," the young man said.

Scott nodded, looking very satisfied for some reason Owen couldn't fathom. "So my question is this: are you, or are you not, a homosexual?"

There was a brief moment where Owen felt it hadn't happened. It couldn't have happened. He looked at the two men staring at each other and there was only the sound of the wind coming over the hill, loudly, it seemed to him.

But then Whit said in a calm, friendly tone: "Yes, Mr. Fitzgerald, I am."

Scott's face seemed to shrink back into itself.

Then Dos Passos and Don Stewart were there and Dos put himself between Scott and Whit, blocking Scott out, and saying to Owen: "I just remembered a few people here I forgot to mention . . ."

Over Dos's shoulder, Scott looked strange, miserable, embarrassed. Sick. Owen thought he might be about to vomit, but Scott just mumbled something unintelligible and scuttled away.

"The Comte and Comtesse de Beaumont," Dos Passos continued affably. "I think I saw her smoking opium in the hedgerow. And those are the houseguests . . ."

Owen looked at Whit, who smiled at him.

"What are their names again, Don?"

"I only remember the lady." Don put his hand on Whit's shoulder. "I'm sorry about that. That was ugly."

"Right." Dos Passos snapped his fingers. "Flora Glass. Some kind of American heiress."

Something surfaced slowly from the drink-soaked recesses of his mind, like a fishing cork bobbing up in a lake. Owen turned to Dos Passos and asked: "What did you say?"

"An American heiress," he said.

"Where?" Owen turned around, scanning the people now dimly lit in the flickering light of the hurricane lamps.

"Over there, by the gramophone," Dos said, pointing to a group of people above them. "The thin one. Well, the young one. Not the other one, that's the comtesse."

○

Sara was standing with Zelda and Gerald, the Comtesse de Beaumont, and one of her houseguests when she saw Scott stumbling up a flight of steps towards them.

She leaned her head in and whispered to Gerald: "Is this party getting quite bad?"

"It might be," he conceded. "Or it might just be Scott."

"This wind," the comtesse was saying. "They said in town that a mistral is coming through."

"We're protected here, on this side of the hill," Gerald said.

"Yes," the comtesse said, "maybe from head-on, but not from above."

She was a striking woman, the comtesse, thin and elegant, but she had a way of always being right that irritated Sara at times.

"They say the mistral makes people go mad," Zelda said, dreamily.

"No," the comtesse said. "It does not. That's only what mad people say to excuse themselves."

Zelda's expression darkened slightly, but she stayed silent.

Out of the corner of her eye, Sara could see that Scott was almost upon them. Gerald saw it too, because he nudged her and whispered: "Incoming."

Scott walked up and stood at the edge of the circle. He fixed his gaze on the comtesse's houseguest, a pretty, drunk girl, who had been swaying silently in their company.

"Who are you?" he asked, staring.

"This is Flora Glass," the comtesse said. "She is visiting from London. She's engaged to Etienne's cousin, Lord Darnby."

The girl nodded. Despite her youth, Sara noticed, there was a hardness to her face, a sculpted quality that was generally the result of age or rough-living.

Scott, who seemed to have lost any interest, turned to Sara and said: "I *have* to talk to you."

"You are talking to me, Scott." She had no desire to get into it with him, and she hoped that if she didn't let him get her alone, he would drop whatever it was. "A wedding." She turned back to the young woman. "How marvelous. When are you to be married?"

"Soon enough," the young woman said.

Sara laughed. "I see."

"Sara," Scott said, but she ignored him.

"They are to be married in September," the comtesse said.

The young woman looked up at the sky.

"Where is your fiancé now?" Sara asked, if only to keep Scott at bay.

The girl shrugged, but didn't move her eyes.

"He's in London. Looking after his affairs," the comtesse said, shaking her head at Flora.

"Sara, why won't you look at me?" Scott grabbed her arm.

"Now, Scott . . ." Gerald began.

"No, it's all right," Sara said. "What *is* it?"

"I need to talk to you."

"Fine," she said. "Come with me to the car. You can help carry some champagne back."

He trailed her as she marched down the path that led to the driveway in front of Villa America. When they reached the car, Scott stopped her and fell to his knees.

"What on earth are you doing?"

"I've realized that it doesn't matter about Zelda," he said, clutching her legs. "Because I love you. You are my perfect woman."

"Get up," she said sternly.

"I won't," he said. "Oh, beautiful Sara. In your beautiful silver dress. *Had I the heaven's embroidered cloths/ Enwrought with golden and silver light . . . I would spread the cloths under your feet . . . Tread softly because you tread on my dreams.*"

"You're being ridiculous," Sara said. "Pull yourself together."

He stood. "Kiss me."

"Scott . . ." but before she could say anything else he planted his lips against hers.

Sara pushed him away. "Now that we've settled that," she said briskly, "take that champagne out of the car. I'm going back to the party."

✴

Owen walked up to the part of the garden where Flora stood, then stopped a moment, watching her. She seemed to hold herself at a distance from the other guests. He'd heard Sara ask her questions and watched her look away.

She looked older. Of course, it'd been ten years, but it was more than that. She was wearing a blue beaded dress and she was still as slight as she'd always been, yet it wasn't the same childish slightness he remembered. It was more a fashionable *thinness*.

He didn't know what he should say, or if he should say anything at all. But he had to know, he decided, briefly wondering if he'd regret it in the morning.

He watched as Sara and Scott walked off together. Flora moved a little further away from the circle and was looking at some of the records by the gramophone. He wished he had another anisette for courage.

He covered the distance between them and stood at her side. She didn't look up. "Hello, Flora," he said.

"Hello," she said, turning the record over in her hand. "I saw you were here."

This was not what he was expecting.

"I was wondering if you were going to say something," she said.

"I didn't know if I should," he said, finally.

"Probably not," she said, lifting her face to his. "But then people often do things they shouldn't. Don't you find?"

He felt his face go hot. "You wrote *me* that day."

"I suppose I did. It doesn't matter now." She shrugged. "I guess you want to know what's become of Charlie."

Up close, he noticed that her lipstick was a startling shade of red, like a gash across her face.

"Well, he's dead," she said, picking up another record. "God, don't they have anything a little more peppy?"

"Charlie's dead?" His own voice sounded far away, as if it wasn't really coming from him. He wondered if it was the liquor or what she had said.

"Yes, fool got himself killed at the front. That, among other things," she said, "did Daddy in. And now," she put the record on the gramophone, "I'm an heiress, fit for a lord. Lucky me."

"Charlie's dead?" He didn't know why he said it again. Maybe he didn't believe her.

"Yes, Owen," she said, her voice like granite. "He's dead. So no more kisses in the barn with my brother, no more love affairs, if that's what you were hoping for after all these years. Look at you." She shook her head. "Sidling up here, pretending we're friends."

He stared at her. He hated her. He wondered if he'd really ever hated anyone before. He couldn't remember having this feeling, not even for the Germans who'd killed Quentin. "I don't think we're friends," he said between gritted teeth. "And I wasn't hoping for that. I would never hope for that."

"No, I suppose you wouldn't," she conceded. "You paid for it, too, in your own way, I guess."

"I'm the only one who paid."

She laughed. "Oh, is that what you think? You think it was all just hunky-dory between Charlie and Daddy afterwards?"

He thought about everything he'd lost, his mother, the loneliness, all the hiding and the shame. And here she was with her snappy talk and her hard face and self-pity. "Hunky-dory? *Hunky-dory?* Fuck you, Flora." And it felt like opium to his blood to say it, a euphoric high.

"Oh, that's charming," she said. "Well, as much as this little reunion has been enlightening, I think we should keep it short and sweet, don't you?" But despite her sharp words there was something in her expression, too fleeting for him to place. If he had to name it, he might have said sorrow.

He watched her walk back to the comtesse, touch her host on the arm and incline her head towards the house, before moving up the path and out of his sight.

❖

The wind had really picked up, and pine needles were whipping through the air, stinging Gerald's face a bit. Above them, the hills had turned bright orange with fire, and the smell of burning eucalyptus that had been perfuming the air for a few weeks now had suddenly become overwhelming.

"I think you were right, Comtesse," he said. "About the mistral."

"Of course I was," she said. "We should be heading back, anyway. I think our young friend has had enough."

He chuckled. "She seemed like she'd had enough awhile ago."

"I don't know what's wrong with young women today," the comtesse said. "No fortitude. Oh well. *Bonne nuit, mon ami.* Will you give our thanks to your charming wife?"

"Of course," he said.

"Where has Etienne disappeared to?" She looked around and, spotting her husband by the table with Dos and Don Stewart, walked down in his direction, raising her hand over her shoulder.

"Good night," Gerald said.

He turned to Zelda, and was about to offer to refresh her drink, but she was staring, transfixed, at the path leading from the side of the house. Sara was walking down it, and behind her Scott was carrying several bottles of champagne.

"There they are," Gerald said.

"Yes," Zelda said. "Why is it so windy?"

"Mistral is apparently coming through. Won't be good for those fires," Gerald said, looking again up into the hills.

"Will they come down here and burn us?"

"I hope not," he said. "No, of course not," he added. It was Zelda he was talking to, after all.

"Well, we have to drench ourselves in champagne, then. Stay wet," she said.

Sara passed to their left. She gave Gerald a look, a slight eye-roll as she went by. Scott followed, doggedly.

"Why did she do that?" Zelda asked. "Why did she roll her eyes?"

"I don't know."

"She mustn't get sick of Scott," Zelda said. "He needs her."

"Of course she's not sick of Scott," Gerald said, soothingly.

"I'm sick of Scott," Zelda sighed. "But that doesn't matter anymore. Maybe we'll all die in a fire."

"Zelda . . ." he began, but she just walked away, down the steps towards her husband.

Sara was right. This party was getting quite bad. It was time to wrap it up, he decided. Re-serve and let go, was the way to do it. He saw that Owen had sequestered himself by the gramophone. He'd intended to speak with him all evening, but had found excuses not to. It seemed, though, that it might be now or never. He picked up the bottle of champagne on the table beside him and walked over.

"Hello," he said.

"Hello," Owen said.

"Look," Gerald said, "I've been meaning to say something to you. Perhaps I should have written. I'm sorry for the way I went on. You know, after you took me up."

"It doesn't matter," Owen said.

"It does matter. To me." Gerald wondered if Owen had decided he wasn't worth it. "I'm not very good at expressing myself, sometimes. It was such a . . . I was very moved by the experience. That's all."

"I'm sorry?" Owen looked at him as if he'd only just realized he was standing there.

"I was just saying . . . are you all right?"

"Yes," Owen said. "No. I'm drunk, I think."

But really, Gerald thought, he looked more stricken than drunk. He put his hand on Owen's arm. He could feel its shape beneath the shirtsleeve.

"Do you ever wonder," Owen said, "if everything you've believed has been the wrong thing? The wrong way around?"

"I . . ." He must be drunk, Gerald thought, to be talking this way. "Everyone makes choices, I think. You can't know if they're right or wrong. All you can do is stick by them."

"No, see, that's the point. We *do* have choices; it doesn't matter if they're right or wrong, that doesn't matter. It's not just luck. Things . . . they don't just happen to us. I used to believe that. Or something like that. But now I see: I was just a coward." He grasped Gerald's hand.

Gerald didn't know if it was the crazy wind or his mind playing tricks on him, but the expression in Owen's eyes reminded him of something. San Antonio. Training camp. The look in Tom Wilson's eyes before the gun went off.

"I don't want to be a coward anymore."

Owen was holding his hand too hard, crushing it, and Gerald yanked it away, as if he'd been burned. Whatever Owen was trying to communicate he didn't want to understand.

He was startled when he felt a nudge and turned to see Zelda standing there.

"Will you hold this, Dow-Dow," she said, passing him her champagne coupe, seemingly oblivious to what was going on between the two men.

He took it, without thinking, and they both watched as she walked over to one of the smaller tables nearby, kicked off her shoes, gathered her skirts around her, and climbed up on it.

Then, standing on her tiptoes, she began to twirl. Her pink tulip skirt flew out with the motion, round and round, lifting higher and higher. She was looking into the distance with enormous concentration, looking neither at them, nor the others below her, who were now turning to watch.

As she gained speed, the pink petals of fabric came above her waist, and in the lamplight, revealed first her bare legs, and then the shock of black satin panties, like the dark disk at the center of a flower.

The group below had started to move up the stairs,

gathering round, as if hypnotized by the spectacle. What struck Gerald at that moment was the dignity with which she performed this scene. She wasn't doing it for Scott or anyone else. She was doing it for herself and there was a supreme nobility to it.

Her spinning slowed, her skirt lowered, until she finally came to rest. She stood still for a moment. Then Sara offered Zelda her hand, helping her down.

Without a look, Gerald left Owen and walked over to Zelda, handing back her glass.

"Thank you, Dow-Dow," she said. She put her shoes on in silence.

✿

No one had to be told that it was time to go home. The wind and Zelda had made that clear. Owen wanted another swig of something, though, before he left, to blot it all out completely. He was about to pour himself a glass from the champagne bottle Gerald had brought over, when Whit Clay walked up.

"I think you've had enough," the young man said.

Owen looked at him.

"Come on," Whit said, softly. "Let's go."

"Where are we going?" Owen asked.

"Your place." He smiled.

"It's not near."

"That's all right, I'll drive. Give me your keys."

Owen reached into his pocket, took out his keys and placed them gently in the man's open palm.

✿   ✿   ✿

It was late and Sara didn't know how long they'd been asleep when there was a knock at the door. She wondered if she'd imagined it, until she heard it again, more violent this time.

Leaving Gerald sleeping, Sara rose and walked through the sitting room, switching a lamp on as she went.

It was Scott, still dressed, shaking. "You have to come quickly," he said. "It's Zelda. She didn't mean to do it."

Sara nodded, still not fully awake, but with that instinct for night emergencies she'd developed since having children. "I'll be right there."

She went back into the bedroom and found her dressing gown.

"What is it?" Gerald was half sitting up.

"Something's wrong with Zelda," she said.

"Wait. I'll come too."

She waited as he rose and searched for his own bathrobe. Then they made their way down the hall.

When the party had ended, Sara had managed to convince Scott and Zelda to stay over instead of driving home, and they'd been relatively quiet on the car trip back to the Hôtel du Cap.

They hadn't even waited with Sara and Gerald on the terrace to take a nightcap with Dos and Don Stewart who were walking back from Villa America. It had surprised her a little at the time—she'd never known the Fitzgeralds to leave when some amusement might still be had—but she'd also been relieved. She wondered now if that hadn't been a portent of some kind.

Arriving at the Fitzgeralds' room, she knocked softly. Scott opened the door. She could tell he was sweating through his clothes and he stank of booze. Over his shoulder she could see Zelda lying motionless on the bed.

"What's happened?" Sara asked, moving past him to his wife.

"She took some sleeping pills," he said, following her.

"How many?" She slapped Zelda's cheek lightly, but her eyes remained closed.

"Well, all of them, I think. I don't know how many were left," he said. "I don't think she did it on purpose. Oh God."

Sara turned to Gerald. "You two get her on her feet. I'm going to get some olive oil."

Gerald nodded, and he and Scott began to lift Zelda up.

Sara ran down the hall and down the main stairs to the lobby. Not wanting to wake the staff, in case there was gossip, she made her way through the formal rooms to the kitchen herself. She was out of breath and panicky as she opened and shut cupboards looking for oil. She'd heard somewhere—where?—that it counteracted the effects of poisons in the stomach.

Finally locating a bottle, she rushed back as quickly as she could. Zelda was awake, barely, and Gerald and Scott were supporting her, practically dragging her around the room.

"I found some," Sara said. "Sit her down."

She poured some of the oil into a water glass. Zelda's head kept rolling onto her chest. Scott turned his face to the wall and started sobbing.

"It'll be all right," Gerald said, but Scott just kept on.

Sara knelt down by the chair, taking Zelda's hand. "Zelda, darling? Drink some of this." Sara lifted Zelda's chin and held the glass to her lips.

"Mmm?" Zelda's eyes slid down, trying to focus.

"Come on," Sara said.

She took a sip, and then spluttered. "No," she moaned.

"It's olive oil. It's going to make you feel better, I promise," Sara said.

"No, Say-ra, no," she said.

"Yes, darling."

"No," Zelda pleaded. "Don't make me drink that, Say-ra, please. If you drink too much oil you turn into a Jew."

Sara tried to put the glass back to Zelda's lips, but she knocked it out of Sara's hand. It fell to the floor, the oil seeping into the rug.

Zelda started crying. "I'm sorry," she said.

Sara looked up. "Scott, fill the pitcher with water. Gerald and I will walk with her."

She and Gerald each took an arm and hauled Zelda up.

"Maybe the hall?" she said.

Gerald nodded and they took her out of the room and began walking her up the long corridor.

"If she doesn't stay awake, we'll have to go find a doctor," Gerald whispered.

Sara nodded, but Zelda said: "No doctors. They molest you with wrenches."

She looked at Gerald and he shook his head.

"Just keep walking, darling," Sara said.

✳

In his rooms above the Café d'Esterel, Owen could hear the wind beating against the bay.

On his bed was the yellow chenille coverlet and so much radiant skin, hard and smooth and curved. Kneeling, he placed his hand against the back of the neck and felt the spot where the barber's blade had mowed down the hair, sharp under his fingers. He ran his hand down, down the spine that bent in, a line of pebbles extending in order of size. Over the ass, his palm following the sweep, hesitating at the small dip before the rise of muscle. Then the spot where the back of the thigh began, between the legs, so soft, fine hairs, the calves like bows. All the way to the sole of the foot, its arch, the tough skin of the heel.

He brought his hand back to the shoulder and turned the body over. He put his lips to the waiting lips. Felt the tongue push into his mouth, brushing the inside. He closed his own lips around it, felt it slip out. He braced himself, looking into the green eyes, the wavy hair framed by the pillow. He pushed the thighs apart.

He reached down, taking one thigh in his hand, lifting him up, positioning him. Owen was ready.

❖   ❖   ❖

Sara had gone back to bed at dawn, but Gerald couldn't sleep. They'd walked Zelda up and down that damn corridor until the sun began to throw light through the window at the end of the hall, casting a rectangular patch on the crested runner.

Zelda had seemed all right, or as all right as she was going to be under the circumstances, and Scott had quietly gathered up their things, solemnly shaken Gerald's hand, and bundled her into the waiting hotel taxi, Tristan at the wheel.

Now, Gerald sat on the terrace drinking a coffee, the early morning sky hazy with smoke blown down the hills by the mistral. His brain felt viscous, stunned. It didn't seem to have the power to form any real thoughts, only shutter through a collection of images: the oil-paint sunset; the unfinished house rising above the grounds; Sara, in silver and white, in the middle of their guests; Owen's face when he held his hand so tightly; Zelda, swirling, black underwear exposed; Scott sobbing against the wall, crumpled and terrified.

He rubbed his face. He'd wanted the party to be perfect, to be complete. To show a glimpse of what their life at Villa America was going to be like, not so much for their friends as for himself. But it had turned somehow, real life poking in, darkness blurring the edges. He wondered how high you had to build the walls to keep the barbarian hordes out. Higher, perhaps, than he was capable of.

He thought of Owen. "I don't want to be a coward anymore," he'd said. Was he, Gerald Murphy, a coward? Perhaps a little. But mainly, he wanted to build a beautiful castle, an idyll with high walls, to keep his children safe, to keep his love for Sara safe. To keep their life safe. From ugliness, and violence, and desperation. But mostly, from confusion. And to do that he had to scotch some of the defects in himself. As best he could.

It suddenly seemed very important that he tell Owen that. Explain his side of things. He rose, leaving the coffee half drunk, and went to his car. He started the engine and began his journey to Agay.

On the drive he rehearsed his small speech, convincing himself that this was not a strange thing to do, not overly intimate. He even managed to keep his conviction when confronted with the *patron* of the cafe, who pointed him in the direction of Owen's rooms. But when he reached the door at the top of the narrow flight of stairs, he faltered, unsure. What was he doing here at seven o'clock in the morning, coming to the rooms of a man who was barely a friend, to answer a question that hadn't even been asked during a drunken party?

He tried to think of his speech, the importance of it all, but it seemed mad now. He stood in front of the beaten wooden door. Then he reached into his pocket for the red fountain pen that had belonged to Fred. He took out one of his calling cards. He would write a note, something casual, in case the *patron* told Owen he'd come by. Then he would leave.

He braced the card against the wall and unscrewed the cap. But his hand was shaking and he dropped the card, which fluttered down the stairs, and then the pen, which rolled against the door. He bent down to retrieve it, but banged his head against the knob. He heard footsteps and knew there wasn't enough time to make an escape.

The door opened and Owen stood there, bare-chested, a yellow coverlet wrapped around his waist.

"Gerald?" He looked confused.

"Hello," Gerald said. "I was just passing by."

Owen nodded.

"I'm sorry. I was just going to leave a note. The *patron* said you weren't up yet."

"No," he said. "It's all right."

Gerald felt an insane kind of relief, joy even.

"Why don't you wait for me downstairs? We can have a coffee. I'll just . . ." Owen looked down at the coverlet. Then he looked over his shoulder.

It was only then that Gerald saw him: the young man from the party whose name he didn't know, naked, asleep, tangled amid the sheets of Owen's bed. He looked back at Owen, but he held Gerald's gaze without flinching.

"I'm sorry . . ." Gerald began. Unable to say anything else, he shook his head and retreated towards the stairs. "I shouldn't have . . . I'm sorry."

He fled, but the image wouldn't leave him. The white cotton curtains sucked through the open window above the bed, the safety razor and box of Three Stars Safety Matches on the bedside table, the young man's smooth body curved like a seashell. And in the foreground of the tableau, Owen, half naked, standing there. Owen.

*   *   *

When Zelda awoke at six p.m., the villa was quiet. She checked Scott's study but it was empty. She rifled through his papers a bit, looking at the handwritten notes, picking up a list of ideas for a title: *The High-Bouncing Lover? Trimalchio? Trimalchio in West Egg? Goldhatted Gatsby?*

She found a slumbering pen, uncapped it and wrote beneath these: *The Great Gatsby*.

Then she took a piece of Scott's correspondence paper and wrote:

> Dear Sara and Dow-Dow,
>> Thank you for the most wonderful party ever.
>>> We must do it again soon.
>>>> Love,
>>>>> Zelda and Scott

1925

Sara was sitting at the small table in Honoria's playhouse, listening to the ticking of the timer and watching the concentration on her daughter's face. In the ten minutes since they'd put the Barney biscuits in to bake, Honoria had tried countless times to open the door of the miniature wood-burning oven to check their progress. Each time, Sara had stayed her hand.

"They'll fall if you open it too soon," she'd explained. "Wait for the timer."

Still, despite having to repeat herself, she took an exquisite pleasure in Honoria's efforts at patience, her inability to delay gratification.

Sara had given Honoria *A Little Cook Book for a Little Girl* at Christmas, and they'd spent the whole summer trying out the recipes in the playhouse that she and Gerald had built for her on the grounds.

The work on the house had finally been completed at the beginning of June and they'd moved in immediately. As the weeks, then months passed, life had taken on its own routine at Villa America. Mornings began early, with the sound of Amilcar, the farmer they'd hired to deal with the livestock and the cash-crops, swearing at the cows, which seemed to delight in kicking him while being milked.

They would all breakfast together, then Gerald would go to his studio to paint, assisted by Vladimir, while the children had lessons with their governess. For her part, Sara would plan meals with their maid and cook, Tintine, arrange the flowers brought in by the gardener and give instructions to the chauffeur for errands, or go with him herself if the shopping list was complicated.

Sometime before noon, Gerald would finish his work and round them all up with the call: "Come on, children. To the beach." And they would set off with all their accoutrements.

After a swim and hors d'oeuvres, it would be time to go home for lunch on the terrace, under the silvery linden tree, the dry sound of cicadas filling the air. Gerald had found a collection of iron bistro tables and chairs and painted them in silver radiator wash, giving their al fresco dining area the look of an elegant stage set.

Afterwards, nap time for the children, as well as for the adults. Then in the late afternoon, when the heat of the day had passed, they would drive to the Hôtel du Cap to swim off Eden Roc.

The only thing that marred Sara's pleasure was a growing anxiety over Gerald. He hadn't really been himself; he'd been impatient with her, with the children. And his painting seemed to be giving him no pleasure, either. There were many times he'd emerged from his studio more frustrated than he'd gone in.

She couldn't pinpoint exactly when this dark mood had begun to descend, but she'd felt it in Paris over the winter, and into the spring. She'd hoped the sunshine of Cap d'Antibes would help lift it, but nothing seemed to have changed.

They had a round of guests coming their way this week, to stay in the Bastide, the little stable they'd converted into a guesthouse: Monty Woolley, a friend of Gerald and Cole's from Yale, followed by Esther, Dos, and Fred's widow,

Noel, who were stopping together on their way back from Pamplona. And, to top it all off, Hoytie, who'd invited herself down out of sheer curiosity about the new house.

It would either be truly gay or an absolute disaster. But she hoped it might be a distraction for Gerald, might bring him back to them a little.

The timer went off and Honoria leapt out of her chair, reaching for the oven door.

"Careful," Sara said, taking a dishcloth and pulling out the muffin pan.

Honoria let out a little gasp, marveling at her first, very-own biscuits.

"We should wait until they cool down a bit," Sara said, but one look at her daughter's face told her this was futile, so she gently removed them and placed the biscuits on a china plate from the shelf.

Honoria took one and then quickly dropped it. "Hot," she said, smiling up at Sara.

"Shall we put some butter on them?"

"Yes, please," Honoria said, but wanted to do it herself.

She sat watching her daughter munching away. Sara felt that they were finally home, in the real sense of the word, and the ebb and flow of people, of their life, was as natural and irrelevant as the tide.

❊ ❊ ❊

Gerald was in his studio working on *Razor*, Vladimir over by the workbench mixing a new batch of red. He had planned on finishing the painting that spring, to show at the Salon des Indépendants. But it had kept nagging at him that something wasn't quite right, and he'd pulled it from the exhibition. He'd been retouching it ever since. This morning it had come to him that the shade of red was too orange. It should be more the color of blood.

He could hear the Russian sighing in the corner. He was tired of this, Gerald knew. In fact, Vladimir had hinted last week that perhaps Gerald should move on to something else, throwing him into a cold rage, which he later regretted.

He didn't understand what was wrong with the damn canvas. *Watch*, which he'd started around the same time, hadn't been a struggle, and that piece had been much more intricate.

Maybe it was that *Watch* grew naturally, organically, from his experience. When they'd returned to Paris in the autumn, it had seemed like an eternity before he would see the Riviera again, and he'd found himself constantly checking the gold pocket watch Sara had given him as an engagement present. As if it kept time in months instead of minutes and hours.

He'd become fascinated by the moving parts. He'd been reminded of his father's railroad standard, which Patrick Murphy had also checked constantly when Gerald was a boy. His father had explained, loftily, that his was a railroad watch, and therefore had been certified by a railroad company as to its precision, down to the second. Just one more way, Gerald thought ruefully, that his father asserted his superiority over everyone else: his timeliness.

So, in his studio on the rue Froidevaux, gray, flat light streaming in, he'd sketched the painting. Much of it was occupied by the inner mechanism, deconstructing the movement into parts: the winding wheel, the crown wheel, the jewels, the regulator, the barrel bridge, the hairspring. But also the case and the crown, and half-moon slivers of the face.

Then he and Vladimir had mixed the colors, echoing the same winter light he was working in, highlighted with golds and honey-browns, the shades of his floorboards. He'd felt satiated by this nitpicky work, its ordered chaos, its almost monochromatic neatness.

But *Razor* was another matter.

Gerald walked over to the workbench and surveyed the color Vladimir was mixing.

"Too brown," he said.

Vladimir looked at him and sighed again, but nodded.

Gerald returned to the large H-frame easel. "Leave it," he said irritably. "I need to do some more sketches. We'll start again tomorrow."

Vladimir, who'd clearly had more than enough already, walked out, stretching his arms into the sunshine outside the studio.

Gerald pulled up a stool and sat down in front of the canvas.

There was a peace in acceptance, he'd been telling himself all summer, but he'd found his temper at times was worse than ever. The Black Service. He feared it and this made him even more angry. At times, the routine of their life here smoothed out his edges, and he felt a sort of beneficence towards his friends, towards his children. But even then it was like he was outside it, looking in.

He'd spoken of it with Scott.

"There are times," Scott had said one afternoon at La Garoupe, "where the pleasure in the writing—in my own, but also that of people I admire—is enough. Really, I feel like that's enough. But then I think: my God, all this work, all the control it requires, and no one's understood what I've been trying to do. Am I a failure?"

Gerald knew that the reception and sales of *Gatsby*

were breaking Scott's heart. Many critics had been glib or even unkind, and Scribner's had informed him that they didn't expect the figures to come even close to *This Side of Paradise* or *The Beautiful and the Damned*.

"I don't know. Maybe work is just one long process of hiding one's deficiencies," Gerald said. "Sometimes, it's as if I don't even understand my own work. As if I'm completely lost in some tunnel, not knowing which way to turn. Which path to take, or how I'm ever going to get out."

"The darkness," Scott said, shaking his head. "And all you can do is keep running so that it doesn't eat you alive."

"The darkness," Gerald said.

They'd sat there squinting into the sun, each thinking their private thoughts.

None of them had ever spoken of Zelda's overdose after that morning, not once. It was a closed subject. The four of them had continued to see each other all through the fall and winter in Paris, and it had been business as usual: grand, playful evenings mixed in with mawkish and sophomoric displays that left both him and Sara irritated.

This summer, however, Scott seemed more introspective than anything else. Dreamy almost. More like Zelda, actually.

One evening last week, when the Fitzgeralds had arrived for dinner at Villa America, Scott had beckoned the children over and taken Honoria onto his lap.

"Reach into my pocket," he'd told her.

Gerald watched as she put her little brown hand in his suit pocket and emerged with two lead soldiers: one painted red and gray, and one painted blue and black. Scott took them from her and held them up for Baoth and Patrick to see as well.

"I have something terrible to tell you that concerns these

soldiers," Scott had said conspiratorially. "There is a princess locked in a castle by an evil witch, and guarded by a fierce dragon."

Three pairs of very wide eyes looked back at Scott. Gerald smiled. He felt Sara's arm go around him.

"And one of these soldiers is a secret prince," he said. "But the other is the head of the witch's evil army."

Baoth nodded, as if this made complete sense to anyone with a brain.

"Now," Scott said, "Scottie is having a party, and at this party . . ." He stopped. "Wait, I've forgotten if you Murphys like parties."

"We do," Honoria said breathlessly.

Baoth laid a hand on Scott's leg and pinched him lightly.

"Oh, I see. Oh, right," Scott said. "Well, at this party there is to be a battle royale, where the secret prince will attempt to rescue the beautiful princess. Would you like to come and see it?"

"Now?" Baoth asked.

"No, not now." Scott laughed. "Tomorrow."

They'd gone the next day of course, the children nearly hysterical with anticipation. Scottie, almost four now with beautiful plump arms, had led the way out to the Fitzgeralds' garden, where they found an elaborate papier mâché castle, all turrets and towers.

"I made that," Zelda had whispered to Gerald and Sara. "Don't the stones look real?"

"Oh Zelda, very," Sara had said.

Around the perimeter of the castle, rubber duckies floated placidly on a small moat that had been dug and filled with water. A foot away stood two armies of lead soldiers, facing each other, ready for combat. And next to all this was Scott, his hands clasped behind his back.

"Look," Honoria said, pointing to a doll with flowing blond hair standing at one of the windows in the tower. "The beautiful princess."

"Yes," Scott said sadly. "She is in great distress. The prince must defeat the evil army to rescue her. Which one do you think is the evil army?"

Baoth marched over, his stolid little body mimicking Scott's stance, hands behind his back. "The blue and black one," he said. "And that fellow," he said, pointing to the gray and red figure Scott had brought to dinner, "he's the secret prince."

"Correct," Scott said. "Well spotted. But that's not all. There is also a dragon that must be vanquished." From behind his back, Scott produced a small wooden cage. The children rushed towards him and peered inside.

"A beetle," Baoth said joyfully. "It's a beetle, Dow-Dow. That's the dragon."

"Ah," Gerald said, nodding.

Scott put the tiny cage in front of the castle and began to narrate the battle, moving the soldiers hither and thither, enlisting the children to help, until finally the gray and red army were able to rush the gates. As Scott had the secret prince open the wooden cage, Zelda cracked two rocks together to simulate the breaking of the lock. The children jumped at the noise.

The beetle, clearly ready to escape, moved in the direction of the secret prince.

"Now," said Scott, "we'll just turn him over on his back, which makes beetles helpless, you know." He flipped the beetle, whose legs wiggled in the air. "Now, the prince can rescue the princess."

While the four children were busy marching the prince

up the side of the tower, arguing over *how* exactly the princess was to be extracted and *where* exactly the evil witch was lurking, Gerald watched Scott.

With a gentleness that he would never forget, and which continued to pain him long afterwards, he saw Scott ever so carefully turn the beetle back over and, cradling it in his palm, place it tenderly under a mound of lavender.

*   *   *

Monty Woolley was having a grand time. "Honk the horn," he instructed the Murphys' chauffeur as they drove through the gates of Villa America.

The chauffeur, whose name he'd immediately forgotten at the train station, gave him a weary look, but obliged.

"Again, if you please," Monty said, only for the thrill of annoying the man.

On the second sounding, Sara streamed out of the house, wearing some sort of gorgeous creation that would have looked well on Madame Butterfly, all silk and delicate printed flowers, with wide, bell-like sleeves.

"Ah, my beautiful Sara, do you come to us from the Far East?"

He smelled her nutty perfume and she wrapped her arms around him.

"Oh, you don't know how glad we are that you're here. We've been desperate for you," she said. Her tan face and lovely almond eyes looked up at him. "Gerald in particular," she said, taking his arm and walking him towards the house. "I think he needs a little cheering up."

"Your wish is my command," Monty said. "Where is my old school chum?"

"He's at Eden Roc with the children. They'll be back soon. Definitely before cocktail hour."

"That's a relief. Now show me this house of yours. I am agog with anticipation."

He had to hand it to them, the house was like nothing else he'd seen in the South of France, or elsewhere really. The floor was all black waxed tile, the sitting room painted a stark white and the furniture covered in, alternately, black and white satin with flashes of steel. The fireplace had been tiled in mercury glass that glinted in the sun streaming through the row of French doors. Dotted around this rather austere and modern palette were flashes of bright color: huge arrangements of hot pink flowers trailing all the way to the floor, a small coral carved elephant on the corner of the mantel, a Provençal cloth draped over an armchair, blue and purple and green Venetian glassware on the bar.

On a side table, what looked like some kind of green lace was fanned out on a golden plate. Monty touched it gingerly.

"Parsley," Sara said, laughing. "Come with me to the Bastide, your very own little farmhouse."

"Oh, please don't put me in with the livestock. I promise I'm housebroken."

"Don't be an idiot," Sara said. "It's lovely. In fact, we're a little too proud of it, I'm afraid."

"Oh, well, in that case."

º

After he'd bathed and changed in the lovely room that Sara had filled with branches of eucalyptus, Monty made his way back to the main house, his gifts under his arm. It was very early evening and he could hear birdsong over the terraced garden.

He hadn't liked the sound of Gerald's mood, as Sara had

described it. But part of him wasn't surprised. How long could someone go on living in denial of some basic facts of one's own personality, even if one was doing the denying in paradise? He had a suspicion that this was at the root of Gerald and Cole's falling out, although neither had spoken to him on the subject. Linda, of course, had her own theories, but he was less interested in those.

Perhaps, though, Gerald wasn't in denial, and *that* was the reason for their disagreement, Monty thought to himself. Perhaps some young man was at the heart of it all. Either way, his two old friends weren't talking and Gerald was apparently in a low place. And he intended to do a little investigating while he was here.

As he skipped up the flight of steps towards the terrace, he could hear Gerald's voice through the open doors, saying something in French to someone offstage. He crossed through into the sitting room, where he found his friend standing at the bar, in what appeared to be deep concentration.

"There you are," Monty said.

Gerald turned and smiled at him, a shaker in his hand. "I'm sorry," he said. "I would have come down to say hello, but we had a bit of a situation with *les enfants*. Baoth, I'm afraid, won't be able to greet you tonight. He's had a spanking and been sent to his room. Honoria, though, is thrilled to see you."

"Blast the children," Monty said. "What have we got to drink?"

"The Villa America Special," Gerald said, returning to his project.

Monty sat on the sofa, placing his parcels next to him. "Don't you have a third?" He lit a cigarette.

"A third?"

"A third child."

"Patrick, you know that. He's been put to bed," Gerald said, his back still to him.

"Well, I guess the presents for the boys will have to wait until tomorrow." Monty pulled a pink glass ashtray closer to him. "So, what projects do you have on the go? Still duking it out with that painting?"

"Yes. But I don't really want to talk about that," Gerald said. A little waspishly, Monty thought.

Gerald brought over two long-stemmed glasses on a tray, before sitting down in an armchair. "The more exciting news is that Vladimir and I are building a boat. Down in Marseille. Or, well, he's designed her and we're having her built."

"A boat? I didn't know you sailed," Monty said, eyeing him.

"I'm going to learn," Gerald said. "And I've bought a motorcycle."

"I think I saw the beast on the driveway," Monty said, taking a sip of the drink. "Delicious. What's in this concoction?"

"Just the juices of a few flowers," Gerald said, smiling over the rim.

"So," Monty said. "You're building a boat, learning to sail, riding a motorcycle. Quite a list. Whatever is it that you're trying to distract yourself from?"

"What is that supposed to mean?"

Before Monty could answer, Sara swept in.

"Monty," she said with mock alarm. "Didn't Gerald tell you? We absolutely do not dress for dinner when we're *en famille.*"

Monty looked down at his evening clothes. "Ah," he said, winking at her. "But I have a surprise. And I wouldn't want the two of you to feel underdressed. But we'll get to that soon enough."

Sara clapped her hands.

"Now," he said, "where's the child who's not asleep and not in trouble?"

Sara walked towards the hall, calling up: "Honoria, come down and say hello to Mr. Woolley."

Monty could hear a thudding noise from somewhere in the interior of the house, and then a few moments later the Murphys' daughter appeared, cheeks pink, clearly fresh from a bath.

"Hello," she said, a bit shyly.

"Now," Monty said, "what have I got for you?" He pulled out a thin parcel and handed it to the seven-year-old.

She tore the brown paper off to reveal the record, reading out the words on the cover: "Jelly Roll Morton."

"You can practice your Charleston to that," he said. "But I'll want a performance at some date in the future."

"Thank you, Mr. Woolley."

"Monty," he said, but she wasn't looking at him; all her attention was on the record. He returned to the pile of parcels next to him. "Now, what else do we have here? I think this one is for the beauteous Sara."

"Me?" she said, putting her hand to her heart, before taking the package. She carefully undid the paper, pulling out a silk wrapper, the color of a peach peony, with a long slit from the collar all the way down the back to the waist.

"This, actually, is from your devoted husband. I'm just the messenger."

"It's for the beach. I sent the design to your dressmaker," Gerald said. "The slit is so that you can sun your pearls, while keeping your shoulders covered."

"Oh," Sara said. "I love it." She slid it on over her dress and twirled.

Honoria held a bit of the hem between her fingers, rubbing it.

"And this," Monty said, "is for you, old chum." He handed Gerald two bulky packages.

Gerald opened them. "Dinner clothes?"

He shrugged. "Again, just the messenger. Your wife had them made up and I retrieved them from your tailor in Paris."

"I know you said you didn't want any down here," Sara said, smiling at Gerald. "But sometimes dressing up can be ever so cheering. And I thought you needed a little cheering, darling."

"The amount of toing and froing for Murphy clothing . . ." Monty said, "I felt like I was in 'Gift of the Magi.'"

"What's 'Gift of the Magi'?" Honoria asked, watching her mother smiling at her father.

"It's a story about a husband and wife who sell their most precious possessions to buy each other gifts," Sara said.

"Why?"

"Because they have no money."

"Why don't they have any money, Mother?"

"They just don't. But they don't mind in the end because they realize that their love is the real gift." Sara sat down on Gerald's lap and kissed his cheek.

"Why?" Honoria said.

"Well . . ." Sara said, throwing her hands up.

"Because O. Henry said so," Monty said. "And because he was a puritanical blighter."

"Who's O. Henry?"

"Goodness, we're literal this evening," Sara said. "All

right, Honoria. Give Dow-Dow a kiss good night. Then up to bed and Mamzelle will read you a story."

"But not Baoth," the girl said. She turned to Monty. "He's been naughty."

"No," Sara sighed, "not Baoth."

Honoria went over to her father, leaning across the arm of the chair and kissing his cheek. "*Bonne nuit*, Dow-Dow."

"Good night, Daughter," Gerald said, and gave her bottom a little shove away.

When she was gone, Sara turned to Gerald: "You go put on your dinner clothes, and I'll wear my wrap and we'll really dine in style."

"I'll man the cocktails," Monty said.

Gerald rose and gathered up his dinner clothes. On his way out, he put his hand on Monty's shoulder. "I am very glad you're here, you know," he said.

Dinner was a real Murphy affair, plenty of gin fizz and fresh food from their garden—some chicken with olives, which Gerald told him came from their own trees.

Sara wore a bathing suit and pearls, covered by her new silk wrapper, the peach glow reflected onto her face in the dimming light. She rested one bare foot on her husband's knee.

Gerald, meanwhile, was all solicitation about whether he had enough to drink, and had he heard this record of rare Negro spirituals, and how was his job going at the Yale drama department.

"So, I'm sure Gerald told you in his letter," Sara said. "But the hordes are descending soon. Hoytie and Esther and Noel and Lord-knows-who-else. We're going to have a real Dinner-Flowers-Gala on Friday."

"I did hear," Monty said. "Unfortunately, I won't be able

to join in the fete. I have to get on to Venice tomorrow. Night train. I promised Cole."

"No." Sara swatted him with her napkin.

"He's very low. Some Russian poet. You might know him. Boris Koch-something?" Monty said. "Dances in the Ballets Russes."

"I don't," Sara said, turning to Gerald. "Do you?"

Gerald shook his head.

"Well, what's wrong with Boris Koch-something?" she asked.

"Doesn't return our friend's very amorous affections, it appears."

"Oh dear," Sara said.

"When's the last time you saw Cole?" Monty asked, studiously keeping his eyes on what was left of his chicken.

"We saw them in Paris, briefly, this spring," Sara said. "At a party."

"And the lovely Linda?"

Sara took a sip of her drink. "Oh yes, she was there."

"I was sorry to hear things are difficult for Cole," Gerald said. "Career-wise, I mean."

"Were you?" Monty asked, giving Gerald a mischievous smile. "Sorry, I mean?"

"He hasn't done anything *to* me," Gerald said, throwing up his hands. "We just . . . something came between us. I don't know what exactly."

"Mmm," Monty said. "Well, there you are."

They sat in silence a moment, and Monty would have given his eye teeth to know what each of the two were thinking. Sara, he knew, would never tell. But Gerald . . . perhaps, if he could get him alone. "What time is it?" he asked.

Sara reached into Gerald's pocket and pulled out a gold pocket watch. "It's dreadfully early," she said. "Only seven-thirty. We would have been more elegant if we'd known you were only staying one night. Would you like to go to the casino? Or . . ."

"You know what I think?" Monty said. "I think Gerald and I should get on that motorcycle and take a spin in town, in all of our grandeur. Then we'll come back, pick you up and get that obliging chauffeur to take us to the casino."

"I'm not sure I'm up for all that," Gerald said.

"Yes, you are," Sara said. "You boys go and have a good time. I'll put on something a little less . . . something."

✧

Many of the shops in Antibes were already shuttered as they whizzed through the winding streets, but there were still plenty of locals out and about, whose consternation Monty enjoyed as he and Gerald flew by, tails flapping, top hats perched jauntily on their heads.

"A drink?" Monty yelled into Gerald's ear above the roar of the motor.

Gerald nodded and in a few more turns pulled the motorcycle up to a small cafe overlooking the old port. They both dismounted and took a table in front of the small crowd sipping aperitifs and ogling the machine.

"Well if that doesn't get their attention I don't know what will," Gerald said, a little grumpily.

But Monty didn't care about the motorcycle now. "I know what's gotten my attention," he said, nudging Gerald.

To their left, sitting by himself at one of the tables on the edge of the terrace, was a tanned, blond man, perhaps ten years his junior. A lovely, well-built specimen, the kind he saw coming off the football fields at Yale, fresh and strong and . . .

"Oh," Gerald said.

Was his friend's face coloring?

"I know him."

"American?" He looked at Gerald. "Well, do introduce us."

Monty watched him get up and approach the younger man. He couldn't hear what they were saying to each other, but after a few seconds the man rose and followed Gerald back to their table.

"Monty Woolley, Owen Chambers."

"Hello," Monty said. "Won't you join us for a drink?"

"Thanks," Owen said, and Monty watched as he eased himself into one of the small cafe chairs.

"So how do you two know each other?"

He watched the two men look at each other, seemingly waiting to see what the other would say, and that's when it hit him. He almost laughed. He didn't need to interrogate Gerald, it was all too clear. This man, this Owen, was Gerald's Boris Koch-something.

"You know what, Owen Chambers, you should join us for dinner on Friday," Monty said, smiling his most disarming smile and ignoring the look on Gerald's face.

After they'd parked the motorcycle back in the driveway of Villa America, Gerald turned to him and said tightly, "You shouldn't have done that. Sara's very particular about numbers."

"Don't be such an old fusspot," Monty said. "He'll make a charming addition. You can thank me later."

Then he went into the house, calling out to Sara: "I've found another guest for your Dinner-Flowers-Gala: an Owen Chambers?"

Sara came into the hallway. "Oh, you met Owen. We haven't seen much of him this summer. How is he?"

"Very nice," Monty said.

"And he's coming?"

"He said he would."

"Don't you arrange everything so well," and she kissed him on the cheek.

"I'm going to bed," Gerald said. "You two can go to the casino."

º

The next morning, Gerald woke with a start. Something was wrong. Only when he had been awake for five whole minutes did he realize what it was. Owen, the dinner invitation.

Sara had already risen and he looked at his watch. It was eight o'clock. She must have let him sleep in. He dressed and went down to the terrace, where breakfast was already in full swing.

Sara was expounding her theories on fresh foods and germs, while Monty sat there nodding.

"You have to wash the children's coins, they carry germs," Sara said. "And on trains, gloves are a necessity. Also, I put disinfected sheets around the compartment." She took a sip of her coffee. "I believe in fresh milk, it's so important. That's why we have the cows."

"*Basta, Violetta*," Baoth, his mouth full of cereal, yelled, doing his imitation of Amilcar.

"Germs," Monty said, slicing into a melon. "You don't say."

"Good morning," Gerald said, primly, then hated himself for it.

"There you are," Sara said. "I hated to wake you. Your face was all mashed against the pillow."

"Well, now I won't have much time for work," he said, pulling out his chair loudly. "And I really do have to keep at it."

Sara poured him a cup of coffee. "Don't forget that Monsieur Trasse is coming at nine. The barber," she said, turning to Monty.

Monty rubbed his beard. "I could use a little attention from Monsieur Trasse myself."

Gerald would have liked to pull that pointy beard right off his face.

"Why is your beard so red?" Baoth asked.

"Because I drink the blood of small children," Monty said, making crazy hands.

"And adults," Gerald said. "They call him the blood-sucker."

"Well, well," Monty said. "Looks like someone got up on the wrong side of the bed."

Gerald could feel Sara's eyes on him, but avoided her gaze.

"All right, children," Sara said. "Time for lessons. Don't keep Mamzelle waiting." She rose. "I'm going, too."

"To putter," he said. "She's a great one for puttering, my wife." He said this last to no one in particular.

"Yes, to putter, Gerald." She gave him a look. "Also called chores."

Gerald drank his coffee, not looking at Monty. He thought about Owen, about seeing him the night before. He felt his face go hot, thinking of himself, all dressed in his dinner clothes, and that foolish top hat. He thought about Monty's theatrical desire, and about his own . . . what? He thought about the morning, almost a year ago now, in Owen's rooms, the body in the bed behind him.

He'd meticulously avoided Owen this summer, or meticulously tried to, sending Sara alone on any errands to the airfield for things she wanted, and making excuses to leave any place he turned up.

If he interrogated himself on this subject, the only con-
clusion he'd come to was that in some way, somehow, he felt
Owen had made a fool out of him. But when he got to the
part where he asked himself *why* he felt that, his mind
would wander, and he couldn't answer.

The work, their life—the realization of all that he and
Sara had dreamed of, had talked of, had planned for during
their courtship—that was everything. That was all that mat-
tered. That was what he told himself.

"I think I'll go for a stroll before your barber arrives,"
Monty said, wiping his lips carefully with his napkin. "Call
me when he's ready for me."

Gerald watched his friend's back as he retreated down
the stairs into the garden. He sat there awhile, being as still
as he could be. Finally, he stood. With one violent movement, he kicked over his chair. He looked at it, and then just
walked away.

It was Sara, not Gerald, who called him when the barber
arrived. From the bottom of the garden, Monty could see
her, leaning out of one of the second-storey windows,
framed by the yellow shutters, waving a handkerchief, with
comic distress.

He made his way back to the house, still pondering
Gerald's mood. Of course, he hadn't intended to hurt Gerald's sense of propriety, but the man was being a dunce. He
himself knew what it was to hide; they all did. A few giddy
postwar years weren't going to change that.

The line between public and private was still clearly
delineated, at least for most of the people he knew, the
ones who lived in the real world, and not in some garret in
Paris or cabaret in Berlin. But that was the point of having

friends. And more importantly, one shouldn't hide from oneself. Monty sighed. Perhaps, though, he had been a little too cavalier. More sensitivity might be required.

He found them on the terrace, the barber setting up his tools neatly on a tray. When the Frenchman saw him he clapped his hands in approval.

"*Une vraie barbe,*" he said.

Monty smiled. "*D'abord, Monsieur Murphy. Après, la vraie barbe.*"

The barber nodded, and opened a bottle of some kind of lotion, which he began applying in a circular motion to Gerald's head.

"What is that strange elixir?" Monty asked.

"I'm going bald," Gerald said tersely. "It's supposed to help."

"Look," Monty said, settling himself into one of the chairs. "Does he speak English?"

"Not really," Gerald said. "But that doesn't give you license to say whatever idiocies you have in your head."

"My God, you could join my graduate dramatics," Monty said. When Gerald didn't answer, he continued: "It's probably none of my business . . ."

"It's not your business."

". . . but I'm going to say it anyway. There are many ways to live one's life, Gerald. It doesn't have to be one thing or the other. You know how much I love Sara. I adore that woman. And I understand what you have here . . . but you're also allowed to have something for yourself. Not like Cole, perhaps, that hasn't exactly been a recipe for happiness," he conceded. "But there may be a way without hurting anyone else."

Gerald looked at him with no anger, but with no warmth either, it seemed. Then he said: "I care for you, I do. You're an old friend and I don't want to argue or hurt your feelings. But you don't know me, Monty. Don't presume to."

         ✿   ✿   ✿

There was a scene unfolding at the house. Sara didn't know if she was coming or going. Hoytie was upstairs packing noisily, and apparently breaking things. The children, who'd been terrors all day, had been sequestered in their rooms. Dos and Noel and Esther had taken refuge at the Bastide. The cook was in the kitchen panicking about the changing numbers for a dinner party that was supposed to happen in less than an hour. And God knew where Gerald was.

The day had started off in a perfectly lovely fashion, and the afternoon at La Garoupe had been one of the best she could remember from the summer. They'd had a Far East costume party on the beach with their houseguests, along with Zelda and Scott, who'd been on their best behavior, and the Picassos had come down, and the Barrys had been there.

Admittedly Hoytie, who'd arrived that morning by train, hadn't wanted to wear a bathing costume or a Far East costume, and had sat superciliously under an umbrella on an impossibly high mound of cushions. She'd only spoken when spoken to, except for muttering occasionally to no one in particular: "Sara did always like the beach. Heavens knows why." And she'd refused to take the photo of them all in their outfits in the canoe.

But other than that, it had been such fun—even Gerald's black mood seemed to have lifted just a little—and Sara had been looking forward to the dinner party that evening. That is, until they'd returned home, and Hoytie had cornered her in the upstairs library.

"This crowd of yours," her sister had begun. "Well, I'm not sure really why you bother. But that's neither here nor there. I have some very good people—whom I know intimately—staying in Cannes. And I've invited them to come stay here at Villa America . . ." She stopped, looking around at the room, as if it were all so impossibly preposterous. "Well, to come to dine and then stay on."

"Hoytie," Sara said, shocked. "How could you? Firstly, there's no room. Secondly, that's not your invitation to give. And finally, I will not have you turn my dinner party into one of your holocausts."

"Holocausts? Holocausts?" Her sister's face was turning beet red.

"When did you invite them anyway?" Sara stormed to the window, as if they might already be banging on her door.

"I just sent out your chauffeur with an invitation," her sister said, a look of smug satisfaction on her face. "The day at the beach convinced me your table needed a little finessing."

"Well, I'll have to send Vladimir after him, then," Sara said. "You know, you're more trouble than you're worth. Are you really so blind to other people's feelings?"

"Ha. That's the pot calling the kettle."

"What is that supposed to mean?"

"Oh, you've always been selfish. You and Olga. The only thing you care about is what's going on in the middle of your own little world. All this . . ." She spread her arms wide.

"Oh, really? My God, Hoytie, you're the most selfish person I know."

"You think you have it all figured, don't you?" Hoytie put her hands on her hips. "Well, you don't. You know, there's great curiosity in Paris about what Gerald's true *nature* may be. Not that you'd notice anything, of course."

"How dare you talk about my husband." Sara was absolutely seething now. "What about your little infatuation with Misia Sert? Although that may be too delicate a word for you to grasp. I believe *lovesick puppy* is the term I've heard used."

Hoytie slammed her palm against a side table. "She adores me."

"I hear she calls you *l'emmerdeuse*," Sara said triumphantly. "God knows what her husband calls you."

"I will not," Hoytie was shouting now, "stay in this backwater house one minute longer. If you won't do anything to keep up your station, I certainly won't let you bring me down with you."

And with that, her sister had stomped to the guest bedroom across the hall and Sara had stomped downstairs, where she found the children conducting their own Salon de Jeunesse on one of the white satin armchairs.

Now, after dispatching Vladimir after the chauffeur, upbraiding Mamzelle, and informing Tintine that she had to take the dinner numbers down, or perhaps bring them up if Hoytie's infernal guests arrived anyway, Sara stood in the hall shaking with anger.

She heard another crash from upstairs and rushed back up and into the guest room. Hoytie was tying up her small case, and the remnants of what had once been a lavender pitcher—one that Gerald had bought for her on his way to training camp in San Antonio—lay on the floor.

"How could you?" Sara asked, pointing to the broken china.

"Things, things," Hoytie said, lifting her case. "All you care about is things." She marched past Sara, who followed her down the stairs.

Hoytie swung the front door open. "I'm going back to Paris," she said. "You can send my trunk on later."

"There's no one here to drive you," Sara said sweetly.

"I'll walk," Hoytie screamed at her face.

"Fine," Sara said, slamming the door after her.

It took all her effort not to cry. There were other guests to think about and she had to dress for dinner.

She walked towards the stairs, past Tintine, who was standing in the doorway of the dining room.

"*La famille,*" Tintine said, shrugging her shoulders.

Sara nodded. "Yes, *la famille.*"

By the time she'd bathed and dressed, there was still no sign of Gerald. Sara sat down in a chair near the bed and tried to calm her nerves. It was rare that she became this shaken, and she knew it wasn't all about Hoytie. She *was* worried about Gerald. She'd hoped that Monty's visit would cheer him up, but they'd had some kind of quarrel. Gerald had said it was about Cole, but she didn't entirely believe him.

Every couple had a dance, Sara knew, one that had to be performed when times got tricky. Gerald didn't like to be confronted, and lately she'd been trying hard to ignore his increasing distance from her. It wasn't there all the time, but when it was, it was like a big hole opening in the earth, threatening to swallow them all up.

She knew things about Gerald that no one else did—although she was aware some people doubted this—and he was schooled in all her deficiencies. She believed, or had come to believe, that in a marriage you uncovered these hidden imperfections—maybe not all at once, maybe little by little—and then you had to make a choice: you could either see them as ugly, as betrayals, as sheer weakness, and gradually come to feel contempt for the person; or you could understand them as vulnerabilities, soft spots in the person you loved, which had to be protected from the outside world.

She'd chosen the latter. And she loved him more, and fully, because of it. And never, for one minute, in all the time they'd been married, had she doubted his love, his loyalty to her. But Gerald was unhappy and she knew it. And she wanted that to stop. The keel of their life depended on it.

❖

Gerald looked at his watch and realized he'd lost track of time. He didn't know how long he'd been standing in his studio, staring at the painting.

He'd also been hiding out from Hoytie, whose tactics of domination and subjugation exhausted him. Her performance on the beach had been enough to make him ask Sara if it was possible to disown siblings. But he couldn't leave Sara to deal with everything alone. Although he would have liked to. Especially the dinner party. He felt entirely too keyed up to think about that.

He would be polite to Owen, but that was all, he decided. He didn't want to draw attention to the situation, but nor did he want to encourage a repeat of this dinner invitation.

He walked back to the house, where he found Sara on the terrace fussing over the table settings.

"I'm late," he said, accusingly, as if it were her fault.

She looked up. "Where have you been? Hoytie's gone off in a fit. She's left."

"Well, thank God for that," Gerald said.

"Gerald . . . I don't think I can stand this much longer."

He heard the desperation in her voice and it stopped him cold. He went over and put his arms around her. "I'm sorry," he said. "What happened?"

"It was awful. She wanted me to invite some terrible friends of hers to stay and when I said no, she just . . . And you weren't here. You've not really been here at all."

"I'm sorry, Sal," he said, kissing her head. He pulled away from her, gesturing to the terrace. "And look how beautiful everything looks. Let me get dressed and I'll come down and help you."

Sara nodded and Gerald felt relieved. *This* he could do. Thank God, because there wasn't much else he felt he could do lately.

*   *   *

It was a strange kind of dinner party, Dos thought. The flaming row between the two sisters had left a kind of indelible mark on the festivities. Sara seemed tense, but like she was covering it up, and so did Gerald, although what that was all about, Dos couldn't say.

He and Noel and Esther were left to carry much of the conversation during the cocktail hour. Then Owen arrived. Dos was glad to see the American pilot again; he'd liked him when he'd met him at the party last year, and he gladly shook hands with him when Sara ushered Owen into the sitting room.

Still, he couldn't quite pin him down. He'd seen him go off with that young writer, Whit Clay, and had been surprised. He hadn't figured him like that. But then, that sort of thing seemed to be going on willy-nilly these days.

Before the war, he supposed he'd never really thought about it. There'd always been what his mother referred to as "neuters"—men who lived with their mothers, never married, and seemed to have an inordinate interest in stamp collecting—or the two spinsters, "best friends" who shared house and home and holidays. But the idea of young, vital men and lovely, wealthy women bed-hopping with each other, well, that was something else. He supposed they were outsiders, too, like so many interesting people, but frankly it disturbed him when it wasn't clear which side of the line someone fell on. Still, now that he knew about Owen, it was all right. He was a good fellow and didn't run his mouth.

"So how's the piloting business going?" Dos asked him at dinner.

"Busy," Owen said. "It's crowded down here now. Used to be only the winter season, but this summer's been pretty good."

"Still over in . . ." Dos snapped his fingers, trying to remember.

"Agay," Owen said. "Yes. But I'm thinking of expanding a bit, looking for some land of my own."

"What did your folks do?"

"Farmers," Owen said.

"Farmers," Dos said. "Bad time for it. What do you think of what's going on with Coolidge? He's making a lot of farmers pretty angry."

Owen shrugged. "All farmers are gamblers," he said. "Double down now and hope next year's better. Just the way they are."

"So it's the farmers' fault?" Dos found his indifference a little provoking.

"It's nobody's fault. It's bad choices. Like most things that go wrong."

"Yes," Dos said, "but so what, you throw them to the wolves? Compound it with negligent policies?"

Owen looked at him; he seemed a little surprised by Dos's vehemence. "Your family, are they farmers?"

"No," Dos said.

Owen nodded. "Well, I don't know that much about Mr. Coolidge's policies, but it's always been tough, farming, for most of the people I knew, anyway. It's the nature of the thing. But I think people have choices," he said.

"Some people," Dos said, "don't."

Owen was quiet; either he'd had enough of the debate or he was thinking, Dos couldn't tell which.

"Are they still at it? Your family?"

"No," Owen said. "They're dead now."

Noel, sitting on his right, turned to him. "Dos, are you expounding your political theories? He's been very political this year," she said to Owen. "His new book is coming out soon."

"Dos has always been political," Esther said from across the table. "He's one of those men that had his conscience shaped by the war, among other things. And now he's an optimistic revolutionary."

"I am not optimistic," Dos said.

Noel laughed. "I don't know. You called us all a lot of fake bohemians at Pamplona last year. And yet you went back. If that's not optimistic, I don't know what is."

"Not all of you," Dos said. "Just a select few."

"You all talk so much about Pamplona," Sara said. "It sounds wonderful."

"It's pretty bloody," Dos said. "And if you go with Hem, Gerald, he'll make you get face to face with a nasty bull."

"Yes," Sara said. "And when are we going to meet Ernest Hemingway? We read his story in the *Transatlantic Review* last year. It felt very . . . new, I suppose."

"He's definitely got something," Dos said.

"Something is right," Noel said, caustically.

Dos chuckled. He knew Noel liked Hem just fine, but

she made *him* nervous: a beautiful, tall, blond woman who had absolutely no interest in his macho antics. And this, in turn, made Noel feel superior. It was a good show watching the two of them together.

Noel rarely talked about Fred's death—all she would say was that she still loved him. She'd bought a place just outside Paris so that she could be near the cemetery where he was buried. But she spent a great deal of time with Esther these days, and there were rumblings from that quarter. She was apparently much admired by her sister-in-law's Sapphic circle.

"His book of short stories is very good," Esther said, lighting a cigarette and bending in on her knee, a favorite pose of hers when she was about to get going. "It's about childhood. Or the childhood of a time we've lost."

"Did you fight in the war, Owen?" Noel asked.

"I did."

"Do you feel that we've passed some age of innocence that can never be regained?" she asked, taking one of Esther's cigarettes. "That seems to be the working theory these days."

"It didn't feel very innocent to me before."

"No, it did not," Dos agreed. "That's a myth."

"I don't know," Gerald said. "I think we all have an inherent innocence inside of us."

"You *would* say that," Dos said.

"Gerald's a romantic," Esther said. "Look at this Garden of Eden he's created for himself."

"Maybe it *is* invented," Gerald conceded. "But can't something invented also be real?"

"I don't even know what that means," Dos said.

"I do," Owen said.

Dos looked at him, surprised.

"About the innocence, I mean. I don't think we're more or less innocent than before we all started killing each other. It was always part of our nature. But so is the other side. What are we supposed to be guilty of, anyway? I don't understand that."

"This from the man who believes in free will," Dos said.

Owen seemed to think this over. "Choices, even bad ones, don't make you less innocent. And maybe you're right: maybe some people don't have a choice."

Dos noticed that Owen was looking straight at Gerald, now.

"I'm not sure what we're talking about anymore," Dos said. "Am I drunk?"

"Gerald is talking about inventing your own reality, which you inhabit as fully as if it were naturally occurring," Esther said. "And Owen is talking about humanism."

"That doesn't help, Esther," Dos said, laughing.

"Speaking of one's nature," Noel said. "Have you heard what André Breton and that gang are up to? They've taken it upon themselves to hold a summit to discuss their feelings on homosexuality."

"And what are their propositions?" Sara asked, laughing.

"The surrealists have decided," Esther said, "that they are favorable to Sapphism, but that between men, such love is both morally and physically repugnant and they condemn it."

"I know some people who do more than just condemn it," Noel said, somberly.

"Jesus," Dos said, "this is taking quite a turn. I don't think I can keep up with all this big thinking." What he actually felt was damn uncomfortable.

"I agree," Sara said, throwing her napkin on the table like

a white flag. "Let's dance instead. Gerald, my darling, will you choose us a record?"

"With pleasure," Gerald said, but it took him a few moments before he seemed able to tear himself away.

They were all dancing to a Jelly Roll Morton—even Owen was doing a sort of shuffle—when Hoytie made her re-entrance.

She stood framed by the French doors leading out to the terrace and dropped her case noisily on the black tile. "Well I'm glad to see that my well-being hasn't been any cause for concern here," she said loudly.

Sara looked up from her dancing, obviously startled. "Hoytie," she said. "What . . . ?"

"It seems there are no trains back to Paris after five p.m.," she sniffed, looking down at her feet.

"Oh Hoytie," Sara said and started laughing. "Honestly." She held out her arms to her sister. "Come out here and join us."

"Come on, Hoytie," Dos said. "Don't stand on ceremony." She could be highly irritating, Sara's sister, but he had to admit she had comic value.

"I'm not dressed for dinner," Hoytie said.

"Oh, for heaven's sakes," Sara said. "I think we've had enough of that for one evening. Just kick off your shoes and come join the beneath-the-salts."

"Oh," Hoytie said, sighing like a world-weary traveler. "Oh, all right."

*

Owen picked up one of the hurricane lamps and made his way down the steps into the darkness of the garden. The beam from the lighthouse on the hill above swept at intervals over the grounds, lighting up the sea beyond, catching the tips of the waves rolling in.

No one seemed to have noticed that he'd taken himself off, or at least no one called out to question him. They were all dancing and drinking cocktails, and pulling Sara's sister around the terrace, in some mock punishment.

He walked down another flight of steps and was now well and truly away, the music coming to him only faintly on the breeze. He ran his hand over the tops of the plantings he passed, thinking about his farm, and how he used to know every stalk, every blade, kernel, bail, bug, burn and quickening. Dos's questions had brought it back. He didn't like to think about it or feel pity, or any of the things Dos seemed to want him to feel, because it hurt him, and now he felt a sadness, despite his enjoyment of the evening.

Owen hadn't been sure whether he should come to the dinner or not. He'd sensed that Gerald hadn't wanted that friend of his, Monty, to invite him. But when a card followed, signed by both Sara and Gerald, renewing the invitation, he'd decided it was all right.

Gerald had clearly been avoiding him this summer. He wasn't exactly sure why, but he guessed that it had something to do with Whit. Whit, who'd changed everything for Owen. The feel of skin beneath his hands, the lips on his lips, real desire, the kind that doesn't stop to see if something's wrong or right, that just *is*. Whit had given him his body back. He'd never thought about things in those terms before, but the experience had overwhelmed him, as if it had altered the chemistry in his brain.

They hadn't seen each other since Whit returned to Paris, although they'd exchanged letters. They were of the friendly sort, though; Owen didn't want anything more than that one moment.

It had, however, made him more conscious of other people like him. He began to be aware of signals that before hadn't appeared obvious to him, like music finally penetrating radio static.

Owen wandered over to the far edge of the garden, to a large shed standing under a maple tree. He held up the lantern to the small window and looked in. It was a studio: he could see jars of brushes and the large easel, a canvas leaning against it. He opened the door and walked inside.

Holding the light up to the painting, Owen saw the parts of it, as if one by one.

A large red fountain pen crossed with a safety razor, like a coat of arms. Then behind it a box of matches, painted yellow and red and black with three red stars in the center. All against a raised platform.

His mind clicked over as he looked at it. Gerald's red pen. The Three Stars Safety Matches, the ones Owen always carried instead of a lighter, ever since the war when he'd been told the three stars meant luck. The ones he always had on his nightstand, next to his razor. He thought back to that morning when Gerald had shown up unannounced, looking through his open door. He'd never known what Gerald had come to ask him, and all this time Owen had figured that Gerald had been disgusted by what he'd seen. But now, in his mind's eye, he could see Gerald's shyness, his embarrassment, then his shock, as if he'd been burnt.

"What are you doing in here?"

Owen turned, and in the light of the hurricane lamp, saw Gerald standing in the doorway. He turned back to the painting. He heard Gerald cross the floor towards him, and then they both stood looking at it.

"I haven't been able to get it right," Gerald said quietly. "I've tried so hard, but somehow I'm not capable."

It was that kind of moment, and Owen knew it. He recognized the feeling, the same one he used to get before making a dive on the front lines. His hands shook. He tried counting in his head. His hands kept shaking.

He handed Gerald the lamp. Then he said: "I have to go," and he walked out, before the momentum became too much.

*

Gerald caught up with Owen in the driveway. He seemed to be searching for his car keys, checking his pockets.

"Owen," he said.

Owen turned.

They were standing very close, and Gerald thought back to the time in the hangar, his thigh brushing against Owen's. And the way he'd felt with him in the plane. And the way he'd felt with him ever since he'd met him.

"It's just a painting," Gerald said. And for some reason he felt so sad.

Then from one moment to the next, Owen was kissing him, his tongue in his mouth, the feel of his stubble against his own shaven skin. And in that dizzying step from nothing to flesh, from before to after, Gerald knew he would never be able to say no again.

1926

Owen was having the dream again, the one he always had about being a blade of wheat, rooted, stuck, at the mercy of the sun and the rain. But this time when he woke, drenched in sweat, he found Gerald's hand in his.

He had to look at him for a while before he could believe that Gerald was really there, lying next to him. It had been nine months since that kiss—that kiss, the taste of saliva, salty like the taste of the sea in his mouth—had illuminated everything for him, had made him see what he'd been blind to: he was in love. And in love not only with a man who was married to a good woman, but a man so different from himself that it still rattled him when he thought about all the ways they weren't the same. And yet, he loved Gerald anyway. Who could say why this happened to anyone? How one chose or got chosen.

He looked at the slim hand resting in his own. They'd never spent a whole night together before, he'd never had the comfort of being unconscious next to someone he loved. But Gerald had fixed it; a trip to Paris had been cut short a day early. Just one night. Owen stared out of the window and could see it was still dark. He wished the morning would never come.

They drove in a cavalcade up to the Villa Paquita in Juan-les-Pins: Sara and Gerald in their car, Ada MacLeish in her own little Citroën, followed by Scott and Zelda. The sun was over the yardarm, meaning it was time to drink seriously, and they were on their way to cheer up Hadley Hemingway with "quarantine cocktails."

May was such a beautiful time of year on the Riviera, Sara thought, as they drove along the cliffs. Paris was still gray and damp, the mold practically seeping into one's bones, while here it was all warm days and cool nights. In the hills, the lavender was coming back to life and the olive trees had shed their old leaves, the young, darker ones burgeoning with sap.

Sara put her hand through her new short hair. She'd had it bobbed and she loved the feel of her fingers sliding through it, slipping out fast at the blunt ends. When Mrs. Pat, all of her theatrics still intact, had come to stay with them at Villa America, she'd remarked sadly: "Just think, all that tender weight gone." But Sara felt cleaner, sexier, happy to be rid of it.

She felt freer this spring than she had in so long. Perhaps it was because the house was finished, or the children were getting just that much older and less needy. Whatever it was, she felt a kind of boundlessness at forty-two that she'd never felt at twenty.

And now they had Ernest's arrival to look forward to. Hadley's visit hadn't panned out all that well, so far. She and Gerald had invited Hadley and their little boy, Bumby, to stay at Villa America while awaiting Ernest's return from Spain. But Bumby had come down with whooping cough. It had sent a jolt of terror through Sara, the danger in her own home, her own children at risk. Luckily, Scott and Zelda were leaving the Villa Paquita for a larger house, and gave it over to Hadley and her son as quarantine quarters.

She knew that Hadley thought her slightly hysterical for pushing them out, but Sara didn't set much store by Hadley's smarts. Anyway, it seemed Bumby was out of any real danger now, thank goodness, and their English doctor—*the best*, she and Gerald had assured Hadley—had said it would definitely be safe by the time Ernest arrived in Antibes.

In the meantime, the Hemingways' good friend Pauline Pfeiffer, who'd had whooping cough as a child, was coming down tomorrow to give Hadley some moral support. Until then, they just needed to keep Hadley's spirits up, and Sara had enlisted Ada and the Fitzgeralds to help her carry on a daily cocktail through the wrought-iron fence of the Juan-les-Pins villa.

When they arrived, they parked in a line on the other side of the road.

Ada slammed her car door, and blew out her cheeks. "Oh, I hate this thing," she said, cheerfully. "Only Archie knows how to drive it."

Sara loved Ada, loved her sunny face, and she had the happiest smile of anyone she knew. A singer with a clear voice, high and light, that reminded Sara of champagne. They'd been introduced to Archie and Ada in Paris a couple of years ago, through Don Stewart, and they'd all slowly become fast friends, as Sara liked to say. Archie, a poet, had started his professional life as a lawyer, a skill he was currently putting into practice in Persia, where he was doing something or other with the League of Nations' Opium Commission. Really, he'd told Gerald, it was a way to see the country.

"*I* love our car," Zelda said, laconically, and Sara had to laugh.

"Scott, do you have the shaker?" Gerald asked.

"Ada and I don't want cocktails," Sara said. "We brought lots of different wines to try. We're going to open every one and take just a few sips."

"That's right," Ada said. "We're going to be sinfully wasteful."

Zelda clapped, delighted.

Across the road, Sara could see that Hadley had already set up a chair and table inside the fence.

From the backseat, she retrieved the cuttings she'd brought along from the garden, while Gerald pulled out camping chairs for the ladies. Then they all traipsed over to the fence—near, but not too near—and set up shop.

Scott, who said *he* wasn't afraid of whooping cough, took a green glass bottle of wine and slid it through the fence to Hadley.

"It's German," Sara said, raising her voice a bit so Hadley would be sure to hear her. "Owen discovered it."

"Oh," Hadley said.

"How's Bumby?" Gerald asked.

"Much better, I think."

"Scott," Sara said, handing him a bunch from her pile of flowers and vines. "Take these and twine them through the fence. I'll direct you."

"Oh, may I have one of the peonies?" Zelda asked.

Sara selected a pale pink one and handed it to her. "It matches your belt."

Zelda pulled a bobby pin out of her handbag and fastened the flower to the top of her head. On anyone else it would have looked comic; on Zelda, it looked marvelous.

"No, Scott," Sara said when she saw him sticking the flowers through in hunks. "A little more delicacy, a little more artistry, please."

He looked quizzically at his display and then tried to pick some of them out.

"I think we should try this blue bottle first," Ada said, holding one out to Gerald.

"The color of your eyes," Gerald said.

"You always say the nicest things, Mr. Murphy," Ada said. "But wine will get you further than flattery with this crowd."

"Yes, my love, stop your bows and scrapes and pour us some wine," Sara said.

"I'm henpecked," Gerald said, turning to Scott. "Do you see how this is?"

"I'm the one who has to put posies in the fence like some schoolgirl," Scott cried, hysterically.

"If you were a schoolgirl, you'd be a very, very bad one," Zelda said. "But Dow-Dow would go to the top of the class. With Al Jolson."

"Quit it about Al Jolson," Scott said, and Sara detected a darkness running through his tone.

Throughout the merriment, Hadley sat quietly watching them. She must be going mad, all by herself. Sara liked Hadley all right, but for some reason she didn't feel the same about her as she felt about Ernest, who was so full of life and thoughts and sheer physicality. Hadley was a plain, handsome woman. A nice woman. And she wanted to love her, but she couldn't somehow. She neither seemed that bright nor that practical, and Sara couldn't help but wonder what she brought to the marriage. Then again, the mysteries of closed doors were unfathomable.

By the time they'd finished the cocktail hour, she and Ada had managed to taste at least four different bottles of wine, Zelda had drunk a bottle of champagne all by herself, and Scott and Gerald had been fairly competitive with their various cocktails. Hadley had sipped at the German wine, agreeing that it was very nice.

Sara emptied the remainders from the wine bottles and handed them to Scott.

"I think that fence still looks a little bare," she said. "Your flower arrangement leaves much to be desired. Let's see how you do with the bottles."

"Oh, with bottles I'm a master," Scott said. He gathered them up and stuck them through the scrolls and whorls in the wrought iron. Then he said: "Hadley, I also bequeath you my shaker," which he shoved in along with the flowers and the colored glass, winking in the crepuscular light.

It looked very gay, Sara thought. "I know it's awful," she said to Hadley. "But it won't be long now. And we'll send the driver up tomorrow with more provisions. Is there anything in particular you'd like? Or anything you think Pauline might need?"

"I think we could use a bit more soap," Hadley said.

"Oh good, you're using it. It's the best one for germs," Sara said. "It's made by monks in Castagniers."

"Any soap will do, really," Hadley demurred. "Don't go to any trouble."

"No," Gerald said. "Only monk soap will do. Sara will flagellate them if necessary. It's our duty to keep you and Bumby clean until Ernest arrives."

"Flagellate them, indeed," Sara said.

"I don't like monks," Zelda said.

"Get in the car," Scott said.

"Oh dear," Ada said. "I don't know how I'm going to get this thing back to the house."

Then they'd all gotten in, with the chairs and the glasses, doors slamming and engines starting. And they were off, waving behind them as they drove back to Villa America,

Sara wondering if everyone else felt as relieved as she did to be away from the locked gate, and the germs floating behind it.

* * *

It was love, the rip-roaring, ecstatic, rejoicing, fear-inducing, all-consuming kind. It was quiet only in that it was secret, and he was full with it and when they were alone together it all burst forth in streams of words and the joy of speaking them to someone.

And it was physical in a way he'd never known, or had been afraid to imagine. And God, that made him happy, too. When he saw Owen, maybe just in town, walking down the street, running errands, Gerald couldn't imagine anyone finer, and then he would remind himself: he's mine. And it made him dizzy.

Or Owen would walk into a room and they would look at each other and *know* what no one else knew, and it was grand and good and wonderful.

For almost a year now he'd felt drunk. It was as if he'd been imprisoned inside his own head, his own body, for thirty-eight years, and he'd only now just stumbled out into the light. That his hands and lips and all the sensitive parts of him were meant to be used like that, to *feel* like that: he hadn't known.

There were other thoughts that came with these: darker, sadder thoughts. About his wife, how he wished he could feel that with her, how he wished that there were no barriers in their bed, in their life. How he wished—how he hoped to God—that, at the very least, he was able to make *her* feel that way. That this wasn't a betrayal of her, of them, of their family, but instead an additional connection in his life. That her love for him wasn't wasted. But these thoughts he tried to push away.

His work was flourishing, his head full of ideas for new paintings. In the past year he'd painted *Doves*, which was for Sara, for her grace and beauty, *Laboratoire*, *Still Life with Flowers* and *Roulement à Billes*, a depiction of an eighteen-inch industrial ball-bearing that Owen had found for him in a disused German armaments factory. Gerald had had it mounted on a black pedestal so that it turned, and placed it on the large ebony piano in their Paris apartment. He loved running his hand over the smooth chrome.

He was currently at work on another piece, *Bibliothèque*, fragments of his father's library, that cold sanctuary he'd at once feared and venerated as a boy. Gerald's happiness was such that even that dark place, his father's shadow, could be turned into something beautiful.

Today he was driving over to La Fontonne, a small village on the eastern outskirts of Antibes, to see the land Owen had purchased. It had been used as a flying school by the Garbero brothers before the war and Owen had said the setup was perfect to expand his business.

Gerald felt awed by Owen's ability to do things for himself, and also a little unsettled by it. Owen was stronger than he was. Gerald knew this inherently. And he sometimes worried that this strength would engulf him, would impress its will upon him. Expose and ruin him. He'd lived so long with the fear of discovery that it had become a part of his nature.

But it was no match for the light and the heat that he experienced when he was close to this man whom he adored with every living cell in his body.

Following the directions he'd been given, Gerald pulled off the old Roman road, through what passed for a village— a *boulangerie*, a laundress and minuscule restaurant, Le Bol d'Or—and took the allée des Cigales. He drove down the small winding path until it finally opened up into a large cut field with two enormous weather-beaten hangars, one leaning precariously, and a dilapidated barn.

As he shut off the motor, he saw Owen emerging from the barn. He watched him move across the field. When he reached the car, Owen leaned over the door and Gerald could smell the plain soap he used rising off his skin in the warmth of the May sun.

"Welcome to my palace," Owen said.

"It's . . ."

"It's a shit-hole," Owen said. "But that's why it was cheap."

"It's going to be wonderful," Gerald said.

Owen straightened and opened the car door. "Come on," he said. "I'll give you the tour."

They kept their hands at their sides as they walked, but Gerald could hear the shift of Owen's cotton shirt as his body moved under it.

When they reached the barn, Owen opened the side door and Gerald saw, among the detritus, a camp bed, Owen's old battered desk and chair, and a small warmer for cooking and heating coffee.

"You cannot live here," Gerald said.

"I am living here," Owen said. "I can't afford the rooms and make a go of this, too. It's fine." He pulled the desk chair over for Gerald. "Sit down. Close your eyes."

Gerald did as he was told.

"At night," Owen said, "it's so dark and so quiet, you can hear insects rustling, grass growing. The crack of an egg hatching. It's like you're in the middle of nowhere."

Gerald, his eyes still closed, smiled.

"You can smell the wood, and the dust and the sea. There's a tree on the edge of the field, and you can see the stars through it. And no one knows you're here, or cares."

Gerald opened his eyes.

"I want you to come here," Owen said. "See for yourself."

"I can't spend the night."

"No," Owen said, looking away.

"Besides," Gerald said, "that camp bed isn't exactly made for two."

Owen nodded. "Sara wrote to me."

"Did she?"

"She wants a waffle iron." Owen smiled.

"She would," Gerald said.

"She read about it in a magazine. It's going to be the first waffle iron on the Riviera, apparently."

"That woman never ceases to amaze me," Gerald said. "She's very excited about Ernest Hemingway coming."

"She mentioned it."

"I, as it turns out, am less excited."

Owen smiled, slowly. "More tests of your manhood?"

Gerald stood up. "I know it's childish," he said, "and I hate myself for it, but I *want* to impress him."

Owen laughed openly now. "Jesus, G. You are ridiculous," he said.

"You haven't met him," Gerald said.

Owen shrugged. He sat down on the camp bed, a green tartan blanket hanging off the edge. "Come here," he said.

Gerald walked over. He found he was shaking. Still now, after almost a year, he was nervous with desire every time. "I can't stay long," he said.

"You can leave whenever you want."

"I don't want to leave."

"No," Owen said. "I don't want you to, either."

And he began undoing the buttons on Gerald's shirt.

* * *

Owen was loading the Fokker, when he heard the hum of an approaching motor. It was early morning, and he was expecting Eugène, the mechanic he'd hired away from the airbase in Fréjus. A good mechanic was as essential as a reliable engine, and Owen had been forced to promise a small share in the profits of the new business—if and when they came—in order to lure Eugène from his steady job.

But when he looked up, he saw it was Sara and Gerald's car: not the touring car the children called Iris, but the one driven by the chauffeur. He walked out of the hangar to greet it.

Sara stepped out of the back, her short hair a halo around her head. "Hello," she smiled.

"Hello," Owen said.

It was the first time she had come here, and he imagined Gerald giving her directions. He wasn't surprised to see her: he'd known she'd turn up sooner or later. And he was glad it was sooner. One of the current complications in his life was his attraction to Sara. It wasn't the physical, the chemical kind he had with Gerald. It was more like standing near a warm fire in a cold room. He felt drawn by her, connected. Yet it unsettled him slightly.

He lifted a tool kit and placed it under the pilot's seat.

"Are you off somewhere?" she asked, raising an eyebrow at him.

"Amsterdam," Owen said. "To pick up some paintings."

Sara looked into the hangar. "Is that it? The new one?"

Owen nodded. Everything was riding on that passenger plane and it made him nervous to talk about her. He'd bought her from a Czech speculator who'd lost his fortune in a mining scam. The cut-rate was the only way he'd been able to afford an enclosed passenger plane like this one, and even then he'd had to take a loan from the bank in Paris. He wasn't sure yet if it was good luck or bad that had brought him to her, but then again, he told himself, he didn't believe in luck anymore. She carried a much larger load, meaning fewer runs, and this way he could charter flights for holidays and such for all the rich Americans and Europeans flooding to the Riviera.

Owen followed behind Sara as she walked over to the plane.

"She's so lovely. Just one big, glorious wing," Sara said. "But you have to sit outside, while everyone else gets to sit inside."

"No frills for the pilot," he said. "I don't mind. I like being out in the air."

"Except when it rains, I'd imagine." She ran her hand over the lettering on the fuselage. *"Arcadia?"* she said, looking at him.

Owen kept his expression still. It had been Gerald's idea, the name, after some French painting he liked. It wasn't the sort of thing he would've chosen himself, but Gerald had gotten so excited, and he'd wanted to please him.

Owen had never been in love before, not like this, so he wasn't sure how it was supposed to go. Only that for people like them it had to be secret. He knew that.

For the past nine months, they'd had to carve out time,

snatched moments. When the Murphys were at Villa America, they met in his rooms above the cafe, hiding from the proprietor, making excuses for the numerous visits at odd hours. They'd also seen each other, all of them together, in Paris, and some afternoons had been spent, curtains drawn, in a hotel room off the boulevard Montparnasse. All stolen hours, and whispered declarations and cries into the darkness.

Owen wasn't an effusive man, so the secrecy didn't bother him that much. But the lying did. He had no idea how it was supposed to end, how it could come out right. Still, he told himself that even if Gerald wasn't married, it wasn't as if they'd be walking down the street hand in hand, or shouting it from the rooftops. They couldn't live together, not in any way he could see. So what did it matter?

"May I look inside?" Sara asked.

Owen opened the door of the plane and set up the small ladder so she could climb up. After looking around, Sara poked her head out: "The upholstery needs a little work. I could find something for you."

"I'm not that worried about the upholstery," Owen said, smiling.

"No, something this marvelous deserves good upholstery." She climbed down. "Anyway, I didn't come to harangue you. Ernest is coming back from Spain next week and Gerald and I want to throw him a party. I want it to be a champagne and caviar party," Sara said. She chewed her thumbnail. "Does that sound pretentious?"

"It sounds very fancy," Owen said.

"Mmm." She seemed to think about this. "Oh, I don't care, it will be good," she said finally. "So, I was hoping you could fly in some caviar from the Caspian Sea. It will be so romantic and funny and different."

"Sure," Owen said. "I could pick some up in Sofia. Tell me how much you want and I'll work out the costs and get back to you."

Sara kissed his cheek. "Thank you."

They started walking back out to the car and Sara stopped at the door.

"Gerald tells me you're camping in your barn."

"I am," Owen said.

"You know we've bought that small bit of land across the road from us. With a little converted barn? It's a sort of guesthouse, now. I was wondering if you might consider staying in it for a little while, to test it out. It would be a great favor to us. There are a few crops and it would be wonderful to get your expert opinion on it all."

"You have a farmer," Owen said.

"Yes, but Amilcar is so busy with everything else . . ." She trailed off. "It would make us all so happy. Gerald loves having you around and Vladimir would be thrilled. And the children. I know it's a lot to ask, but it would be such a great help."

"Thank you for the offer," Owen said. "But I'm fine here."

"Just think about it," she said, opening the door and getting into the car. "Oh, and you must come to the party for Ernest. I'll send along the details. It's going to be pretentious and horrible and disgusting, and we'll have a grand time."

"I'm sure it will be great," he said.

"Bon voyage," she said.

He watched her drive away. She was a riddle, he thought. What she knew, what she didn't know. How guilty he should feel. But he was tired of all that. He'd decided, when it became clear that it wasn't going to stop, that they couldn't or wouldn't stop, that life was too short to blame himself for the things in his nature that made him human. If he had a choice, which he did, this was his.

*   *   *

Ernest had arrived late in Juan-les-Pins and after being picked up by Pauline and Hadley at the station they'd headed over to Villa America. They arrived after dinner-time, but Sara served them a summer vegetable stew and they sat under the linden tree on the terrace eating and drinking a good bottle from the Murphys' cellar.

The car ride had been hell. All the feelings he'd been trying to scotch in Madrid came back twofold. He wanted Pauline, wanted to touch her; he felt guilty about Hadley; guilty about Bumby; and furious for being made to feel guilty. If Hadley would just either do more or do less, he might not despise her so much. But her sad acceptance made him feel spiteful.

So, arriving at Sara's house, with its fine things and peaceful quiet, and her good looks and sweet smell, had been a relief.

Gerald was prattling on, as he liked to do, and Ernest was ignoring it, listening instead to the nightingales in the garden.

"I'll never forget how kind you were to me in Schruns," Gerald said. "About the skiing."

"Well, you *were* graceful," Ernest said. And he had been, but Christ, the man never let anything go.

Ernest didn't know how Gerald had caught a fine woman like Sara, but there you were. Where Sara had a sort of understated way of thinking and speaking, Gerald was like a schoolboy eager to please. He didn't have the patience for it right now.

As if she'd read his mind, Sara said: "Come with me. I have something for you."

They walked together into the cool of the house and he felt his mind hush a little. He followed her up the stairs and into a library.

"It smells nice in here," he said.

"It's eucalyptus," Sara said, turning, obviously pleased. "The smell always reminds me of big airy rooms and gentleman's soap."

He watched her as she walked over to a small, straight wooden desk, saw the outline of her hips through the gauzy material of her dress as she bent forward and retrieved something. He wouldn't mind sinking into those thighs, drowning in them, all quiet and calm and untroubled.

She handed him a small, black, leather-bound diary. He opened it, elegant Spanish script covering the pages.

"The dealer on the rue Saint-Sulpice said it was the authentic diary of *le grand matador* Pedro Romero Martinez," she said. She laughed. "Although, I don't know if that's really true."

He turned it over. The leather was very worn and soft.

"It doesn't matter, it's a wonderful present." He pulled her into his arms. "You're so lovely."

She laughed and pulled away. "Come along, now," she said. "I can't keep you all to myself."

When the Hemingways and Pauline had left, Sara walked Ada to the Bastide and said good night, before deciding to take a stroll in the gardens. She walked down to the farthest edge of the property and looked out into the darkness, listening to the sound of the tide coming in far below.

She thought about the day, the feel of the leather diary in her hands, of Ernest's body against hers, of the smell of the inside of Owen's plane. There was something about Owen. Something between them that she couldn't yet give voice to, but that hung in the air like a musky perfume. She would have called it attraction, except it was closer to the intensity she used to feel for some older girls at school she admired. It wasn't the same thing that she felt when she touched Ernest, or sensed *him* watching her. That was the kind of electricity that could only happen with men.

Ernest. Sara toyed with her pearls, feeling the silkiness of the beads between her fingers. Thinking of being so near him in the library. That nothing could ever happen between them didn't mitigate the pleasure she experienced when she was close to him, she decided, a sort of perpetual anticipation that might never be fulfilled. That had its own kind of thrill.

But with Owen, no. It was more complicated than that. Of course. Despite all the reasons why they might not be friends, there was nonetheless an understanding between them. She loved the way, when she'd shown up today, that he'd accepted her unexpected arrival as natural. More than that, as welcome. She never needed to explain herself around him. That was a rarity. He allowed quiet unspoken things to happen between people, and she didn't know another single person like that. He was special, and not just to Gerald.

She wondered about Gerald and Owen and *Arcadia*. About why she'd invited him to stay at their little farm. It wasn't that she felt sorry about where he was living. It was something else. To have him here at Villa America, to have him inside the circle, rather than dangerously battering down the gate from the outside.

Intimacy was difficult to talk about, especially for her, who had so very little experience in articulating it outwardly. She knew her marriage, her family, was the one thing she had to protect from life's vagaries, and that to do so, she might have to allow for complications. And for love. For love to expand, she supposed. She wasn't sure if she could do it, but she knew she had to try.

※

After Sara had gone to bed, Gerald took one of the bicycles and rode to Owen's field. He found him in the barn reading by the gas lamp.

He looked up and smiled at Gerald.

Gerald leaned his bike against the wall. "I loved you more this evening than I ever have."

And it was true what Owen had said about the sound of the grass growing and the smell of the dust and the sea. And the happiness of being with your heart's desire on a late spring night in the South of France. And how no one else knew you were there, and no one else cared.

※   ※   ※

Ellen Barry was leaning against the terrace wall of the Casino Cléo in Juan-les-Pins with Ada MacLeish, surveying the party. She adored the out-of-season season here. All the passions and rows and fun that lay ahead this summer, she thought with a smile; life was too dull if someone wasn't sparking off about something.

It had turned out neatly, Sara and Gerald's soiree for Ernest, not least the surprise of caviar in the summer. Nobody, absolutely nobody, ate caviar this time of year, as it spoiled on the long train ride from the Caspian Sea. But leave it to Sara to find some pilot willing to lug it back here for Ernest. And then bottle after bottle of crisp, beautiful champagne.

It was a fine warm evening and the casino owner was hovering around the table where the Fitzgeralds and the Hemingways, along with Sara and Gerald, were sitting.

"He's like an excited gnat," Ellen said, eyeing the owner.

"Well, if this is a success, it will be a boon for him, won't it?" Ada said.

"You can say that again."

"Speaking of gnats." Ada waved a plump, smooth arm over her head, clearing a swarm of them. She looked at her glass. "Empty," she said. "Oh, I wish Archie were back already. All this coupledom is wearisome alone. Where's Phil?"

Ellen jerked her chin towards the fountain, where her husband was talking and talking to Hadley's friend, the lovely and shockingly thin Pauline Pfeiffer.

"Speaking of coupledom," she laughed.

"Oh, I wouldn't worry about that," Ada said. "Pauline has bigger fish to fry."

"Mmm," Ellen said. It was what it was, but she thought the fact that Pauline was supposed to be Hadley's friend made the whole thing in poor taste. "I blame Ernest, though, really."

"I'd blame anyone you like if I thought it would do any good," Ada said, smoothing down her yellow evening dress. "I said something to Sara about it, how strange the three of them are together, you know—the looks, the silences, *the flirting*—and she just stared at me like I was off my head."

"Sara likes a very male animal," Ellen said.

"And then there's dear Gerald," Ada said.

Ellen shrugged. "Well, some women might like to eat an

elegant slice of lamb all week long but dream of a bloody steak on Sunday night. Nothing wrong with that."

"I think Archie's more like a drumstick," Ada said.

Ellen looked across at the table full of their friends and had to laugh. There was Ernest, big and dark and smiling and chatting to Sara, who was obviously delighted and scooping up spoonfuls of caviar. And then on her other side there was Scott, like an apoplectic puppy, his head about ready to explode. "Scott's going to have a breakdown if they keep on like that," she said.

"Scott," Ada said, laughing her silvery laugh and shaking her head. "You know, he's always trying to make love to her. I saw him do it in a taxi once. And you know what she said to me? 'Oh, Scott's in love with everyone. What's a little kiss between friends, anyway?'"

"Ha," Ellen said. "I love Sara."

"Madly," Ada said.

At the table, Ellen saw Sara turn away and say something to Gerald, while Ernest continued to look at her. And he wasn't just looking, Ellen realized, he was observing, calculating. "It's not just Scott," she said.

Ada looked, too. "No," she said. Then she sighed. "But the thing about Sara is, she's just incorruptible."

"Ah," Ellen said, as a waiter appeared at their side carrying a fresh bottle. "Please, sir, may I have another?"

✦

Scott watched Sara. He felt sick in his bones, in his heart. How could she? There was Ernest, all flattery and smiles and stories, but Sara was better than that. *He* loved her. Ernest was just an interloper in this love that existed between himself and Sara and Gerald and Zelda. Though, Zelda, he felt distanced from her lately. There was darkness

319

in her, and sometimes he thought she was trying to kill him. Zelda said he was drinking too much, but what the hell? That wasn't the point, that was a ruse.

Sara in her shimmering gown with her hard and lovely face and golden bob and rope of pearls and silver spoon. He wanted to write her, to draw her, to show what it felt like to be near her and adore her. He would, he would. If only Ernest would stop talking to her.

He was talking about Pamplona and Sara was enraptured. Ernest was describing the nobility of the matador, and she said: "I can't wait to see it with you."

He hated that they were all going to Pamplona together. He hated that Ernest read his manuscripts to Sara and Gerald, and they said: "Oh, how new. How fresh. How exciting." They never said that about his work. Ernest's work *was* good, it *was* fresh and new. And Scott wanted the world to know that. But that didn't mean they had to love Ernest more.

Scott turned to Gerald, sitting on his right, and said: "Sara's being mean to me."

"Don't be ridiculous," Gerald said, and Scott didn't like his tone.

"Don't talk to me like that," Scott said, but Gerald looked beyond him, concentrating on Ernest's story. Scott hummed a little tune to himself. But it didn't work.

Ernest had Hadley *and* Pauline, what did he need Sara for? Just to take her. That was the way he was.

"So," he turned back to Gerald, "I suppose you have some special plan for all of us tomorrow, do you? Something special, that includes costumes and a hat and dance and a flying elephant and . . . something that no one's ever seen before and we're all going to be amazed and in awe of you?"

Gerald ignored him.

"Sara," he said. "Look at me." But she didn't.

"There are all sorts of reasons a matador can be second-rate," Ernest was saying. "But the good ones, the ones that are second-rate not because of cowardice or weakness, they'd rather die than live that way."

"Is second-rate so bad?" Sara asked, and Scott could tell she was teasing, and he hated it.

"Not if it's just bad luck," Ernest said. "But any other way, yes."

"Well," Sara said, pushing her hands through her hair. "I suppose then we must all be very careful not to slip into that status."

"I don't think you've ever had a second-rate moment in your life," Ernest said, smiling at her.

"Don't make my pedestal too high." She was smiling, too.

"Sara," Scott said, but too quietly for anyone to hear.

Then that American pilot was there and Scott's head felt heavy as he lifted it up to look at the man's face. "It's you," he said. "The man from the mystery place. The pilot who knows pilots who steal people's wives. Owen. That's the name."

"Hello, Scott," the pilot said, but then he also turned away.

Well, that was it. If even nobody-pilots were pretending he was invisible, something had to be done. Scott pushed back his chair and managed to get himself upright.

He stumbled through the terrace doors into the casino, where he tripped on a small rug. He managed to balance himself on the door frame and stared down at the offending object. "You," he said to the rug.

Then he picked it up and put it over his head. If he was going to be forced into the role of supplicant, then supplicant he would be. He got down on his hands and knees, rug over his head, and began crawling back to the table.

When he reached what appeared to be Gerald's legs, Scott grabbed one. "Hello, I'm just a poor supplicant. I've come to beg for attention."

Gerald looked down and Scott felt that icy coldness that he used so effectively sometimes. "Get up."

"Sara's being mean to me," he said to Gerald. Then louder, to the whole table: "Sara's being mean to me."

"Scott, get up."

"I won't," Scott said, clutching the rug tighter around his head.

"I don't know why, but you're trying to wreck this for us. Stop it."

"Fine," Scott said, standing and throwing off his head-dress. "But the only thing I'm trying to wreck is a champagne-and-caviar party that is beyond a doubt the most affected piece of nonsense I've ever seen. I, sir, am doing you a favor. Saving you from your own ridiculousness."

Gerald stood. "You stay if you want. I'm leaving."

❖

Scott wasn't aware of anything after that, until the next morning, when, in the bright sunshine, he awoke in the back of his car next to Zelda. Looking around he saw they were parked in the middle of a trestle bridge, the one used for the streetcar, the sea glinting far beneath them. At the end of the bridge there appeared to be a peasant-type person, who was waving his hands frantically at them. Scott tried to clear his head. And then, from somewhere behind him, he heard it. It was growing louder: a rumbling on the tracks.

The evening after the party for Ernest, Sara was alone in the library. The children were long asleep, Ada had been fed and sent off to the Bastide and some kind of order had been restored.

"There you are."

She turned to see Gerald crossing into the room.

"I've just written Scott a very tough letter," she said. "I think it should set him straight."

"Better you than me," Gerald said, sitting in one of the chairs.

"You were absolutely right to leave, and I told him so."

"Thank you," Gerald said. "I'm sorry I abandoned you. I just couldn't."

"No," she said. What Scott had said about Gerald being ridiculous had been unnecessarily cruel. She could have clocked him.

She went over and sat in the chair across from Gerald. "Are you tired?"

"A bit." He held his hand out to her and she took it.

"You know," she said, "I talked to Owen about moving into the little farm."

"You did?" He let go of her hand.

"It seemed awful to have him camping in that falling-down barn when we have so much space."

"I suppose," Gerald said, but he didn't say anything else.

"And I saw his new plane."

"Oh?" He was picking at something on his trousers.

"*Arcadia*," she said.

"Mmm."

"I didn't want to mention it to him, but I wondered if it wasn't a rather dangerous name for a plane."

"Dangerous?"

"Gerald," she said, a little sharply. "Don't be obtuse. An unattainable paradise? Anyway, it struck me as odd."

"He probably doesn't know what it means, not in that way, at least," Gerald said.

"I wonder," she said, looking at him and thinking of the Poussin painting, the one with the tomb, that her husband admired so much. "Shockingly," she said, "I could use a nightcap. I feel quite awake."

"A sherry?"

"Yes. Why don't you bring one up to bed for me?"

"I'd be delighted," he said.

She hadn't put on her nightgown and instead lay naked under the covers. She couldn't say *why* she'd done that, she'd just felt like it. Why was she doing anything these days?

When Gerald came upstairs with the little glass of sherry, she didn't sit up, only continued to lie on her side, her head on the pillow, watching him.

He placed the glass on the nightstand next to her. He looked at her.

"Get undressed and turn out the light," she said softly.

And while they made love, Sara thought of first-rate matadors, with rough hands and red capes, who slaughtered bulls with enormous care.

⁂

Sara woke up early, before anyone else, and she wanted to get out. She'd been dreaming about her mother and her sisters and father and their trip to India. She felt wonderful, and she didn't want to share it with Gerald or the children or Ada or anybody. She wanted only to savor it before it disappeared into the routine of the day.

She dressed quietly and slipped out of the bedroom and down the stairs. She took the touring car to drive herself, which she never did anymore. Her driving had never been very good and after a few run-ins with bushes, she'd all but given herself over to their chauffeur.

She made her way through the town, asleep except for a few women hanging washing. The June air was cool and she wished she'd worn something warmer. Climbing up the Roman road, she drove through a small village and turned onto the allée des Cigales. She was going to see the one person she knew who never required any explanations.

When she pulled her car to a stop on the edge of the field, she could see a man in front of the hangar watching her, the mechanic she supposed, and on the other side of the runway, Owen emerging from the barn, already dressed himself.

She walked quickly across the field to him and met him at the barn door.

"Hello," she said.

"Hello," Owen said. "Would you like a cup of coffee?"

Sara nodded and followed him inside. She saw the sagging camp bed and old blanket, that desk he'd brought from the airbase. He pulled out the chair for her and then poured a cup of coffee from the speckled enamel pot sitting on the gas warmer.

She knew why Gerald had been worried about Owen's living situation, but this morning his arrangement looked like heaven to her. Simple, clean, just for one person.

"No milk. I'm sorry," Owen said, handing her a sort of camping cup that matched the pot.

"Oh, I don't care," Sara said. Then: "I'll bring you some from our cows, if you like."

"Sure," he said.

He lowered himself onto the camp bed and they sat there together in silence, sipping their coffee. After a bit, she could hear doves and the creak of the barn shifting. She put down her cup.

"Will you do something for me?"

"Yes."

"Will you take me up in your plane?"

"If you'd like."

"I want to be outside, though, like you."

"The Spad," he said.

"Yes," she said. "Not the one called *Arcadia*."

"No," he said. He put his cup on the ground and stood, offering her his hand. "You'll need a jacket, though."

She nodded.

He handed her a horsehide jacket and carefully buttoned her into it. She stood still and let him, as Honoria might have done.

Then they walked together to the hangar and she watched as he and his man pushed the plane out onto the field. Owen helped her climb into the passenger seat behind the cockpit, before getting in himself.

He and the Frenchman exchanged shouts as Owen started the engine and the man spun the propeller. Then they were moving down the field, then lifting. Then she was flying.

It was loud and brutal and wonderful and it vibrated through her bones. She leaned over the side and saw the town below and the Roman road and the golden-pink cliffs in the morning light rising like ladies' bosoms from the sea.

She could see the back of Owen's blond head and the strong shape of his neck. She placed her hand on his shoulder. He reached back and briefly clasped it.

He took her out over the open water and she wondered how anyone had ever looked at that blue expanse with no end and believed that there could possibly be something on the other side.

The plane circled wide and as they began to approach the shoreline she could see the Cap, with its fingers spreading, and the spot where their house was, where her husband and her three children were dreaming, cocooned in sleep.

After they'd landed and the plane had come to a stop, Sara sat for a moment before letting herself be helped out.

"Oh Owen," she said, when they were face to face.

He unbuttoned her jacket and she slid out of it.

"I want to do that all the time," she said. "I want to be like you. I want to fly my own plane."

"You could," he said.

"Do you think so?"

"Why not?"

She shook her head. "No, I don't know. I'm not that person, I suppose." She looked around and out at the horizon. "I just wanted to be this morning." She put her hand up to his cheek, cold from being up in the air. "Thank you."

He nodded. "Anytime."

*   *   *

Owen had heard someone at the casino the other night pronounce that the Murphys had invented summer on the Riviera. He'd laughed at the time—God, what a fucking oily thing to say—but maybe there was something to it.

He hadn't had any intention of joining their craziness when he went over to the house earlier that morning. He'd only gone to drop off the waffle iron. But they'd all been so involved in their preparations for La Garoupe and Sara had insisted and somehow he'd just been swept along.

He watched Gerald now, his limbs long and brown, the white bathing suit belted high at the waist, his straight sharp nose. The chin he always protested was weak. Owen had a memory of running his hands down that body two nights ago, for a few hours in the barn, on top of the scratchy wool blanket spread out on the ground.

It was a strange thing, to know him then, and to know him now, here at the beach, in the middle of everything, in his public life, his other life. His life with Sara.

He never asked Gerald if he and Sara still made love. He didn't want to think about that, he didn't want to hear about it. It wasn't just jealousy, but a kind of effort not to get involved in their marriage. To leave that to them, and to keep himself and Gerald somewhere else. Separate. Unrelated.

But it only seemed to get more and more complicated, more and more messy. There was Sara, of course. The other thing, though, if he was completely honest, was that he didn't want to be swallowed up by the Murphys. Didn't want to become a cog in their machine. But he needed Gerald, and therefore Sara. Because the truth was, no matter how he tried to convince himself otherwise, there was never going to be anyone else. Not for him, anyway.

He watched as Sara sat on a blanket in the sand unpacking a small trunk—swimming costumes, a collection of hats, a miniature tea set, colored jars for collecting beach glass, two small rakes and a shovel, a box of tin soldiers, and a set of watercolors. Gerald stood above her taking the items from her one by one, and finding spots for them on small tables, under umbrellas and inside the striped tents they'd set up. Owen wondered how G. chose which place was the perfect one for every little thing. He loved the mystery of his mind, the way it seemed to have its own order, one that no one else had in their head.

It was pretty much the same crowd that had been at Ernest's party, along with a few others who had already been camped out at La Garoupe when they'd arrived—a collection of European aristocrats staying at the Hôtel du Cap, and other people Owen didn't recognize.

The children, brown and naked, were splashing around in the water. There was a gang of them belonging to the various parties and they made Owen think of some of the boys he'd known on the island when he was young, though he wondered if they'd ever played like that. There was always work to be done, chores to get back to.

To his left, Scott, who definitely appeared sober, was sitting out of the sun under an umbrella, speaking with Ada and Hadley. Gerald came over and handed Owen a sherry.

"Scott looks recovered," Owen said.

Gerald nodded. "Sara was furious with him."

"You didn't seem so happy about it, either."

"It's hard with Scott," he said. "Because there's always a part of him, even buried, that's the good part, the quiet part. Where the writing comes from, I suppose."

"But . . ."

"But, really, all the antics. It was trashy. I think under the circumstances, a little distance might not hurt."

"The antics," Owen said, thinking about the pageantry Gerald and Sara themselves created.

It was hard to keep track of the rises and falls in the Murphys' circle. Of course, it didn't really have anything to do with him, but for some reason the shifts in favor made him uncomfortable. He didn't doubt their loyalty to their friends, or their generosity. But then, it was also clear that it could be withdrawn.

Ernest, who'd been swimming with the children, came over in broad strides, joining them on the edge of the circle of blankets and tables. He was still wet from his swim, drops of sea water running down his bare chest.

"Hello," he said, grinning at Owen. "I'm Ernest. Sara tells me you're a pilot."

"Owen," he said, holding out his hand. He hadn't really spoken with him the other night and he was curious about this man who seemed to have such a powerful effect on everyone around him.

"So, what kind of plane do you fly?"

"I have a couple, a Spad and a Fokker."

Ernest nodded. "Good planes," he said.

Owen wondered how he could know that, without knowing their specifics, but said nothing.

"They're amazing machines, the engines in particular," Gerald said. "There's a kind of grace to them, in all their complexity. I think you would understand them completely."

Ernest ignored him. "How long have you been flying?"

"Awhile. Since before the war."

"I went up in a plane for the first time a couple of years ago," Ernest said. "You know, it was only then that I began to understand cubist painting."

"Oh," Owen said, nodding.

He could see what Gerald meant about the man's physicality; Ernest was standing very close to him, hands on his hips, chest stuck out. He wasn't bigger than Owen, but he seemed to take up more space.

"The man who took me up, you'd like him, knows his stuff," Ernest said. "I'd like to go up again."

"You should," Owen said.

"Owen took me up," Gerald said. "I've never been able to describe it adequately, but I've never been so moved."

Owen smiled at Gerald, although he wished he would stop doing whatever it was he was doing.

"Some of the things you've talked about when you talk about Pamplona," Gerald continued, "that's what I felt up there."

"Well," Ernest said, finally acknowledging Gerald, "I suppose if you experience something very intensely, it can feel the same. Sometimes, I feel that way when I watch Jack Dempsey fight. Don't you?" He looked at Gerald, his eyes narrowed, and smiled.

"I don't know," Gerald said uncertainly.

He must know Gerald knew nothing about boxing. Owen felt his temper quicken a little.

"Well, if you've never seen a fight, you should. That's when you really understand what it means to be brave."

Owen laughed.

Ernest turned on him. "Do you box?"

"No," Owen said. "No, I don't box."

"No," Ernest said.

"Ernest's written the most wonderful book," Gerald said. "About Paris and Pamplona and men and women."

Owen didn't know what to say. He hated this whole conversation and wanted it to stop. He just nodded.

Ernest looked embarrassed. "You shouldn't say things like that," he said. "It could jinx it."

"Nothing's going to jinx the talent you have," Gerald said. "It couldn't."

Ernest began backing away from them a little, and Owen realized this man's weak spot, his vulnerability under all the boxing and flying and bullfighting: he was superstitious.

"Well . . . I should go see if Hash needs anything," Ernest said.

"She's been such a valiant soldier," Gerald said.

"She has," Ernest said. "Bumby's lucky to have her."

"We all are, and we love her."

Ernest looked at Owen. "Nice to meet you. If you change your mind about the boxing . . . I mean it's real boxing, because you can't really do it any other way. But I'm sure you'd be fine."

"Thanks," Owen said. "I'll let you know."

When Ernest was out of earshot, Gerald said: "Do you see what I mean?"

"I do," Owen said. "Especially about him making you nervous."

Gerald looked unhappy.

"Never mind, G. Just don't . . . I don't know. Just be careful what you say around him."

The afternoon unwound: there was swimming and group photographs; there were records on the gramophone and Ernest and Phil Barry raced each other and Sara showed them a jig she'd learned as a girl. There was lunch, including stuffed squab, glazed with honey and served with a garland of thyme.

Afterwards, Owen was lying in the sand next to Sara, her bathing suit straps pulled down around her shoulders, her short hair fluffy and curling from the salt water. Next to her, under an umbrella, Ada MacLeish was knitting and talking about her husband, Archie, who was finally returning from Persia that evening on a boat landing in Marseille. There seemed to be a plan to meet him, the whole group of them.

"Gerald's fixed it with one of the officers of that ocean liner docked in the harbor," Sara was telling Ada. "You know the big one from New York? Well, Gerald's lined his palm so that we can get aboard and make a scene on their deck."

"He didn't," Ada said, looking up from knitting and smiling her big, broad smile. "Isn't your husband clever."

"Isn't he just?" Sara said.

At the shoreline Owen could see Gerald playing with Scottie, who'd refused to lie down with the other children. He watched as, after a while, Gerald stood and offered his hand to the little girl, who took it, and they began walking back. When they reached the others, Gerald settled Scottie under Ada's umbrella, covering her with a linen cloth.

"Now remember our deal," he said.

The little girl nodded.

"That's a good girl," Gerald said.

"What have you been getting up to now?" Sara asked when Gerald sat down in front of her, at her feet, Owen noticed.

"We made a good pact," Gerald said. "It seems Scottie's been watching a very mystical light that shines from the Cap, across the bay and into her bedroom window at night. She wanted to know what it could possibly be. So I explained to her that, naturally, it was the lighthouse run by fairies. And if she promised to lie down for her nap, I promised to take her there to see them one of these nights."

Sara leaned forward and kissed Gerald on the cheek.

Owen felt a pain in his chest, a shortness of breath, from the openness of that kiss. It was everything he'd never be able to do. And in it was the striking truth that Gerald's body belonged to her, really. He turned away.

*

Later, with the sun setting over the harbor in Marseille, Owen watched as Ada and Gerald and Sara stood on the deck of the ocean liner in feathered headdresses, faces painted in red stripes, carrying makeshift tomahawks, whooping. They were doing a war dance for Archie as his boat pulled in. Really, though, it was a dance of welcome for one of their tribe, a missing part of the Murphy circle returned to them.

Owen wondered, briefly, if they would ever do a dance like that for him. Then he wondered how you knew whether, in a certain moment, you were inside or outside.

❖   ❖   ❖

They were sitting at the Bar Gaucho, Gerald and Sara, Ernest and Hadley and Pauline. Ernest, Gerald noticed, seemed to know everyone in Pamplona, even the pilgrims and peasants who'd traveled to the festival. He ordered them *pintxos* from inside and small plates kept arriving; a dinner of deliciously oily anchovies, cured ham, *tortilla de patatas* and stuffed peppers, all atop slices of crusty bread and speared with a toothpick.

They were drinking a young white wine, also chosen by Ernest, who seemed to be consuming most of it.

The night was hot and dusty, and despite the late hour, the small cobbled streets were still buzzing with people who had gathered earlier to watch the procession of the statue of San Fermin and his relics.

It had been a strange and thrilling sight for Gerald, that procession. Not only were clergy and councilmen and town folk part of the parade, but there were also the magnificent *gigantes y cabezudos*. "Giants and Bigheads," Ernest had translated. Fourteen feet high, richly garbed, with papier mâché heads, carried on the shoulders of men.

They included four pairs of wooden kings and queens, representing the four corners of the earth: Europe, Africa, Asia and America; the African queen with a face as black as ebony. And with them, their entourage of Bigheads, representing a mayor, a councillor, a grandmother and, strangely, two Japanese figures, as well as others for protection.

Gerald had been so enchanted he'd inquired about getting one made to ship home. Of course, Ernest had just shaken his head, making Gerald feel crass.

There'd also been *jota* dancers accompanied by skin-covered *bombos* and guitars and castanets, hands on their waists, feet kicking in front of them, like a rustic blend of a waltz and a volta.

It had been a heady experience, the Spanish sun beating down, the language Gerald didn't understand, the fusing of pagan and Catholic rituals, a Catholicism so different from the cold catechism he'd grown up with. The smells of people who'd traveled a long way in the same clothes, the wandering merchants carrying skins of wine, selling replica relics, shawls, and musical instruments.

Gerald was thinking he would like to be here with Owen, to see this with him, to eat *pintxos* together on a hot night in Pamplona while next to them men crowded around wooden barrels drinking. There were so many things he'd like to do with him, things they probably never would. But he was also glad to be here with Sara, whose delight in things human and new was like a drug to the system.

Sara, of course, had hung on Ernest's every word, many of them at this moment dedicated to tomorrow's running of the bulls, and the amateur bullfight, and finally the bullfights themselves with the matadors he so admired.

"I wish I could run," Sara said, leaning back and fluffing her bob. "My hair is almost short enough."

"I don't think your hair is the problem," Gerald said.

"Ah," she said, smiling. "It's my matronly curves, is it?"

"Matronly is not the term I would use," he said.

"Pauline could do it. You're as lithe as a boy." And she said it in such an admiring way there could be no doubt that it was a compliment.

"Or as lithe as a daughter," Pauline said, smiling at Gerald, her smooth cap of dark hair falling in one eye.

In Antibes, he'd started calling Pauline "Daughter" after she'd remarked to him one day: "I love that you call Honoria 'Daughter.' I love the way you say it, the way it sounds in your mouth." In turn, she'd begun calling him Dow-Dow.

"Running is the tradition of men here," Ernest said, and his tone sounded a little annoyed.

He had that habit of changing his moods quickly and since they were all outsized, the effect was always immediate.

"You *should* run, Gerald," Hadley said. "I think there're ways of staying out of danger."

Gerald smiled. He hadn't made up his mind yet and he didn't want to talk about it in front of Ernest because somehow he'd end up doing it even if—*especially if*—he didn't want to. To his relief, a well-dressed man sitting at the next table interrupted them.

"Excuse me," he said. "You're Americans?"

"Yes," Gerald said. He liked the man's gabardine suit, the way the trousers were cut from the waist straight down to the ankle.

"Ogden Summers," the man said. "Consul General to Barcelona. I'm very glad to have found some compatriots."

"Join us," Sara said, scooting her chair over a bit to make room.

Ernest rose suddenly, saying he was going inside to get another bottle, and disappeared into the brown sliver of a bar.

"It's unusual to see any Americans here, although I think I met your friend last year," Ogden said, indicating Ernest's back. "I'm here with some of my local staff—they intro-

duced me two years ago to all this wonder—but I've let
them have the evening to themselves. Not much fun spending it with the boss." He winked.

"Our guide is practically a local himself," Pauline said.
"And a marvelous one at that."

Gerald noticed Hadley shifting in her seat.

It seemed Pauline did, too, for she added, hastily: "Oh,
you too, dear Hash. Of course, you've been coming as long
as he has. I always forget that. Anyway," she turned back to
Ogden, "we feel positively Spanish after only one day here."

"That can happen. It seems it happens more in Spain
than anywhere else. So," he said, turning to Gerald, "running tomorrow?"

"I haven't decided."

Sara squeezed his hand.

"Well, if you do decide to, I can give you some tips. If
you'd like, of course."

"Actually, I would," Gerald said, thinking that this man's
tips would likely be more beneficial to his health than
Ernest's.

"Wonderful," Ogden said, clapping his hands together. "I
do like giving advice."

Sara laughed. "Oh, we can use it."

"Well, you'll want to be aware of the timing of the shots,"
Ogden said, settling himself back as if he were going to tell
them a bedtime story. "That's something they never tell you.
You know, of course, there are six bulls, led first by six steers
and then followed by three more?"

Gerald nodded and Ogden rubbed his hands together.

"Right, well, the first shot—" here he raised his fore-
finger and thumb like a pistol—"tells us that the first bull
has left the corral, while the second shot announces the last

bull has exited." He clapped, as if closing a gate. "Now if the shots are close together, it's likely to be a less hair-raising run for the likes of you and me, because it means the bulls are being well guided by the steers and therefore less likely to get lost and become distracted and angered by silly things like people."

It was hard for Gerald to imagine this man with his dramatic gestures and groomed hair and fine clothes doing anything as strenuous and elemental as running with a pack of crazed bulls.

"Now, a longer period between shots, and you might find yourself face to face with a disoriented bull. Which I don't recommend. Also, if you see a bull falling, stay out of the way, because they are not happy when they get back up."

His emphatic expression made Gerald chuckle.

"No, no." Ogden wagged his finger theatrically. "It's no laughing matter, I assure you."

This made Sara start laughing too.

"Oh," he said, as if he'd just remembered something, though Gerald doubted it was off the cuff. "Another import-ant thing to remember: when you hear the bulls behind you, *don't look back*."

"What will happen?" Pauline said. "Hades will snatch you back down to the underworld?"

"Indeed, Miss . . . ?"

"Pfeiffer."

"Indeed, Miss Pfeiffer, something like that." Ogden leaned in and lowered his voice. "What runners fear most is not being gored. Being gored is . . ." he raised one hand with a flourish, "an honorable experience. But being trampled, well, that's just pitiful. Clumsy. Ridiculous."

"I can't say I'd relish either of those," Gerald said.

"I should think not," Sara said, pulling a printed scarf tighter around her neck. "But goodness, it's brave."

"To avoid such a fate," Ogden said, "you only have to read the faces of the men running in front of you. You see, people will naturally turn as the sound gets nearer, and all you have to do is study the expression on their faces to know how close the bull is. And that way you won't trip. The fear in those faces tells you everything you need to know: run faster."

Sara shivered, a smile on her face.

Gerald noticed Hadley looking around. "Where's Ernest?" she said nervously.

"I'll go fetch him," Pauline said. "Not to worry."

She hopped up, her white cotton dress slim and fine as a slip, and walked towards the bar, Hadley's eyes fixed on her back.

"I think that performance deserves a drink. On us," Sara said.

"No, no," Ogden waved this away. "You've done me a favor. And now, I must retire if I'm going to be fresh for the challenge tomorrow." He stood, then turned. "I've just realized we haven't been properly introduced."

"Hadley Hemingway," Gerald said, indicating Hadley, who nodded distractedly. "Her husband, Ernest, is inside. I'm Gerald Murphy and this is my wife, Sara."

"Wonderful. Hopefully I'll see you all tomorrow. Until then, *buenas noches*." He picked up a light brown fedora from his table, perched it at an angle on his head and strolled off in the direction of the Plaza del Castillo.

"What a marvelous character," Sara said. "It was like listening to Vladimir tell the children stories. But we were the children. Jerry, do you really believe that man runs with the bulls?"

"Do you think it was a put-on?"

"It did have something of the fictional in it," Sara said, twining her fingers in her scarf, a mischievous look on her face.

"God," Gerald said, laughing. "I hope he hasn't just sold us a bunch of hoodoo. That's all I need."

Pauline returned, pulling Ernest by the hand, his face wary.

"Has he left?" Ernest asked.

"Who? Our storyteller?" Gerald said, smiling.

"It seems Ernest has something against Mr. Consul General," Pauline said, her face tipped up to his.

Ernest sat down and poured himself what remained of their bottle of wine. Gerald noticed that he hadn't brought a fresh one.

"Storyteller?" he said, looking incredulously at Gerald. "The man's a goddamn queer."

* * *

Gerald woke up early the next morning and said to Sara: "I'm not doing it."

Sara turned over, propping her head on the pillow, and looked up at him. Finally she said: "Are you sure?"

"I just don't think it's for me."

He watched as she sighed and rose, throwing back the curtains and opening the doors to the little balcony that looked out over the Plaza del Castillo.

They were staying at the Hotel Quintana, at Ernest's insistence. It was the bullfighters' hotel and their room was across the hall from the rooms of Nino de la Palma and Nicanor Villalta. The latter, Ernest had told them, had only a month ago walked out of the ring in Madrid with the highest award ever bestowed in that arena: the ears of both bulls he fought that day.

They'd yet to cross paths with either man, but they were sure to see them in the ring at some point. Gerald had bought the best tickets, the *barrera* seats, for every day of the *corrida* as a surprise for Ernest.

Gerald could hear that the day had already begun on the streets below. He checked his watch. It was six a.m. The runners would be breakfasting before making their way to the Cuesta de Santo Domingo to say a prayer to the golden statue of San Fermin nestled in a niche in the wall.

"Of course, we'll go cheer Ernest on," Gerald said.

Sara didn't move from the balcony.

"Do you wish you'd married someone with more derring-do?" he asked.

When she didn't answer he got up and went to the closet, carefully laying out the clothes he would wear that day. It had taken him awhile to choose the appropriate outfit to bring here, but he felt fairly satisfied with the pearl-gray lightweight suit. The hat had been problematic: he didn't want to wear a panama, it wasn't right somehow. So he'd dug up his father's old flat cap, a kind of golfing cap he'd always loved, and which he'd lifted before they'd moved to Paris.

Then he took out his shaving kit and arranged everything on a small wooden table next to the stained sink.

When he'd done all this, he walked over to where she was standing and put a hand on her shoulder. "Sara?"

"I'm sorry you won't run," she said, finally turning. "I think it would be a great feeling afterwards."

Outside, the town had set up wooden post-and-rail fences along the route of the bull run, in the places where the treacherously narrow streets didn't provide natural barriers. Sara and Gerald took coffee, strong, dark stuff in small, creamy cups, at a table under the stone arches of their hotel.

Not finding Pauline or Hadley there, they made their

way to the corner of the Calle Estafeta to secure a spot to watch the run. Once they'd seen Ernest pass, they'd decided, they would make their way along the back streets to the Plaza de Toros, to cheer his arrival.

They stood behind the wooden fence, jostled a bit by the people around them, and waited. They heard the first shot. The street, its slender six-floor stone and stucco buildings, the people standing on the balconies, the crowd at the barriers—all of it was hushed. The second shot went off. Sara clasped his hand and he could feel the current running between them.

"I don't know why, but I'm nervous," she whispered in his ear, as if they were in church.

He nodded.

Then the first man, dressed in dark pants and a dark coat and white shirt, came into sight, running down the cobbled street. When he passed, they could feel the rush of air his movement created.

Behind him, six more, one with his hand out, fingertips almost brushing the buildings, as if feeling their texture. Then the sound, a sort of rumbling. It was hard to tell how far away it was.

He could feel Sara's hand tightening around his own. When he looked at her, her lips were slightly open, her breasts pressed up against the top rail. He was filled with a kind of sadness, looking at her like that. All that was earthy about her, about her sexuality, was lost on him. At that moment he truly wished he were a different man.

The people around them started shouting and a group of fifteen or so men came streaming down the street. Among them, Gerald could pick out Ernest's shape, barrel chest out, arms held close to his sides, face lit up with a kind of joy.

Pounding after them was a line of steers, which passed

the men, strongly but dumbly. Then came the bulls. Sixteen hundred pounds of shiny black coat and muscle, and horns the color of shells worn down by the ocean, their tips black as if they'd already been dipped into blood. All running with single-minded purpose.

They were all mixed up now, the men and the bulls, and the sound of shouting and the Spanish morning sun. The bulls feeling the heat of the steers, and the men, fear and confusion. How small and fragile even Ernest suddenly looked compared with this thundering mass of brawn and sinew.

He heard a cry escape Sara's lips, a call of excitement or pleasure or a blend of the two. He wanted to cry out too, but the cry was trapped in his throat. He saw a bull stumble, and catch its balance, and make an upward thrust of its head in frustration. And he saw how it was that men got gored so often: that arc that could disembowel the soft flesh of a man ' was just part of the natural state of being a bull. Some people just got in the way.

He was thinking this and holding Sara's hand and feeling her heat and his own, and all at once, the bulls and the men were past, and it was over. And then the sun went away and the sky opened up and it began to rain.

They reached the ring too late to see Ernest come in; Gerald had stopped back at the hotel for his raincoat and Sara an umbrella. When they got there, though, he was waiting, smiling broadly. On either side of him stood Hadley and Pauline, like bookends.

"Oh, we saw you," Sara said, "running like a little boy, so very happy. And those bulls."

"They're tough," Ernest said.

She shook her head.

"You," Ernest said, pointing at Gerald. "You may have escaped the running, but I have a surprise for you."

"Oh good," Gerald said.

"You know," Ernest said, surveying him, "that cap is just the right thing."

Gerald touched the brim and was disgusted with himself for being so flattered and so relieved.

"Anyway," Ernest said, "after the run, the tradition is for the locals to test their strength against the young bulls in the ring. I signed us both up." He grinned.

"Marvelous," Sara said.

"Mmm," Gerald said.

Gerald followed him down the steps and was forced to swing himself over the barrier as Ernest did, trying not to slip in the fine dust that had turned a bit soupy from the rain. It was barely drizzling now, but Gerald realized he was still clutching his raincoat in his hand.

Young Spaniards were dotted around the ring, taunting the juvenile bulls, and Gerald saw one get tossed up in the air.

"Don't worry," Ernest called to him. "Those are small horns. And they're padded for the ladies."

The crowds were obviously enjoying what to them looked like comedy. Gerald hoped no one could see him shaking.

Ernest was standing several feet away, but Gerald could see he was watching him out of the corner of his eye. At that moment, besides his fear, he felt hatred. He was thinking of leaving, but he couldn't, and then he heard Sara yelling his name. He turned and saw there was a bull coming straight at him.

There was something hideous about the way the animal looked with its head down like that, coming to cut a swath through him. And there was Ernest watching, watching, always watching. And Sara.

Gerald lifted his raincoat, out of some perverse sense of showmanship, and held it in front of him.

"To the side," Ernest was yelling. "To the side."

It was almost upon him, almost too late, but he managed, somehow, to process Ernest's words, pulling the raincoat to his left, and the bull followed, just passing his body.

Ernest was suddenly next to him, slapping him on the back, saying something about doing a veronica, but Gerald could only hear the buzzing of blood in his head.

He looked up and saw Sara clapping and smiling. Ernest saw it, too, and then he was gone from his side. Gerald watched as Ernest waved down a bull, and when it charged him, threw himself over its horns in a kind of insane somersault, landing on its back.

The bull bucked once, stopped, swayed for a few moments, before falling to its knees under the burden of Ernest's great weight.

And the crowd yelled: *"Olé."*

*

It was early evening and they were all making their way to the ring to watch the *corrida*, Sara's heels clacking on the cobblestones. The sun, which had made a reappearance before lunch, was still high in the sky, casting short shadows onto the street.

It was her first bullfight and they were going to see Villalta, whom Ernest knew and admired so much. The run had been . . . well, she couldn't even put it into words. It had been hot and mean and beautiful all at once.

She didn't know if she would ever love something as

much as she loved Pamplona. If there would ever be anything so visceral again.

After lunch, she and Ernest had walked through the maze of merchants and unicyclists and men performing feats of strength, while the others had decided to stay and lounge at the Café Iruña and watch the world go by.

She wanted a guitar for Baoth. While Honoria was like a perfect blend of both herself and Gerald, and Patrick was like a little Gerald—"more Gerald than even Gerald," as Archie liked to say—Baoth was her. Or a boy version of her younger self: strong and sturdy and naughty and fearless. And he, out of all of them, would love a Spanish guitar the most.

After dismissing some of the plainer ones, she found the perfect specimen: small, its face inlaid with mother of pearl, vines engraved into the finger-board. Ernest bargained the price down for her, but in such a dignified way that none of them, including the merchant, felt badly when it was over.

"Now," Ernest had said, afterwards, "we have to find a *bombo* for you."

"My own little drum," Sara said, "to bang whenever I want."

He insisted on choosing it himself. It had a polished red wooden base with a top-skin as white as snow, and waxed woven cords securing the top to the bottom. He carried it back for her.

"Do you know what I think would be wonderful?" he'd said.

"What?"

"I think you should put on all your diamonds this evening and a silk dress and wear them to the *corrida*. And with the late sun, the diamonds will flash, and you'll flash, around your neck and on your ears and your lovely wrists, and we'll watch the man who may become the greatest killer of his generation do his honor by the bull."

She'd felt lightheaded when he'd said this. The idea of herself the way he saw her.

And now, here she was, on her way to see Villalta, in a silk dress the color of sea-foam, and every single diamond she'd brought.

A group of Spanish couples pointed at Gerald as they passed.

"What are they saying?" he asked Ernest, and for a moment her heart stopped.

"They call you the 'man in the silver suit,'" Ernest said.

"Oh," Gerald said. "Do they approve?"

"They think it's fine," Ernest said. "But I prefer the cap."

Sara exhaled silently.

When they reached the Plaza de Toros, Gerald handed the man their tickets and he showed them to their seats: Sara on the outside, followed by Ernest, then Hadley, Gerald and, finally, Pauline. They were practically in the ring.

"These are good seats, in the shade for the true *aficionados*," Ernest said. "Still, it's not quite the same as being poor, or the first time you come."

"No," Sara said. "But nothing is ever like the first time, is it?"

"The mistress of understatement," Ernest smiled down at her. He leaned over and called across them to Pauline: "How are you feeling, all the way down there at the end, Daughter?"

It surprised Sara a little to hear him call her that, but then, Gerald's language had always been infectious.

Pauline raised a hand. "I'm just fine and dandy, as always," she said. "God, this is going to be a smash, isn't it?"

The *paseíllo* began, the constables on horseback in their black velvet caps topped with glorious red plumage; then the three matadors, their *traje de luces* encrusted with gold, each clad in a different color silk, black, pink, and blue; followed by their teams of *subalternos*: three *banderilleros*, shimmering in silver, and two *picadores*, in gold like the matador. They lapped the ring, making tracks in the burnished dust, before saluting the *presidente*, and finally departing again.

Sara had carefully written down all the Spanish words in a black book she'd brought with her. Now she rolled them over her tongue.

A trumpet sounded, and Villalta and his three *banderilleros* came into the ring, their capes flashing. The matador was tall and slender and walked on the tips of his toes like a ballet dancer. He crossed himself, while the *banderilleros* spread their magenta capes wide and the bull entered the ring.

They goaded the animal into attacking, making passes, exposing the gold lining of their *capote*. Villalta, meanwhile, studied his opponent, the way the bull moved, its reactions to his assistants' maneuvers.

Then he stepped forward into the center and called the bull himself. His stance was set: arched back, head forward, chin down, one foot planted, the other on tiptoe, as the bull circled and passed.

Something about his height, his profile, perhaps, reminded Sara of Gerald. The matadors were not bulky in a traditionally masculine way, and yet these men were the killers of bulls. They commanded by grace and skill, rather than brute force.

It was like an opera, with its three acts, and the staging and the bright colors and the arias of movement. Its noble, somehow tragic hero. Ernest had explained to her that there was no hatred in the matador's killing of a bull; he respected the bull and would only fight a worthy and honorable opponent.

From another entrance Sara saw the *picadores* enter, their long lances held in one hand. She was rather shocked to see the condition of the horses they rode. They looked malnourished, broken-down. They were blindfolded.

She looked over at Ernest. He was leaning forward, elbows on his knees, his face set hard in concentration. She touched the diamonds around her neck. They were slightly warm from her skin, though not exactly sparkling in the shade of their seats.

The bull had noticed the horses too, and now went for one of them. Head down, it endeavored to thrust its horns into the poor animal, while the *picador* turned the horse, poising his lance.

The bull's horns ran the horse through its rib cage. Sara looked again at Ernest. "Why doesn't it make any noise?" Sara whispered.

"They cut their vocal chords," Ernest said, without even looking at her, a slightly irritated tenor to his voice.

She was suddenly quite angry that he hadn't told her about this part. There was no honor in sacrificing a completely defenseless and worn-out animal in this fashion. There was nothing operatic about this.

The bull backed up ever so slightly and dipped its head. Its horns pierced the horse's stomach at the same time that the *picador*'s lance pierced the bull's neck. But the bull didn't disengage. And then all at once, the horse's stomach tore open and its bowels dropped into the dust, the horse and the *picador* dropping with it.

A *banderillero* came from the side to distract the bull so

349

that the *picador* could escape. But Sara had seen enough. She was disgusted.

Clasping her handbag, she stood up and walked quickly and furiously out of the ring.

Back at the hotel, she removed each piece of jewelry, carefully placing them back in the case. For a while, she studied the bracelet and necklace, lying straight out and still, like dead things, in their tray. Then she shut and locked the tiny casket and put it at the back of the dark wooden wardrobe, locking that too.

She lay back on the bed and stared at the ceiling.

She heard footsteps in the corridor outside and sat up quickly, smoothing her dress, touching her fingertips to her hair. The door opened. It was Gerald. She lay back again.

"Sal?" He came over and looked down at her.

"He didn't even notice that I'd left, did he?" She saw there was a piece missing from the ceiling rosette.

"Who? Ernest?"

She propped herself up, looking at him. "He didn't, did he?"

"No," Gerald said, a little sadly. Then he offered her his hand. "But I did."

"Yes," she said, taking it and smelling it, the lovely, clean odor of her husband. "You did."

❖   ❖   ❖

On the last night of the festival, Hadley was sitting outside at the Café Iruña, watching Ernest and Pauline and Sara and Gerald dancing the *boleras* with a crowd gathered in the Plaza del Castillo.

Tomorrow she and Ernest would travel to Madrid, then

on to Valencia and San Sebastian. Pauline was going back to Paris. Hadley wondered if she could even risk feeling glad about that, or if what was so wrong with them would pursue them through their travels in Spain.

Ernest had said it was her fault, for asking him in the first place if he was in love with Pauline, said she put the idea in his head. What could she do after that? She'd been forced into acceptance. No, *more* than acceptance. She'd felt she had to go so far as to arrange for those two to be together, just to prove that she didn't believe it.

That, of course, had led to the awful *menage à trois* in Juan-les-Pins: living together, swimming together, eating together. All the while, Hadley's heart was breaking. And in Pamplona, things only seemed to get worse, although Ernest's admiration for Sara softened the situation a little.

She felt for Gerald, too. He was certainly uncomfortable around her husband. She could sympathize with his position. Ernest was the kind of man to whom men, women, children and dogs were attracted. It was something. And he could make you feel lower than those dogs if he didn't respect you.

Although, with Gerald, it was a little more complicated than that. Hadley had noticed that Ernest had started calling Pauline "Daughter," and he clearly didn't like it when Gerald used the nickname himself, which was his to begin with, for goodness' sakes. Aside from the fact that it made her feel sick to her stomach to hear him call Pauline that, it also flagged up to her that there was some part of Ernest that was jealous of Gerald Murphy. Even if her husband would never admit it.

She watched them now, dancing in a large circle, Ernest holding Pauline's hand tightly, while she looked at him, obviously smitten. Pauline seemed so small next to Ernest, and Hadley thought of her own bigger, stronger body, one that her husband had loved and admired for its ability to fish and hunt and ski and make love. What did he see when he looked at it now?

She supposed she'd thought that the trip to the Riviera might banish her fears about her marriage. She'd arrived at Villa America with high hopes. Ernest would join her and Bumby, and they could be a family again. And that house, and the Bastide, with its white-painted floor and crisp sheets and vases of flowers and soaps made by monks; anything Sara touched became exquisite, it seemed. How could bad things happen there?

But then poor little Bumby had become so sick and she was cast out. No, that wasn't fair. She could remember the look of sheer terror on Sara's face when the doctor told them it was whooping cough. And she'd heard all about her, how Sara hung her own sheets in train compartments before letting the children board. She really didn't think the Murphy children had ever had any of the usual childhood illnesses. So, while Sara's reaction might have been over the top, it was genuine.

Ernest let go of Pauline's hand and moved out of the circle, and for a brief shining moment Hadley thought he was coming to get her. Her heart even raced a little.

But then she saw he was gathering a few people from the crowd and talking to them, a big smile on his face. His up-to-something face. Whatever he was saying was spreading through the crowd and they began to circle Gerald and Sara, who looked a little alarmed. The group started clapping. Then they began to chant: *"Dansa Charles-ton. Dansa Charles-ton. Americanos, dansa Charles-ton."*

Ernest had put them up to this and Hadley knew why.

On the train journey down, Gerald had been going on about how they'd hired a professional American vaudeville group touring the Riviera to come to Villa America and teach them all, including the children, how to do the Charleston. This was Ernest's revenge, his way of punishing Gerald for this luxury, this knowledge. It made her sad.

But then, the band seemed to catch on and they started playing something resembling jazz, and the Murphys looked at each other, Gerald holding a hand out to his wife, and they began to dance. And they did it beautifully, two dark blonds, like a matched set. And then fireworks lit up the night sky, and Hadley wondered if there was anything they couldn't make come out right for themselves, anything that could leave a mark on them.

* * *

When he touched down onto the field, Gerald was waiting for him. Seeing him there, Owen knew what happiness felt like: it was the person you loved finally returning to you.

Gerald felt it too, saying with a kind of surprise, or wonder, in his voice: "My God, it's you. I can't believe you're real. Are you real?"

"I'm real," he said, pulling his overnight bag out of the cockpit.

"Are you still mine?" Gerald asked quietly.

He turned to him. "I'm still yours."

"Thank God. Thank God for that."

They started walking towards the barn.

"How was Spain?"

"Horrible, wonderful," Gerald said. "As Sara said on the train back: 'Isn't it a relief *not* to know how we feel about it?'"

"Do you not? Know how you feel about it?"

"I'm not sure. It was a pageant, a beautiful, bloody circus. There were things . . . but then, of course, there was also Ernest. He was wonderful to us, I'm not saying he wasn't. He knew everyone. Took us everywhere. But I felt, more than ever, a sort of contempt coming off him like a bad smell."

"Fuck him," Owen said.

Gerald smiled. "What about you? What have you been doing?"

"Took a run to Berlin," he said. "Met a man who flew with the Lafayette Corps. Not in my escadrille, but we knew some of the same people. He's a pilot now for a new German airline. Doing runs to Paris and Zurich. And making a lot of money at it."

Gerald stopped. "But you wouldn't want to do that. You have this, the business to run."

"I know," he said. "But still. It's a lot of money. Not many pilots know how to fly these planes."

"If you need help . . ." Gerald said.

Owen looked at him. "Don't."

"I'm sorry. That was arrogant."

They started walking again.

After a moment, Owen said: "It's not that I don't appreciate it. You know that, G. But it can't be like that between us. Like it is with you and Sara and all those artist friends of yours. I'm not a collectible."

"I'm sorry," Gerald said. "I'm sorry this is all so difficult."

Owen shook his head. "It doesn't have to be."

But Gerald just looked down at the ground.

This wasn't how Owen had wanted this to go. He'd missed him, he'd wanted to see him on the edge of that field every goddamn day since Gerald had left for Spain. "Forget it," Owen said. "Come on. I have some German wine in my bag."

Afterwards, they lay on the blanket on the ground, their bodies entwined. He could still taste Gerald's sweat, his insistence. Owen pulled back a bit and studied his lover's body. He ran a finger over Gerald's lips, his eyelids. He ran his hand down over his hip bone, over his thigh.

"I wonder if I measured every inch of you and added it up what it would come to." But what he really meant was: *Would I know you any better if I could add the sum of your parts?*

Gerald smiled at him. "I shudder to think," he said softly.

Owen lay back. He was thinking of the evening he'd spent with the pilot he'd met in Germany. It had been easy time, a few beers, talking about planes, about how it was during the war—not the bad stuff, just the funny stories. It had been a relief to meet someone like himself, after these people who weren't his own kind. These people who courted complication, who made a life—made a religion really—out of their confusion.

It was Gerald who was studying him now.

"You look like the matador I saw in Pamplona," he said. "Nicanor Villalta. Magnificent. When he was fighting, he arched his back from here." Gerald slid his fingers under the small of Owen's back and pressed on his spine. "His rooms were across from ours at the hotel and when I came back one afternoon during the *siesta*, his door was open and he was lying there on this cot, still and straight like you, but his hands were folded over the counterpane . . . like this." Gerald took Owen's arms and crossed them over his chest.

"He was surrounded by candles, with a sheaf of gladioli next to him, and statues of his saints. We'd watched him perform the day before. The bull had pierced his jacket without touching him. They have these outfits with hundreds of gold bullion coins sewn into the silk and they call them 'suits of light.'"

And listening to him, Owen began to forget all the reasons why this thing, this passion, was too complicated, wasn't right. There was only this handsome, lean man next to him, who could find beauty amid ugliness, who found such joy in pageantry. Who wanted to make him happy and tell him all the things he'd seen since they'd been apart. Wanted Owen to be able to see the visions in his head, wanted to share those things with him. And then his hands on his body and the way that made him feel.

"Next to him, on a stool, his sword boy, his *mozo de espada*, was mending it. And he showed us the hole. And when I held that jacket in my own hands, its weight was startling."

Owen pulled Gerald towards him. "Enough. Enough talking," he said.

❊   ❊   ❊

When they arrived at the Casino Hollywood in Juan-les-Pins, Scott and Zelda were nowhere to be seen, so Gerald arranged a table by the doors to the terrace and led Sara through the main room with its columns and flashy chandeliers.

They each ordered a champagne cocktail and Sara drummed her fingers on the tabletop.

"I hope they're not going to stand us up," she said.

They hadn't seen the Fitzgeralds since they'd returned from Spain and Gerald knew that they were both a little nervous about what they would find. May and June had stretched their patience with Scott. Zelda, on the other hand, had been a sort of question mark: she hardly ever came to the beach or to the house and, when they did see her, she was somehow still strangely absent.

They'd left for Paris before he and Sara had departed for Pamplona. Scott had said they were going because Zelda needed an appendectomy, but the way he'd said it had made Gerald think that it wasn't an appendix she was having removed. Of course, he hadn't pressed the matter.

Sara picked the maraschino cherry out of her coupe and popped it in Gerald's mouth. He loved them; she thought they tasted like sweet gasoline.

"Thank you," he said, chewing.

She was wearing a dress he'd had made for her in Paris: blush- and silver-colored beaded chiffon, floor length, with large draped sleeves, and a sash. When she ran her hand through her hair, the tips of the sleeves dropped down her arm to her shoulder, in a lovely fluid movement.

"There they are," she said.

Gerald followed her gaze and saw Zelda and Scott crossing the casino towards them. Zelda looked like she was floating above the ground, in a white satin gown. She had a pale pink rose, fat and open, with what looked a hundred petals, pinned to her shoulder. She looked like that rose, Gerald thought.

Scott had his head leaning into hers and they were obviously talking as they walked. Gerald could see that they had that look, that tonight they were companions, they were drawn together, inseparable, they were waiting for something to happen, expecting it. Something *had* to happen, something extravagant.

He looked at Sara and he knew she'd seen it, too; she looked tense.

When they arrived at the table, Scott said: "No, no, no. We have to have a table outside. All the good people are outside."

"Oh, all right," Sara said, standing. She kissed Zelda, looked at her. "There are those eyes," she said. "I've missed them."

"Oh Say-ra," Zelda said. "How come you look like something to eat?"

Gerald embraced her as well. "*You* look like something from the garden."

"Dow-Dow," she said. "Oh Dow-Dow. Where have you been all our lives?"

"We *have* missed you," Scott said. "Paris was dull and expensive." He looked at Sara, then caught her wrist. "Can I have this wrist?"

Sara gave in and kissed him on the cheek.

"Have you forgiven me?" Scott asked her.

"Don't give it another thought," Sara said. "I haven't."

And then the four of them went out to take a table on the terrace under the stars of the Riviera.

They drank—or really Gerald and Sara and Scott drank —copious champagne cocktails, too many, and Gerald was glad they'd brought the driver with them. Zelda hardly touched hers, although, somehow, she seemed high, too.

Scott had been telling them about the new book he was working on, *World's Fair*, but in the middle of a moderately torturous explanation of the plot, he stopped and turned to Sara.

"So how rich are you?"

Gerald nearly spat out his drink, but Sara continued sipping hers calmly, answering: "Oh, my father knocked over the Federal Reserve, didn't you know?"

"Seriously, how rich, really?"

"Oh and then, of course, he was in on the World Series fix. That's how we could afford Villa America."

"I *need* to know," Scott said, whining a little.

"Scott," Gerald said. "Let's put it this way, you're richer than we are."

Scott shook his head, saying, "That's not possible."

"Don't be a bore," Gerald said.

Zelda put her head on Scott's shoulder. "My husband is never a bore."

Sara shrugged. "You're a good woman, Zelda. A better one than I."

Zelda lifted her head. "Say-ra, did I tell you I'm thinking of taking up ballet again?"

"Again?" Sara said.

"I was very good as a child. Everyone said so."

"Everyone at the playground in Montgomery, Alabama," Scott said.

"I think that's wonderful," Gerald said, more to stave off a fight than because he believed in the wisdom of this endeavor.

"Well," Sara said, "if that's the case, then you might be interested to know that Isadora Duncan is sitting at that table over there."

"Where?" Zelda asked breathlessly, and Sara used her glass to indicate the dancer.

"Her?" Zelda said. "But she's fat and old . . . and her hair is purple."

Gerald burst out laughing. It was true the famous dancer's hair seemed to match her purple dress, and maybe she did look a little shopworn, but she wasn't exactly *old*.

"Well," Sara said, "nonetheless it is she."

"Oh Say-ra," Zelda said, putting a hand over her mouth, "I'm not going to look like that when I'm a dancer."

"I think she looks wonderful," Scott said, his gaze fixed on the woman.

They watched in amazement as he rose and walked over to her table. Gerald couldn't hear what Scott was saying to the dancer, but whatever it was she nodded, and he sat down at her feet, gazing up at her adoringly.

Then, improbably, Isadora Duncan started running her fingers through Scott's hair, and above the chatter, Gerald could hear her calling him "her centurion."

"Is this just about the weirdest thing you've ever seen?" Gerald said, turning to Sara.

"I'm at a loss," Sara said. "Zelda, darling, do you want me to retrieve your silly husband? Or shall we leave him where he is and run up his tab?"

They were both looking at Zelda, but she was looking at Scott. When she did turn to face them, she had a peculiar look in her eyes. Vacant, almost, Gerald thought. She got up slowly and stood on her chair, and before either he or Sara could say anything, she leapt—a ballerina's *grand jeté*—across their small table, clearing Gerald's lap, and over the parapet behind them, the tip of her white satin sash fluttering after her.

"Oh my God," Sara said, and was up in a flash.

Gerald, whose back was to the small wall, looked over it and saw her crumpled on a steep stone stairway leading from the terrace down to gardens below.

"She's landed on the stairs." But when he looked back, Sara was already running towards her.

He rose himself, and went over to where Scott was sitting. "I think you might want to get up. Your wife's just thrown herself over the wall."

To his credit, Scott did look alarmed and he followed meekly behind Gerald. When they reached the top of the staircase, Sara was helping Zelda up the stairs, blood seeping through Zelda's white dress at the knees.

"She's fine," Sara said. "A little bruised and bloody, but in one piece. You are in one piece, aren't you, darling?"

Zelda didn't respond, just looked at Scott, then, pushing Sara away, walked straight past them and into the casino.

*

They were all quiet as they drove down the coast toward Antibes. Zelda had informed them that she and Scott were staying at the Hôtel du Cap. When Sara had asked about their villa, Zelda had replied that there were bats living there, and no one said much after that.

Gerald looked out into the darkness. He was thinking about how still it would be now in Owen's barn. No one would be drunk or throwing themselves off parapets or interrogating their friends about their finances. And yet . . . he couldn't help remembering their last conversation, lying on that blanket on the ground.

"You call it a circus," Owen had said. "But could you live without it?"

"What do you mean?" he'd asked, pretending he hadn't understood what Owen had so clearly meant.

"Without the spectacle and the costumes and the fucking disguises. The *ideas*, Jesus, the endless conversations about ideas, and the misunderstandings. Could you live without that? Could you, G.? Because I could. I can. I do."

Gerald had felt angry and had turned away. "Why are you asking me impossible questions?"

"Well, then what are we doing here? Is this it? Me, here in this field, you in your house. *Your* house. *Your* life. And what? I get to stand at the window and press my face against the glass, like some beggar? I'm not a beggar, G."

At that point, Gerald had risen and begun to dress.

"You know," Owen said, standing too, naked, "you pretend like you built that house and that wall around it to keep your family safe. But you're lying to yourself."

Gerald had turned on him. "What about you? Oh, forgive me, I forgot, you're in control of everything. No good luck, no bad luck, just choices. Isn't that what you say? And look how far you've come," he'd said, spreading his arm around the barn, the shoddy camp bed. "Have you told anyone what *you* are? Not just *what* you are, but *who* you are? And don't presume to talk to me about family. What on earth would you know about family?"

And with that, he'd turned and left, and he hadn't looked back.

"Scott." Zelda's voice brought Gerald back to the automobile. "Scott. Do you know what we have to do now?"

Gerald looked at Scott, sitting across from him.

"Scott." Zelda said it again. Gerald could tell by her tone it wasn't a question; it was payback.

Scott lifted his head and looked at his wife. "What do we have to do?"

"Don't you think, Goofo, it's the perfect night to jump off Eden Roc?"

❖

They were standing, all four of them, on the highest rock, looking down into what would be the sea below if they could see it in the darkness. A thirty-five-foot drop. Gerald knew this from Archie who took pride in his swan dives off here, thrilling the children. That was when the sun was up.

Zelda stripped down to her underpants, ruffly, he could tell from their outline against the night sky, her dress a pool at her feet. Then her shoes, cast behind her.

Gerald was standing next to Scott, who even in the very dim light looked whiter than usual. He could feel him shaking. Gerald thought of being in the ring with the young bull in Pamplona and wanted to tell him: *you do not have to do this.* But he felt he couldn't interfere with what was going on between the two of them. It was beyond him, or he was beside the point.

Sara had said nothing either; she must have felt the same way.

"Goofo," Zelda said.

Scott sat down and took off his shoes. Then he removed his socks, carefully placing them inside. Slowly, a little unsteadily, he stood back up and took off his dinner jacket, handing it to Gerald, like something you'd give a friend before a fistfight.

He looked at Zelda. "You first," he said.

"Don't worry, Scott, my nerves never fail," Zelda said.

She walked towards the edge.

"Wait," Sara said suddenly. "No, this is mad. You could kill yourselves."

Zelda turned to her and said: "Oh, but Say-ra. Didn't you know? We're not conservationists." And then she jumped.

They heard a splash.

Scott looked at them, and he had the saddest look in his eyes that Gerald had ever seen. He looked down at his bare feet, and then, without a word, he followed her off the cliff.

✻

Gerald and Sara were standing in the lobby of the Hôtel du Cap. Scott and Zelda, soaking wet, had made their way up to their rooms.

"Well, it seems she can dance, after all," Gerald said.

"Don't," Sara said, shaking her head. "That was . . . awful. They're becoming unbearable. I can't watch."

He pulled her into his arms and she kissed his neck.

"Let's go home," she said into his collar.

Gerald moved back. "You take the car. I still have Scott's jacket. And I think I should talk to him," he said. "I'll get the hotel car to drive me home."

"Are you sure?"

"Of course."

He watched her walk out and then handed Scott's dinner jacket to the bellhop. "Make sure Monsieur Fitzgerald gets this," he said. "And I need a car."

When the car stopped at the end of the allée des Cigales, Gerald turned to the driver and said: "Please wait. I'll only be a few minutes."

He walked first to the tree on the edge of the field and stood under it. Between the leaves he could see the stars in the sky, like jewelry on a woman's neck. Then he made his way to the barn.

Inside it was dark, but he knew by memory where the cot was. He went over and kneeled down, putting his hand on Owen's shoulder and gently shaking him.

Owen sat up.

"I'm sorry," Gerald said.

Owen was silent.

"I can't stay. But I wanted you to know: you do have a family."

He couldn't see his eyes, but Gerald could feel his gaze.

"Will you come with me tomorrow? Out on the boat? I want to be in the middle of the ocean with you. I want to be in the middle of somewhere with you."

"Yes."

He nodded and stood. He made to leave and then turned back and said: "I love you."

*

Vladimir toweled off and sat down on the hatch, leaning his back against the *Picaflor*'s mast. Gerald lay naked on the deck in front of him, as was his way, while Owen, still in his swim trunks, lay on the starboard side, drying off in the midday sun. They'd dropped anchor near a small peninsula so that they could swim in the open sea before heading back to Antibes.

They'd eaten their lunch early—cold roast chicken, its skin encrusted with salt, slices of preserved lemon and plums for dessert, all packed up by Sara, who'd waved them off from the harbor in the Old Town.

Gerald turned his head to the side and opened one eye. "Tell us a story, Vladimir."

Vladimir thought a moment. He had a story for them, but he wondered if he should tell it. It was one that he had been saving for Owen alone. He couldn't deny that he questioned the wisdom of what his two friends had embarked upon. Changing the alchemy of one's life was a dangerous thing to do, something he didn't believe should be undertaken unless absolutely necessary. But some tales were predestined, their endings already written. And if he'd been asked now to tell a story, perhaps there was a reason.

"I heard a story," he said. "About your land, Owen. About when it was a flying school."

Owen lifted his head. "The Garbero brothers," he said.

"Yes, when they owned it, but it's not about them," Vladimir said. "It's a love story. It is Proust's love story."

"Is this going to be a tragedy?" Gerald groaned and Vladimir could hear Owen laugh.

"Who can tell?" Vladimir said. "What is tragedy and what is destiny?"

"Christ, Vladimir," Owen said.

"All right, just tell it," Gerald said. "And we'll vote on it afterward."

Vladimir nodded. "I will tell it. It begins like this: Marcel Proust, he was in love with his chauffeur, a man from Monaco whose name was Alfred Agostinelli. He had met him first when Agostinelli was just a boy. But fate, being what it is, had them cross paths again when the boy had blossomed into a young man in his prime. Proust's desire for him was then ignited, and he became convinced that he adored him and he could not live without him.

"He hired him as his driver and even allowed Agostinelli's pear-shaped woman to move in with them. Little by little, Proust ended up not only paying for Agostinelli and his lover, but for the chauffeur's whole family, such was his desire to keep the young man near him.

"One day, however, Proust awoke to find the house in Versailles empty: no Agostinelli, no woman, money missing. Proust was heartbroken. Driven by desperation, he hired a private detective to find his amour. After some time, he was discovered in Antibes, enrolled in the Garbero brothers' flying school, under the name Marcel Swann.

"Why, thought Proust, when this had been related to him, would Agostinelli choose a name that conjured the very essence of Proust himself—his first name and the last name of his most famous character—if the young man did not love him? So, believing this to be true, he sent his secretary down to Antibes to beg Agostinelli to return.

"But, alas, Agostinelli would not. The young man, it seems, had decided that his destiny was to become a great pilot. So Proust offered to buy him an airplane of his own, and even a Rolls Royce, anything he wanted, if only he would return. The answer was still no. Distraught, Proust finally sent his secretary down to Monaco to offer Agostinelli's father whatever sum he desired if he would force his son to come back to him. A third time, he was refused.

"The day of his first solo flight—embarking from your land, my friend—Agostinelli flew out over the bay and immediately dropped like a stone into the water. Those that saw him say the plane floated for a few seconds, while Agostinelli stood on the wing screaming, before being sucked into the water below.

"Now it was Agostinelli's family who came to beg Proust: they needed cash to pay to have him pulled out of the sea. Proust agreed. And when they lifted his body, rotting, from the water, they found that his pockets were stuffed with the money he'd stolen from Proust. Why had he called himself Marcel Swann? What had happened to the plane? These things were never known. All that was known was that the young man had refused love and fallen into the sea."

Gerald sat up as Vladimir finished the story and clapped. "I don't care if that was a tragedy. Bravo."

But Owen, Vladimir noticed, said nothing. His friend's eyes were still closed, his face expressionless, but the silence was enough to tell him that he hadn't liked it.

Owen stood up. "I'm going for a swim," he said, and dove into the water.

On the way back to Antibes, Owen sat next to Vladimir at the tiller. "Where did you hear that? All that about Proust?"

"From a man in town," Vladimir said.

Owen shook his head, his expression hard. "Some people talk too much."

*   *   *

Owen had run into Sara in town and she'd asked him up to the villa for a drink.

"We're feeling rather bereft," she'd said. "Archie and Ada are ensconced in their own house. And Bob Benchley and Dottie Parker aren't arriving for two weeks. And the Hemingways, well, they're coming in a few days. But it does seem awfully empty. Come keep us company."

He pulled his car into the driveway and looked at the house a moment. From the front it always seemed so quiet, except for the row of bicycles leaning against the wall. Life happened on the other side.

He got out and went to the door, opening it without knocking, and then wondered when he'd started doing that.

Tintine came scuttling out of the dining room. Seeing who it was she smiled. *"Ils sont dehors,"* she said.

Owen walked down the hall and out the French doors to find Sara and Gerald sitting at the table under the linden tree.

"Oh, good, you came," she said.

Gerald rose, hand on Owen's shoulder. "Whiskey sour?"

"Thanks," Owen said, kissing Sara on the cheek and sitting down at the table.

In the center of the table was a light blue bowl filled with white eggs. Sara was turning one over in her hand. The china was so thin it was partially translucent, and in the late sun, the shells of the eggs were too.

"Pretty big omelet," he said, smiling.

"No," she said. "We're not . . . no, they're for decoration. I just thought they belonged together, the bowl and the eggs."

He nodded.

"You must find us awfully silly sometimes," she said.

"No, I don't find you silly at all."

"I think some of the most beautiful things are the things that aren't used in the way they were intended," she said, continuing to turn the egg in the cradle of her hand. "It doesn't matter what it was *supposed* to be, what it was born as. It's what you make of it."

Owen put out his own hand and she passed the egg to him. He looked at it, felt its weight. "This taught men how to build airplanes," he said. "To make them efficient. A plane's skin, not an internal structure, supports the load, the same way an eggshell bears the weight of the egg."

"Is that true?"

"It is. You're right, it depends what you use it for." He looked up at her; their eyes locked.

"Fascinating," she said.

Gerald came through the doors, carrying a frosted glass on a silver tray. He placed the whiskey in front of Owen.

"I heard Vladimir had quite a story for you on your boat trip," she said, when Gerald had sat back down.

"He did," Owen said. He wondered why Gerald would have told her that story, that secret love story. Not for the first time, he wondered what went on behind these closed doors.

"It made me anxious," she said. "You will be careful, won't you?"

"Don't worry, I'm not going to fall out of the sky."

"Don't even say that," she said, twisting her hands together.

"This is what I do for a living," he said. "It's all right. Nothing's going to happen."

"Something can always happen," Sara said. "Especially when you think you're safe."

"Oh, that was just Vladimir," Gerald said. "You know how he is about stories."

Sara didn't answer, just kept her eyes on Owen.

"We went up the other night to tuck the children in," Gerald continued. "And there was Vladimir recounting a story in French about a boy named Mowgli who's raised by wolves and a bear named Baloo. They thought he'd made it up and there he was telling them the whole of Kipling's damn *Jungle Book*." He laughed.

"Yes," Sara said, smiling now, too. "It was funny. They think he's some magical genius. I didn't tell you this," she turned to Gerald, "but last week, he was telling them the story of how the Cossacks shot his father. Can you imagine? Of course, it was a sanitized version, but still."

"I suppose they loved it, though," Gerald said.

"They adored it," Sara said, taking a sip of her drink. "I didn't have the heart to scold him."

Gerald laughed out loud, as if tickled by the whole idea, and by Sara's soft-heartedness.

Owen looked at his drink. He didn't think he could take it.

"Dow-Dow?"

Honoria was standing in the doorway, holding Patrick's hand.

"Speak of the devil," Gerald said.

"We heard voices," the child said.

"Little busybodies," Sara said. "Isn't it bath time?"

"We've been practicing something for you," she said, shyly, scuffing her feet a little.

"Well, show us," Sara said. "I'm sure Owen would like to see, too."

"Dow-Dow has to put this record on," Honoria said.

"Your wish is my command," Gerald said, rising and taking it from his daughter.

When he'd placed the record on the gramophone, he called out: "Ready?"

"Wait," Honoria said, and pushed Patrick over a bit, whispering something in his ear.

"Now?"

"Yes, Dow-Dow," she said.

The needle hit the record and a hoppy tune filled the air.

The little girl and her brother began to dance, their arms circling furiously, feet passing behind each other. Every now and then, they would slap their hands on their behinds. Honoria was a little more adept, while Patrick's lack of balance meant his was mostly an arm dance, and his sister kept eyeing him and mouthing "No." After a while, though, she seemed to stop caring and she just looked at the adults, her face shining, manic, joyful.

All at once, when the slide trombone cut in, Baoth jumped out from behind a curtain onto the terrace, holding some kind of elaborate guitar, and started playing it, loudly and out of tune, and hopping around, until the song ended.

"Goodness," Sara said, when it was over, "that was marvelous." She kissed Baoth's collarbone, and he leaned against her, winding an arm around her neck.

"It was the Black Bottom dance," Baoth said.

Gerald stood and clapped. "We're going to have to sell you to a dance troupe, you're so good. Also, we really could use the money."

"No, Dow-Dow," Honoria shrieked.

"No, Dow-Dow," Patrick repeated, and ran over and clung to Gerald's leg.

His head was so small, Owen noticed. Everything was so small. And fragile. How had he never noticed that?

"Well, what do you say, Sal?"

"Oh, I don't know," Sara said. "I quite love them. Maybe we should keep them for ourselves."

"Oh, all right," Gerald said.

"What did you think, Owen?" Sara said, turning to him.

"It was great," Owen said. "You were great." He stopped. He felt like he'd been punched in the stomach. "I'm sorry, but I just remembered, I have to meet my mechanic. Go over some things." He stood up.

"Now?" Gerald looked at him, surprised.

But Sara just held on tight to Baoth.

"Yes," Owen said. "You know, I'd just forgotten. But thank you, for everything."

"I'll walk you out," Gerald said.

"No, stay," he said, but Gerald followed him out anyway. Owen got in the car and shut the door.

"Owen," Gerald said.

"Don't," he said, turning the engine over. "Not for a while." And he quickly backed out and drove away from Villa America.

*

The next morning, sitting at his desk, Owen went over the books. Three months running they were making money. That was good. He had standing orders that would take them through October, at the least. Tallied against the cost of fuel and Eugène's share and the payments to the bank, they would come out in the black.

It was safe for now. He took out his writing paper and wrote two letters. One he addressed to the Fréjus airbase, and the other to Berlin.

Then he got in his car and went to post them.

*   *   *

Gerald had waited a week. Well, in a way. He had gone up to Owen's place the next morning, but hadn't found him there. He wasn't sure if it was the type of circumstance in which one should wait, or in which one should definitely not wait, because he wasn't clear as to what had actually happened. Only that something about them all being together at Villa America that evening had upset him.

When his effort to see Owen had failed, he'd decided that perhaps he should respect his wishes and stay away until Owen came looking for him. Yet the look on Owen's face when he'd driven off haunted Gerald. There'd been a kind of desolation etched across his features that had at first stunned, then panicked him.

He'd tried writing him a letter, but he hadn't known what to say. There was nothing, really, he could say to make it come out the way Owen wanted it to.

So, he waited.

Things were also gearing up at the house: the Hemingways had arrived that afternoon and, of course, Sara had planned a Dinner-Flowers-Gala for them, with the MacLeishes, the Barrys and the Fitzgeralds.

Gerald, in honor of the occasion, had concocted a new cocktail, which he'd named a "Bailey," calling for Booth's gin, lime juice, grapefruit juice, torn mint and a great deal of ice. He was perfecting the first round now, and making notes in his bar book.

Sara, already dressed and smelling beautiful, came up behind him and wrapped her arms around his waist.

"There's something going on between Ernest and Hadley," she said. "What is it with married people these days? What do they all *have*? I don't think I can stand another shock."

"What do you mean? What kind of shock?" he asked, turning around. "Wait. Don't answer. Try this first." And he handed her a sip of the drink.

"Perfect," she said. "Oh, I don't know. Whatever's going on with Scott and Zelda. And now this."

"Now what?"

"They aren't even looking at each other," she said.

"Well, maybe they just had a row."

"No, because Ernest took me aside and said he had something to tell me."

"Of course he did."

"What does that mean?"

"Well," Gerald said, "maybe he wants to introduce you to someone. You'll probably like him, *he's tough*."

Sara laughed. "Oh, shut up. He's just attracted to those sort of people."

"Fine, but does he always have to finish his description with that? If I hear one more word about someone or something being tough . . ."

Sara sighed. "Never mind that, Jerry. I'm telling you, there's something going on."

Now it was his turn to sigh. "I'm sure we'll hear about it tonight, if that's the case. I think I'm going to restrict our guests to two cocktails before dinner."

"Isn't that a bit cheap?"

"It's called survival," he said.

She rubbed his earlobe. "You have lovely ears," she said. "May I have a drink now? One that doesn't count towards my two?"

"I trust *you*," he said, and poured her a Bailey.

❈

Gerald had taken a small group down to his studio to show them *Bibliothèque*. Archie had expressed an interest in his work-in-progress, and then Zelda, perhaps suspecting something exciting, had joined in and Scott had tagged along because she did, although Gerald knew he had absolutely no interest in paintings.

Archie looked at the canvas thoughtfully. "It's severe, I'll say that."

"It's my father's study," Gerald said. "Or rather, my impression of it."

"There are no titles on the book spines," Archie said, peering a bit closer. "Or country names on the globe. Learning for learning's sake?"

"Perhaps something like that," Gerald said.

"Who is that creepy bust?" Zelda asked, mildly interested. "He looks like he's spying on you from behind that column."

"Caesar?" Archie said.

Gerald laughed. "No, not Caesar."

"Ah," Archie said, smiling. "I believe that's Gerald's *pater*."

Scott yawned.

"It's not finished yet." Gerald replaced the drop cloth.

"It's very effective," Archie said, as they walked back out into the soft evening air.

They picked up their cocktails, left in a row, like soldiers, on the wall outside the studio.

"I have to talk about Ernest and Hadley," Scott said, suddenly animated, anxious even. "I know we shouldn't, but I can't stand it."

"What about them?" Archie asked.

"They're breaking up," Scott said. "You didn't know? None of you?"

Gerald had seen Ernest talking quite seriously with Sara in the living room before they'd come down to the studio, but he hadn't thought too much of it.

"They're divorcing?" he said now. He couldn't believe it. Of course people divorced, but he'd never been close to anyone who had. Not really. It felt momentous.

"It's all cracked up between them." Scott looked genuinely upset. "I can't understand it, though. There's some mess with Pauline. Ernest thinks he's in love with her. Hadley's making him choose."

"Oh, I think she'd be lucky to get rid of that one," Zelda said, and Scott shot her a dark look.

"Well, I'll be damned," Archie said. "I'll be goddamned. Poor Hem."

"Poor Hadley," Gerald said.

"Yes, her too," Archie agreed.

The three men leaned back against the wall, contemplating this, while Zelda practiced *pliés* on the path in front of them.

"I suppose they always were an odd match," Gerald said.

"Why do you say that?" Archie asked.

"She was so, I don't know, naive? Basic? None of those are the right words, but Ernest seems to have more drive in him, I suppose."

"Huh," Archie said. "It never occurred to me that they were unhappy. Or mismatched, as you put it." He exhaled loudly and then swallowed the rest of his drink. "I hate finding out that things are different than what they seem."

Gerald looked at him.

"We have to help him," Scott said.

"Not much we can do there," Archie said.

"Well, about his work, then."

"Yes, this new book. I suppose *you* can do something. I don't know what," Archie said. "What's it about exactly?"

Before Scott or even Gerald could answer, Zelda, in the middle of an *effacé*, said: "Bullfighting, bullslinging and bullshit."

"Zelda," Scott said fiercely. "Don't talk like that. Say anything you want, but lay off Ernest."

"Try and make me," Zelda said.

"What have you got against Ernest?" Gerald asked.

Zelda stopped her movements, coming to rest on both feet, and looked at Gerald straight on. "He's bogus," she said, and then walked off up the path.

"She doesn't know what she's talking about," Scott said. "Ignore her."

But Gerald was rather astonished by her comment. He never would've described Ernest as bogus: intimidating, yes, overbearing, definitely, perhaps overly concerned with masculine pride. But a fake? He wondered if, with all his own disguises, he had no accurate perception of the disguises of others. He felt a dread come over him.

Back up on the terrace, the strangeness of the evening, and Gerald's unease, only continued to deepen. As he carried on a halfhearted conversation with Phil and Ellen Barry who, fed up with New York and with Broadway, were considering moving permanently to Antibes, he couldn't help eavesdropping on an extraordinary conversation Scott and Zelda were having with Hadley. He saw now that the latter did indeed look drawn, and unhappy. What had he thought before? That she was tired? Archie's comment about things not being what they seemed echoed in his head.

"Well, you know that I had an affair," Zelda was saying, her face very solemn.

Hadley looked as if an ice-bucket had just been dropped on her head.

Scott, standing with his arm around Zelda, nodded. He looked even paler than usual. "His name," Scott said, "was Edouard Jozan."

"He loved me, passionately, dearly," Zelda said.

Scott's face took on an expression of distress, but, to Gerald, it looked rehearsed.

"But it was hopeless," Zelda said. "Hopeless, hopeless, hopeless."

"Because Zelda could never truly love anyone but me," Scott said and Gerald thought he saw tears in his eyes.

"And when Edouard realized this . . ." Zelda stopped and looked at Scott.

"He committed suicide," Scott said.

Gerald had to make a concerted effort not to burst out laughing. This was patently untrue; in fact, he'd seen Jozan last year in Antibes, alive and well. He'd told Gerald that he was leaving the Riviera for a post in Indo-China.

But then it came to Gerald why they'd concocted this narrative, and then he didn't feel like laughing at all: the idea of Jozan killing himself was the only way they'd been able to survive the realization that, perhaps, they weren't fated to be, that circumstance, not destiny, had brought them together.

Hadley, however, didn't seem to understand why she'd been singled out for this horrific story, and obviously hurt, just backed away from them.

Gerald decided to rescue her. "Another cocktail?"

"I thought there was a two-drink limit," Hadley said. "Sara informed me."

"We're very understanding here," Gerald said. "Exceptions can always be made."

"I can't go in there," she said, indicating the bar in the living room, where Ernest and Sara were still deep in conversation, ensconced in the white satin sofa.

"No," he said, "of course not. I'll fetch it."

"No," she said. "Don't leave me alone."

He put his hand over hers. "I'm sorry, I wasn't thinking. I won't leave you."

"Actually," she said, "I'm quite tired. Would you mind walking me to the Bastide? I don't want to worry Ernest, but, for some reason, I don't want to walk in there by myself."

Gerald offered her his arm. "I don't like to walk alone, either," he said.

❈ ❈ ❈

Sara looked down the length of the table where her friends and husband were gathered. The cloth was dotted with small bouquets of pink roses and yellow mimosa from the garden, and in the middle, her mother's silver and glass candelabra threw warm light on her guests' faces.

She had been very sad to hear what Ernest had to tell her. He was obviously torn about what to do and she only wished she could somehow make it better for him. She was glad, though, that if he had to go through heartbreak, he was doing it here, among people who loved and admired him. Hadley, it seemed, had skipped out on dinner, but she could understand that.

In her heart, Sara felt that Hadley should never have

forced him to choose between two kinds of love. The only reason for asking the question "do you love X?" was to be told "no." Or, for the questionable vindication of being right when told "yes." And what good came of that?

She felt a husband and wife should make each other happy in as many ways as they knew how. But what you do not do, even for a second, is allow the possibility that another could supersede you, could break you, or wreck you. It wasn't denial, it was survival in a long relationship. But even as the thought crossed her mind, she wondered if she was fooling herself.

Gerald, who had put a Schubert record on the gramophone, returned to his seat and raised his glass.

"To my wife," he said.

"To Sara," came the murmur from the table.

She clinked with Archie, seated to her right, and Scott seated to her left. Tintine served the first course of artichokes with a poached egg in the center and they all began to eat.

Afterwards, when the music had stopped, Sara said: "I can hear the nightingales. I love that. I love that we can always, always hear them."

"They went so well with the Schubert," Ada said, smiling from the other end of the table.

"They did, didn't they?" Sara looked at her friend. "Would you do something for me?"

"Anything," Ada said.

"Will you sing something for us?"

"Now?"

"Mmm."

"No," Ada said, and Sara could see her coloring a little in the candlelight. "I don't want to be responsible for ruining your evening."

"Come on, Ada," Archie said. "Don't be shy. You never are at home."

"Or in public, for that matter," Ellen Barry said.

"Oh, yes, well, for the less discerning public," Ada said. "That's one thing."

"No, please," Sara said. "I want to hear your beautiful voice, singing with the nightingales."

"You shall never be invited back if you don't sing for your supper," Gerald said.

"Oh, all right."

Sara watched as she rose and stood back from the table, disappearing a little into the darkness. The table hushed, and there was only the sound of the candles hissing and the cicadas and the birdsong as Ada placed her hand on her diaphragm.

She drew in her breath, and Sara, reflexively, did the same, holding hers.

"An die Musik." To Music. Ada's *voix blanche*, clear, pure, unwavering, rose and floated over them, expressing all the sweetness, the gratitude, all the sadness of Schubert's music.

> *"O lovely Art, in how many gray hours,*
> *When life's fierce orbit ensnared me,*
> *Have you kindled my heart to warm love."*

Sara knew it from her youth, traveling around Chicago, New York, London with her mother and Hoytie and Olga. The warm realm of that still time, she just a sleepwalker then. She knew it from the concerts played at the house in East Hampton while she ran on the lawn, down to the beach, her hat falling on the grass behind her. She knew it from the drawing rooms in which she and Gerald had fallen in love; knew it from houses in which they'd made love. All that time forgotten that had brought them here, to this moment.

When Ada finished none of them spoke. Sara realized that she had tears coursing down her cheeks. Ada sat back down. It took a moment before the gentlemen started clapping and Ellen Barry, her eyes wet, too, reached across Scott and took Sara's hand.

"Do you know, I'm just so very happy right now," she said.

Sara could only nod.

Gerald stood: "To Ada."

"To Ada," they cried.

*

By the time dessert had been finished and cleared, and Tintine had brought out the coffee and brandy, Gerald was feeling a little more relaxed. Whatever currents had been at work earlier in the evening seemed to have lessened and some kind of peace had settled over them, starting with Ada's singing.

He was chatting to Ada about music, when he heard Scott's raised voice. They both turned, Ada leaning forward a bit.

"What is it, Scott?" she said.

"I'm trying to talk to Gerald," he said.

"Well, you're at the other end of the table," Ada said, laughing.

"Gerald," Scott said, and Gerald had a sinking feeling. The timbre of Scott's voice indicated that he had passed the point of social conversation.

"Yes, Scott. What can I do for you?"

He saw Sara try to take Scott's hand, presumably to distract him, but he waved her away, saying: "I *will* ask it."

From the end of the table, Sara gave Gerald a little warning shake of her head.

"Gerald," Scott began again. "When did you and Sara first have sex? Did you do it before you were married? Sara won't answer me."

Next to Gerald, Phil groaned, putting his head in his hands. "Not this again."

"I don't care what *you* think, Phil Barry," Scott said. "This is between me and Gerald."

"Scott," Gerald said. "Really . . ."

"Do you still have sex? Or are you the kind of man that is more concerned with your art? That kind of man. Or the kind that gives so much of himself that there's nothing left over for your wife?"

"Christ, Scott," Gerald said, but he felt he had to say something to shut him up. "Sara and I are very happy." He could now feel Ernest's eyes on him, boring holes in him.

"Yes, but do you have the essence left in you?"

Gerald just stared at him. "What essence?"

"The essence of a real man, of a physical man, who can love a woman."

Gerald felt the blood leaving his body.

Before he could react, Sara stepped in.

"Scott," she said, her voice cold and hard, "you think if you just ask enough questions you'll get to know what people are like, but you won't. You don't really know anything at all about people."

Even in the candlelight, Gerald could see Scott's face drawing in on itself, the skin tightening, rage flushing over him. He rose, shaking, from the table and pointed a finger at Sara.

"How *dare* you? No one says that to me."

"Really?" Sara said, arching an eyebrow. "Is that right, Scott? Would you like me to repeat it?"

Scott seemed to have no response to this, so Sara stood,

slamming a palm on the table, and said, enunciating slowly: "You . . . don't . . . know . . . *anything* . . . about . . . people."

Scott stared at her. He picked up his wineglass, one of the Venetian ones Sara loved so much, and threw it over the side of the wall. He looked back at her, as if to make sure he'd hit his mark. Then he picked up Ellen's and snatched Ernest's clean out of his hand, and did the same.

"Scott." Gerald stood, too, sheer fury coming over him. "Stop that right now."

Scott hurled another.

Archie got up quickly and grabbed Scott. He started dragging him off, but Scott ripped away from him.

"Scott," Archie said. "I think you should behave."

Scott sneered, mimicking: "'*Scott, I think you should behave.*' You know what I think?" Scott asked, and threw a roundhouse punch at Archie, hitting him square in the jaw.

Archie rubbed it a minute. Then, calm as anything, he clocked Scott—the sound like the pop of a cork—and knocked him out cold on the terrace.

"Oh my God," Phil said. "It's just like college."

"But better," Ellen said. "I never went to college."

Archie and Gerald carried Scott out to his car, Zelda trailing behind them.

"I'll drive them home and come back for Ada," Archie said.

"Dow-Dow," Zelda said.

"Zelda," Gerald said coldly. "Put him to bed. And when he wakes up tell your husband he is not welcome here for three weeks. And not to bother writing."

Zelda sighed, but nodded and got in the passenger seat. "Will you tell Say-ra that I had just the most splendid evening?"

Gerald shook his head and left Archie to it.

Back inside the villa, Gerald leaned against the front door, Owen's words running through his mind: *Could you live without it? Without the spectacle and the fucking disguises . . . the endless conversations about ideas, and the misunderstandings . . . Could you, G.?*

It was a question without an answer. Could he live without Ada's singing "An die Musik" on a warm August night? Could he live without Baoth playing the guitar, one plump arm wrapped around Sara's golden brown neck? Could he live without his wife slamming her hand on the table and giving Scott Fitzgerald a run for his money? But, then, could he also live *with* the endless search for double meanings in his friends' words, the fear of being just a bit *too* this, or just a bit *too* that, of wasting his essence, as Scott had said, on a frantic performance? Could he live with being not what he seemed?

"There you are."

Of course it was Ernest.

"Just bundled them off to the pulse of a motor car," Gerald said. "Our charming mutual friends." Did he sound breezy and nonchalant, or did he sound . . . something else?

"Archie's pretty tough," Ernest said. "I had no idea. Those glasses hide it pretty well. Then again, Scott's a soft touch."

"I suppose we must be grateful for that," Gerald said.

"Mmm," Ernest said. "So why are you hanging back here?"

"Just recalibrating," Gerald replied.

"He said some awfully hard things." His dark brown eyes, almost black really, regarded Gerald lazily.

"I was sorry to hear about you and Hadley. Is it decided?"

"I don't know," Ernest said. "In a way I guess it doesn't matter: she's always been a kind of truth to me. A part of growing up, of where we came from. That won't change."

"I suppose there are different kinds of truths," Gerald said.

"You think so?" Ernest put his hand near Gerald's head, leaning his weight against the wall, his face closer than Gerald would have liked. He looked at him awhile and then said: "Do you think Scott's a fairy?"

"No," Gerald said.

"Me neither," Ernest said, not taking his gaze off Gerald. He could smell his breath, sour from the booze.

"You know, I don't mind a fairy like that pilot friend of yours. Owen." His mouth went round when he pronounced the "O."

Gerald stared at the opposite wall, silent.

"Do you mind a fairy like that?"

"No," Gerald said.

Ernest looked at him a while longer, then smiled. "I didn't think so," he said and pushed himself away, chuckling. "That's exactly what I thought."

✲

Gerald was awoken the next morning in the touring car, damp from sleeping in the open air of Owen's field. He'd driven up the night before, after everyone had gone to bed, determined to wait for him, but had apparently fallen asleep.

Now it was Owen's man, the mechanic, Eugène, who was shaking his shoulder, calling "Monsieur Murphy."

"Yes," Gerald said, sitting up as straight as he could, wiping some spit from the corner of his mouth. Somewhere he could hear church bells ringing. It was Sunday. He looked at Eugène. "I was looking for Monsieur Chambers," he said. "I . . ."

"Monsieur Chambers is gone," Eugène said.

386

"Gone?" Gerald was trying to shake himself into a semblance of normalcy. "Where did he go?"

"I don't know." Eugène shrugged.

"No, I mean . . ." He stopped. "What do you mean you don't know?"

"He's gone, gone," Eugène said. "You must not be here."

"I'm sorry, what are you saying? What does gone, gone . . . ?"

"Monsieur Murphy." Eugène rested his hand on his shoulder.

Gerald looked at it.

"Monsieur Chambers, he has left. He received a telegram and he . . . *il a engagé un autre pilote* . . . for this." The mechanic spread his arms towards the field. "He is not coming back."

"I . . ."

"You should go."

"Did he leave a note for me?"

"You must go, Monsieur Murphy."

"Damn it, Eugène. Where has he gone?"

"I'm sorry," Eugène said.

"What . . . what am I supposed to do?" Gerald asked.

But the Frenchman just shook his head, unable or unwilling to answer.

1927–1928

M. Gerald Murphy
Villa America
Antibes
France
Nov. 3, 1927

Herr Owen Chambers
Gossowstraße 13
Berlin-Schöneberg
Germany

Dear Owen,

I don't know if this is the correct address, but like Proust, I have been searching for you and was able to finally track down something resembling a place of residence. Eugène is blameless in this; he was as good as his word (or what I assume was his word to you) and never breathed even the smallest hint about where you were.

But I do know *something* about you, having loved—and still loving—you as I do. I have never forgotten a single word of what we've said to each other—not even seemingly innocuous comments about how much pilots could make in Berlin.

I won't say that I don't understand why you went away and left me without a word, a note, an explanation.

Our whole time together is explanation enough, what it meant to you and to me, and what was impossible.

More than a year has passed, a whole year in my life where some essential part of me has been wasted, is atrophied like an unused muscle. A winter; another spring, with the sound of birds' eggs cracking in your field in the silence of the night; a summer full of the smell of eucalyptus and all the shades of blue in the sea and in the evening sky; and a fall, the grasses turning brown and cold winds coming down from the Esterel Mountains, across your bay in Agay; all of this has passed. And now I face another winter, another season without you.

I won't write to you of all the small things that remind me of you every day, which serve only to break my heart a little more each time. Or about the children, who are growing, or the new boat that has never had your body on it and is therefore useless to me, or the people I have seen who ask of you. Why would you want to know about these things?

What am I to you? I often ask myself this and have no answer. Could I will you back, with the kind of will you so believe in? Can my poor heart call you back to me out of sheer loneliness?

My language is changing, I notice this sometimes, and I think of you. I am quiet more often now, I do not always want to talk about everything, wear it all out through exposure—*the endless ideas*, as you called them once. This is your language, this silence, this watchfulness. You have altered me, and now I carry you with me. You are part of me. But you are also lost to me.

If I could call you call back, through a letter, a word,

a signal on the wind or the image of a small camp bed
and a woolen blanket in a leaning barn, then I call you
back now. If volition is all there is, if it is as strong as
you say, you will come.

G.

*

M. Gerald Murphy
Villa America
Antibes
France
February, 1928

Herr Owen Chambers
Gossowstraße 13
Berlin-Schöneberg
Germany

Dear Owen,

I don't know if you are receiving these letters.
This will make four, and I am beginning to feel as if
I'm writing into a void. Or maybe they are slipping
through the letterbox of some Hausfrau in Berlin, who
is wondering what is wrong with this crazy American
man. Perhaps, in between her washing and cooking,
she sits down and puzzles over my words, eking out
their meanings, and pondering the fate of this other
American, the pilot. What has become of him? Has
he found someone else? Is he dead? I don't know why
in my mind these are the only two options. Except,
perhaps, it's that they're the two that would crush me,
once and for all.

Here, France—our France, anyway—is changing.
All of the people we counted on as immutable, as *like*

us—as family, I suppose—seem to be leaving, returning to America, called back by some mysterious tie that neither Sara nor I feel. We ask ourselves sometimes if we are missing some critical loyalty or understanding of our home country. How is it that we feel we could never return, when everyone we love has left or is leaving?

(Do you feel this, too? Do you ever yearn to go back, to your island, or anywhere else? I wish I knew what you were thinking, and seeing, and feeling. My love.)

Pauline is pregnant and she and Ernest are leaving soon for Key West. They want their child to be born on American soil, Ernest tells Sara. Archie and Ada have bought a farm in Conway, Mass., and are also departing. Zelda and Scott are in Delaware (although, who knows? They may turn up, like a couple of bad, but dear, pennies). And the Barrys and Don Stewart are bound for New York.

Then there is Dos, who remains blessedly nomadic: he's headed for Russia soon, to study socialism, and is as idealistic as ever, which comforts me and gives me hope for the future.

So there it is: the tent is folding, the circus moving on.

Vladimir, good man that he is, is still here, although we never speak of you. I don't know why. Maybe he knows where you are and what you're doing and is under orders not to tell me. If that is the case, then you may already know that he is courting a woman in town, though I'm not sure if it's really all that serious.

As for Sara. Do I write about her? Do I tell you how she is just the same? How she said to Scott in Paris last spring when he tried to kiss her (again) that "you really should stop that, you might catch something."

The thing is, I must tell you of her, because she is a part of us, too.

I think perhaps you always thought it was you on the outside, me in the middle, and Sara on the inside. But there have been many times when I felt that I was the one on the outside: you and Sara are both strong; you believe in yourselves and in your ability to choose your own life, in a way that I have never been capable of. And she, too, must have felt at times like the odd man out. Have any of us been well served by this?

The idea of family is one I continue to cling to, despite the fact that the one I grew up with means nothing to me, and the one made up of my peers is now seemingly disintegrating. Only the one that I have created with Sara remains constant.

Lately, I've begun to wonder if perhaps that tie is stronger than I think, strong enough for me to at least tell her the truth about myself, about us. Some people say that's what makes a man; I still don't know how one identifies that mythical and elusive figure. I know what Ernest would say, but when I think of a man, I think of you.

I think of you all the time, Owen. I still have no answers, no solutions to the problem that drove you away from me. But I feel that I'm beginning to at least see it more honestly. Is that worth anything to you? I may never know. Wherever you are, whatever you're doing, whomever you're loving, I remain constantly yours,

G.

*

                                        M. Gerald Murphy
                                          Villa America
                                            Antibes
                                              France
                                        July, 1928

Herr Owen Chambers
    Gossowstraße 13
        Berlin-Schöneberg
            Germany

Dear Owen,

I can't tell you what it meant to get your letter.
And what you said about what you feel for me. What
you feel still. And that you're alive, with me on this
planet. And that you'll come back. You'll come back.
Is it possible?

I know I can't expect more than the visit you promise
in August, but all I want is a moment, just to sit and be
quiet with you and know you're there beside me. Not to
have to turn to make sure you really exist. Just to know.

What you said in your letter, about that one night—
the only whole night—we were able to spend together,
in your rooms above the cafe in Agay. How it was the
only time since you were a child that you awoke to know
that someone you loved was beside you. That you could
dream, even terrible dreams, without fear, with the
certainty that there was another who would hold your
hand, who would wake you up if you cried or called out.
I know what it means. It is how I feel about you being
alive.

I am afraid to write more about this now, afraid that
I will revert back to that person in the spectacle, with
the costumes and the fucking disguises. Those words you

said haunt me even now, and in *my* nightmares, that is what I hear.

So we will talk of other things. How La Garoupe has been taken over by Riviera *arrivistes*, who seem completely unaware that this beach belongs to us. To remedy this, Sara has encouraged the children to throw wet sand and seaweed around in a wanton manner, and to let the dogs run wild over their picnics.

Bob Benchley and his wife Gertrude will be coming to stay at the Ferme des Orangées, which is what Sara named the little farmhouse across the road, the one she tried to persuade you to move into. Benchley calls it the Ferme des Derangées. I thought that might amuse you.

I have also started a new painting, *Portrait*. I don't want to say anything about it just yet, only that it is different, at least it feels different, than the others. There's something in it . . . yet, I don't know if what I can imagine in my mind is achievable on the canvas. We shall see.

As for your news, of course we *know* that politics exist, but the tensions you describe in Berlin are not visible here, nor on the streets of Paris. Nor New York, at least from what I've seen. Poverty, yes, but not in the way of smashed beer bottles and strange militant rallies and such. Although, perhaps we are just not in the path of such things. Dos would know, though.

His reports from Russia are fascinating, and I wonder what those German Communists you describe would make of it. If that is the dream they're fighting for. He writes that he is as of yet undecided whether the extreme hardship is a necessity, in order to cleanse the past and make way for something greater, or whether it is only the sad result of that banal evil: centralized

394

oppression. I certainly didn't know how to respond to *that*.

Lastly, I've been up to your land and the tree on the edge of the field still stands, and you can see the stars through it at night. I just thought you should know.

None of this seems real. It won't until you are returned. I am afraid, and happy, all at once. I should stop, I am stopping, before I ruin it.

Just come back.

G.

＊

Mr. Gerald Murphy
Savoy-Plaza Hotel
767 Fifth Avenue
New York
November, 1928

M. Owen Chambers
Chambers Field
La Fontonne
Antibes
France

Dear Owen,

We have just arrived in New York and I am currently sitting at the desk in our rooms, looking out over Central Park, the trees bare and grim. I have an awful sense of déjà vu, images from a childhood nursery and the loneliness and the bleakness of that house, where in a top room I sat at a small desk by myself arranging stories in my head of a happier life.

The happier life I am now dreaming of resides with you, back in Antibes. Images of these past months are

seared on my brain and I keep them locked up, and
only take them out and turn them over when I need
to remind myself of what I'm doing all this for. If I'm
completely honest, there is also an enormous sense of
guilt and foreboding. How will I tell Sara? How will
we arrange our life? As you know, I cannot leave her
and the children. But I must be honest with her. She
is my best friend and my wife. And these lies are
poisonous, and a prison for us both. I know she must
be told.

Monty Woolley once said to me that there are many
ways to live one's life. It doesn't have to be one thing
or the other. For his wisdom and his trouble, I gave him
the cold shoulder. But now I wish I had listened more
carefully. I have always been good at arranging things,
but this is one fantasy I don't know how to bring about.
I am afraid of destroying everything I spent my life
building, but I am also afraid of not actually living
my life.

It is strange being back in America, knowing that
we will be here for four months—the longest period
since we left seven years ago. And in Hollywood, too.
I wonder what we will make of it.

Before we set sail I received a letter, a poem, really,
from Archie, from his new home in Conway. He wrote:

This land is my native land. And yet
I am sick for home for the red roofs & the olives,
And the foreign words & the white of the sea fall.
How can a wise man have two countries?
How can a man behold the sun & want
A land far off, alien, smelling of palm trees
And the yellow gorse at noon in the long calms?

How indeed? I am a man who wants two countries. Your love, your body is a country to me, a land far off, now.

Tonight we will dress in our finery and go off to see Phil Barry's new play, *Holiday*, and Don Stewart's acting debut. Then tomorrow, we board the *Super Chief* for Hollywood and the studios and the madness of filmmaking that awaits us.

Scott insists that King Vidor is a serious man, despite his profession, and that my work on *Hallelujah!* will also be taken seriously. King *says* he wants his story of black sharecroppers to be authentic, and that my help with the score and photography will be indispensable, but I have heard enough about the movie business to take that with at least several grains of salt. Vladimir, however, feels very optimistic about his role as a production assistant. God help us.

How are things on your end? I wonder if you have your running water yet, or if "Antibes Time" is rolling as slowly as ever.

Tonight I will be thinking of you, of lying with you, of holding your hand and of my fingertips feeling the place at the base of your neck. I will be thinking of all of us, too. Of the treasure hunt we took, your happiness and the happiness of the children, and of Sara's beautiful face on the deck of the *Honoria*, when it seemed possible that we could live together, that perhaps joy could be assembled out of a variety of parts, that we could build our own instrument of precision. Of all the days since you've come back, that is my favorite. Do you think of it, too?

Do not forget me. I will return.

G.

1929

Honoria leaned her hot head against Dow-Dow, as the train rattled along the tracks. She'd been dreaming they were already there, home, but then she'd awoken to the movement and Dow-Dow's hand feeling her forehead.

The doctor in Paris had been kind, but Dow-Dow had looked funny after he came out of his office, and he'd made the taxi driver stop at a telegraph office before going on to the Gare de Lyon. He said he'd only cabled to tell Mother that they'd arrived safe and sound. And how they would all be together again soon.

Honoria didn't want to go back to Switzerland, where they'd already been for a month, which seemed like forever. Back to that place full of sick people, the Hotel Palace, huge and dark and dull-looking. Where Patrick was so ill he couldn't get out of bed and they all had to be quiet as mice all the time. Where Dow-Dow was always angry and sad, and Mother looked like a piece of string pulled too tight. Where Dottie Parker tried to cheer them up, but always ended up slurring her words and crying a little when she thought no one was looking.

And it was cold all the time, because tuberculosis patients like Patrick had to sleep in an unheated room, the doctors said. And his room was next to their rooms.

Dow-Dow wasn't around during the day very much; Honoria would spy him sometimes on the balcony where

Patrick spent his days outdoors, bundled up. Or she would see her father slipping by, carrying things for Patrick—a chamber pot, fresh pajamas, another blanket—wearing what he called his Swiss Peasant outfit: brown britches and a green felt apron with a wonderful bronze chain.

Sometimes she would hear him yelling at the doctors. And once, when she had hidden behind Patrick's sickroom door, she saw the doctors giving Patrick the gas injections, a huge needle, the fattest Honoria had ever seen, pushed under his armpit, and Dow-Dow just standing there crying. It was to collapse the bad lung, immobilize it, and stop the spread of the TB, she'd heard her father tell Dottie. Patrick had only one good lung, and they didn't know how long that one would last.

She knew Mother was trying hard to keep them happy, and distracted. She'd had their dogs brought up from home. Well, really it was Dottie who'd driven all their things, including the animals, from Villa America, all the way to Montana-Vermala in her shiny green car, because Mother and Dow-Dow had to go on ahead for Patrick. And now there was also a pet monkey named Mistigris, and Dottie had brought them a parrot, which took big bites out of Dow-Dow's ear and made them all laugh. Mother said Ernest and Pauline would come up for Christmas and that Ernest would teach them how to ski and they could shoot a goose and go on mountain adventures. But it didn't feel like happy news.

Honoria knew, at almost twelve, that it was her job to help Mother and not to complain, but she hadn't felt very well herself lately. Still, it hadn't been all bad. They had just celebrated Mother's birthday, with a cake and champagne. Honoria was allowed to have a sip. And Dow-Dow toasted Mother, and then they entwined their arms and drank their champagne, as if each was drinking from the other's glass. And then Dow-Dow kissed Mother very gently. And there were doctors and nurses there, and they all clapped, and even Patrick smiled.

Although, later, when Honoria had asked when they would be going home for good, Mother had answered: "Not just yet." And she'd known that that meant not for a long time. And she also knew then that Patrick would die. Even if Mother and Dow-Dow didn't believe it.

✿   ✿   ✿

Owen was waiting for them at Villa America. He'd gotten there early, long before they were expected to arrive, and had been sitting in Gerald's studio, looking at his work, and reading and rereading the letter from Hollywood, the one he had begun to carry with him everywhere, like a talisman.

Gerald was returning today from Montana-Vermala, where the Murphys would now live indefinitely in a sanatorium atop an Alpine glacier while they waited to see if Patrick would live or die.

Gerald had stopped in Paris to bring a feverish Honoria to a specialist there, to see if she'd been infected with TB, as well. They believed Patrick had contracted it in America. Where they never should have gone. And now they were on their way to Antibes. To close down Villa America.

✿

It had been eight months since the letter from Hollywood had been sent. And in eight months, it had all come crashing down, and Owen found himself waiting, waiting still, while this horror played out. Owen turned the letter over in his hand. It was strange, he thought, looking at the words on the page, a message from the past.

M. Gerald Murphy
1737 Angelo Drive
Beverly Hills, Ca.
United States
February, 1929

M. Owen Chambers
Chambers Field
La Fontonne
Antibes
France

Dear Owen,

Well, we'll be making our way back to New York shortly, and from there, finally, to Villa America. It can't be too soon, as I think you must have gleaned from my previous letters. Still, I feel like every day I am struck anew by the inauthenticity of where we have been stranded these last months.

Home to the Skippety Crickets Cake Shop, Le Naughty Waffle Drive-In, Barkies Sandwich Shoppe (complete with the huge drooping head of a dog atop their sign) and a disturbing chain of grocery stores called The Piggly Wiggly Stores. And oh, the doughnuts —or Do-Nuts, as they like to call them here. This is the pinnacle of what our country can produce.

Dottie Parker and Bob Benchley have been instrumental in keeping us somewhat *compos mentis*, for they, too, are feeling the strain of living in this god-awful way-station of life.

Six weeks was all it took to do Vladimir in. I'm not

sure if he has made his way from Paris to Antibes yet, but when he does I am certain he will regale you with his feelings on the subject. A moral desiccation, is how he described his ailment.

We have just concluded a visit to Sara's sister Olga and her husband Sidney in Carmel, which cheered Sara considerably. The two haven't seen each other in a while, and Hoytie isn't a very good advertisement for sisterly love.

We all stayed in their log cabin and it made a wonderful change from the holocausts we endured at Marion Davies' house and the work on the ghastly *Hallelujah!*

Resigning from that film may have been the best thing I have done for the saving of my Irish soul. A month into production, they had it so full of "Lor sakes!" and "Oh, no'm, Miss Georgia, you cants eat dem chitlins" and banjoes a-strummin' . . . well, they might just as well have put the cast of one of Cole's musicals in blackface and had done with it.

Since my last letter there has also been disturbing news from two different quarters. First, Pauline wrote to tell us that Ernest's father committed suicide in December. We then received a strange letter from him, full of bravado on the subject, but also darkly hinting at his own similar demise. I still don't know what to make of it. But it rattled us.

Secondly, it seems Esther is getting married. The gentleman in question is John Strachey, an English politician. I had only just received a long letter from Noel, detailing my sister's obsession with Nathalie Barney, when Esther herself rang up to tell me of her impending nuptials.

It has made me think about a lot of things, all the complicated strands of our familial tie. I realize that I have perhaps been hard on her over the years, most likely because her proclivities rubbed up against my own personal concealments.

But now that she is doing what I would have urged her to do, I am heartbroken for her. I feel her life is a very sad one, the work left undone, the book she never seems able to finish, the love unconsummated, or unreturned, and now this flight even further from herself, from her true nature. Esther, an English politician's wife? Can this really end happily? You are the only one to whom I can tell the whole truth of my feelings about this.

Then again, maybe she knows what she's doing. Perhaps this is her arrangement of life. As for myself, I don't want any more disguises, not to the people that matter. And you and Sara and the children are all that really matter to me.

I was happy to hear that the works at the field are going according to schedule, and that you will have a decent and fit place to live in before long. Although, I wonder if anything will ever be as beautiful as that run-down barn, and the plaid blanket and your coffee hot from the gas burner. Promise me that you'll keep them, and bring them out once in a while.

I wonder—sometimes with optimism, and sometimes through blackness—how everything will turn out for all of us. Can three people truly share love? My God, I hope so. Because if happiness truly exists, I believe we have all deserved some piece of it.

Until I see you, I am sending all my love,

G.

The November air inside the unheated studio had made Owen's fingers go numb and he fumbled a bit as he folded the letter back up and put it into his pocket. He thought of a time long ago when he used to take a horse and cart out before the sun had even risen, and deliver milk and eggs to people on an island that used to be his home. The way that the cold used to freeze smell, so that the world became almost odorless.

In front of him, he'd propped up two paintings. The first was *Portrait*, the one Gerald had written to him about in Berlin.

There was a ruler running down the center dividing it in two. To the left was a huge eye. To the right, a foot. Below, lips. There were also three sets of fingerprints. All these, he knew, were parts of Gerald's own body, meticulously copied and enlarged on the canvas.

But there was also something else. In the left-hand corner, next to another, smaller ruler, was a profile. Owen's profile.

I wonder if I measured every inch of you and added it up what it would come to. Would I know you any better if I could add the sum of your parts?

Owen put his hand over his eyes. Sometimes he wondered why he had ever come back. It wasn't that he'd been so happy in Berlin, but this . . .

He supposed he knew: it was the possibility, however slim, that everything might come out right. It was Gerald's belief in this dream of some sort of paradise for them all.

Spring and summer had passed in a haze of sex and love and the potential of what might come afterwards. They'd talked about loving Sara, and telling Sara. Sometime. Sometime in a future that would never come. He couldn't believe he'd ever thought such a fantasy could really come true, that there could be an outcome with no responsibility, no pain. It was crazy. Worse than crazy. It might have brought bad luck.

And now. Well, if he looked at it now, he saw a man who wanted to steal a father away from his family while a child's life hung in the balance. That's what had come out of all this. That's what *he* had become.

He took his hand away from his face and forced himself to look again at the second painting, Gerald's latest, *Wasp and Pear*.

A ripe green pear, split in two, one half showing its core, its seed, the other half its skin. And a huge and intricate wasp with curving wings, fastened onto it, hooked into it with its mouth, feeding on its sweetness.

Was he, Owen, the wasp? Sara and Gerald, the two parts of the pear? He felt sick. Perhaps, if he was honest, that's all he'd ever been. To Charlie and Flora, to Sara and Gerald, to Quentin. An unthinking, insentient creature that fed on the insides of fuller people. Carrying with it, in its tail, death and pain.

Sometimes, lately, he wondered about that day, during the war, when he killed that boy in the tunnel. What if it had been the other way around, what if he had died and the boy had lived? Would the boy have gone on to do better than him? Be a better person than he was? But he hadn't died. He'd lived. And these people had brought him back, cut open the cocoon he was living in. And a wasp had flown out.

What disgusted him most, though, was that despite knowing all this he had hope. It grew like a weed when nothing else would grow, defying inhospitable weather, an insult to the real crops that withered before they even had a chance to take root.

*

Owen was waiting in the driveway when their car pulled in. Gerald stepped out first, then reached in, scooping his daughter up in his arms, and carried her straight past Owen into the house.

He'd moved quickly enough that Owen hadn't been able to get a good look at him. But when Gerald came back down the stairs, Owen saw that his face had changed. All the features were sharper, older.

"The doctor says she's been exposed," Gerald said, looking at him, but also looking through him somehow. "She has speckles on her lungs. We're leaving tomorrow for Switzerland. We'll know more in a week."

Owen nodded. He knew he shouldn't touch him. Didn't dare. The body that had been his to touch was gone, replaced with another Gerald, one that belonged to someone else.

In the living room, all the white furniture was cast pale gray in the November light. There was a bronze bucket full of now-dried eucalyptus sitting on the coffee table.

"Would you like a drink?" Gerald asked, as if half remembering an old habit.

"Yes," Owen said.

Gerald rose and went to the bar. "I don't have anything fresh," he said, looking helplessly at the bottles. "Whiskey?"

"Whiskey's fine," he said.

Gerald brought the drinks over and sat down in a chair across from him, crossing his legs, arranging his tie, trying to smooth down his crumpled white shirt.

"How's the business?" he asked Owen. "Is the Panic affecting it?"

"I don't know yet," Owen said. "The bank's not saying anything. You?"

"We're not sure. Hoytie's lost her shirt. Our man's trying to see through the dust. But none of that matters now."

"And Sara?"

"Not good," Gerald said. "But she's being very brave. We're both . . . we're both trying."

They were silent for a while and Owen wondered if Gerald wanted him there at all. He'd asked him to come in his telegram. But now it felt wrong. "How's Patrick?"

"He's a very sick little boy," Gerald said, looking down at his glass. "And he is so little, Owen. But the stoicism . . . I've never known such patient, such private determination." He stopped. "I've never been quiet like that. It's what will help him survive."

"They think he'll get better?"

"What do they know?" Gerald asked, slamming his glass against the table and standing suddenly. "What could they know about life and the terms on which someone is prepared to meet it?"

Owen said nothing, just watched Gerald pacing the room. He stopped in front of the French doors, staring out at the terrace, now covered with dead leaves from the linden tree. Minutes passed.

"We're selling the house," Gerald said, finally. "Patrick will never be able to live at sea level again."

Owen rose and went over to him, standing close behind him, but not touching him.

"I've written the advertisement for the agent," Gerald said. "I think it's pretty good. Of course, it can never say what really went on here . . . never describe . . ."

Owen put his hand on Gerald's shoulder. "G. . . ."

"No," Gerald said, turning, something desperate in his eyes. "I can't. Not anymore. It's all gone. I have nothing left for anyone else."

Owen looked at him.

"It was all . . ." Gerald waved his hand around, encompassing the room, the terrace, the tree. "It was all invented. It was the best part, but it wasn't real."

Gerald began to shake and Owen held him, held his long, lean body until it was still again.

"I saw your paintings," he said quietly. "I saw *Wasp and Pear*."

Gerald looked at him, not understanding. "Those," he said. "Oh. I can't even remember those."

"They're good," Owen said. "*Portrait*, too."

"No, they're nothing. They mean nothing. I won't ever do that again."

Owen wasn't certain if he meant painting, or something else.

Gerald looked back out across the garden, towards the sea.

"Patrick sits on a balcony all day, looking at the mountains. That's all he's allowed to look at," Gerald said. He drew a deep, wavering breath. "So that's all I look at, too."

Owen recognized this, what Gerald was doing. He'd seen it before, in the war. In the planes of men who refused to jump. Complete immolation.

"Do you know what he says to me, about the view, in his serious, small-boy voice?" Gerald asked, his eyes wild, darting. "He says: 'Melancholy skenery, Dow-Dow.' That's what he says." Gerald gripped Owen's arm hard. "Jesus Christ, my son." And then he sank to the floor, sobbing.

Owen sat while Gerald slept on the sofa, and the afternoon hours slipped by. He'd put his hand in Gerald's and held it, the way he had done for Owen once. He'd been listening for sounds of Honoria, in case she might need something. He didn't know what a little girl might need, he just knew he had to be watchful. But Villa America was silent.

Then, when the sun began to dip down low in the sky, Gerald woke, sitting up slowly, unfurling himself, disengaging his hand.

"There's something I have to do," Gerald said. "I have to go to Juan-les-Pins, to see Scott and Zelda. I have to keep a promise I made to their daughter. To Scottie."

"I can stay and look after Honoria, if you'd like."

"Vladimir is supposed to be here," Gerald said. "I told him to take my paintings away. Perhaps you could stay until he comes?"

"Yes," Owen said. "I can do that."

Gerald rose and disappeared upstairs. From the living room, Owen could hear water running through the pipes, the sounds of doors opening and closing, and hushed whispers. After a while, he heard footsteps descending the stairs and Gerald reappeared, dressed in fully pressed, beautiful evening clothes, a top hat in one hand and silver cane in the other.

He walked over to where Owen was sitting and looked at him. Then he bent down and kissed Owen on the lips. A long, almost chaste, kiss. Just the feeling of Gerald's flesh pressed against his own. Then Owen tasted salt in his mouth, tears, and Gerald said softly, almost too quietly for him to hear: "I'm sorry, my love."

Then he was gone.

✧　　✧　　✧

Gerald held Scottie close to him as he drove, kept her tucked under one arm. He could smell her little-girl smell, warm skin, soap, starch from her dress. He thought of Honoria. It wasn't the same smell; Honoria smelled like

Sara, somehow, blood and love bound together in the skin. But the warmth, the stillness of the girls was the same.

"Would you like to hear about the lighthouse again?" he asked.

Scottie looked up and nodded.

"Well, as you know, you can see its light shining into your room at night, can't you?"

"Yes," Scottie said.

"And you know about the fairies."

More nodding.

"Would you like to hear about them again?"

"Yes please, Dow-Dow."

Gerald felt a piercing of his heart. "Well," he said cheerfully, "the lighthouse is run by a band of very special fairies. Sailors' fairies, actually. They live there and their job is to turn the light on at night and help guide the ships in safely to the port."

"Are they good fairies?" Scottie asked, a little suspicious.

"Of course they're good fairies," Gerald said.

The hills were shrouded in darkness as they drove along the coast towards Cap d'Antibes.

"Some people say that they are girl fairies who have fallen in love with sailors and every night they turn the light on, hoping their beloveds will return to them."

"Like princesses?"

"Not like princesses, exactly," Gerald said, smiling down at the pink, frothy princess's dress Zelda had sewn for Scottie to wear on this occasion. "Because fairies are magical."

"Oh," Scottie said, as if this explained everything. "Do they sing?"

"Do they sing? Well, they *do* sing. But their voices are so high and sweet, that humans can't hear them."

Gerald made the turn on the boulevard de la Garoupe and began the ascent up the chemin de Calvaire.

"We're getting close," he said, smoothing his hand over her hair, thick like Zelda's, but silkier, smoother. A little cap. He thought of Patrick's hair, fine like his own, these days always damp, and lank, sticking to his feverish skull.

Sometimes, when Patrick was sleeping, he would slide his palm under his head and feel its shape, and its weight. His small son's agonizing weight, all the bones, like a bird's, and organs and flesh, none of it heavy enough yet.

When he pulled the car up next to the stone lighthouse, he cut the engine and looked at Scottie. The white beacon circled, lighting up their faces in flashes as it swept by. The area was cloistered by *pines maritimes*, which spread themselves around an old chapel off to the side. Notre Dame des Amoureux.

"Are you ready to go find the fairies?" Gerald asked, leaning over her and releasing the door handle.

Her eyes, wide as saucers, were fixed on the lighthouse. She swallowed and nodded.

Gerald got out and put on his hat, adjusting it tightly around his crown. He gripped his cane and pulled his shoulders up, straightening his spine for this one last act of magic that he would perform here.

He walked around and lifted the little girl lightly out of the car, setting her on her feet. He then took her hand and they began walking.

As they approached the entrance, Scottie stopped. Her sweaty hand gripped his own so tightly.

"Is everything all right?"

She looked up at him, that childhood expression of panic that signaled either fear or the need to pee, painted on her face.

"You know what I think," Gerald said. "I think the fairies might be busy." He picked her up and her arms went around his neck. "I think we should sit on that wall over there and that way we can watch from close by."

He carried Scottie over to the wall and they sat, hand in hand, and watched the beacon sweep like clockwork across them, across the car, the chapel, the pines, the hills of Cap d'Antibes, the Baie des Anges, all the way into the empty bedroom of a small child.

1930

Dorothy Parker
Hotel Palace
Montana-Vermala
Switzerland
January, 1930

Mr. Robert Benchley
The New Yorker
25 West Forty-Fifth Street
New York, NY

Well, Fred, still here on this godawful glacier, trying
to keep it together, while the Murphys go to hell.

They are solemnly turning these rooms in the
sanatorium into Heidi's grandfather's cabin, all reindeer
skins and cuckoo clocks and other horrible decorations
that are meant to make you want to run out and yodel
atop the highest peak. All this forced merriment, all this
goddamn bravery, well it just about breaks your heart,
Fred.

Last night, as we all sat at the table, up to our
teeth in mufflers, because it's so goddamn cold,
Gerald spoke of you, Fred, and of their other friends,
everyone they've left behind in their real world, and
then he said: "That's all right. No, that's all right, though,

because when I think of them, my heart is full." Ahh, Mr. Benchley . . . I don't know if I can stand it.

And I don't know how long Gerald can bear it, either. He's pouring every bit of life he has into making that child well. There's something in his refusal to acknowledge that the boy is ill. But there's something else, too. I'm not sure exactly what's eating him, but it began before, during this summer in Antibes, and it's also connected with his giving up painting. He won't even have it mentioned now.

Poor Gerald (and those lights are out in the Hippodrome, Mr. Benchley, when you think of Gerald Murphy as "poor Gerald").

There isn't anyone in the world worth a damn except you, Mr. Benchley, and the Murphys. I didn't know that until now . . .

                            Donald Ogden Stewart
                                Chalet La Bruyere
                                Montana-Vermala
                                Switzerland
                                September, 1930

Mr. Philip Barry
12 Washington Square
New York, NY
United States

Dear Phil,

I hardly know what to write about what I've found here in the Murphys' Switzerland. Bea and I came to visit on the understanding (in the form of a letter from Sara) that Patrick was improving. What we've found,

instead, is that they are biding their time in a Magic
Mountain resort with death hovering just outside,
waiting to undo the two people who have been our
models of how to live.

Sara and Gerald (along with Dottie Parker) have
installed themselves in a chalet—granted, much better
than the awful Hotel Palace, which is no hotel at all,
but a place of dying. They've also taken over a house
in the village which they have turned into a bar
(heartbreakingly called "Harry's Bar," after the one at
the Ritz where we all spent many happy hours getting
sloshed).

On any given evening you can find a Munich dance
band, and people lighting cigarettes with embossed
matches that Gerald has had printed God-knows-where,
and rattan furniture . . . And the worst is late at night,
sometimes, Sara and Gerald take over the piano and
sing together, and it's like a shadow passing over your
grave.

She seems to be holding it together for both of them.
He's not well, Phil. It's like all the air has been sucked
out of him. But he soldiers on. And she keeps him from
cracking up entirely. Sara is everything we always
thought she was, and more now.

When I think of *Holiday*, of that fine play you wrote
(and which I nobly starred in), I can't believe how far
things have gone, in the other direction. How much of
Gerald was in Johnny Case, and how much of that man,
with his insouciance, who mixed "just the juice of a
few flowers," has been wiped out, or at least obscured
for now.

Last night, Sara and Gerald sang "An die Musik" at
the piano, and Bea had to get up and leave. The memory

of that—of the once blithe, sparkling Murphys from Antibes, singing sweetly into the face of death—will remain one of the most frightening of my life. But, Phil, it will also remain one of the Murphys at their most beautiful, at their most courageous . . .

1931

Archibald MacLeish
Fortune Magazine
Chrysler Building
New York
January, 1931

Ada MacLeish
Uphill Farm
Conway, Mass.

My Darling Ada,

It can't be too soon until I get back to you and our
farm and our garden. I am beginning to wonder how
I ever let Henry Luce seduce me into this godawful job
of reporting on all the squalid desperation that our
government and the stock market and fate and even
the weather is now inflicting on its citizens. It can make
a man sick to his very bones, the despair. But enough.
You've heard this diatribe before and no doubt you'll
hear it again. I miss your voice, singing in the music
room, making me feel as if not all the lovely things
have been leached out of this place we call America.
Because there is you.

I did not see Gerald on his trip here, after all. He
skulked around like Lon Chaney in *The Phantom of the
Opera*. Instead I received a letter. And what a doozy it

was. Of course I *think* I know what he's saying. But does one ever really know about another person? I wish you were here to read it over my shoulder. But I am including the most relevant parts:

"I owe you an apology for avoiding you when I visited New York last. It was a cowardly thing to do, and I'm sorry if I hurt you. But you see, in one moment, in one infected breath, my whole life changed—all the joy, all the things that went into making it a life, have been sucked out. And I find myself more a cut-out than a living, breathing man.

I do not say this because I pity myself; I have only myself to blame. I have concealed myself, my true nature, from almost everyone who loves me, and now when I need strength and nourishment from those friendships, I cannot receive it, because I haven't been honest. I am coming to realize that I have not had one real, honest, full relationship in my life.

I have been aware of my defects since the age of fifteen, when I made a deal with life: I would fight them, scotch them, as best I could and in return life would look the other way. Not for one second have I been free from the feelings of those defects. Despite all the beautiful things that filled my world, despite Sara. But I tried my best to find a way. Now, though, life has broken with me, and my shortcomings seem to be all I have left. I am morally bankrupt.

So, not seeing you or Ada on that visit, it was a way of preserving our friendship, the way you see it, of keeping it safe from my own realities. I hope you can understand that. That you can understand what I am trying to tell you.

One more thing. Don't worry about anything I've

said. Everything is perfectly all right. Frankly, I am long
since bored by my own unhappiness."

So, my love. Put your fine mind to that. I will be
back soon . . .

❖

Scott Fitzgerald
Les Rives de Prangins
Lake Geneva
Switzerland
September, 1931

Ernest Hemingway
  L-Bar-T Ranch
   Wyoming

Dear Ernest,

I am waiting at the clinic to take Zelda away from
this place, this clinic that has been our home for a year.
She is so much better. Not only am I *told* this, but I *feel*
it, too, and Dr. Forel says that her condition *may* be
kept on an even keel, if she avoids conflicts. I will do
my best to help her with that, but she has always had
her own will in these things. Are these conflicts of ours
continually to be laid at my door?

From here we will motor to Paris, and hope to
recover or rediscover some of that which sustained us
in our early, happier years together.

We have recently returned from a visit to the
Murphys at a house they took for the summer in Bad
Aussee, Austria. A great big hunting lodge sort of
establishment, with sanded floors and animal heads
(though not a patch on your specimens). And we swam
in the lake and rode bicycles like madmen. It was,

overall, a wonderful time and Zelda handled everything beautifully, except at the end. And, of course, *I* got blamed for that.

There was a situation over the bath water, where it seemed the nurse was bathing Scottie in the dirty water left over from the Murphy children. Zelda looked calm, but it was up to me to kick up the fuss, and it turned out that it was bath salts, not dirt. But the damage was done, and Zelda spent the night locked in a circle of thought about Scottie falling ill. I took her away very early, before anyone was up. I hope we can just forget about it, and that it won't prove something that will prey on her mind later down the road.

How did I find the Murphys? I found them better than you described from your visit at Christmas. But, well, they are different and they are the same. Sara is as beautiful as ever and she has real courage, to always take the hardest road, even when all her resources are spent. But I believe her resources are spent, and I'm not only talking about money.

We stayed up very late one night talking, and even through her own pain, she managed to speak so eloquently on the subject of Zelda. She said: "Zelda has a violence that I sympathize with. I believe she has been thinking terrible, dangerous secret thoughts. Keeping in pent-up rebellions. But who doesn't?" This she said with those intense, slanted eyes, hair golden brown. Then: "Hers, I suppose, are just more impenetrable."

Words like that, Ernest. There are so many things I wished at that moment to tell Sara, in return, about herself: that if all her worldly possessions were taken from her, if she was stripped of everything she loved, everything she'd created, if it was all burnt on the pyre of life, she would go on. Because she is part of our times, of who we are. Perhaps I *will* tell her this one day. I only tell you, because I know you feel the same. For now, all I can say is that my time with her has only gone further to helping with the novel, bolstering it, giving it shape . . . she is in there, by God, in every line.

As for Gerald, well . . . he sleeps in a separate bedroom, one of the maid's rooms, all cloistered up like a monk's cell. But I will never forget his great tenderness in coming to see Zelda at Prangins this past spring. He was the first person, apart from myself and Scottie, that she asked to see of her own free will. And I know he was terrified, but he was kind and asked her about her basket weaving, and was generally the gentle soul I know him to be. Even if there is—and always will be—something of the hysteric in him.

I do think that his affliction, which we've discussed, goes on. I heard some whisperings from the Riviera about that American pilot, the one who was always so silent—morbidly silent, if you want my opinion. You, of course, saw it first. But you've always been so right about people. Still, there's no indication that the connection has survived their move to Switzerland, so that's one thing to be thankful for, if only for Sara's sake. Christ, the couples this universe makes up for us.

Oh, one last note. Hoytie Wiborg's visit coincided with ours. God, what a bitch (and I know you always thought her so). One afternoon, I'd agreed to go with the children and Hoytie in the car into town to pick up some supplies. She insisted on driving. And then because she has absolutely no talent for it, she rammed into some Austrian fellow's car. Well, instead of just apologizing and driving on, she got out and started yelling: *Jude! Jude!* at the man.

Whether he was a Jew or not, this really got him sore, and he leapt out of his own car and made a run at her, to hit her. Sadly, Hoytie was too quick and managed to get back in and drive off before anything else happened. But when this little episode was reported to Sara, there were fireworks, as you can well imagine, knowing Sara as you do. She insisted Hoytie track down the man and apologize. We didn't stay long enough to find out how that one ended. But I knew you'd get a kick out of it . . . .

✻

Vladimir Orloff

Chalet La Bruyere

Montana-Vermala

Switzerland

December, 1931

Owen Chambers

Chambers Field

La Fontonne

Antibes

France

My dear friend,

I was happy to get your letter and to hear your flying business hasn't been destroyed by what seems to be a great tide sweeping over the world and swallowing everyone's riches. I hope you will remain safe, and not take chances, in the rising swells.

I understand that you have not written to Gerald. Sometimes he asks for news of you, but I have not known what to say, or if one should say anything at all. I would not like to give advice on this matter, only to tell you that I have seen with my own eyes many letters begun, with your name on them, that have ended crumpled in the basket in his solitary room.

I am not a spy, but a mere helpless observer. I remember a time, years ago, when I thought you and I had become like two old men on a porch, watching the world go by, with no stake in this game, only a search for peace after the tumult and destruction of war. But I was naive. I see that now, my friend. You were waiting to live, for once truly and fully, and I . . . perhaps I was just waiting to be swept along on my next adventure.

It is sad here, to see these lives still together, but now so divided. I will go away soon, to Normandy, where I will pick up the new boat, the *Weatherbird*, named after that piece of jazz music they love so much and that they still dance to, from time to time. I will sail her down the coast, through storms, no doubt, to bring her home to Antibes. You will not believe this creation—there is a refrigerator and bathtub belowdeck. Such comforts, after the simplicity of the *Honoria*. Life changes, does it not?

Villa America will not sell, it seems, and so Sara and Honoria will go down in the spring to stay.

Gerald is just back from America, his father lying cold in the grave. He died as Gerald was crossing the Atlantic. And while this loss seems to have been absorbed in the black hole of his spirit, he is very angry over the inheritance. It seems the company, which is all there is, was left in the charge of Mr. Murphy's mistress of many years, one Lillian Ramsgate. She is

now president of the company, and Gerald resigned.
I wonder at the prudence of this. Only time will tell.

And Patrick . . . there is the heart of all this. He gets
better, then he gets worse. The bad lung is very bad, and
he is once again confined to his bed. But he is a brave
boy, and finds things to keep himself amused. At present
he seems interested only in statistics, statistics of any
kind: sports, hunting, and any sort of probability. It is
his battle with death, and that probability, I believe,
that has brought him to this.

I will be sailing the *Weatherbird* in to Antibes at the
end of March or beginning of April. I will wire and let
you know before I set off. Will you fly your plane over
me, as I come in, to greet an old friend . . . ?

1932

Stella Campbell
     Beverly Hills, Ca.
          United States
August, 1932

Sara and Gerald Murphy
     Villa America
          Antibes
               France

My Darlings,

I felt I would burst if I didn't write directly upon my return to thank you for the most glorious moments spent at your slice of heaven on the Riviera. Can you really be serious about selling it? I think not . . .

When I saw the lanterns in the garden all lit up for Patrick's visit, well, my heart just fairly grew two sizes and I am so proud to have been part of that celebration. Then all the trips on the beautiful *Weatherbird*—how happy I was on that yacht of yours. Rooms painted different colors for each guest (does one call them rooms on a ship?). No matter.

I just wanted to say that you both—and together— make everything cool and sweet and lovely around you. (And thank you for the check—my landlady is most grateful that I am now able to pay my rent.)

Now, you told me to "hunch for luck for Patrick."
I don't know what hunching is, but if it means hoping
and praying that he gets better and will be up and about
again as he should, enjoying life, then you will find me
"hunching" all the livelong day . . .

✿

Archibald MacLeish
Uphill Farm
Conway, Mass.
August, 1932

Gerald Murphy
Hook Pond Cottage
East Hampton, N.Y.

Dear Dow,

I think you must have all already left for Ernest's
mountains in Wyoming. I can imagine you and Sara and
Honoria and Baoth have such a damn good time there.
Sorry to hear that Patrick won't be able to be with you.
He is always in our thoughts, and Ada and I would love
to have him anytime he needs a get-away.

However, one of the reasons I'm writing is that we've
been cooking up a plan we hope you Murphys will agree
to: could we possibly entice you all to Uphill Farm for
Christmas? Ada is exhorting me to tell you (bully that
she is), that she will do the sweet potatoes if you will
bring the wine.

I am also writing to tell you that it came upon me
today—as I felt the last of the summer sunshine—that
it has been a long time since we sat under the linden
tree together and listened to the mourning doves and
spoke of the things that are important to us. This letter
is mostly to say, simply, that I miss you . . .

426

Noel Murphy
La Ferme des Anges
Orgeval
France
October, 1932

Esther Murphy Strachey
10 York Terrace West
London

Dear Esther,

In answer to your letter: yes, it is love with Janet
Flanner. It is not, perhaps, the same as that I feel or felt
for Fred, but it is both passionate and calm. She comes
on the weekends and we have friends and I cook and
we sunbathe nude and she writes while I deal with the
farm. (She calls my accent Park Avenue Peasant, for
all the cooking and farming I do.) There are also no
problems with Solita, who seems to have taken her
lover's shift in affections with a grace I'm not sure
I would possess. But she has also started visiting the
farm.

I feel a little guilty writing this to you, knowing that
your own marriage is coming to a rather painful end.
But, despite your many gifts, housekeeping and wife-ing
were never going to be among them. And perhaps,
although a wrench now, it was what you needed at the
time, when things with Djuna were driving you mad.
Now that can all be finished with.

I wouldn't worry about what Gerald will think.
Who cares, honestly? It is your life to lead, and you
know best how to do that. Besides, I think Gerald
may be finished with all those judgments of his. Life
has dealt a cruel blow to him, to be sure, but he wore

his blindness to his own nature like a badge of honor.
I do not approve of throwing stones when living in
glass houses. The world is too full of other things to be
concerned with than arbitrating the personal affections
and private complications of our fellow men and
women.

Speaking of complications, I, for my part (and Janet
agrees), was glad to see your John (or should I say
ex-John) had broken with that Oswald Mosley and his
British Union of Fascists. I don't like that man one bit,
even if he was the best man at your wedding. And if you
think that's harsh, you should hear Dos on the subject.
(Marriage to Katy certainly hasn't softened *him*.)

He passed by to see us awhile back, fresh from the
Democratic National Convention, ranting about
Roosevelt and his theme song "Happy Days Are Here
Again," while lines of "grimy men" who "have lost the
power to want" camped outside in cardboard boxes . . .

❁

Vladimir Orloff
21 rue du Château d'Eau
Paris
October, 1932

Owen Chambers
  Chambers Field
    La Fontonne
      Antibes

My dear friend,

And so despite my efforts, you slipped through our
grasp once again. You were gone by the time the family
arrived at Villa America, only to return, I hear, after

they'd departed for America, for good this time, I fear.
I am now living in Paris. I will never again return to
America after the horrors I endured there. I have met
someone, someone I believe who is special and nurturing
to my life, but I will save that until I know more. That is
for another letter.

This letter is to do what I promised I wouldn't, to
meddle in your affairs. To ask you simply, will you not
write to him? Not to bring back what it was you had
and lost, but to bring comfort and light to someone you
once loved. There is so little of that in the world, it is
a grave sin to waste it on pride.

I will say no more, but will include their new address
in America. And some news of the family.

Sara, well, she is lost and lonely, but she is like a
warrior against death. Patrick is iller than ever, the
other lung diseased now, as well. They believe a new
climate, out west perhaps, may be the solution. Honoria
is growing into a beautiful young woman, so like Sara,
and getting too old for my stories. Baoth's nature
remains unchanged. He brings light to his mother,
as that is his way.

As for Gerald, there was a strange scene earlier
this year that I will relate. It has to do with Baoth and
the German boarding school he was in. He wrote Sara
a letter, which disturbed her greatly, about how he
and his classmates were forced out into the snow at
5:30 each morning in only their underclothes to repeat
over and over "*Heil Hitler*." It seems the school has
some connection to this political man. Of course, after
hearing that they decided to remove Baoth immediately.
So, Gerald and Scott and I took the train together to
retrieve him. (Scott is a fine man, an honorable man.)

Once there, however, Gerald found himself in a very passionate argument with the headmaster. He railed against cruel childhoods. It was very beautiful, and a bit Russian. But also very sad, as it seems anger is the only emotion he is capable of touching these days . . .

1933

Zelda Fitzgerald
Downstairs in the living room
La Paix
Towson, Md.
July, 1933

Scott Fitzgerald
Upstairs in the study
La Paix
Towson, Md.

Dear Scott,

I know you are hard at work on *Dick Diver's Holiday*,
or whatever you're calling it now. But I am downstairs
and just had a question for you: another summer is
half-over, and we are here, and do you think we will
ever have sunburns again from sitting out too long at
La Garoupe? Will there ever be sherry at noon and
cocktails at yardarm time, and do you suppose they still
have nightingales in Antibes? And will we ever be full of
happiness—the kind when you know something is over,
but that it will all begin again tomorrow?

I don't want to go back to the clinic. But, oh Goofo,
I need you to love me, please—life is too confusing.
Zelda

1934

Ada MacLeish
Uphill Farm
Conway, Mass.
United States
April, 1934

Ellen Barry
Villa Lorenzo
Cannes
France

Dearest Ellen,

I am just fresh back from a tour of Key West—a very drunken tour, I might add. Sara and I ditched our husbands—lamb cutlet and drumstick—and jetted down like two debutantes to stay with Dos and Katy and visit with the Hemingways.

Buckets of frozen lime cocktails were consumed and Sara and Ernest and I danced like drunken sailors in the Hemingways' lovely living room to Sara's records and we went out fishing and swam and Dos and Ernest argued about politics, and Pauline cooked marvelously and it was perfectly lovely. And dear Katy made sure we all had something nice for our hangovers in the morning.

I know it was a relief for Sara, to have some real fun.

But I am still worried for her; things don't seem to be getting any easier. There are, of course, real money problems now, and they can't seem to move Villa America (although between you and me, I wonder if they're really ready to let it go, even if Sara has come to refer to our times there as "the era"). Then there is the sorry Mark Cross business—it seems that fancy lady of Gerald's father is running it into the ground.

Of course, Patrick's illness and the expense weighs heavily. But—and for heaven's sakes don't read too much into this—it seems that there is a lack of connection between Sara and Gerald. She says very little—because, Lord knows, she is the world's most loyal woman—but reading between the lines, I believe there has been a loss of, shall we say, marital affection. And it tolls heavily on her, I think. She is such a warm, affectionate sort of human and, well, we all need to be loved . . .

❈

> Owen Chambers
> Chambers Field
> La Fontonne
> Antibes
> August, 1934

Vladimir Orloff
21 rue du Château d'Eau
Paris

Dear Vladimir,

I'm writing to you at this address, but I guess you could be anywhere now. I'm glad your adventures, as you call them, have finally brought you back to the sea, where you belong. The *Weatherbird* sounds like a fine ship, and I imagine you happy at the helm.

Life in Antibes goes on, but my business is failing, like so many others. Business in and out of Germany is getting more difficult, so the contacts I made there aren't worth much. It's hurt. As a pilot friend from Berlin describes it now: "With Hitler, everything is coming under the rule of arbitrary will." It's not the kind of will I used to put so much store in, the kind I felt I'd fought for. I wonder sometimes how many more things I still have to learn about the way things are. Or maybe it's time to just admit that there are no ideas that last, so there is nothing to learn.

I never wrote to Sara or Gerald, as you may or may not know. There are so many reasons, and I don't want to go into them. But your words did not go unheard . . .

           ✿

           Ernest Hemingway
             Hotel Ambos Mundos
             Havana
             Cuba
           September, 1934

Sara Murphy
    Hook Pond Cottage
        East Hampton, N.Y.
           United States

Dear Sara,

I had a tremendous dream about you and about Key West. And I wanted to write immediately and tell you that I love you very much. And I often think of how fine a woman you are. You have been so brave and I guess you'll just have to go on being brave, good kind beautiful lovely Sara. We can't let the bastards grind us down.

About Scott's novel, you were right to say that the book, which is a bad one, bears no resemblance to you. All flash with nothing important at the heart. But Poor Scott.

I am also writing because I would like to send Patrick one of the African heads we're having mounted. Which do you think he'd like best—a Gazelle or an Impala? You could put it somewhere where he could see it while lying in bed. I think an Impala, all clean and light and lovely. They're the ones that sort of slip along in the air as they move. The one I'm thinking of weighed approx. 151 pounds, was killed with one shot, 6.5 mm Mannlicher, at 217 paces. You can tell him that for his statistics collection.

It's raining here, I wish you were with me . . .

◊

> Archibald MacLeish
> Uphill Farm
> Conway, Mass.
> October, 1934

Patrick Murphy
  Doctors Hospital
    170 East End Avenue
      New York

Dear Patrick,

Last night it was dark coming up from the pond. I was tired coming up and not paying attention and when there was a little rustling in the leaves in the woods I hardly looked . . . something almost the same

color as the elm leaves. It barely ran. I thought as
I carried it that it was very hot in my hand but then
I thought too that small animals always feel hot to us.
When I came into the kitchen under the bright light
over the sink I saw what it was. It was a young flying
squirrel, sick or hurt or for some reason unable to move.
I went back into the woods and put it in the bole of
a great maple covered with leaves. It lay still there.
All night in the brilliant moon I thought of it there
and wondered about it. Its fur was softer than any
squirrel. My love to you . . .

Owen Chambers
Chambers Field
La Fontonne
Antibes
France
December, 1934

Sara and Gerald Murphy
Hook Pond Cottage
East Hampton, N.Y.

Dear Sara and Gerald,

    I'm not sure where to even begin with this letter.
It's very late. Is it enough, as a friend, to say something,
even if you say it very late? I wish I had more words
to tell you how much I've thought of you both, and of
Patrick and Baoth and Honoria, over the years that have
passed since we all last met. Especially Patrick.

    I can't explain why I didn't write right away, except
that I felt like I couldn't do anything to make things
better, only things that would make it hurt more. Then

a year passed, then another. I guess that's the way these things work.

I've heard some of your news from Vladimir over the years, and was always happy when it was good.

The thing is, I'm writing now because I saw you. You didn't see me. It was August, at the casino in Juan-les-Pins. I was having a drink. And you both were there, with Honoria and a tall girl, her friend, I guess.

Sara, you were wearing a black dress like something from the movies, and you were sitting with the other girl and you gave her your lipstick. She looked very happy about it and put it on. It was the color of those brush fires in the hills we talked about when we first knew each other.

And Gerald, you were on the dance floor, moving your daughter across it. She looked beautiful, like a woman, and you were talking to her and she was smiling at you. And when you came close to my table, I could hear you say to her: "Keep your hand light on my shoulder. Keep your body light like you're treading water."

I left because I was afraid you'd see me. And because I realized what a coward I've been, what a coward I am. You both gave me so much that I will never be able to repay, and which I didn't even try to give back. You even gave me these words, things I would never be able to say, let alone write, if it weren't for knowing you. I'm sorry. I don't really know what your life is like now, but you were good and real and very, very much alive in that casino. Whatever's going on, you've survived. And that's the important thing.

Later, at home, I thought about the times we flew together. And I thought about the happiest time, the trip to Saint-Tropez and the treasure hunt. I won't say more about that, because I can't. Besides, sometimes there isn't much to say that hasn't already been felt.

I will be leaving Antibes in the spring. My business is all gone back to the bank. It doesn't matter, because I had it once, and it was good. And I think I might have stayed too long here.

I don't know if our paths will ever cross again. But, my God, I'm glad they crossed at all.

Love,

Owen

1935

Gerald Murphy
539 E. Fifty-First Street
New York
United States
February, 1935

Owen Chambers
Chambers Field
La Fontonne
Antibes
France

Dear Owen,

It has taken me a while to be able to reply properly
to your letter. Sara and I were both so moved by it and
spoke for some time about how much has changed since
we were all together, and how sad we felt that you
watched us from afar and didn't feel you could come
over and greet us.

This is not a reproach, only a meditation on the
chasms that have opened in all of our lives. I am so sorry
to hear about your business, that is indeed a blow, and
I can't imagine you doing anything else but being up in
the sky. That is how I've imagined you all these years.
The propeller in movement, the roar of the great,
precise engine as it started up, the back of your neck,

tan, in the sun, as I watched from behind, and then
made a fool out of myself afterwards by over-talking it.

What you said about giving you words—I shudder
to think. I wrote you once, many years ago, about how
I felt my language was changing because of your
influence. Your silent influence, because it was your
silence I admired most. But if I have acted on *you*,
if that is what enabled you to write those words, then
I am glad.

It is the strange alchemy of two people coming
together. When Sara and I began our life together, our
marriage was our crowning achievement. How we found
each other and knew we should marry is still a wonder
to me. But we did. And what resulted—whatever good
things we created—had more to do with the alchemy
I speak of than it had to do with what is deemed a
"happy marriage." Each person changes the other, for
good. And then you can't change back.

Loving Sara changed me, then loving you changed
me. But what I never realized, because it had yet to be
tested, was that the love for my children changed me
the most. It made me vulnerable to life in a way nothing
else could, so that life could destroy me if it so chose.
I do not want you to think there is anything direly wrong
with me; I'm all right. I just wanted to explain
to you how I think about things these days.

Patrick goes on. For how much longer, I cannot say.
This is something that Sara and I do not talk about. She
can't bear to believe that she can't save him. And her
fight is all-consuming. I cannot help her and she cannot
help me. I have come to understand that only one's
pleasure in life can be shared. Grief cannot.

The other children are as well as can be asked for.

Honoria, as you saw for yourself, is ravishing and a bit rebellious at school (Rosemary Hall). Baoth seems quite pleased at St. George's, although he is currently suffering from measles, poor fellow. His sense of humor is intact, however. The letter I received from the infirmary was signed: "The Leaning Tower of Baoth."

Sara, meanwhile, is in Key West at the moment, getting some much deserved rest with the Hemingways and the Dos Passoses, who are the same. (Did you know Dos got married? I've forgotten . . .)

As for the other parts of our life, the tedium of money and such, well, we're broke. However, I have (shockingly) managed a coup at Mark Cross and have taken it over and will be trying to pull it back from the brink of ruin, so that both Esther and I may have something to live on. I can't imagine what my father would say to this.

This brings me to another reason that I am writing to you now. I am leaving for Europe on March 8th. I will be coming directly to Villa America, for a few days, before going to London on a trip to see our suppliers.

If you will still be there, I would like to come see your field one last time. I would like to see you, my dear friend, my love. I know it is not possible to bridge the distance that lies between us now, but how I would like to see your face again, to shake your hand. There are so few things that mean anything anymore, but what we had is one of them.

I will be arriving in Antibes on March 14th. There is no need to reply to this letter. I will come up to the field. If you are not there, I will understand.

Until we meet again,

G.

P.S. I don't know if you've read, or even heard of Scott's
new book *Tender Is the Night*. It is a curious rendering
of our life at Villa America. He says he used much of
us in it, although Sara, after reading it, was outraged.
For myself, I think there are many good parts in it, and
some true things. When I told him this, Scott seemed
for a moment like the old Scott, before everything
happened to him and Zelda, to us. He looked at me
with that look, the one he used to reserve for Zelda
when they were about to do something extraordinary,
and said: "Yes, it has magic. It has magic."

* *

Owen woke up late that morning. He wasn't sure why; he
was always up with the sun. He hadn't slept well, though.
Maybe it was Gerald's visit. He bathed and went outside.
The field was spongy from the rain the night before. It was
one of those warm March days on the Riviera, when it
seemed spring had already arrived.

Eugène was already there, outside the hangar, as usual.
He'd put on the gramophone, his second great love next to
airplanes, and was listening to a Mozart piano sonata and
smoking a cigarette.

Owen looked up at the sky, clear blue. The soft notes of
the music rising and falling in the air. He closed his eyes.
Just for a moment. He was late. He'd left a note for Gerald,
saying that if he got there before Owen was back, to wait for
him.

She was outside the hangar, patient, still. Just one last
time in *Arcadia* before the Spanish buyer came to collect
her. She wasn't worth much anymore, but she'd do if you

needed a plane. And Owen needed to pay Eugène something since the bank had taken everything else.

Owen opened his eyes. He made his way to the plane.
Eugène raised his own eyes skyward.

"I know, I know, I'm late," Owen said, fastening his old
flight jacket.

He would have talked to her, run his hand down her
body, like he used to do. But he was late. He didn't want
Gerald to get the note. He wanted to be there when he
arrived. So, he pulled down the ladder and climbed into the
cockpit.

Eugène began cranking. They didn't have to call to each
other anymore; slight head movements were all they needed,
they knew each other so well.

As *Arcadia* crossed the field, bumping along the track, he
looked back and waved at Eugène. Then she was off, up into
the sky. Her noises, her reactions to his touch, so familiar to
him.

The air was colder up here, the softness of the morning
lost below. Beneath him, he saw green things beginning to
grow again in the ground and he remembered his dream
from the night before, which had woken him when it was
still pitch dark and he was alone. The same one. Always the
same dream. The wheat, the sun.

He thought of Gerald, as he crossed out over the sea.
Thought of his face, so loved, his lean body. Thought of the
warmth of his hand. There had never been anyone else.
There never would be.

Before him, the expanse of blue-gray water disappeared
and it all rose up before him, the past. Like the piano music
had risen in the air of the field in the warm spring morning.

Was it because of this that he didn't hear the changes in
Arcadia? Was it that face in front of him, so dear, so lost to

him, that kept Owen from realizing that her engine was failing, that he was falling, that his hand outstretched was touching air, and not another human being who was reaching back for him so clearly in his mind's eye?

When the plane hit the open water, she broke all up. The fuselage floated a minute, resting on the waves like a bright blue buoy. And then, all at once, what remained of *Arcadia* and its pilot was gone, sucked down into the sea.

❄   ❄   ❄

The room at Massachusetts General Hospital was kept dim, because the light made Baoth scream. His body, the body she had made and loved and held, was now smattered with purple welts, his neck twisted to the side, his head covered in bandages from the five brain operations, the seizures which wracked him coming without warning, shaking him, until they had passed and all that was left were the tears of pain streaming down his face.

Sara held his hand.

"Breathe, Baoth. Breathe."

There was no sign that he heard her except that his will to live came through. And he went on. If she could have breathed her own life into him she would. *Her* child. Fifteen years old and not yet a man. Still had the scent of a boy on him sometimes. And the naughty smile of the child who had played the guitar for her on the terrace of Villa America. That smile, the solid feeling of him when he hugged her hard, and then pulled out of her grasp. She could have held him forever.

Disaster had come through the back door while she had been guarding the front. Small and insidious: just measles.

444

Then: just an ear infection, and an operation to relieve the pressure.

Some minuscule bacterial organism, too insignificant to be seen by the naked eye, had snaked its way in, floated on his blood, torn a path straight through her son into his spine and into his brain. Meningitis.

Where had she been? Key West. Taken in the middle of the night by Ernest to the mainland, on the plane with Ada, still unable to believe that what Gerald said could be true. But he hadn't gotten on the boat to Europe. So she'd known, no matter how much she hated him for telling her, that he wasn't lying. Because for a moment she hoped he might be.

Baoth could not die. She would not let him die. *He would not die.*

"Breathe, Baoth. Breathe, Baoth."

She could feel Gerald next to her. He was quiet. He didn't say anything to Baoth. He was calm, resigned, as if all this was inevitable. She wanted to scream at him for giving up. She wanted to shake him and call him a coward for laying down his arms so easily.

Honoria was shrinking against the wall. Part of her knew it was her job to hold that child, as well, but she couldn't. Not yet. Everything had to go to Baoth. Until he was saved. Until they were all saved from what it would mean to lose him.

Baoth's face. That face so like her own. Twisted into a silent scream. Why was it so still? Why wouldn't he look at her? Oh Baoth.

"Breathe, Baoth. Breathe, Baoth. Breathe, Baoth."

No one seemed to move. And then Gerald did. Gerald who had made Baoth, too. She felt his hand on her shoulder.

She shook him off. Angry. She put her face into Baoth's neck, warm. And smelled him. Antiseptic, sweat, decay. She inhaled as deeply as she could and there was, beneath all that, a trace of him, of the living boy.

Another hand on her shoulder, the doctor. He held a needle in his hand.

"Mrs. Murphy."

She took Baoth's face in her hands. "Breathe, Baoth, please breathe."

She felt the shot in her arm, Gerald's hand still on her shoulder.

Where, she wondered, would all her love go?

❖   ❖   ❖

WESTERN UNION

TO: ERNEST AND PAULINE HEMINGWAY AND KATY
AND JOHN DOS PASSOS

BAOTHS ASHES WERE LAID TO REST BESIDE HIS
GRANDFATHER UNDER THE WILLOW TREE AT THE
CEMETERY IN EAST HAMPTON ON SUNDAY OH THIS ISNT
HIM AT ALL THIS ISNT ANY OF US PLEASE OH PLEASE
KEEP US IN YOUR HEARTS WE LOVE YOU

SARA AND GERALD

1937

Archibald MacLeish
Uphill Farm
Conway, Mass.
January, 1937

John Dos Passos
571 Commercial Street
Provincetown, Mass.

Dear Dos,

I heard from Gerald that you stopped by to see them the day after Patrick died. Gerald said he'd been so moved, when Sara opened the door, to see you there, bags in hand from your recent trip to South America. You said to her: "I just wanted to be with you."

It is the only thing we can do for them now, and of course you would know that. Just be with them.

I saw them at the house in Saranac Lake shortly before he passed. It was different from the terrible ordeal of Baoth's hospital death. They were home. Even if it isn't the home I always imagined them in. And they sat in Patrick's room, and this time she held one of the boy's hands and Gerald held the other and they just kept saying to him: "You're fine, Patrick. We're right here with you." Until he went.

What a horror these years have been for them. I can't

447

help thinking that all that beauty they created under the linden tree can't begin to make up for what they lost, and it seems, more than anything, a rebuke rather than a consolation.

We have all tried to capture them in our work—you, me, Scott, Ernest. And yet they have eluded us. I think that is because their gift is not one of giving beauty, which might be captured, but of revealing it. Don't ask me how . . .

*

Scott Fitzgerald
Tryon, N.C.
January, 1937

Sara and Gerald Murphy
Camp Adeline
Lower St. Regis Lake, N.Y.

Dearest Sara and Gerald,

The telegram came today and the whole afternoon was so sad with thoughts of you and the past and the happy times we once had. Another link binding you to life is broken and with such insensate cruelty that it is hard to say which of the two blows was conceived with more malice.

But I can see another generation growing up around Honoria and an eventual peace somewhere, an occasional port of call as we all sail deathward. Fate can't have any more arrows in its quiver for you that will wound like these.

The golden bowl is broken indeed, but it was golden . . .

WHAT WAS FOUND

1928

The *Honoria* was making her way down the coast. It was midday and they'd already cleared Cannes and were approaching Saint-Raphaël. It was the apex of summer, the heat making the water shimmer and below them, schools of brightly colored fish, gold and silver and blue.

In the distance, off the starboard side, they could see the Riviera, the craggy cliffs, the flashes of white cove, the scrubby pines, all below a perfect blue sky.

Sara was cranking up the gramophone, a Stravinsky record in her lap. Vladimir was at the wheel, while Owen and Gerald stood nearby, to help the mate, Henri, who'd been hired to crew.

Baoth stood on the port side, his body leaning against the rail, a small makeshift harpoon held aloft in his hand.

Lying on his stomach on the deck, his chin on the edge, Patrick was counting the fish and keeping a tally.

Honoria sat next to her mother, her head on her shoulder. When the music started to play, Sara twined her fingers through her daughter's hair.

"When your father and I were young this ballet caused a riot in Paris," she said.

"Why?" Honoria asked, tipping her face toward the sun.

"Oh, I don't know. It's hard to explain, but it was *new*."

Baoth ran past Owen, knocking him.

"There's a big one, maybe a small shark," Baoth said, by

way of apology. "He's gone under us. I might be able to get him."

"Don't run on the boat," Gerald admonished.

"Dow-Dow, a shark . . ." Baoth repeated, exasperated.

"I'll feed you to the shark if you don't stop running."

"I know a story about a big whale," Vladimir said.

Owen smiled.

"I'll just bet you do." Gerald grinned. "A white whale by any chance?"

"Ah," Vladimir said. "I've told you this one before?"

"Vladimir, honestly," Sara said, leaning back, propping her heels against the deck to get sun on her legs. "What are we going to do when they go to school and tell everyone all these stories you've 'made up'?"

"What do you mean, Mother?" Patrick asked. He was like that, always listening while the others were off in their own worlds.

"I . . ." Sara looked at the men.

"Your mother means that Vladimir is a teller of tall tales," Gerald said.

"I'm never going to school," Baoth shouted, the shark lost somewhere under the sea.

"Dow-Dow," Patrick said. "Can I look at the map again?"

"Yes, Dow," Baoth said. "We need to be prepared."

"I think Owen has the map," Gerald said.

"It's in my bag, belowdeck."

Gerald watched Owen as he moved slowly toward the hatch, his shoulders set against the cliffs in the distance, his blond hair bleached almost white from the sun.

When Owen reemerged he sat down on the deck and the boys closed around him. He pulled out the small rusted metal box and opened it, removing the piece of parchment, with a map of the coast of France drawn in faded ink. In one

spot, above a cove in Saint-Tropez, there was an "X" marked
on the map in what looked like dried blood.

Baoth quickly took the map from Owen, but allowed his
brother to look at it over his shoulder.

Above their heads, Owen smiled at Sara.

The seeds of this trip had been planted in the children's
minds a week ago, when Gerald had gathered them round
one morning to say he'd received a mysterious letter in the
post, informing him that there was an old map buried in
the garden of Villa America, which showed the location of
buried pirate treasure.

The children, mad with anticipation, had dug in the indicated spot, killing a few of Sara's peonies in the process, to
reveal the box and map.

"Hopefully, Vladimir will know how to navigate us to the
right spot," Gerald had said when they'd presented him with
their findings. "And we might get Owen to fly over the area,
beforehand, for reconnaissance."

They'd spent a week preparing for the voyage, Sara
buying special foods and camping kits, Gerald finding tents
that they could pitch on the beach. The children had been
exhorted to "say nothing to anyone. We don't want to arouse
suspicion."

Then, very early that morning, when it was almost still
night, they'd left in search of treasure buried somewhere in
the hills of the Riviera.

"Do you think there'll be jewels?" Honoria asked, going
over to inspect the map with her brothers.

"Nah," said Baoth. "Spanish bullion, most likely."

Owen laughed. "Sounds like you know a lot about buried
treasure."

"I read about it. That's the kind of treasure pirates
carried," Baoth said, as if everyone knew this.

"There might be jewels," Sara said, laying out brightly colored linen towels in the cockpit. "From beautiful women captured by the rogue pirates."

"See?" Honoria said, shoving Baoth a little.

Sara began opening the picnic basket. "All right, children, Dow-Dow, Owen. Lunch *est servie*."

They gathered round, the children wrapped up in the linen towels to protect them from the sun, and ate: gnocchi, salad and fresh peaches with cream. When Sara cut a pear in half and placed it on the deck, Gerald watched as a wasp landed on it and pierced it with its proboscis, trying to drain the fruit of its sweetness.

"Isn't that just like life," he said, watching the wasp eating the pear.

"Isn't what just like life?" Sara asked.

But Gerald just shrugged, unable to articulate. Instead, he went over and picked Patrick up and held him for a minute, the notes of the *Rite of Spring* speeding them along on their journey.

✤

It was evening when they reached the cove. Anchoring, Vladimir rowed Owen and Gerald and the supplies ashore, then turned back for the others.

Owen and Gerald hauled the tents and food and gramophone and records and all the other necessities farther inland, to escape the tide. There was a cave carved into the rock surrounding the half-circle of beach, and they put the supplies inside and pitched the tents nearby. There were two tents: one for the children, and one for Vladimir and the mate. Sara and Gerald and Owen would sleep outside under the stars, they'd decided.

Once they'd finished the setup, Gerald poured them

each a glass of wine and they sat watching Sara and the children coming over the water in the dinghy.

"Thank you for coming with us," Gerald said. Then more softly: "Thank you for coming back."

Owen nodded, not looking at him.

When they were all together, they built a fire for Sara to cook over and sat around it as the sun dipped below the horizon.

"I think it's time for some pirate stories," Gerald said.

The children's faces, flickering eerily in the light of the fire, all turned toward him.

"Wait," Sara said. "We have to set the mood."

She went inside the cave and cranked the gramophone and put on Debussy's "Engulfed Cathedral," its deep, haunting notes swelling inside the cave and echoing out over their camp.

"We think this treasure that we hope to find tomorrow may have been part of Captain Kidd's loot," Gerald said. "And that cave was most likely used to shelter the captain and his villainous crew."

"Why were they so villainous, Dow-Dow?" Patrick asked.

"Because they were a band of vicious men. All pirates live by a code," Gerald said. "And the penalty for breaking that code was brutal. One of Captain Kidd's crew was strung up by his arms and drubbed with a drawn cutlass for helping himself to a huge ruby. For others, it was the plank."

"What was the code?" Baoth asked, chewing the cuticle of his thumb.

"A code of how to behave aboard the ship. And how much treasure each man was allowed for himself."

"What happened to Captain Kidd?" Honoria asked, her voice trembling a little as she moved closer to her mother's body.

"Well, that's a good question, Daughter. By all accounts Captain Kidd was a savage pirate and when he knew that he was close to being captured, he began burying his treasure, either so that he could return later for it, or to use it as bribes to get out of punishment. But when he was tried and convicted, and sent to the gallows, the whereabouts of his treasure was lost forever."

"And this is *our* treasure?" Patrick asked.

"It may well be," Gerald said. "That's why we have to be careful not to let anyone see us when we find it."

"Will we be sent to the gallows?" Patrick asked.

"No," Gerald said. "But like the pirates, we must live by a code of secrecy about what we find buried. It's *our* secret now."

When the children had been put to bed in their tent and Vladimir and Henri had retired, Gerald and Owen, Sara in the middle, sat wrapped in their blankets on the sand, drinking the wine.

"The story I heard about Captain Kidd when I was a boy was a little more bloody," Owen said.

"Really?" Sara said.

"Mmm. We used to go camping out by these swimming holes up island and tell pirate stories. The way I heard it, when they hung him, the rope broke, and they had to do it all over again. Then they took his body and nailed it to a post and hung it over the Thames for three years, as a warning to other pirates. First it rotted and swelled, and birds pecked his eyes, and then his skin and muscle started to drop off and rats ate it. You know, it went on like that." Owen took a sip of his wine, laughing.

"Heavens," Sara said, grasping Owen's hand. "That would be enough to put me off pirating."

"I know," Owen said, turning to her, smiling. "You would

think so. But you know how it is, somehow those stories make it even more exciting to boys. The worse they are, the more you think you'd like to be a pirate."

"I never heard any pirate stories," Gerald said. "At least none that I remember."

"Did you hear *any* stories, my love?" Sara said, running her hand down his arm. "I can't see either of your parents, or that horrid nurse of yours, telling you anything beautiful or magical."

"No," Gerald replied. "They weren't ones for that kind of thing. I had a dog, and I told *him* stories."

"Well, now you have us. And you can tell *us* stories." Sara turned back to Owen. "You know, we're so glad you came back."

Owen smiled at her. "Thank you."

"It's like something's missing when we don't have our friends around us. Promise me you'll never stay away so long again." She squeezed his hand.

"Your very own pirate code," Owen said.

✿

The next morning, the children were up before anyone else. At first they sat in their tent, whispering.

"I hope we find the very large, red ruby," Honoria said.

"Gold bullion," Baoth said. "I'm telling you."

"Whose blood do you think was used to make 'X' on the map?" Patrick asked.

"Maybe the man they killed with the cutlass," Baoth said.

"What's a cutlass?"

"You don't know what a cutlass is?" Baoth laughed. "You don't know anything."

"It's a sword," Honoria said. "And *you* don't know anything, Baoth. Mother said there would be jewels."

"She said there *might* be."

"Shhh," Honoria said. "I hear something outside."

"Do you think the pirates are here to kill us?" asked Patrick.

Baoth picked up his small harpoon. "I'll kill *them*," he said.

Honoria peeked out. "It's Dow-Dow," she informed her brothers. "He's getting firewood."

"Breakfast," Baoth said, triumphantly.

"Breakfast," Patrick repeated.

They sat out on blankets, while their mother boiled milk for their cocoa in a pan and coffee for the adults in a dented metal coffee pot.

"That coffee pot looks as old as the pirates," Vladimir said.

Owen smiled. "It's getting there."

"But it's so useful," Sara said. "Thank you for bringing it."

They ate bread and jam and fruit for breakfast, while their father pored over the map.

"All right, children," he said when they had finished eating. "It's time."

They crowded around him while, with his finger, he traced a line on the map leading from the cove into the hills.

"We have to take this path. Everyone ready?"

Leaving Vladimir behind to 'defend against marauders,' they walked up the beach and started climbing the path. Their mother held Patrick's hand to keep him from stumbling over the rocks and roots along the way. Baoth ran ahead.

After a while, their father stopped suddenly. He pointed to the parchment map.

"I believe this is the spot."

Owen, shovel in hand, began to dig into the sandy soil,

the dry top layer skittering away. They heard a chink, as his shovel hit metal. He dug around it to reveal a metal box.

"That's too small," Baoth said. "That can't be a treasure chest."

"I hope we haven't been led on a wild goose chase," Gerald said.

"Oh, that would be a shame," Sara said, her face a mask of disappointment.

"Well, maybe we should just open it," Owen said.

"Maybe it's just one large ruby," Honoria said, kicking dirt at her brother.

"I think Patrick should open it," Sara said.

Owen handed the small box to Patrick, who sat down on the ground to get a better handle on it.

Patrick finally managed to pry the box open and put his small hand in and pulled out a skeleton key with a parchment tag attached, a skull and crossbones drawn on it.

"The sign of the pirates," Gerald said.

"There's more," Patrick said.

"Really?" Sara said.

"Let me see," Baoth said, crouching down next to his younger brother.

Patrick pulled out another piece of parchment paper.

"'Walk two feet uphill from this very spot,'" Baoth read aloud. "'Then five paces to the west. Then ye shall be standing directly over the spot where ye should begin digging again.'"

They carefully made their way as directed. Then Gerald handed Baoth the shovel, and the boy started attacking the ground, throwing soil in every direction.

"Baoth, do be careful with all that dirt," Sara said.

"Pirate treasure, Mother. No time for niceties."

Sara laughed. She leaned over to Owen and said quietly: "I'm so excited I can barely stand it."

"The moment of truth," he said.

"I hit something hard," Baoth yelled, his ruddy face full of joy.

Honoria stood impatiently watching the shovel, while Patrick just kept his wise little head still, focused.

And then, all at once, there it was: the pirates' treasure chest.

The children seemed stunned to actually see it, as if they'd willed it out of their imagination into existence and were awed by the power of their own fancy.

"I think your mother should open it," Gerald said, handing her the skeleton key.

"No," she said, "I think Owen should open it." She handed it to him.

Owen looked at it, turned it over in his hand, felt its weight.

"Yes," Honoria said. "Open it."

He bent down and fit the key into the lock. It made a small click.

"The lid's going to be heavy," he said. "I think we'll need to open it together."

The children, along with their parents, each put a hand on the lid and pushed. The lid fell back on its hinges and all was revealed. Stones and beads of every color, cuffs of gold and silver, garnets and bloodstones, and turquoise, deep enough to push your whole hand through, brilliant and glittering in the French summer sun.

"Rubies," Honoria said.

"And diamonds and emeralds," Patrick said. "How many do you think there are?"

"There's enough for everyone," Sara said, straightening up.

The children would never know about that treasure, how Gerald had searched out old parchment paper from the galleries on the rue La Boétie in Paris. How Sara had hunted all over the Left Bank for a treasure chest, and combed the flea markets for jewelry and beads. How Owen had gathered it all up in his plane on his return from Berlin, and flown it down to Antibes. How Vladimir had gone on a mission to bury the chest and the box weeks in advance.

And while Honoria and Baoth and Patrick marveled at what Captain Kidd had left behind, Sara and Gerald and Owen stood watching.

The morning had broken so clear up in the hills, and they could see straight over the pines and palms and olive trees, bending like women curtsying in the breeze, out over the sea to the three islands in the gulf, the Îles d'Or. The Golden Isles, shining in the distance, just out of reach.

Author's Note

Writing a historical novel based on the lives of real people is a tricky business. Lines between the writer's imagination and biographical fact become blurred, and the past becomes ambiguous. One of the major differences between historical fiction and biography is that where, in biography, gaps in the known narrative can only be filled with supposition, in fiction, they are where the story lives. The author's job is to dramatize what the biographer is only permitted to guess at. The result is a work that is framed by fact, but is ultimately fiction. *Villa America* is such a novel.

But first, the facts—for this book wouldn't exist without the painstaking and brilliant research undertaken by a group of journalists, biographers and family members.

I initially became aware of the existence of Sara and Gerald Murphy while writing my MA thesis on F. Scott Fitzgerald's *Tender Is the Night*, which was—and remains—one of my favorite novels. Intensely romantic and tragic, it is dedicated: "To Sara and Gerald, Many Fêtes."

As I began my investigation, I realized that the Sara and Gerald to whom he was referring were the Murphys, great friends of Fitzgerald's, and the models, he claimed, for Nicole and Dick Diver in the novel. I would also discover that the Murphys themselves, and in particular Sara, found that suggestion absurd—even slightly insulting.

My real introduction to their lives, however, came through

reading Calvin Tomkins's beautiful and heartbreaking *Living Well Is the Best Revenge*. The book is expanded from a *New Yorker* article he wrote based on his extensive interviews with the Murphys, who also happened to be neighbors. And because he knew them and quoted them at length, his account was my first taste of their unusual voices, their way with language. And I fell in love with them. Here I found the story of how Gerald first knew he wanted to be a painter, walking down the rue La Boétie one day; of the beginning of his friendship with Cole Porter at Yale; of the infamous scene at Villa America where Scott threw wineglasses, and ultimately a punch, and was banned. It was my first glimpse of Vladimir and his White Russian background and of the way Villa America looked in the 1920s and of Zelda throwing herself off a parapet, or jumping off Eden Rock.

Living Well Is the Best Revenge is a gem: small and perfectly formed and, for anyone interested in the lives of the Murphys, a must-read.

However, for a fulsome biography of Sara and Gerald, Amanda Vaill's amazing *Everybody Was So Young* is the first and last word on the Murphys. Meticulously researched and brilliantly written, it manages to bring to life all the texture—from the delicate details to the sweeping glamor to the awful tragedies—of their lives.

Her book informed much of what I know about the early lives of the Murphys, their youth and courtship. And her thoughtful interpretation of their marriage and their family life, as well as the complicated nature of some of their friendships, greatly inspired my treatment of them in *Villa America*.

And it was while reading Vaill's account of the caviar and champagne party given in honor of Ernest Hemingway that the idea of the character of Owen Chambers was born. Vaill notes in her biography that the caviar had to be flown from the Caspian Sea by a pilot, and it was in that small gap—an unknown pilot—that the fictional narrative began.

That Gerald Murphy struggled with his sexuality is well documented through letters he wrote both to Sara and to friends. However, what exactly that struggle consisted of is unknown. There is no suggestion that he ever engaged in a love affair with anyone outside of his marriage. The invention of Owen and their subsequent relationship is part of that shadowland where historical fiction lives; the affair is a way of dramatizing Gerald's struggle, of writing action, where only absence exists.

For readers who wish to peruse those letters, I highly recommend *Letters from the Lost Generation*, edited by Linda Patterson Miller. That collection, which skillfully illuminates the web of friendships among this group of talented and difficult people, inspired many of the letters that appear in the novel.

Aside from Vaill and Miller, another rich source of letters is the memoir penned by Sara and Gerald's daughter, Honoria Murphy Donnelly, *Sara & Gerald: Villa America and After*. Providing a firsthand account of life at Villa America as well as documenting a treasure trove of correspondence, Donnelly's book was indispensable in gaining a clear and realistic picture of the Murphys, the details of their everyday life, of their love and affection for their children. In particular, her extremely moving description of the tin soldier battle at Scott and Zelda Fitzgerald's villa, as well as the treasure hunt that makes up the final section of the novel, were crucial when writing those scenes in *Villa America*.

The letters in *Villa America* are, for the most part, invented. However, some of them echo real letters, some of them contain a line from a real letter, and a few of them are reprints of the originals.

For example, in the series of letters exchanged between Sara and Gerald while she is visiting India, his comment to her: "I can't very well chat to the men I see about such a small thing, without being thought effeminate. Wilson, Panama, and the Cadillac 1914, yes," was inspired by a line in a real letter, quoted in Vaill, that he wrote to her while she was traveling, which reads: "how few men there are with whom I am able to carry on more than a five minute conversation . . . these dinners out, during coffee,—get so far with the Panama situation, or Wilson,—or the 1914 Cadillac vs. the 1914 Ford,—then sit back . . . Any mention of some important exhibition, concert, book . . . is at once allied with effeminacy."

Similarly, Sara's letter to Gerald dated March 20, 1914, in the novel is based on a real letter she penned him from Rome. In the original letter, Sara says: "What do you mean by never writing? What have you all been doing, and what were your costumes like at the costume balls? Having been to the ends of the earth, we'd like some news . . . India was the wildest success." Compared with the fictional letter, the echoes are clear, however in the novel this letter is intended to cover up the fact that she and Gerald have been writing in secret to each other, which colors the tone.

Again, when Gerald writes Sara in the novel that he is coming to ask her father for her hand in marriage, the fictional letter was inspired by three separate letters he wrote to her shortly before declaring his intentions. In the first, he describes a meeting from the previous evening that "left me impressed, uplifted, awed (no word!) as I have never been. It may be strange," he continues, "for a man to admit of this—but I could never take what occurred to us last night casually." In the second, he says that "I cannot live alone with this feeling much longer." And in the third, Gerald writes that he can no longer bear to have their courtship kept a secret and that he will come to "ply my suit with your respected male parent."

And in the next letter in the novel, the line "Think of a relationship that not only does not bind, but actually so lets loose imagination. Think of it, my love—and thank heaven" comes directly from a line Gerald wrote to Sara when they had first become secretly engaged, the only variation being the substitution of "my love" for "Sal."

Similarly, Gerald's letter to Sara that he writes from San Antonio in the novel is greatly inspired by part of a real letter he wrote to her when he was at the training camp, in which he said: "It gives me such courage now to think of us established as a little family. I believe so in us—it is my creed—we can do anything ourselves."

In other cases, expressions or words that Sara and Gerald favored have been used in the letters, such as the description of their future children as "humorous, lithe and clean" or referring to the decorating fashion of the day as "Smart Apt" or Gerald's "feeling of being 'inspected' when with a group of men."

In the other large series of letters in the novel, which are exchanged between 1928 and 1937, there are several cases where real letters have been used. Firstly, the lines by Archie MacLeish that Gerald includes in the fictional letter to Owen, beginning "This land is my native land" comes from a real letter MacLeish wrote to Gerald upon his return to the U.S. MacLeish later turned the letter into a poem, entitled "American Letter," which appears in the collection *New Found Land*.

MacLeish's heartbreaking letter to Patrick Murphy about the sick baby squirrel he finds in the woods is a real letter he wrote to the boy, which appears in Donnelly's memoir, with lines cut to make it shorter. Finally, Fitzgerald's poignant letter to the Murphys upon the death of Patrick Murphy, which begins "The telegram came today and the whole afternoon was so sad with thoughts of you . . ." is an original letter. A few lines have been cut for brevity.

Other letters in this series in the novel, while fictional creations crafted to advance the narrative, were inspired in part by real missives, as well as by the general style of the various writers to whom they are fictionally attributed. Gerald's description of his time in Los Angeles, for example, written in a letter to Owen, contains echoes of one Gerald wrote to MacLeish on the subject, including the infantile nature of the culture (as evidenced by the silly restaurant names) and his experience with the racial stereotyping on the set of *Hallelujah!*

Other letters that are inspired by the real-life writings of the authors include Donald Stewart's letter to Phil Barry, which draws on Stewart's description of a visit to the Murphys, given to Calvin Tomkins, and that can also be found in his own auto-biography, *By a Stroke of Luck!*. The invented Archie MacLeish letter to his wife, Ada, which includes a passage of a letter from Gerald to Archie, also falls into this category. And the fictional letter from Dorothy Parker to Bob Benchley was inspired by a description Parker gave of her time in Switzerland with the Murphys, and the line that begins "Poor Gerald . . ." is taken from a real letter she penned to Benchley.

Similarly, Fitzgerald's fictional letter to Ernest Hemingway includes a description of his feelings about Sara that echoes words Fitzgerald wrote to her in a real letter several months after Baoth's death. The short fictional letter Zelda Fitzgerald writes to Scott was inspired by part of a letter, cited in Nancy Milford's fantastic biography *Zelda*, which she wrote to her husband during the period when she was living at the psychi-atric facility Highlands Hospital.

Hemingway's fictional letter to Sara was inspired in part by a letter he wrote to Sara in 1934, after a trip to Africa. His offer of a stuffed impala or gazelle's head, his insistence that it is "clean and light and quite beautiful to look at when you're in bed," and his description of how impalas "are the ones that float in the air when they jump," all inspired the fictional letter that appears in the novel.

All the works cited above were invaluable to the writing of this novel and I am indebted and extremely grateful to their authors for setting me upon this frustrating and wonderful and heartrending journey. I cannot recommend these works enough: *Living Well Is the Best Revenge*, *Everybody Was So Young*, *Letters from the Lost Generation* and *Sara & Gerald*. Read them.

I also owe thanks to Yale's Beinecke Library, which houses the Sara and Gerald Murphy Papers, for their help in my research and their patience in teaching me how to handle rare manuscripts.

Acknowledgments

There may be nothing harder for a writer than writing into the void: it's a lonely business at the best of times, but when no one gives a damn, it's even lonelier. Conversely, there is nothing more joyous than writing a novel amid the cheering sound of encouragement and support. And when it comes to support for this book, my cup runneth over.

Firstly, I am evermore indebted to my editors Kate Harvey at Picador and Judy Clain at Little, Brown, who washed this novel with all the taste and style and brilliance in their arsenal. Whatever its flaws are lie with me; but when it comes to any of the high, gleaming moments, so much credit goes to those two talented women. Thank you, thank you—I can't say it enough.

My agent, Caroline Wood, a woman of truly startling honesty, has been an amazing shield and an incredible companion on the path we've travelled together over the last four years. Thank god I found you.

So much gratitude goes to my U.K. publicist—and my friend—Emma Bravo, who wages one hell of a campaign. Long may our capers continue. And also to my U.S. publicist, the incomparable Sabrina Callahan, whose humor and tirelessness has made tromping around the United States a real joy.

My thanks to the whole team at Picador, who've become a bit like my very own pirate gang, and in particular to my lovely

Acknowledgments

publisher, Paul Baggaley, for all his gracious support of this novel.

To the folks at Little, Brown—I send my heartiest thanks and devotion from this side of the pond for the hard work, eagle-eyed attentiveness, and astounding support.

Also deserving of so much love and acclamation are the long-suffering writers in my workshop group: Emma Chapman, Tom Feltham, Liz Gifford, Carolina Gonzalez-Carvajal, and Kat Gordon.

Finally, to my family: Thank you. I love you.

picador.com

blog
videos
interviews
extracts